Maggie Rose

Maggie Rose

A NOVEL BY SHARLENE MacLAREN

WHITAKER
HOUSE

MAGGIE ROSE
Second in The Daughters of Jacob Kane Series

Sharlene MacLaren
www.sharlenemaclaren.com

ISBN: 978-1-60374-075-3
Printed in the United States of America
© 2009 by Sharlene MacLaren

Whitaker House
1030 Hunt Valley Circle
New Kensington, PA 15068
www.whitakerhouse.com

Library of Congress Cataloging-in-Publication Data

MacLaren, Sharlene, 1948–
 Maggie Rose / by Sharlene MacLaren.
  p. cm. — (The daughters of Jacob Kane ; 2)
 Summary: "Maggie Rose, Jacob Kane's middle daughter, moves to New York City
to work at an orphanage, where she nurtures needy children and falls in love with
a newspaper reporter whose lack of Christian faith and painful past create various
obstacles to overcome—by the grace of God"—Provided by publisher.
 ISBN 978-1-60374-075-3 (trade pbk. : alk. paper) 1. New York (N.Y.)—Fiction. I.
Title.
 PS3613.A27356M34 2009
 813'.6—dc22
             2009011958

1 2 3 4 5 6 7 8 9 10 11 12 **ᴎ** 17 16 15 14 13 12 11 10 09

To Alexis Joy Brady (Grandma's *beautiful* girl)…

when I first laid eyes on you,
I thought my heart would burst wide open!

Chapter One

August 1904

Maggie Rose Kane settled her temple against the smudged window, blinked hard, and fought back another wave of nausea as the smoke from her seatmate's cigar formed cloud-like ringlets before her eyes and floated past her nose. Why, her lungs fairly burned from the stench of it, as if she'd been the one chain-smoking the stogies for the past five hours instead of the bulbous, gray-haired giant next to her. Even as he was dozing this afternoon, slumped with one shoulder sagging against her petite frame, the vile object hung out the side of his mouth as if permanently attached. She couldn't even count the number of times she'd wanted to snatch it from him and snuff it out with the sole of her black patent leather shoe.

"Next stop, Albany," announced the train conductor, making his way up the aisle.

With a quick intake of air, Maggie lifted a finger and leaned forward. "Excuse me, sir."

The conductor stopped, turned, and tipped his hat to her in a formal manner. "Yes?"

"Is this where I should disembark in order to change over to the New York Central?"

Tilting his head to one side and slanting a reddish eyebrow, he released a mild sigh that conveyed slight annoyance. "If that's what your ticket says. You're goin' to New York, aren't you?"

She gave a hasty shake of her head and adjusted the plume hat that had barely moved in all these many hours. Surely, by now, the slight wave in her hair, as well as the tight little bun at the back of her head, would be flatter than a well-done pancake. "Someone's to meet me at Grand Central," she explained.

He nodded curtly. "Get off here then and go to the red line, then put yourself on the 442." This he said with a matter-of-fact tone, as if anyone with a scrap of common sense ought to know about the 442.

Sweaty fingers clutched the satchel in her lap as she peered up at him, debating whether or not to admit her ignorance. "Oh, the 442." She might have asked him at least to point her in the right direction once she disembarked, but he hurried down the aisle and pushed through the back door that led to the next car before giving her a chance. The train whistle blew another ear-splitting shriek, either indicating that the train was approaching an intersection or announcing its scheduled stopover in Albany.

"What's a pretty little miss like you doin' going to the big city all by yourself?" asked the man beside her. Not wanting to invite conversation with the galoot, especially for all the smoke he'd blow in her face, she had maintained silence for the duration of the trip. Still, it was her Christian duty to show him respect, so she pulled back her slender shoulders and tried to appear pleasant—and confident. After all, it wouldn't do to let on how the combination of her taut nerves and his rancid cigar smoke had stirred up bile at the back of her throat. For the twentieth time since her departure on the five a.m. that very morning—when her entire family, including her new brother-in-law and adopted nephew, had bid her a tearful farewell—she asked herself, and the Lord Himself, if she hadn't misinterpreted His divine call.

"I've accepted a position at the Sheltering Arms Refuge," she replied with a steady voice. "I'm to assist in the home, and also to work as a placing-out agent whenever trips are arranged."

He quirked a questioning brow and blew a cloud of smoke directly at her. She waved her arm to ward off the worst of it. "It's a charitable organization for homeless children. Using the U.S. railway system, we stop in various parts of the Middle West and place children in decent families and homes, mostly farms. Surely you've heard announcements about trains of orphans coming through?"

He looked slightly put out. "'Course I heard of 'em, miss, just haven't never run across anyone actually involved in the process of cartin' them wild little hooligans clear across the country." He took another long drag and, fortunate for Maggie Rose, blew it out the other side of his mouth so that, this time, it drifted into the face of the man across the aisle. Apparently unruffled, he merely lifted his newspaper higher to shield his face.

"Where you from, anyways?"

"Sandy Shores, Michigan." Just saying the name of the blessed lakeshore town made her miss her home and family more than she'd imagined possible. Goodness, she'd left only this morning. If she was feeling homesick already, what depths of loneliness would the next several months bring?

"Ah, that near Benton Harbor?"

"Quite a ways north of it, sir."

He seemed to ponder that thought only briefly. "What made you leave? You got home problems?"

"Certainly not!" she replied with extra fervor, offended he should think so. In fact, she might have chosen to stay behind and continued life as usual, helping her dear father and beloved sisters at Kane's Whatnot, the family's general store. But God's poignant tug on her heart would not allow her to stay. *I sincerely doubt Mr.—Mr. Smokestack—would follow such reasoning, though, so why waste my breath explaining?* she thought.

"Well, you can see why I asked, cain't you? It's not every day some young thing like yourself up and moves to a big place like New York, specially when she don't even know her way around."

"I'm sure I'll learn quickly enough," she said, trying to put confidence in her tone. "I hear there's to be a big subway system opening soon, which should help in moving folks around the city at great speeds."

He nodded and took another long drag from his dwindling cheroot. "Sometime in the next month or two, is what I hear," he said, blowing out a ring of smoke. "That'll be somethin', all right. Before you know it, there'll be no need for any four-legged creatures." He chuckled to himself, although the sound held no mirth.

As they approached the station, the train's brakes squawked and sputtered, and the mighty whistle blew one last time. Outside, steam was rising from the tracks, and Maggie Rose noticed a couple of scrawny dogs picking through a pile of garbage. Folks stood in clusters, perhaps anxious to welcome home loved ones or to usher in long-awaited guests. A tiny pang of worry nestled in her chest at the sight of such unfamiliar surroundings.

When the train came to a screeching halt, the passengers scrambled for their belongings, holding onto their hats as they snatched up satchels and crates bound in twine. Some of them were dressed formally; others looked shoddy, at best, like her seatmate with his week-old beard and soiled attire. Another puff of smoke circled the air above her, and it was all she could do to keep from giving him a piece of her mind—until the Lord reminded her of a verse she'd read the night before in the book of Proverbs: *"He that oppresseth the poor reproacheth his Maker: but he that honoureth him hath mercy on the poor"* (Proverbs 14:31).

Was she not traveling to New York out of a sense of great compassion for the city's poor, lost children? And if so, what made her think the Lord exempted her from caring for people of all ages? Moreover, why had she spent the better share of the past several hours judging this man about whom she knew so little?

My child, you are tempted to look on his countenance and stature, whereas I look on the heart. The verse from 1 Samuel came to mind—oh, how the truth of it struck her to the core. Without ado, she looked directly at her seatmate, smoke and all. "And where might you be headed, sir?"

"Me?" A look of surprise washed over him. "My sister just passed. I'm goin' to her funeral in Philly."

A gasp escaped. "Oh, my, I'm…I'm sorry to hear that." Silently, she prayed, *Lord, give me the proper words, and forgive me all these many hours I might have had the chance to speak comfort to this poor soul.*

He dropped what remained of his cigar on the floor and ground it out with his heel, stood to his feet, and retrieved his duffle from under the seat with a loud sniff. "Yeah, well, we weren't that close. She quit speakin' to me after I married my wife, her bein' a Protestant and us Catholics." He followed that up with a snort. "My brother died last year, and she still refused to acknowledge me at his funeral, even though my wife passed on three years ago."

Blended odors of sweat, tobacco, and acrid breath nearly knocked her over as she stood up and hefted the strap of her heavy leather satchel over one shoulder, but newfound compassion welled up in her heart, lending her fortitude. The line of people in the aisle was moving at a snail's pace, and she decided to make use of their extra seconds together.

"But you're going to her funeral anyway?"

He nodded halfheartedly. "It's my duty to pay my respects. She won't know it, but I will."

"Yes, and you'll feel better afterward for doing so." Suddenly, she had more to say to the man, but the line of anxious passengers was picking up speed, and he squeezed into the tight line. She followed in his wake, doing her best to keep her footing as folks shoved and jabbed. *My, such an impetuous, peevish lot*, she thought, then quickly acknowledged her own impatience.

"Watch your step, ladies and gentlemen," the conductor said. One by one, folks stepped down from the train. Her fellow rider took the stairs with ease, then turned abruptly and offered her his hand. Another time, she might have pretended not to notice and used the steel hand railing instead. Now, however, she smiled and accepted his grimy, calloused palm.

"Thank you."

Drooping eyes looked down at her. "New York, eh? You sure you don't want to purchase your ticket back home? Ticket booth's right over there." He hooked a thumb over his shoulder, and for the first time, she sensed that he was toying with her.

"Absolutely not!" Pulling back her shoulders, she gave her head a hard shake, losing a feather from her hat in the process. She watched it float away, carried by the breeze of passengers rushing by. "When the Lord tells a body to do something, you best do it, if you want to know true peace," she said, lifting her eyes to meet his. "This is something He told me to do—to come to New York and see what I can do about helping the deprived, dispossessed children, just as I'm sure He prompted you to attend your sister's funeral."

Surprisingly, he chuckled and bobbed his head a couple of times. "Can't say for sure it was the Good Lord Hisself or Father Carlson, but one of 'em convinced me to come, and now that I think on it, I'm glad."

Out the corner of her eye, Maggie Rose sought to read the myriad signs pointing this way and that, hoping to find one to point her in the right direction. Slight queasiness churned in her stomach. *Dear Lord, please erase my worries about finding my next train*, she prayed silently. The man ran four grimy fingers through his greasy hair. Absently, she wondered if he intended to clean himself up before attending his sister's burial service.

"You take care of yourself, little lady. It's a mighty big world out there for one so fine and dainty as you."

A smile formed on her lips. *Fine and dainty*. Had he made a similar remark to one of her sisters, Hannah Grace or Abbie Ann, an indignant look would have been his return. She extended her hand. "I'll do my best, Mr....."

He clasped her hand and gave it a gentle shake. "Dempsey. Mort Dempsey. And you are?"

"Maggie Rose Kane."

He gave a thoughtful nod. "Has a nice ring to it." Then, tipping his head to one side, he scratched his temple and raised his bushy brows. "At first glimpse, you look a bit fragile, but I'd guess you got some spunk under that feathery hat o' yours."

Now she laughed outright. "I suppose that's the Kane blood running through me.

We Kane sisters are known for our stubborn streak. It runs clear to our bones."

Several seconds ticked by. Mr. Dempsey glanced around. "You got any more baggage, miss?"

"My trunk's due to arrive at the children's home the day after tomorrow." She gave her black satchel a pat. "I'll make do with what I have till then."

In the next silent pause that passed between them, a pigeon swept down to steal a crumb, a stray dog loped past, and in the distance, a mother hushed her crying babe. Mr. Dempsey removed his pocket watch. "Well, listen, little lady, my train for Philly don't leave for another hour yet. What say I take you over to the red line? Number 442, was it?"

"Oh, but you needn't...."

He'd already looped his arm for her to take. The man's stench remained strong, yes, but Maggie Rose found that, somehow, in the course of the past few minutes, her nose had miraculously adjusted.

My, but the Lord did work in wondrously mysterious ways! Why, just this very morning, Jacob Kane, her dear father, had prayed that God might send His angels of protection to lead and guide her on her way, and now look: Mort Dempsey was taking her to her next connection.

Imagine that—Mort Dempsey, God's appointed "angel."

They parted ways at the Albany platform where she could board Number 442.

K

When she arrived at New York City's Grand Central Terminal, Maggie Rose saw a confusing mass of railroad lines converged in a place that also contained more people than she thought inhabited the earth.

Mr. Dempsey may have been an unlikely angel, but her next escort fit the bill with utmost perfection. She scanned the crowd and saw a pleasant-looking man, probably not much older than she, standing to one side and holding up a hand-printed sign that read: "Miss M. Kane." Dressed in an evening suit, a bowler cap, and a bright-red bow tie that was almost blinding, he was searching the crowd with expectant eyes. When their gazes met, a broad smile formed on his face.

"Miss Kane?" he asked, greeting her with the warmth of a clear summer morning.

"Yes!" She had to tell her feet to walk in ladylike strides, even though her travel-worn body wanted to slump into the nearest bench with relief. They shook hands, and he introduced himself as Stanley Barrett, an employee—but more of a lifelong resident—at the children's home. The Binghams had welcomed him through their doors many years ago when he'd lost both his parents in a fire.

"You must be tired," he said, freeing her of her satchel without a moment's hesitation, which suited her just fine. As it was, her shoulder ached from the weight of the bag, which held important papers, several personal possessions, some toiletry items, and the changes of clothing she would need until her trunk arrived.

Dusk had settled on New York City, so, without ado, Mr. Barrett led her like a pro through the throngs and straight to their carriage, waiting with numerous sets of nearly identical horses and black carriages lined up in long rows outside the terminal. Such efficiency impressed Maggie Rose, and she told him so. "I grew up here, so getting around is easy for me," he explained, helping her onto the carriage. "You'll catch on, especially once the subway station opens. But don't worry; we usually travel in pairs or larger groups, anyway."

Driving the carriage, he kept up his constant prattle as he dodged fast-moving streetcars, stray dogs, scurrying pedestrians, and the occasional motorcar. Even at this late hour, the city buzzed with activity such as Maggie had never seen. *Why, in Sandy Shores, everything closes up tighter than a drum at five-thirty,* she thought—*that is, everything but the several saloons and restaurants.* Here, though, people of all genders, races, sizes, and ages roamed the streets. Some were selling wares, others begging for quarters; some were huddled on street corners, others sitting on crates or boxes, perhaps looking for a place to lay their heads for the night.

"I can imagine what you're thinking," Stanley said as he maneuvered the carriage onto Park Avenue, heading north, and clicked his horse into a slow trot. "You've probably never seen anything like this place. Mrs. Bingham says you hail from some little town in Michigan. What part?"

"The west side, smack on the shores of beautiful Lake Michigan, about halfway up the state. The town is small, yes, but thriving. We have one main street running east and west—Water Street—with lots of little stores and businesses on either side. Don't be running your horse too fast going west, though, or you'll fall into the harbor," she joked. "'Course, the railroad docks and barges would stop you first, I suppose."

He chuckled, and she decided she liked the smooth tenor of his quiet laughter. "Of all the orphanages in the city, how'd you decide on the Sheltering Arms Refuge?" he asked. "We're a lot smaller than the Foundling Hospital and the Children's Aid Society."

"Someone seeking financial support for your fine organization spoke at our church more than a year ago. I believe his name was Mr. Wiley."

"That'd be Uncle Herbie—Mrs. Bingham's brother."

"He showed us a few pictures and talked a great deal about the destitute children wandering the city—'street Arabs,' he called them. Ever since then, the Lord has kept up His constant nudging, so after much correspondence back and forth, not to mention the process of convincing my father to let me loose, I've finally arrived!"

Stanley glanced casually in both directions before urging his horse through the intersection at East 50th and Park Streets, crossing streetcar tracks and skirting a good-sized pothole. Their amiable conversation continued, but she had to concentrate to drown out all the commotion going on around her, not to mention the smells—a blend of fried food, gasoline, manure, and rancid garbage. And the sounds! Why, the very streets seemed to reverberate with the clamor of loud conversations, tinny barroom music, thudding horses' hooves, barking dogs, and the occasional baby's cry from some upstairs flat.

Stanley Barrett veered the carriage onto East 65th Street, crossed Lexington, 3rd, and 2nd, and made a right on Dover, driving another couple of blocks before directing the horse up a long drive to a stately three-story brick structure. Maggie's very senses seemed to stand on end. "Is this it?" she asked, feasting her eyes on the edifice, which appeared bigger than what she'd imagined from looking at the few photos she'd received.

Stanley guided his horse to a stop, breathed a sigh, and tossed the reins over the brake handle, turning to her with a smile. She decided he had a pleasant one, tainted only partially by a set of crooked teeth. "This is it. What do you think?"

She gazed at her surroundings—a brick house situated on a sprawling plot of land and surrounded by numerous trees, a stable, and several outbuildings. Who would believe that just blocks from this serene setting lay a whole different world? "I think—it's beautiful." Unexpected emotion clogged her throat. She looked up to see a head poke through the curtains of one of the upstairs windows. One of the orphans?

"Beautiful? Well, it's old, I'll give you that. Ginny, er, Mrs. Bingham inherited the historic place from her wealthy grandfather back in the 1880s. She and the Mr. have been operating it as an orphanage for the past seventeen or so years. In fact, I was one of their first residents. But I'm sure you'll get the whole story, if you haven't already, when you're more rested." He winked, gave another low chuckle, and jumped from the rig with ease. "Come on, I'll help you down."

With his assistance, her feet soon landed on solid ground. She lifted her long skirts and stepped away from the carriage, eyes fastened on the three-story structure and the aging brick fence that surrounded the property's borders and was covered by lush blankets of ivy.

Stanley allowed her a moment's peace as she stood before her new "home" and tried to picture its interior. Suddenly, the front door swung open. In its glow stood a portly woman with an apron tied about her waist; grayish hair hung haphazardly about her oval face, and a smile stretched from cheek to cheek as she lifted her hand to wave.

"Well, glory be, come and look who's here, Henry. It's the little miss from Michigan!"

Chapter Two

L uke Madison raked a hand through his straight, chestnut-colored hair, yawned, and tried to keep his eyes from crossing as he scanned what must have been his hundredth document of the day. As usual, he was looking for closure. Rolling his shoulders, he tried to work the stiffness out of his back and neck. Sitting for hours and downing bottomless cups of coffee had a way of wreaking havoc on the muscles, not to mention his stomach, which hadn't consumed anything nutritious in more days than he could remember.

The clock above the newsroom door ticked off the lateness of the day: a quarter past nine. He'd slept exactly three hours last night, and he didn't hold out much hope that this pattern would change anytime soon. What was the point in going back to an empty apartment where all he could do was roam from room to room?

His eyes fell to the commentary he'd been reading. He snatched it up, folded the paper in half, and began reading again.

Not withstanding the declaration of the first mate of the General Slocum that his effort to fight the fire was made useless because the hose had burst

in many places, and the testimony that the canvas
covers of life belts had rotted, the local officials of
the United States Steamboat Inspection Service
yesterday declared the life-saving appliances were
in good order.

"That's hogwash!" Luke mumbled to himself. "Nothing
about that lousy excursion boat was safe." Moving his lips
with determined fervor, he continued to read from the article
of June 17.

Robert S. Rodie, the Supervising Inspector of
the Second District, in which is situated this port,
said the inspection of the Slocum, made on May
5 last, was complete in every way, and that the
boat in every respect fulfilled the requirements
of the law as to machinery, hull, and the various
apparatus used in the saving of lives and putting
out of fires.

"More hogwash! No one wants to take responsibility!" he
spat, tossing the *Times* article aside and watching it land at the
top of the heap of other similar findings regarding the senseless
burning of the *General Slocum* on June 15, some two months
ago. The tragedy had resulted in the drowning and scorching
deaths of more than a thousand women and children. His
mind rehashed the hellish day, as it had a million times before.
He seized his coffee mug from the corner of his desk, thinking
to gulp down what remained of the black brew, but the dead
fly floating on the surface made him decide otherwise.

"Argh!" he growled, nearly retching with the mere
thought of swallowing something so nasty, never mind that
his cold coffee, thick with grounds, would have turned his
innards anyway. He nearly flung the entire thing in the
wastebasket, but instead, he plunked it back on his desk
with disgust. Overhead, a ceiling fan droned, stirring the

stale air in the fifth floor newsroom of the New York World Building. Overlooking the space, dimly lit desks revealed die-hard reporters poring over some hot story or another for the next day's *World*. A low hum of indecipherable conversation was interrupted by the occasional ring of a telephone or the shuffle of footsteps.

He swiveled in his chair, folded his hands behind his head, and gazed out the closest window, which looked out over the city. A burning stomach and nagging muscle aches reminded him of his sorry state.

He didn't know how long he'd been sitting there, staring at the city lights, and dreaming of days past, but he returned to the present at the sound of someone clearing his throat. He spun back around in his chair and started shuffling papers.

Owen Perry stood looking down his beak-like nose at him, suit jacket hanging askew off his shoulders, tie coming loose at the collar. Suspenders did their job of holding up his pants, but his stout gut and his sagging belt kept his shirt from staying tucked in properly. A tight frown creased his forehead.

"It's time we talked, kid," Perry said, pushing up his wire-rimmed spectacles with his index finger. He pulled out a chair on the other side of Luke's desk and sat down with a noisy grunt.

Luke hated when Owen Perry called him 'kid,' like he was fresh out of school and knew nothing of life. In his head, he cursed his boss. He knew more than most twenty-seven-year-olds, maybe even more than Perry himself. "What's up?" he asked, shoving aside a stack of papers to make room on the desk for his elbows. Something in the man's expression told Luke he didn't want to know the answer.

Owen took his time pulling out a cigarette from his inside coat pocket, lit up, and took a couple of long drags. Raking a hand through his thinning head of gray hair, the middle-aged fellow blew out two perfect smoke rings, settled back in his chair, and leveled Luke with a penetrating look. "Here's the thing. I'm pulling you off this *General Slocum* story."

Luke lurched forward. "What?" Sudden outrage made his voice shriek at an unnatural pitch. He quieted. "You can't do that."

Owen's frown deepened as he shifted in his chair. "I can, and I will."

Of course, he could. He was the managing editor of the *New York World*, not to mention Luke's boss. Luke back-pedaled as calmly as he could. "Why would you do that? Look at this mountain of data. My findings indicate the Knickerbocker Steamboat Company's had to pay a slew of fines in the past."

"So what?"

"So, they've been found to be negligent."

"Not this time. There's been no trial yet."

"There will be. And when there is, somebody will pay."

"Yeah, somebody will, and that's why we have a court system. It's not your battle."

A bitter taste burned the back of Luke's throat; his nerves were a jangled mess. "It is my battle, and you know it," he growled. "It's everybody's battle—shoot! The entire city's battle!" He swallowed hard and slammed the tall stack of papers on his desk with his hand. "I've got more evidence right here, Owen. Life preservers fell apart in the victims' hands. The lifeboats had been bolted in place, even though the ship's inspector, Henry Lundberg, had certified the ship safe one month before. My bet is, he didn't probe too deeply, being as he got paid per inspection. He might've even gotten some pressure from certain influential people to overlook a few things."

Owen's look of apathy made Luke forge ahead. "And why didn't the captain beach the ship on the Bronx shore instead of going clear to North Brother Island? Think of the lives that might've been saved!"

Owen Perry's left eyebrow shot above his wire-rims. "Or not. Chances are, it wouldn't've made a bit of difference, kid. Captain Van Schaick has a fine reputation. With the lumber-yards and gas storage tanks lining the Bronx shore, he feared the threat of spreading fires and explosions. He had to do some fast thinking. Don't be so quick to judge the fellow."

"Hundreds of lives were lost, Owen, and somebody'd better take the blame."

"The city's got their finest investigators working on it. Make no mistake, there will be plenty of court trials."

"They still haven't given us the official body count, but it's a known fact some 1300 people were on that excursion boat, and fewer than three hundred are alive and accounted for, which means…."

"I know what it means, kid. I can do the math. The point is, you're off the case."

"But—why?"

In the pause that followed, the air between them nearly sparked with tension.

Perry took another puff of his cigarette and blew the smoke out his nostrils. "Look at you. You're a mess. Bet you haven't slept one full night since it happened." He had him there. "You're not lookin' good. You've lost weight; it's obvious. You're pale and worn-out, and your colleagues have been carrying your load."

"What?" Anger crept up Luke's spine. "I carry my own weight. I'm here more hours than anyone else in this newspaper." At his indignant remark, Luke felt the stares of several newsmen. He was shocked by their lack of rebuttal.

"Being here in body doesn't equate to being here in mind, kid. Remember that shooting up on Lafayette last week? I asked you to cover it, but you couldn't lay aside your *Slocum* investigation long enough to ride up there and ask a few questions. Moore had to do it for you."

"He was glad for the footwork. He's the one who came and asked me if he could cover it. He's a rookie. I thought the experience would be good for him."

"Without my authorization? I told *you* to do it. And what about the investigation into Lewis Blackwell, the New York congressman who's up for reelection this November? There's talk he's been involved in some shady income tax deals, not to mention a sticky divorce. Where did your inquiry wind up—or did you pass that off on someone else, as well?"

Perspiration beaded on the back of Luke's neck. Lewis Blackwell ranked low on his list of priorities, even though the fellow did warrant thorough scrutiny. He reached up to loosen the top button of his collar, then rubbed the back of his neck where a sudden knot had formed. "Okay. I'll admit, I've slacked off a bit in a couple of areas. But...."

"More than a couple," Owen cut in. "Want me to list them?"

He knew there were more. He didn't need a list. Luke sucked in a heavy, labored breath and wiped his sleeve over his sweat-soaked face. *Blast, why can't we get more air moving in this steamy newsroom?* he griped to himself. "I'll do better, Owen," he said, hating the desperation creeping into his voice, hating even more the traces of sympathy stealing over his boss's countenance. Yes, he'd been lax, but for good reason. He had to get to the cause of that massive fire. Couldn't the man see that? On that fateful day, he'd lost his fiancée, Annalise Engel, the love of his life, not to mention his future mother-in-law, Zelda, and his aunt, Frances Connors, the woman most responsible for raising him from a very young age. It was his duty—his consolation—to get answers.

"You need to pull yourself together, young man. Move on."

Move on? If ever he wanted to strike somebody, it was now. How did one "move on," much less work, after a loss like that? Come to think of it, how was all of Little Germany even functioning? Last he heard, they weren't. Many of the men who'd lost their wives and children had committed suicide. Others had deserted the neighborhood in hopes of escaping their unbearable pain and misery. Even Annalise's surviving family—her father, Heinz, her two brothers, Stefan and Erich, and their wives—were considering pulling up stakes, selling the family restaurant, and moving elsewhere. Before anyone knew it, there'd be nothing left of Little Germany.

Owen Perry shook his head. "You can't be objective, Luke." At last, he had dropped the 'kid,' but using his first name was no improvement. "It's hitting too close to home for you. We need somebody neutral working on this story, somebody not so…personally affected. That's not you. You know it's not you."

"I can do it, Owen." That old burning in his gut fired up like a raging furnace.

Owen's bulky frame shifted in the chair. "I've got something else in mind for you," he said through the half-smoked cigarette hanging out the side of his mouth. He scratched his head with one hand and tapped the fingers of the other on the edge of Luke's desk, hard lines etched into his harried-looking face.

"What are you talking about?"

"A human interest story. I think it'd be a good change of pace."

Rebellion started running a fast course through his veins. "What sort of human interest story?" Human interest stories didn't strike him as challenging, especially after having spent the past eight or so weeks hashing out the gory details of the *General Slocum* tragedy.

"The city's got a real problem with homeless waifs; a whole rash of crimes is stemming up on every side because of them. Orphanage doors are wide open, but beds are filling fast."

Luke didn't like the sounds of this. "That's nothing new. Street Arabs have been running rampant for decades."

"And something needs to be done about them. I was thinking you could go out on the streets and talk to some of these children—figure out how they survive, what put them there in the first place, visit an orphanage, maybe catch the next train heading west with orphans and watch the process of them finding new homes and getting a second chance at life.

"Ila, my wife, you know, has befriended a woman by the name of Virginia Bingham. She and her husband own and operate a children's home somewhere between Midtown and the Upper East Side by the name of—let's see here—Sheltering

Arms Rescue, no, Refuge. I have the name and address right here." He pulled a rumpled piece of paper from his side pocket and squinted at it through his spectacles. "Sheltering Arms Refuge," he read before tossing it on top of Luke's desk. "Seems she inherited the old estate from her wealthy grandfather and turned it into a home for waifs. Ila met her at a charity benefit last year and hit it off with her. They've kept in contact. Anyway, Ila says Mrs. Bingham is expecting you."

"What do you mean, she's expecting me?" Luke folded his arms, leaned forward, and tried to appear calm.

Owen didn't blink an eye. "She's got some ideas for your news piece."

"My news piece."

"Yeah, I think it'll be a winner, should do well all around, be good for both you and the paper. The *World*'s new editor-in-chief wants stories that speak more to the audience. In years past, we've taken a hit for printing sensationalism. Oh, we publish the news, no question there. But Cobb wants more stories that grip the emotions—not in a negative way, though, as some of our stories have done—like that one where we focused on the tenement housing and all the deaths that occurred after that heat wave in '83."

"And how would a story about destitute, homeless urchins wind up any differently? It has yellow journalism written all over it."

Owen Perry moved in closer, his eyes flashing in the dimly lit room, his spectacles sliding further down his sloped nose. "You'll print the truth as you see it and not some hammed up version concocted to drive up circulation. The *World* is not a rag anymore, and it's reporters like you who've helped turn the tide. Those waifs out there need a voice, Luke, and you can be that voice."

"The *Slocum* victims need a voice, too, as does the entire German neighborhood of families those women and children left behind."

"They have plenty of voices, Luke. Like I said, there's intense, probing research taking place right now. Hey, I feel for those poor folks, I really do, but there comes a time when you need to step aside and allow the story to run through the proper channels. You are a news reporter, not an officer of the law. Leave the investigation end to the detectives or, I swear, you'll lose your mind."

That old pinch in the gut returned. Would he ever regain a sense of stability, of normalcy? He looked at his pile of research. Annalise's oval china-doll face flashed before his mind's eye—her rosy cheeks, pert nose, raven-black hair, and chocolate-colored eyes she'd inherited from her German father and Polish mother. The memory of her feather-light laughter played at his senses until he had to give his head a quick shake.

"I don't know," he murmured, picking up a pencil and drumming the eraser on his desk. "I owe it to Annalise and my Aunt Frances and...."

"I'm not giving you a choice here, kid," Owen said. "Plainly put, I want you out of the office for a while."

Luke's head shot up with this last bit of news, a huge ball of tension rolling around in his chest. "What do you mean, 'out of the office'?"

Owen Perry took one last puff of his cigarette and then snuffed it out in the clean ashtray on Luke's desk. Unruffled, he heaved a loud breath and pushed himself up from his chair. Suddenly, it seemed like every head in the newsroom was turned their way. Certainly, all movement ceased, as if they'd all been waiting for this moment.

"It's for the best, kid. You'll be as good as new in a few months."

"In a few mon—." In a frenzied gesture, Luke raked back several loose strands of hair off his forehead and glanced about the room, making eye contact with his friend and colleague, Nathan Emory, whose desk was stationed a mere twenty feet from his. Had Nathan seen this coming and failed to tell him? Nathan dropped his gaze almost immediately, burying his head in a stack of paperwork. Luke shook his head and hissed a curse. Then, through clenched teeth, he murmured, "What is it you expect me to do, Owen?"

"I told you. I want a story, just not one about the *General Slocum*. Take as much time as you need; in fact, I don't want to see your face around here for three months. Think of it as a…a leave of absence. A paid one, of course. I'm being generous here, Luke. Ila said this Bingham woman has a spare room for you, 'case you want to bunk up there 'stead of in that empty place of yours."

"A spare room," Luke repeated.

"Might do you good to get a change of scenery. 'Sides, your getting inside the heads of some of those penniless street urchins could give you a whole new outlook on things; make you realize you still got some purpose left in you."

Purpose? As in, a reason to continue living? Luke wiped his face with his hand, feeling the roughness of his day-old beard. His nerves were so rattled that the pencil he was holding started to quiver, so he tossed it down and tucked his hands deep inside his trouser pockets. He would have cried if he'd a clue how to muster up his tears, but he hadn't shed as much as one at the several funerals he'd attended in June. No, his pain festered and brewed in other ways—namely, rage and discontent.

Silence hovered between them like a nameless ghost as a thirty-second stare ensued. Looking weary from his fifty-some years, Owen sighed and leaned forward, fingers steepled on Luke's desk, and muttered quietly, "You'll be okay, kid. You just—you need to step back a bit and regain your focus."

It must have been a vacant nod Luke returned, for he surely felt dead inside. "Yeah, sure," he managed.

After Owen made his leave, Luke grabbed several items from his desktop and drawers in a mindless flurry, tossing them into a small wooden crate. Several pairs of eyes watched from afar, but he refused to acknowledge them.

Finally, Nathan Emory cleared his throat. "Hey, Luke, I'm sorry, man."

"We all are," Walter Wertz chimed in from the back of the room.

"We didn't see it coming, Madison," said George Peterson in his usual gruff voice, this time softened by a hint of sympathy.

"No?" Eyes on his task, Luke refused to look up. He just kept tossing items into the crate—pencils, pens, pads of paper, a box of paperclips, a spiral notebook, the address of the Sheltering Arms Refuge, and all his files of research. A photo of Annalise—the last one he'd taken of her, down at the marina—went on top of the heavy heap. "Seems like you would have, seeing as you were all carrying my load for me."

"Luke, listen," Nathan attempted, pushing back in his chair, its legs grating on the wood floor. He stood up and faced Luke just as he picked up the crate and started for the door. "It's probably for the best. Mr. Perry's right, you know; you need some time away."

"We'll be thinkin' about you," said Walter.

"Save your breath—all of you," Luke said, turning. A part of him hated the way he was leaving things. These were good people; he had no business treating them with disrespect. But something else in him, a bear-like persona, rose up in defense. Who did they think they were? As if they could sum up all his needs in a neat little nutshell and send him on his way! Three months away from the office? Three *years* wouldn't cure him of his heartbreak, but that didn't mean he'd quit showing up for work. Anger—no, fuming rage—boiled up within him.

He pushed through the door and headed down the long corridor, passing the elevators. He needed the stairs tonight. He needed to take them at a run.

"Luke! Wait up!" Nathan's breathless yell forced him to a stop.

He turned and shook his head. "Don't—say anything."

Nathan adjusted his shirt collar with a fidgety hand and cleared his throat. "If it's any consolation, none of us complained to Mr. Perry. But, Luke, you gotta face it, man. You're in bad shape." Luke rolled his eyes toward the ceiling and shifted the weight of his load from one arm to the other. Why did everyone keep telling him that? "Losing Annalise and your aunt had to have been about the worst kind of pain you could have endured, but you have to find a way to go on." Nathan put a hand on Luke's shoulder. Luke flinched, wanting to throw if off.

"Look, I gotta go."

"I know."

"Thanks."

"I'm—praying for you."

Luke couldn't help it. A harrumph flew past his lips. "Good luck on that one."

Nathan gave his head a slight shake and smiled. "Luck has nothing to do with it, my friend. I'm hoping that someday you'll see that, in the middle of your pain, there is a balm to be found. You'll find it the day you start trusting Christ."

A throbbing head and burning eyeballs had him squinting in the dimly lit hallway. He looked at his friend, finding himself at a complete loss for words—and too tired to scrounge for any. A shudder moved up his spine, and he quickly turned. "I'll see you around, okay?"

"You know where I live if you ever want to talk."

"Sure, okay," he said, nearly running down the hall and through the door marked "Stairs."

He didn't stop running till he pushed through the big double entrance doors of the New York World Building. A blast of hot, heavy air hit him square in the face. Across the street, the lights of City Hall cast long shadows on Park Row. Evening traffic produced whizzing streetcars, bustling horse-drawn carriages, and strolling pedestrians, everyone moving with purpose and intent.

It struck him then that the city still functioned, as if it hadn't just lost some one thousand women and children mere months ago—as if no one knew a nearby German neighborhood lay nearly in ruins.

He tossed his head back and looked up at the darkening sky. Then, breathing deeply, he started the ten-block walk to his barren brownstone apartment.

Chapter Three

S omething pulled at Maggie's senses, urging her to open her eyes. But foggy thoughts and utter weariness kept her eyelids shut tight as fiddle strings—until the sounds of faint whispers had her working all the harder to ignore them.

"She's sleepin'."

"She ain't. She's fakin' it. Look, her eyes is movin'."

"She sure is pretty."

"She's okay."

"Mrs. Bingham says we're not to bother her; says she put in a long day of travel yesterday."

"We ain't botherin'. We jus' lookin', is all."

With careful effort, Maggie raised her left eyelid slightly, long enough to see two pairs of big eyes—one set of blue and the other of cocoa brown—situated just inches from her face.

"Haww," one of the scalawags murmured. "She seen us. Come on."

Maggie heard their retreating steps, and for an instant, she considered letting them go. But curiosity got the best of her. "Wait." She blinked and sat up, letting out a big yawn as she focused on the little intruders. One was dark-skinned, the other as pale as the day is bright. Both girls looked to be six or seven, younger than Jesse Gant—well, Jesse *Devlin*, now that the Sandy Shores sheriff, Gabriel Devlin, and her older sister, Hannah Grace, had married and adopted the orphan boy. "What're your names?"

The blonde mite hesitated at the door, but the dark-skinned girl skipped back to her bedside, at least a dozen or more jet-black braids bound with red barrettes bouncing with every step. "I's Millie, and that there's Audrey. We already knowed you're Miss Maggie Rose Kane. Mrs. Bingham tol' us you was comin'."

Audrey hung back at the door. "We best go, Millie, 'fore Mrs. Bingham gives us the business for disturbing Miss Kane."

"Oh, don't go," Maggie said. "You're not disturbing me one bit. Truth is, I want to hear all about both of you. Come, sit up on the bed with me." She patted the twin-sized mattress, knowing they'd have to squeeze together to fit. The upstairs bedroom she had been assigned wasn't even half the size of the attic closet she had shared with her younger sister, Abbie Ann, back in Sandy Shores. In fact, tiny as a teacup described it best.

Besides the twin bed, the furniture consisted of a small oak dresser with beveled mirror, a bed stand with a single drawer, and in one corner, a small, armless, wooden rocker with a brocade seat. Draped over the back of the rocker was a handwoven lap blanket, and above it hung a painting of a young girl seated in front of a vanity and combing her long, blonde tresses. In the corner opposite the rocker stood a narrow wardrobe that almost reached the ceiling, and in the wall next to that was a double-pane window overlooking the backyard. Lacy curtains and a matching valance adorned the window, giving the square little room a feminine touch and making her wonder about its history.

Without waiting for another summons, Millie leaped on the bed, jarring the springs, but Audrey still hesitated at the door, her wispy, blonde hair pulled back in a ponytail, eyes a wildflower blue. "You're welcome to join us, Audrey," Maggie urged, fluffing the pillow behind her back and pulling the comforter up to her waist. Millie stretched out her spindly legs, pressed the wrinkles out of her calf-length gingham dress to make it lie flat, and folded her hands in her lap. Taking baby steps, Audrey approached the bed and crawled up on the side opposite of Millie, sandwiching Maggie between the two of them. From downstairs, the aromas of bacon and eggs wafted up through the floor registers. Maggie could hear the rattle of pots and pans and a low, pleasant-sounding conversation involving two voices, male and female. In response, Maggie's stomach rumbled with hunger, while her chest beat with eager anticipation.

Thank You for bringing me here, Lord. And thank You for the peace that comes from simple obedience. Yes, Jacob Kane had been hesitant to release his daughter into the big city, but once he'd accepted that her calling was from God, he'd had little recourse. "One doesn't argue with the Lord, I suppose," he'd relented after a long discussion in April as to whether she should travel to New York.

She'd leaped to her feet and run across the room to hug his neck. "I'll write often, Papa," she'd said.

"Twice a week, at the very least," he replied, kissing her forehead before pulling her close. After that, it was a matter of making final preparations for beginning the job, packing and organizing, and finally looking into the best means of travel.

"How old are you?" asked Millie, pulling her out of her private thoughts.

"How old do you think?" Maggie threw back on a playful note.

"Forty-one?"

"What?" She gasped and pressed a hand over her mouth. She must look a sight, she realized, with her blonde hair falling haphazardly around her face, her eyes still droopy with fatigue, and her left cheek creased and wrinkly from prolonged pressure against her pillow.

"She don't know her numbers very good," Audrey put in, half mortified, if her gaping mouth was any indication. "I'd say you're more like fifteen—or twenty-four."

Maggie giggled. "Nope. Both wrong." Then, crooking her finger to invite the girls closer, she whispered, "I'm sixty-five."

"Haww." Millie pulled back and gasped, the whites of her eyes a stark contrast to her berry-brown skin. "You're joshin' us. Ain't she joshin', Audie?"

Maggie laughed as she put her arms around both girls and gathered them close, marveling at the immediate love she had for them, inspired the more that neither seemed eager to pull away. "Yes, I'm joshing. I was born in January 1884. There, now, can either of you figure out how old that would make me?"

"Nope," Millie answered at once, unwilling to do the math.

Audrey squinted, and Maggie imagined the wheels of thought spinning madly in her feathery blonde head. "This is 1904," she announced. "So, that'd make you...." She extended both hands, spread her fingers, and mentally counted each digit. "Twenty!" she squealed.

"My! Aren't you the smart one?"

"She gots good grades at school," Millie said, seeming proud of the fact. "Miss Marble sa' she reads better'n anybody."

"Miss Marble?"

"Ar' teacher from las' year," Millie offered. "We both went t' Public School 62. It's thataway."

She pointed at the wall. Maggie grinned. "Do you walk there?"

"Nope," Millie said, seeming to enjoy her role as spokesperson. "Mr. Stanley drives us little ones ever'day, but the bigger ones takes the train."

"Mr. Stanley." For a moment, she'd forgotten about Stanley Barrett, the nice young man who'd picked her up at Grand Central the previous day. She wondered briefly about his role at Sheltering Arms Refuge, realizing that she had much to learn. Goodness, she wasn't sure of her own role, let alone Mr. Barrett's. She had not received a work contract outlining her responsibilities; the refuge had simply sent a letter of welcome, saying they had read and approved her application for employment, and that, after diligent prayer, they believed she would fit their needs perfectly. She knew they had hired her to work with the children in the orphanage and to assist as a train agent when the need arose, but after that, she hadn't a clue what was expected of her. For all she knew, she'd be washing tonight's dinner dishes—and enjoying every minute of it. The Lord had called her to Sheltering Arms Refuge for a reason, and she meant to avail herself of every opportunity. "We are impressed by your desire to serve the

Lord in this capacity," Mrs. Bingham had written. "This can be a thankless job at times, as destitute children tend to come and go from our place, but we continue to seek out servants who are willing to assist us in loving them. We sensed your strength of character, Miss Kane, and your heart of faith, and so it is with eagerness that we await your arrival at our humble estate."

A girl who looked to be twelve or thirteen paused in the doorway, straggly brown hair that looked like it hadn't seen a comb in a few days falling helplessly about her oval face. Her azure eyes, the color of the sky, narrowed on all three of them before she gave her head a slight shake. "You girls best get down to the kitchen and eat your breakfast. Mrs. Bingham won't be happy if she finds out you was botherin' the new lady," she scolded.

"Oh, please, they're no bother. In fact, you're welcome to join us. What's your name?" Maggie asked, eager to learn as much as she could about the residents at Sheltering Arms.

"That there's Maxine Ward. She hasn't lived here very long," Millie answered for her. "She gots a short temper sometimes," she added in a whisper.

Maxine's brow pulled tight. "Millie Sargent, don't go talkin' 'bout me t' other folks."

Maggie cringed at the mounting tension.

"I'm just sayin' what's true," was Millie's pert reply, even as she moved closer to Maggie. Audrey kept her lips sealed. "You was mean as a alley cat when you first comed here."

Maxine pulled back her diminutive shoulders. "Well, maybe I had reason to be."

Maggie prayed that a batch of wisdom would rain down on her, instinctively knowing this would be far from her last such prayer. "Well, girls, maybe you should go have some breakfast now. I'll get dressed and join you in a bit, how's that?"

The girls slid off the bed, Audrey making a beeline for the door, Millie not as eager to leave. Maggie put her hand on the child's shoulder and urged her toward the door. When Millie disappeared around the corner, Maxine huffed a noisy breath. "Sometimes, that Millie Sargent gets on my last nerve," she muttered.

Disregarding the remark, Maggie padded to the bureau to survey herself in the mirror. Dark circles under eyes of blue and a head of disheveled blonde hair spoke clearly of her restless night's sleep. "Ugh," she muttered at her reflection, watching from the corner of her eye for Maxine's reaction.

The girl edged further into the room, taking care not to let down her guard.

"Would you like to show me around the place later?"

One shoulder raised a few notches. "If I got time. It all depends on what jobs Mrs. Bingham's got lined up for me. I'll probably be pullin' weeds out o' the back garden."

"Really? Oh, I'd love to help you." Maggie leaned closer to the mirror, feigning interest in her appearance when, really, it was Maxine's deportment she found most fascinating. Who was this child, and what had brought her to the refuge? She pinched some color into her cheeks. "We have a garden back home, and—."

"I like doin' my chores alone, mostly. 'Sides, I won't know for sure what I'm doin' till I check the wall chart."

"The wall chart?"

"Yeah, us kids have different chores every day. We have to check the chart after breakfast."

"Oh, well, that's good. Everybody has to chip in—sort of like a family."

Maxine shrugged. "I guess. If that's what a family does."

What an intriguing comment, Maggie thought. She wanted to probe, but she decided to let the girl talk on her own terms. She straightened, turned, and opened the valise she'd carried on the train. It held two changes of clothing and a few items to tide her over until her trunk arrived.

The sound of approaching footsteps made both girls turn. Mrs. Bingham stopped and stood in the doorway, her expression warm enough to melt frost off a windowpane. Last night, Maggie had loved her at first sight. Even though she looked nothing like her Grandmother Kane with her rounded frame and less-than-put-together features, she held the same kind of compassion in her eyes as Grandmother's did, along with an underlying patience and sympathy for the pain of others.

"Well, I see you two have met," Mrs. Bingham said, a smile creasing her already wrinkled lips, hands tucked deep into her soiled apron pockets. As early as the hour was, a quarter past eight, the woman's hair had already begun to fall from its tightly woven knot at the top of her head, making Maggie question what time she started her day. "Hope Audrey and Millie didn't disturb your much needed rest, the little rascals."

Maggie would hardly call Audrey a rascal, but Millie— well, she had potential.

"They was right up on her bed," Maxine quickly informed her. "But I chased 'em down straightaway."

"Well, that's good, then. They needed to get started on their breakfast. Did you check on the other girls?"

"They're startin' t' rouse. Little Emily still has that cough."

"Yes, I know." Mrs. Bingham's brow arched in worry. "Dr. Hesselbart's making his rounds this afternoon. I'll have him check on her again."

Footsteps paraded loudly on the floor overhead, sounding like a herd of wild horses. Mrs. Bingham looked up. "Stanley must be bringing down his band of wild banshees. Naturally, they'll be hungrier than a pack of wolves. I best get back to the kitchen." Mrs. Bingham turned to leave, then quickly stopped and pulled an envelope from her pocket, thrusting it at Maggie. "Mercy, I almost forgot. You got a letter from home already. Mr. Langley, the postman, dropped it off this morning."

Maggie gasped. "I did?" Eager fingers grasped and promptly tore open the envelope in their midst. But then, remembering her manners, she stopped and clutched the unread missive to her chest.

"You go ahead and read your letter, dear. Come along, Maxine. Let's give Miss Kane her privacy." She looked at Maggie. "We'll get down to brass tacks later as to your responsibilities around Sheltering Arms, but right now, I got many mouths to feed."

Just then, a procession of marching feet thundered down the staircase nearest the kitchen. "Slow down, Billy Harper," came the familiar voice of Stanley Barrett. "Your breakfast's not going anywhere."

"Stop pushin'," came a whiny command.

"Then don't stop halfway down," was the harsh response.

"Give me that," said another.

"It ain't yours."

"Boys!" Stanley issued, his voice smooth and unmoved. "Get back in line."

Apparently, they complied, for the noise level dropped immediately.

Mrs. Bingham sighed and shook her head. "See what I mean?"

Alone at last, Maggie unfolded the silky stationery and started to read.

My Dear Daughter,

Are you surprised to receive a letter so soon upon your arrival at Sheltering Arms Refuge? I wrote it before you even left just so you would have something to remind you of home. I wouldn't want you getting so wrapped up in your work there that you forget about your loving family back in Sandy Shores.

A tiny tear rolled down her cheek. How could she possibly forget her precious family? Silly Papa.

I wanted you to know how proud I am of you, Maggie Rose. We all feel the same, of course, but as your father, I want to be the first to express how very much I admire your courage and spunk, not to mention your fervor for the Lord. It makes me feel as if your grandmother and I did something right in raising you. (I admit, it still pains me to think about your mother dying so young.)

It took a bit of convincing on your part to bring me over to your side, did it not? New York City is such a big place, especially when compared to where you grew up. As you are well aware, I didn't want to let you go. I've already lost one daughter to marriage, not that I am not tickled for Hannah Grace to have found such a wonderful husband in Gabriel Devlin. Still, my heart does weigh heavy thinking about this big house appearing emptier

*than usual. But what am I saying? I'm sure that Abbie
Ann will more than make up the difference with her endearing humor.*

At that, Maggie wiped her damp eyes and actually laughed
aloud. He certainly had his youngest daughter pegged to a
tee. Abbie Ann was nothing if she wasn't a jokester.

*Now that you find yourself at Sheltering Arms Refuge,
you must rest assured your family will keep you in their
daily prayers and that I, my daughter, have given you
my blessing. The Lord certainly has great plans for you. I
have always had an inner sense that the Lord would call
you, of my three girls, into service. It was more a need for
me to relinquish you into His capable, loving hands, and
now that I have, I am confident you are exactly where
He wants you to be.*

*Keep your eyes upon your heavenly Father as you seek
to do His will.*

Do not keep us waiting long for your first letter home.

*Love,
Papa*

K

On Manhattan's Lower East Side, Luke Madison lay
wide-eyed, watching a huge gray spider make its way across
the ceiling. He was amazed at how it could walk upside down
without falling into space. Had Aunt Frances known a spider
was crawling freely through the apartment, she'd have had
a conniption. She'd always kept the most impeccable house,
and even the hired maid, Mrs. Jennings, had never quite measured up to her high standards of cleanliness. But since his

aunt's passing, Luke had let Mrs. Jennings go, valuing his privacy more than a clean dwelling. Now, the place resembled the aftermath of a storm—dishes towering in the kitchen sink, soiled laundry strewn about the floor, papers stacked in ubiquitous piles. Again, Aunt Fran would bemoan the fact her house had lost its sheen.

Luke tossed his lightweight blanket aside and crawled out of bed, ran a hand over his unshaven face, and shuffled down the long hall to the washroom. A wealthy and generous woman, his aunt had left him not only her luxurious, comfortable, two-story brownstone on Houston Street, three blocks from the East River, but all her assets, as well. Shoot, he didn't need that blasted newspaper to earn a living. Thanks to Aunt Frances, he could while away the hours doing nothing and still have plenty of money to live out the remainder of his days on earth—if that's what he wanted to do.

Unfortunately, reporting to work at the New York World Building gave him a sense of purpose, something he felt sorely lacking these days. How dare Owen Perry steal away the one thread of meaning he still clung to with all his might? Now, rather than report to the *World*, rather than investigate what had caused the deaths of those dearest to him, he was to go in search of some orphanage that went by the name of Sheltering Arms Refuge, run by some woman named Virginia Bingham and her husband. How was he to glean anything worthwhile from this pursuit?

Drained from a lack of sleep, he leaned over the pedestal sink and gave a loud groan at his reflection in the mirror. He had a darkish beard that grew fast, so going a day without shaving had never been an option. The current trend seemed to favor facial hair, but he chose not to follow it. Lately, everything he did felt like a chore, and taking out his Solingen straight-edged razor was no exception.

While lathering up his square-set face, he thought about ways to attack the day.

He'd intended to go visit Heinz, Annalise's father, during his lunch break, but since Owen had given him an assignment in the upper Midtown region, backtracking at noon would be too much of a hike. He'd have to put off visiting him until the weekend. He worried about the fellow, who'd lost his beloved wife of thirty-eight years and his beautiful, twenty-three-year-old daughter, but at least he had Stefan and Erich and their wives to cling to for support and courage. The question remained, though, as to whether the family would hang onto the restaurant, particularly since Annalise and Zelda had played such key roles in keeping the business running smoothly—efficient Zelda, always smiling, and Annalise, so full of life and animation, attracting attention without intending to, her charcoal hair flowing freely with every toss of her pretty head, her black diamond eyes sparkling like hot coals. Truth was, most folks who came into Engel's did so to get a glimpse of the women who ran the place. The German cuisine at Engel's was good—great, actually—but the Engel women truly made the place. He should know; he'd been awestruck by Annalise from the moment he first strolled into Engel's with Nathan Emory. At Annalise's recommendation, they'd ordered *Linsen und Spätzle*, a dish with thick egg noodles, dumplings, lentils, and Vienna sausage. Thereafter, it'd been his favorite meal, always accompanied by their famous, fresh-baked pumpernickel bread, Zelda's own recipe.

But business at Engel's had slowed considerably, the very life having gone out of it the day Annalise and Zelda perished in the *General Slocum* disaster. Now, when Luke walked through its doors, a cloud of gloom hovered almost tangibly. The clientele, mostly men, spoke in low tones or sat alone, sipping mugs of beer or coffee with the *World* or the *Times* folded in front of them, their vacant eyes scanning the daily news. Even the smells of pumpernickel bread baking had vanished, another point of grief for many.

Sometimes, Luke wondered why he kept returning there, but down deep, he knew. *She* was there—if not in body, then in spirit. It was his one way of finding that tiny connection. And, of course, there was Heinz. He had to go back for Heinz.

While shaving, he made a mental agenda. Catch a taxi to that homeless refuge and see if he could find a story there. He refused to sit around and do nothing. Owen Perry wanted a human interest story, and Owen Perry would get one.

He figured writing a first-rate piece might put him in Owen's better graces, maybe even get him back in the office sooner.

A three-month leave of absence? He'd go mad hanging around a bunch of homeless waifs that long! And really, who would want to read about them, anyway? They were old news, those little hooligans who ran up and down the streets selling matchboxes, shining shoes, and begging coins off rich folks. Nuisances, they were, but not what one would call newsworthy. Somehow, though, he'd have to manufacture an angle worthy of Owen's critical eye.

He rinsed his straight edge under the hot water faucet and dried it on a towel before folding the blade into its finely crafted wooden handle and setting it back on the cabinet shelf next to Aunt Frances's "health pills" and powders. At least, that's what she'd called them—health pills—but more likely, they were intended to ease the pain of her frequent bouts of arthritis. Laudanum, maybe? Aspirin powder? The bottles had no labels, so for all he knew, they were homemade concoctions. One never quite knew with Aunt Fran. When she had her aches, she kept them to herself.

According to Aunt Frances, most modern medicines were of the devil and should be avoided at all costs. Health pills, she'd say, had their finer points, although Luke was never to learn what they were. Mostly, when she suffered from severe joint pain, she'd sit in her rocker with her Bible in her lap, eyes closed, chin pointed heavenward, sometimes a hand uplifted while her lips moved in silent prayer.

Aunt Frances had been big on prayer. She wasn't so big on open affection, but one never doubted where she stood in her faith.

Personally, Luke had never quite discovered the point of it, that religious lingo, even though he'd attended church services all his life—first to appease Aunt Fran, more recently to appease Annalise. Not anymore, though—not since the senseless deaths of hundreds of women and children on the *General Slocum*.

Why worship a God who would allow a tragedy of such magnitude?

Chapter Four

Maggie unfolded her hands and rose from her kneeling position. She had been saying her morning prayers, the door to her room closed to prevent further distractions. If there was one practice she'd determined to maintain every morning, it was reading her Bible and saying her prayers. The day always went better for her when she invited Christ to lead her steps. And something told her working at Sheltering Arms Refuge just might require a good deal of His faithful leadership.

With one last glance in the mirror and a quick collar adjustment, she primped her hair, pulled back on each side with silver barrettes, smoothed down the wrinkles of her cotton skirt, which she'd failed to remove from her satchel until that very morning, and tugged the sagging belt at her tiny waist a bit tighter. She supposed she looked halfway presentable for her first day on the job—but then, what did it matter, considering most of the residents probably owned very little in the way of fancy dresses, skirts, or dungarees?

Downstairs, she heard clanking dishes, running water, clattering mouths, shuffling footsteps, and a male voice (Mr. Bingham's?) issuing orders. She pulled her shoulders back, taking a deep breath for courage and uttering one last prayer before heading down the wide hallway toward the back stairs, which led down to the kitchen. At one time, these stairs had probably been used mostly by the service staff. Now, everyone in the household seemed to use them, including the boys on the third floor, when mealtime drew near.

The kitchen was a flurry of activity when Maggie entered. Mr. Bingham stood at the stove, flipping pancakes and then piling them one at a time on a large platter. Mrs. Bingham poured what looked like strawberry syrup from a pan into a pitcher while instructing a couple of boys, who looked to be in their young teens, to set more plates and silverware on the table. To three girls, ranging in age from about eight to ten, she gave orders to shake the rugs in the washroom and then start their dusting chores. Apparently, they'd already eaten, indicated by the smudges of strawberry syrup around their mouths. Out of sight but within hearing range, a baby cried. My, but this was a busy place!

At the slight clearing of her throat, everyone turned. "Good morning, everyone," Maggie managed.

Mrs. Bingham set down the pitcher and wiped her hands on the front of her apron, her round face bright as the August sun. "Well, my stars, here she is, folks."

In less time than it takes a bird to soar from one branch to the next, a dozen bodies, big and little, appeared in the doorway connecting the kitchen and dining room. Audrey, Millie, and Maxine were among them. "Didn't I tell you she was pretty?" Mrs. Bingham said. "I hope all this commotion down here hasn't given you second thoughts. Children, this is Miss Kane. Say good morning."

"Good morning," they chimed in unison.

Maggie's heart swelled at the sight of them as she looked from one pair of eyes to the next, some curious, others wary.

"This isn't all of them by a long shot," said Mr. Bingham, his own eyes twinkling with merriment.

"Me and her already met," said Maxine, her bored expression seeming to indicate displeasure at having to greet her twice in one morning.

"And it was my pleasure," Maggie said with a smile, quickly turning her gaze on the roomful of children. "I'd ask you all to tell me your names right now, but I'm afraid I'd forget them on the spot. Except for Audrey and Millie, whom I met earlier." The little girls stood taller, beaming with pride at being singled out.

A brown-haired sprite with freckles plastered liberally over her nose and cheeks stepped forward. "I'm Rose," she announced in a tiny, yet clear, voice.

Maggie's soul soared at the sight of her—there was something about her oversized red-and-white jumper, its front stained with smudges. Two perfect braids (probably plaited by one of the older girls, Maggie figured) hung clear to her skinny waist, one flung over a bony shoulder, the other hanging straight down her front.

Maggie stepped closer and bent at the waist, coming within inches of the child's precious face. "Well, isn't that something! You and I share the same name. I'm Maggie Rose, and you're Rose…Rose….Do you have a middle name?"

Rose's hazel eyes grew round as dinner plates. "Marie. Rose Marie Kring."

"Maggie Rose Kane and Rose Marie Kring. Now, don't we sound like a pair?"

Several more children, having overheard the commotion in the kitchen, came bounding down the stairs and around the corner—boys and girls of all ages, shapes, and sizes. Maggie straightened and, without warning, felt a twist in her heart. How was it possible, outside of God's divine leading, to have fallen in love instantly and effortlessly with all these children?

"Now, don't go crowding her," Mrs. Bingham said. "I declare, you'll scare her clear back to Michigan!"

"Where's Michigan?" asked a young lad who might have been six or seven.

"It's several states west of...." But before Maggie could complete her sentence, Stanley Barrett rounded the corner.

"It's directly north of Ohio, Indiana, and Illinois—and surrounded by water on three sides, which makes it not an island, but a peninsula," he finished for her with a wink and a nod, looking considerably less formal this morning than he had the night before in his Levi work jeans and cotton shirt, sleeves rolled up past his elbows. A straw hat was tucked under one arm. Three young boys ran to him, and he playfully tousled their hair. "Who's going to help me muck stalls today?"

"Ewww," the boys protested unanimously.

"Somebody's got to do it."

"Go look at the chart on the wall," said Mrs. Bingham, turning back to her task of scooping up the syrup pitcher in one hand and the platter of pancakes in the other. "Anyone who hasn't eaten yet, skedaddle to the table. There're dishes to wash and dry later and potatoes to peel for supper."

"Who's peeling potatoes?" asked Maxine, her rounded shoulders sagging.

If Mrs. Bingham noticed her lackadaisical attitude, she didn't let on. "Like I said, check the chart," she hastened, leaving a breeze in her wake when she bustled into the dining room.

"What can I do?" Maggie asked, eager to get started with her responsibilities.

A trail of children followed Mrs. Bingham into the dining room and started pulling out spindle back chairs around the long oak table. Maggie found herself falling into line with the children. The plump woman surveyed the table, tended to a few noisy boys, assisted a younger one with cutting his pancakes, and then turned to Maggie.

"You, my dear, will sit down with the children and have some breakfast." She pointed at a chair. "While you're doing that, I'll go get that squalling baby from the nursery. Later on, you and I will sit down at the kitchen table and have us a cup of tea. How would that be?" Maggie gave a blank nod. "Now stop looking so worried. Everything will be just fine."

And at precisely 10:30, that is just what they did. Maggie and Mrs. Bingham sat at the table, sipping hot mugs of tea and talking, while a baby slept in Mrs. Bingham's arms. They were also joined by a two-year-old, playing on the kitchen floor with an assortment of wooden spoons and measuring containers. Three girls raced through the kitchen and bounded up the stairs. "Slow down," Mrs. Bingham called after them in a stern but patient manner. They did.

Mr. Bingham swept into the room, bent to place a light kiss on his wife's head, then straightened and winked at Maggie. "She's all bark and no bite, my wife, but don't tell the children that."

Maggie smiled, marveling at the older couple over her cup's rim. Twenty-three children, some orphaned, some abandoned, lived in Mr. and Mrs. Bingham's house, and neither acted like that was anything unusual.

During the course of the morning, she'd learned that the woman who had preceded her, an aging spinster named Miss Tuttle, had moved to Florida to be with her sister. Another woman, whom she had yet to meet, worked on the main floor, tending to the children four years of age and younger, but that she was visiting relatives for a few days. Stanley had lived with the Binghams from a very young age, and they considered him as a son more than as an employee. She also learned that an assortment of volunteers came in every day at noon to assist with various household chores, like putting the young ones down for naps, helping to plan weekly menus, and shopping for pantry staples. She, Maggie, would assume the position of house mother, responsible for tending to eight girls, five years of age and older, who resided on the second floor. In September, she would travel as an agent with the children on a train heading west, helping to find homes for as many Sheltering Arms residents as possible.

"So, all these children will be leaving the house in search of new homes, new families?" she asked Mrs. Bingham while the woman bottle-fed the home's newest resident, a six-month-old girl with wispy brown hair and long eyelashes.

"Well, I daresay, most of them will, and all we can do is pray the Lord will provide them with suitable matches. The Reverend Miles over at Dover Street Chapel has many contacts with churches in the Middle West. He calls ahead to arrange things, and we send the children off with a prayer that God will work in divine ways to arrange the best possible placement for each of them."

"But can't they continue living here?"

Mrs. Bingham shook her head. "We are more of a holding tank, if you will. Several of your larger city agencies and hospitals use us as overflow when they can't find a proper place to put the children. They come in off the streets by the droves, you know, some havin' been kicked out by parents who can't afford them anymore, some running away from physically abusive situations, some starving and lost, and others just plain scared and alone." She leaned closer and whispered, "Poor Maxine suffered the worst kind of abuse when her uncle sold her to a brothel up on East 74th Street. She managed to escape in the dead of night by sneaking out through an upper story window, crawling across the steep roof, and then climbing down a tree. Thank the dear Father in heaven, He led her straight to our doors."

Maggie had put a hand to her mouth to cover her uncomely gasp. No wonder Maxine carried a boulder-sized chip. Mrs. Bingham reached over and patted her arm. "I don't mean to shock or frighten you, dear, but it's important to understand the sad realities of life as an orphan in New York City."

Maggie nodded solemnly and watched as Mr. Bingham poured himself a steaming cup of coffee, wondering what had driven him and his wife to devote their married life to serving homeless children. So many questions arose in her mind that she could barely sort them all out. Mr. Bingham turned, took a sip from the cup, and let out a light chuckle. "Maggie—may I call you Maggie?"

"Of course, please do!"

"And you must call us Henry and Ginny."

"Oh, but—are you sure?"

His quiet laughter grew. "We are going to be fast friends, so we better get ourselves on a first-name basis. Living under the same roof makes folks family around here. But as I was about to say, you look perplexed. You mustn't try to figure everything out at once, you know." Had he read her mind? Sensed her need for reassurance? "These children will tax you of all your energy, if you let them—they're very needy, as you can imagine—but bear in mind, we're here to guide and help you. Be sure to come to us if you have any concerns. And, of course, you can always go to Stanley. He has a way with these youngsters, that boy." He gazed over his cup at Mrs. Bingham. "Ginny and I are just overjoyed you're here, and we hope you won't regret your decision to come."

"I believe God laid it on my heart to come to Sheltering Arms. The very name drew me like a magnet. One night, some months ago, Mrs. Bingham's brother, Mr. Wiley, came to our church to share stories about the children at Sheltering Arms. He told us how they came to you quite destitute and in need of food, clothing, warm beds, and unconditional love."

"Ah, yes, Herb," Mrs. Bingham said. "The children here call him Uncle Herbie. He stops in every so often, bearing gifts of candy and toys. He's very zealous about traveling the countryside and speaking to various churches and charity organizations on behalf of our orphanage. His passion is quite contagious, I must say. God has used him in marvelous ways. Because of him and the donations he's generated, we are able to keep Sheltering Arms afloat financially."

"Well, he certainly stirred my heart. Almost from the second he said you needed more workers, I felt God's gentle tugging to leave the comforts of my home and family. Of course, it didn't happen overnight, and it took time to convince my father."

Mr. Bingham gave a warm, toothy smile. "It can't have been easy for your father to send you off. New York is not the ideal place for a pretty young woman, but he should rest assured you will not be venturing out on your own."

Just as Maggie opened her mouth to reply, a horseman called out a loud, "Whoa!" Following that came the sound of carriage wheels squeaking to a stop.

Mr. Bingham moved to the window and pulled back a frilly curtain. "It's a taxi. The passenger's paying his fare. Might be that young newspaperman you've been expecting, Ginny."

"Oh, good. I'd hoped he'd come today. Tell me, what does he look like?"

"I don't know," Mr. Bingham said with a shrug, leaning closer to the pane. "I'm never good at that. Dapper-looking, I suppose. He's studying the house, as if trying to decide whether it's smart to proceed. I might even go so far as to say he looks a little ornery."

"I'm not surprised by that. He's had a rough go."

"So you've told me. Ah, here he comes. I'll meet him at the door, then."

K

Sheltering Arms Refuge. It didn't look like an orphanage to Luke, but there was the painted sign to prove it. Actually, it more closely resembled a fine old estate in need of a few repairs. Massive described it well, but then, this was an ancient neighborhood, and most of the homes here stood tall and elegant amidst aging oaks and elms. In the 1850s and 60s, New York had been a city filled with contradictions. Its promise of success drew masses of pitiable immigrants and wealthy investors alike, resulting in the poorest of slums but also affluent East Manhattan neighborhoods such as this one. Looking at the preserved shade trees, the tall fences surrounding peaceful properties, and flocks of birds chirping in four-part harmony, one could barely believe a burgeoning city lay just blocks away. He heard the loud, boisterous voices of children at play behind the house.

Luke swallowed hard and heaved a healthy dose of air for fortitude. Straightening his shoulders, he headed up the gravel walk to the colossal, four-columned entryway with the double doors and brass lion's head knocker. He climbed the broad front steps, carrying a briefcase under one arm, and he raised the other arm to knock on the door. But just as he did so, the big oak door swung open wide, revealing a rather stout man with a big smile and a gap in his front teeth. Gray hair, parted down the middle, showed signs of impending baldness. In fact, he appeared to have more hair in his muttonchop whiskers, which extended from ear to ear via a thick moustache, than he had on his head. Luke's immediate assumption was that this was the butler, but this was an orphanage, not the home of the city's mayor or some wealthy banker or physician.

"Well, hullo there, young man. Might you be the reporter from the *World?*" the man asked, extending a big, strong hand. "I'm Henry Bingham. Come in, come in," he said, pulling Luke through the big portal before he even had a chance to utter his first word. "We've been expecting you—well, my wife has, especially," the man said with a sly grin, directing him through the vast foyer and over a large, well trodden Persian rug.

Owen Perry had spoken accurately. It made him wonder how much these folks knew of his situation—the grief he

was suffering at the loss of his aunt and his beloved fiancée—
and what exactly their motivation was in inviting him to this
refuge for homeless children. Was he just another one of their
projects, a challenging undertaking they'd set out to heal and
reform? Moreover, what kind of newsworthy story could possibly lie within—or without—the walls of this huge estate?

Upon entering the spacious kitchen, he discovered a
plump, silver-haired woman with a baby in her arms. Seated
next to her at a round table was a young woman, probably several years younger than he, with wispy, blonde hair and large
oval eyes the color of the sea on a clear day. She had a childlike expression that made Luke instantly wonder who she was
and what her place was here at Sheltering Arms. Her naïve
demeanor told him she certainly wasn't a New York native.

He pulled his shoulders back and sought to put on a
friendly front. "Luke Madison, ma'am," he said, stepping
forward and bowing his head at the older woman, evading
the younger one's eyes. The baby squirmed and yelped but
promptly stopped when the woman started rocking back and
forth. Unruffled by the baby's fussy state, she gave Luke a
wide smile and poked a hand out from under the baby.

"I'm so happy to meet you, Luke. I'm Henry's wife,
Virginia. Call me Ginny, if you please." Awkwardly, he bent
down to give her hand a brief shake. He couldn't imagine calling her by her first name. It seemed too personal, considering
he had no intention of hanging around long enough to get to
know these people on that kind of level.

Out the corner of his eye, he watched the young woman
fiddle with her napkin. She took a dainty sip from her teacup,
then brushed a few strands of hair out of her eyes with a
delicate finger. In the same instant, Mrs. Bingham clucked
at herself. "Forgive my poor manners. This is Maggie Rose

Kane. She just arrived from Michigan yesterday, our newest employee."

So, his hunch had been right. This was no city girl. He turned his gaze on her, and for some unknown reason, he found her pristine appearance an annoyance. Sunlight shining through the window made her long hair shimmer like gold, and her high cheekbones glowed like pink pearls. He forced his smile to stay in place. "Nice meeting you," he said, surprised by his own brusque tone. She lifted her small chin a notch and put a courteous smile on her full, rose-petal mouth.

"My pleasure, as well," she replied.

An awkward lull followed. "Well." Mrs. Bingham cleared her throat and rocked a little harder, then looked at her husband. "Isn't this a blessing, Henry, having Luke join us at Sheltering Arms for a spell?"

Whoa! Join them? A tiny knot of tension formed in his chest. Owen had mentioned the possibility of him staying here in some spare room, but he'd given the notion no thought since then. He had a home, albeit empty, bleakly quiet, and located several miles south of Sheltering Arms. But it was his private domain, his hiding place from an unpleasant world. The last thing he wanted to do was stay under the same roof as a bunch of squalling waifs.

Just what kind of scheme had Ila Perry and this Bingham woman cooked up on his behalf?

He straightened and clasped his hands behind his back. All kinds of warning bells were sounding in his head, but he managed not to react, even while everything in him rebelled against the notion of being anybody's mission project.

A hint of abashment skipped over Mr. Bingham's expression. "A blessing indeed," he said, winking at Luke. "How about some coffee, young man?" He brushed past him and moved to the stove.

Was it his imagination, or was Henry Bingham also intrigued by his own wife's workings?

Chapter Five

"S it down so we can have us a chat, Luke," Mrs. Bingham suggested, gesturing to the chair next to Maggie. The girl edged over to make way for him, and as his gaze lingered on her, he realized she was more woman than girl—young, yes, but 100 percent woman. He scolded himself for noticing.

He pulled back a chair, its legs protesting loudly on the hardwood floor, and sat down gingerly, situating his briefcase next to his feet. Through the door bounded a freckle-faced boy, sweaty and breathless. He speedily helped himself to a cup of water, gulped it down in three seconds, and then left as quickly as he'd come in.

Luke must have looked perplexed, for Mrs. Bingham chuckled, lolling her head back. "The children come and go as they please from the kitchen, Mr. Madison. They all have their own cups, and when they get thirsty, we encourage them to come in for a cooling drink of water. They've got their morning chores to accomplish, and, once done, they are free to roam the fenced-in property at will, read or play a game in the library quarters, or go upstairs to their bunks. You probably heard several of them playing on the swings and slide out back when you arrived. The bigger children know to watch out for the smaller ones, of course. They're very protective of one another. That's something they learned from life on the streets of New York. Otherwise, they wouldn't have survived." She looked down at the now sleeping baby. "Especially these tiny ones."

Confound it if she hadn't spiked his interest! "And how'd that one happen along?" he asked, nodding at the infant.

"I found her in a basket out on the front porch with a note pinned to her blanket," Mr. Bingham answered for his wife, handing off a cup of scalding coffee to Luke before plopping into the chair opposite him, between Maggie and Mrs. Bingham. His face pulled into a frown, making his curled-up mustache wiggle at the ends. He gave his head a despairing shake. "It was nothing but a poorly scrawled message saying something like, 'Can't do it anymore. No money. Please find a good home for my little Christina, someone who will love her in the way she deserves.' That was about a month ago."

Maggie freed a shaky sigh.

"Any idea who she was?" Luke asked, that old reporter instinct crawling to the surface even as a sick feeling churned in his stomach.

Mrs. Bingham waggled her head back and forth. "No clue, other than the letter F, which she had signed at the bottom. She doesn't want us to know her identity, and I expect we never will know, nor will we ever understand the utter desperation that brought her to this point. It's an act of sacrificial love, really, when a woman gives up her baby so it can live. She's putting her child's needs ahead of her own."

Mr. Bingham cleared his throat and took a sip of coffee. "Good chance someone abused the woman," he said. "It happens time and again, and mothers don't want their babies harmed, so they drop them off at some safe place, like Sheltering Arms. It'd be better if they'd identify themselves so we could help them, but they usually refuse. Instead, they run back to their abusive situations, terrified of the consequences if they don't, I suppose."

It seems preposterous, a man beating a woman, Luke thought, but it happened all the time. Most people just turned their heads to the problem, and he acknowledged he was no exception. Even the police usually didn't get involved unless the woman promised to bring up charges, which she rarely did.

"As it is, we don't even have a birth certificate for this little one," Mr. Bingham added. "Truth is, she probably doesn't have one." Now it was Mr. Bingham's turn to sigh as he gazed at the forlorn little creature. "She will forever be a question mark in our minds."

A gentle, cooling breeze blew through the windows, billowing the kitchen curtains and bringing welcome relief from the grueling heat of the past few days. Unable to help himself, Luke stole a glance at the pretty Maggie Rose Kane from Michigan. She must have sensed it, for their eyes met and held for the briefest moment. *You won't last long here, little lady*, he said with his penetrating gaze, doubting she read it. She looked about as sturdy as a cracked crutch. Even now, her eyes showed tears around the edges—whether from fright, homesickness, fatigue, or plain shock and disbelief at the baby's circumstances, he couldn't say.

Yep, she'd be heading back to Michigan in another week or so.

He looks about as mad as a caged gorilla, Maggie thought to herself, and his firmly set jaw, square chin, and rigid brow proved it. Wisps of hair the color of cocoa powder fell over his forehead, nearly reaching the thick eyebrows that shielded his inky, black-brown eyes. Not a glimmer of friendliness shone in those eyes, either, even though he'd forced his generous lips into a smile.

Drops of moisture clung to his brow, probably signifying tense nerves, for it surely wasn't a particularly hot morning. Stubborn and bitter were the first words that came to mind when she dared to snatch a hurried glance at him—stubborn and bitter and, well…terribly attractive, too. As a matter of fact, he was just about the most handsome man she'd ever seen, although her brother-in-law, Gabriel Devlin, ran a very close second.

"How long have you been working at the *World*, Luke?" Mr. Bingham asked.

The switch in topics made Maggie expel a quiet sigh of relief. She could take stories about these destitute children only in small doses, for it broke her heart to hear them. Besides, the question would now grant her the opportunity to give the mysterious Luke Madison a legitimate appraisal.

"Owen Perry, my boss, hired me fresh out of college," he said. "So, it's been six years total." He leaned forward in his chair, hands clenched on the table.

With some mental calculations, Maggie put the man at roughly twenty-six or twenty-seven. She wondered if he had a wife.

"Owen Perry. Ila's husband," Mrs. Bingham said in a thoughtful tone. "I met Ila some time ago at a charity luncheon downtown. We sat next to each other and had a lovely conversation. Sheltering Arms Refuge was that month's focus, and my brother was the featured speaker. Ila wanted to know all about us, so she and I made a point to meet again. Well, now we meet every so often for coffee. She's been a faithful contributor to our organization, too. I'm sure Mr. Perry must have told you that."

"He didn't mention that, but he did tell me his wife and you were acquaintances. Apparently, she suggested I pay you a visit."

"Oh, more than that. You're welcome to stay here—if you'd like to, that is." She readjusted the baby in her arms. Maggie wondered if she ought to relieve Mrs. Bingham of her small burden, but then, what would she do if the baby started squalling? *It's best to ease into this job*, she told herself. She concentrated instead on the conversing pair, looking mostly at the gentleman with the midnight eyes.

"Living among the children should give you plenty of fodder for your news story, wouldn't you think?" the woman continued, bright-eyed. "You are going to do a story, correct? Oh, it will be so wonderful to give your readers a picture of what goes on in the streets of New York. Henry and I figure most people don't want to trouble themselves with homeless children, but that could be due mostly to their lack of knowledge. Once they read your story, I'm convinced folks will wake up and take more notice of the misfortunate around them."

Luke shifted in the wooden chair and pinched the bridge of his nose, looking flustered—or perhaps annoyed—she couldn't tell. "I—I hadn't figured on staying here."

"Nonsense. We've plenty of room. Fact is, there's a spare room at the end of the hall on the third floor. It went empty about a month ago, when Morris Hampton left us. He got married, you see. Stanley will certainly appreciate the extra help with those eleven rowdy boys of his…at least for the time being, while you work on your research."

"Stanley?"

"Yes, he's been with us from the time Henry and I opened this place—seventeen years ago." The Binghams' gazes met for a brief moment, long enough for Maggie to recognize the deep and tender love they had for each other. She wondered if Mr. Madison had noticed, doubting so from the way he wiped his brow and glanced nervously up at the ceiling.

"I…this is all new to me," he mumbled, sweeping his hand over his whiskered jaw. "I just found out last night about this…new assignment." He hesitated, choosing his words carefully.

Mrs. Bingham raised her left eyebrow a notch. "Oh, I see. Well, then, you'll probably want to take a few days to think about it."

"Yes." Relief skipped across his face.

"What say I get the room ready for you, anyway? In my humblest opinion, it would make more sense for you to work from here. After all, you'll want to spend time with the children in order to hear their stories and learn their backgrounds." She fingered the corner of the soft blanket stretched over the sleeping baby, then tipped her face at Luke. "I understand you live in the Lower East Side—in an apartment? That's going to be quite a trek for you if you plan to take the taxi back and forth. And since you won't be going to the *World* every day, I'd assume you'd be coming here. Right?"

The slightest smile played at the edges of his mouth as he dipped his chin and scratched the side of his nose. My, what a transformation one tiny smile made on this man's dark face,

Maggie realized. "I see you and Mrs. Perry have talked a fair bit about my situation."

"Well, no. I mean, Mr. Perry told Ila about you, yes, and she did enlighten me somewhat. She thought, that is, we both thought, perhaps…." Now it was Mrs. Bingham's turn to squirm. "Well, a news story about Sheltering Arms Refuge could be such a wonderful thing, don't you think? Both for the children and for the city." She looked to her husband for reassurance. Mr. Bingham chose that moment to lift his coffee mug to his mouth and swallow several mouthfuls. Over the rim, his brow flickered with amusement.

Maggie sat back in her chair and started to relax. This was an entertaining exchange indeed.

～K～

Luke might have chuckled at the woman's discomfiture if he hadn't been so blasted annoyed with Owen Perry for putting him in this position. He didn't want to stay here, and yet this Bingham woman had a point: he wasn't going back to the *World*—not for the next three months, anyway. And if he were going to write a meaningful story, he'd have to put in some significant time doing research. Any reporter worth his weight knew a good story required hours, maybe days, of investigative study. But at an orphanage? The idea didn't set well, and he had to concede it was due to the emotions it stirred.

Shoot, he could probably write the story now, if he wanted to—no research necessary. He'd already lived it; he knew the pain of growing up parentless. Yes, Aunt Fran had loved him, having taken him in after his parents perished in a train accident, but she'd never quite mastered the notion of mothering him. She often left him with Mrs. Jennings, the housekeeper, so she could run off to her various benefits, com-mittee meetings, and charity events. Aunt Fran's benevolence stretched into the far-reaching needs of the community, but at times, it skipped right over the little boy living under her roof. Widowed after only five years of marriage to a wealthy bank owner twice her age, she'd had no children—until Luke came along. Not that she'd once complained about his pres-ence in her sprawling two-story apartment, but then, that was probably why. The place was big enough that he never got underfoot. If anything, he learned to stay out of her way, and for that reason, they had never been terribly close. In fact, her attending the church picnic with Annalise and Zelda the day the *General Slocum* went down had been out of obliga-tion more than amusement. Luke had convinced her that she needed to become better acquainted with his future wife and her mother, being as their upcoming marriage would throw them all together.

"I cannot communicate with Mrs. Engel," Aunt Fran had complained. "Her English is still so poor. One would think, after all these years, that she would have made a greater effort to adapt to our customs—at the least, learn our language." That had always been a point of contention with Aunt Frances. Oh, she welcomed the immigrants with widespread arms, but they had better learn the American way and waste no time in the doing.

"Annalise will be there to interpret," he'd said on that bright June morning before heading off to work, not in any mood to belabor the topic. Arrangements had already been made for her to go, and he didn't want her backing out.

"You know, I'm missing my library meeting, and it's an important one. We're discussing the possibility of adding another wing."

"I'm sure the discussion will be tabled for another month," he'd assured her. "Believe me, they won't be making any decisions today, not in their biggest donor's absence."

That seemed to have appeased her, so he'd grinned, kissed her on the forehead, and told her to try to have a good time. She'd harrumphed something as she adjusted her floral hat in the mirror, and out he'd gone, never again to see her alive.

Mrs. Bingham's chatter brought him out of his reverie. "Besides, I would think you'd welcome a change of scenery, not to mention a slower pace," she droned. "My goodness, don't you grow weary of fighting all that city traffic day after day? And that awful stench!"

She did have a point, he realized. Most days, he walked to work, and he didn't mind the trek, except for the inescapable odor of horse dung. Street sweepers worked around the clock to remedy the problem, but they couldn't keep up with the rate at which the ubiquitous animals relieved themselves.

"Virginia, give our poor guest some room to breathe," Mr. Bingham admonished, setting down his coffee cup and shaking his head at her, that ever-present twinkle in his eye. "It will remain Luke's decision whether or not to stay on at Sheltering Arms. Naturally, he'll be welcome here, but if he prefers to make the drive back and forth…well, that will be his choice."

"Well, of course it will. I'm merely pointing out the definite pros in staying," she responded, smiling sweetly at Luke.

Her attention returned to the babe in her arms, and Luke took the opportunity to glance at the striking young lady sitting next to him, back straight, shoulders squared, and just the tiniest glimmer of merriment in her eyes. Had she found the conversation humorous? What sort of thoughts churned in that blonde head of hers? Did she even have the slightest idea what brought him here this morning? Yes, Mrs. Bingham had alluded to his present job predicament—his "reassignment." But did Miss Kane know about the circumstances surrounding it—the grief that overtook him daily, driving him to concentrate more on his work and, ironically, perform it in a perfunctory way? He hoped not. He lost the love of his life, as well as a portion of his sanity, and he preferred not to talk about it.

A little tyke wearing a red-and-white checked jumper came skipping through the door, breathless and flushed. Chestnut-colored braids reached down her back, each fastened with a red ribbon. "Can I have a drink?" she asked in a small voice, her blue-green eyes round and innocent as rain. Luke couldn't imagine she was more than four or five, and his heart felt an odd, unexpected tingle at the sight of her.

Mr. Bingham jumped up and rushed to the sink, as if he had been born with the singular purpose of serving this child. "Well, I should say you can, little angel mine." He turned the spigot until a flow of water came gushing out. "Which is yours?" he asked, gesturing at the cups all lined up on a shelf beside the sink, each one bearing a child's name. She recognized hers and pointed to it.

"That's the one!" Mr. Bingham said, beaming with pride.

While the child drank with gusto, Luke and Maggie's gazes connected for an instant. He produced a brief, polite nod, she a tiny smile.

"There, now, out you go," Mr. Bingham said, taking the child's fully drained cup and patting her on the shoulder. She turned on her petite heels and made for the door like a frisky filly.

"Close it—quietly," Virginia said, more as an after-thought, as the screen door hit the casing with a loud thud. She shook her head in hopeless surrender. "They'll never learn to close doors properly."

"What brought little Rose Marie to Sheltering Arms?" Maggie asked, her eyes still trained on the door, voice soft and croaky from prolonged silence.

Mr. Bingham walked back to the table and sat down with a heavy sigh. He folded both hands and thought about his answer, blinking twice. "She's a half orphan, meaning she still has a father. Her mother passed on a year ago—bad case of diphtheria. Her father's a drunk and completely incapable of taking care of her. Matter of fact, someone found her in an alley this past spring, shivering in the cold. In a drunken stupor, her father had locked her out, thinking she'd already gone to bed. Instead, she'd been out begging for bread. Poor thing had nearly starved to death before we got her. She's still a skinny little mite, but we're trying to put a little meat on those bones."

"Does her father know where she is?" Maggie asked.

"Oh, he knows, and he's happy as can be about it," Virginia put in. "Even signed over his parental rights, admitting he doesn't have the resources for keeping her." Virginia eyed Luke with a sideways glance. "And she's only one sad story out of twenty-three."

A chill ran the length of Luke's backbone, raising the hair at the nape of his neck.

"What about Maxine?" Maggie asked, wrapping her hands around the mug of tea she'd been slowly sipping.

"Now, there's a story," Mr. Bingham mumbled, fingering his muttonchop whiskers.

"Mrs. Bingham said she came from a bordello, that her uncle had—sold her? I didn't even think that sort of thing went on anymore," Maggie half-asked and half-stated.

"Oh, my dear, it not only goes on—it's prevalent. Folks just don't know, or more likely, don't want to know," Mr. Bingham amended. "The less they know, the less responsible they need to feel."

More chills ran up and down Luke's back. What had Owen Perry gotten him into, anyway? He didn't like these creepy, chilling emotions gnawing at his heart. Houses of prostitution lined the streets of New York; they weren't explicitly advertised as such, but men seemed to know which "saloon" or "massage parlor" to enter if they sought a woman's touch. To date, though, he'd fallen in with the crowd that preferred ignorance—until this very moment, when he felt himself being pulled out of apathy.

Young girls being sold? He shifted uneasily, which made Maggie turn her gaze on him. He succeeded in not granting her a glance in return.

"Her parents emigrated from England when she was just a young thing," Mr. Bingham continued, leaning back in his chair. "But like so many immigrants, they couldn't find jobs. They struggled for the next few years, but discouragement drove her daddy to drinking, and her mama wound up running off with some other man, never to be heard from again.

"By then, Maxine was about eleven and fending for herself as best as she could. One day, out of desperation, she went knocking on her uncle's door looking for food, even though she knew he was about as honorable as a block of salt. He let her stay with him for a year or so, and during that time, he introduced her to some of his male friends. He'd accrued

some nasty gambling debts, and in order to pay them off, he...
well, he used her as collateral, one might say, and she even-
tually wound up at Miss Violet's Saloon, an establishment
some dozen or so blocks from here, just east of the corner of
74th and York." He made a sneering sound at the back of his
throat. "Miss Violet runs a house of ill repute under the guise
of saloon."

Maggie covered her gaping mouth with her linen napkin.
"Can't the police shut the place down?"

"Not without clear evidence, I'm afraid. An investigation would require firsthand information; something Maxine
and most other girls aren't quick to share. Poor thing is terrified that if she divulges too much, someone will find her and
make her pay.

"I'm sure they threaten bodily harm to anyone who so
much as thinks about ever snitching on the operation, but
without clear evidence, there is little any of us can do, even
though we strongly suspect other girls like Maxine live in similar places around the city." Mr. Bingham shook his head and
gazed at his coffee cup. "It's a tragedy of untold proportions."

A bilious taste gathered at the back of Luke's throat as a
kind of newfound rage boiled up from his gut. He thought
he'd reached the pinnacle of anger after the *Slocum* went
down, but this—this was stirring it to new heights.

He resisted the urge to leap up from his chair and run
outside for a breath of fresh air. *Don't make a fool of yourself,
Madison. Ride it out. Don't let them see your grief.*

"You all right, young man?" Mr. Bingham asked.

"What? Oh sure, I'm fine, just—taking it all in." He
forced a casual tone.

When a moment had elapsed, Mr. Bingham cleared his throat. "Well, then, what say I take you on a tour of the place, inside and out? I could use a good stretch."

"Um, sure, that would be great."

He pushed back his chair, leaving his coffee, cool and untouched, on the table.

A tour? Why had he consented to a tour when all he wanted to do was escape this house of haunting, unthinkable stories?

Chapter Six

Dear Papa,

Thank you for writing to me before I'd even left Sandy Shores. Your letter brought tears to my eyes, especially when you told me how proud you are of me. Papa, I was worried I'd disappointed you with my desires to come to New York to help these homeless children, but now I see I was wrong. You have actually given me your blessing. Thank you again, Papa. It meant so much to me to read your words of reassurance.

Some of the children are here under such dire circumstances. Why, one girl in particular escaped from a bordello. Can you imagine? She remains distant and wary around people, but can you blame her? Others are here because their parents simply could not care for them, and some because one parent died, leaving the other destitute. These are called half-orphans. Most half-orphans' single parents have already signed over their rights to the children. Papa, I would have to be on my deathbed before I would do such a thing, but then, I suppose many of these parents are. Consider precious Jesse, for instance. His mother had to send him to a home when she was *dying. Oh, I cringe to think what might have happened if he and Gabriel had not found each other. He's such a darling boy and has adjusted so well since joining the Kane family—or rather, the Devlin family.*

A newspaper reporter from the New York World came to Sheltering Arms today. Apparently, his boss sent him to our orphanage for purposes of researching and reporting about street urchins and, in particular, life at Sheltering Arms. This man appears rather unfriendly, not to mention unhappy. Mrs. Bingham has alluded to his having suffered some difficult circumstances, but since it's none of my business, I haven't inquired further. I will say he's quite nice looking, which is unimportant, of course.

Well, I'm starting to ramble. Papa, please do tell everyone to write to me, as I miss and love you all so terribly.

Give Jesse a squeeze from his aunt Maggie Rose.

Best regards,
Your loving daughter

⁓ K ⁓

Luke did not return in the next two days. Mr. Bingham thought they'd scared him off with all the talk about Christina, Rose Marie, and Maxine, but Mrs. Bingham said she thought he might be taking a few days to let their stories digest, that maybe he'd already begun his article and needed time away from the house to formulate his thoughts.

Maggie decided Mrs. Bingham was an optimist. In her opinion, Luke Madison would sooner eat a shoe than write a story about Sheltering Arms. After his tour of the place, he'd phoned for a taxi, and when it arrived not ten minutes later, he took his leave with barely a cordial farewell. He looked slightly green about the gills, making Maggie wonder if he had taken ill. She mentioned this to Mrs. Bingham, who shook her head and replied, "More likely, he suffers from a sickness of the heart—the kind that heals only with time and prayer."

Maggie hadn't asked for details. While she was rather curious, she had a houseful of children who needed her undivided attention. Learning about a mysterious man's hidden heartaches did not rate high on her priority scale.

Saturday morning ushered in a thunderstorm, bringing brisk winds that lingered all morning and into the afternoon. They calmed, at times, then picked up speed, dictating that the children play inside. An exception was made for the few boys who went out to help Stanley Barrett with the chores— mucking stalls, milking the cows, Roberta and Henrietta, feeding the chickens, and tending to the horses.

After helping put the younger children down for their naps, and seeing that the rest of them had found quiet activities with which to occupy themselves, Maggie took advantage of the lull by walking out to the barn herself, thankful that the rain had slowed to a light mist and the worst of the wind had settled. There, she found Stanley brushing down a horse; ten- and twelve-year-old brothers Stuart and Ricky Campbell were feeding the barn cats, and young Billy Harper was making a game of chasing the chickens that had made their ways into the barn and were looking for grain. In the back, she heard some of the bigger boys talking about starting up a game of baseball if the sun came out. Stanley joked around with the boys, claiming that he could hit farther and run faster than all of them put together. They made comebacks and enjoyed several seconds of sparring while Maggie watched and listened from the doorway. When she feigned a light cough, Stanley looked up in surprise, grinned, and returned the horse brush to its hook on the wall.

"Well, if it isn't the pretty Miss Kane."

"Maggie, please."

"Well, all right then, Maggie it is." He patted the horse's hindquarters, then exited the stall, closing the door behind him. The horse whinnied and pawed a front hoof in the hay.

"You don't have to quit on my behalf," she said.

"I just finished. Perfect timing. So, are you doing a little exploring?" He removed his straw hat and plunged a soiled hand through his brown hair, then plopped the tattered thing back in place. His bib overalls hung loosely on his long, angular frame, and the sleeves of his blue plaid shirt were rolled up to his elbows, revealing muscular forearms.

"Yes, after feeding the little ones their bottles and snacks and putting them down for their naps, I finally found myself with a bit of time to walk the grounds. Mrs. Bingham says she'll be relieved once Charlotte Decker returns from visiting friends and relatives, as she has primary responsibility for the children four and under."

The tiniest flicker of some elusive emotion skipped across Stanley's face, but Maggie didn't think she knew him well enough to inquire. Besides, he recovered quickly enough, eyes brightening when he pulled a watch from his pant pocket and looked at it.

"Well, what do you know? I have some time, myself. Would you happen to want a guide?" he asked, stuffing the timepiece back where it belonged.

She laughed. "I think I'd like that very much."

He gave her his slanted grin and held out an arm for her to take. She accepted it, smiling back, and let him lead her out of the barn. Outside, they circled the backyard gardens as he told her about Virginia Bingham's grandfather and how he'd accumulated great wealth by investing in the Baltimore and Ohio Railroad Company back in the 20s, afterward building a mansion for his small family.

He told her how Virginia, then twenty-five, and Henry, then thirty, had met at a church social, quickly fell in love, and were married four months later, even though Virginia's sickly mother and aging grandfather hadn't approved of Henry's lower social status. Henry and Virginia had determined to live independently, surviving on love alone for those first several years. Henry worked at a bakery for meager wages, and Ginny cleaned houses. They had wanted children of their own but discovered it wasn't part of God's bigger plan for them, and so they'd dreamt of the next best thing—fostering a whole houseful of homeless children. When her grandfather passed away, no one was more surprised than Ginny to discover that he'd left her his entire estate. Yes, she'd been his only living heir, but she had always been sure he would will his riches to a charity or to the local hospital, not to his granddaughter, from whom he'd basically estranged himself after her marriage.

They walked past the vegetable garden, where thriving cornstalks stood, ears waiting to be picked, ripe, red tomatoes hung from tired vines, sunflowers pointed their smiling faces to the sky, and flowering Corfu lilies spread their leafy wings like angels of mercy. "Ginny often says, 'When God has a plan, no one stands in His way,'" Stanley said. "I'm sure she believes God softened her grandfather's heart so that Sheltering Arms Refuge could ultimately come into being."

Maggie nodded in agreement. She walked with Stanley past several outbuildings, and his voice droned on, explaining what each one housed. Maggie listened intently, relishing the chance to relax and breathe in the scents and smells of a New York summer.

Overhead, the clouds parted just enough to reveal a hint of the afternoon sun, its rays glancing off the wet blades of grass that bordered their brick-laid trail.

K

Luke passed one abandoned business after another, each representative of the wife, mother, sister, or daughter a family had lost, as well as the men who could no longer face the challenge of remaining in the neighborhood of Little Germany. To Luke, it seemed a matter of time before the entire district would close down. Long faces showed up at every corner, and he knew with poignancy the pain behind those empty expressions. A woman and her child left a grocery store just two doors down, and for a second, he wondered what had kept them away from the ill-fated *Slocum*, thereby preserving their lives. He then reminded himself that not everyone in Little Germany was a member at St. Mark's Lutheran Church on the Lower East Side, the church that had chartered the boat that fine June day for its annual picnic trip to Locust Grove on Huntington Bay.

The sign for Engel's Restaurant came into view, and Luke headed across the street, halting to allow a sequence of wagons, horse-drawn carriages, and motorcars to pass in front of him before stepping up to the sidewalk. One block ahead, a newspaper boy stood at the corner and chanted the headlines, desperate to rid himself of the last of his stack so he could go home, get some rest, and start all over again at dawn. A steady stream of pedestrians, some sauntering, others moving with purpose, brushed past him in the opposite direction. Breathing deeply of the moist air, he glanced up to see that the worst of the rain had passed; a tiny slice of sunshine was peeking through gray clouds.

An elderly couple exited Engel's just as he pulled open the screen door, so he raised his chin at them and held the door. Heinz stood at the rear entrance of the long, narrow eatery, talking quietly to a patron, his stout body silhouetted against the doorway so that Luke couldn't tell which direction he faced. Hazel, a middle-aged woman who came in on weekends, smiled and waved when Luke slipped through the door, her brown hair pulled into its usual tight bun at the nape of her neck, her plain gray dress bearing breakfast and lunch stains. She scooped up some crumbs from a table, straightened the salt and pepper shakers, pushed in a few chairs, and then walked to the sink behind the lunch counter. Luke bypassed the available round tables with the red-and-white checked tablecloths and slid onto a bar stool instead. It was mid afternoon, and very few patrons inhabited the place.

"Coffee?" Hazel asked, wiping her hands on a rag and reaching for the coffeepot.

"I'm trying to lay off the stuff, thanks."

She turned a teasing gaze on him. "Just checking. You want a Coca-Cola, then?"

He let a grin sneak past his stiff lips, so unaccustomed to smiling these days. "Now you're talking my language."

She went for the icebox under the counter and retrieved a glass bottle of the caramel-colored soda, popped off the lid, and plopped it down in front of him. Then, she leveled him with a steady gaze. "How you doin', Luke?" Gone was the banter.

He took four or five deep gulps and set down the bottle with a *clunk*, blowing out a loud breath. He looked up at the painting on the wall behind Hazel, which featured a German passenger ship bearing the name *Hamburg Amerika Line* sailing over rough waters. It was the ship known for carrying German immigrants, the Engels' ancestors included, across the seas to Hoboken, New Jersey, beginning in the 50s. Heinz and Zelda had followed their aunts, uncles, and cousins across in the early 80s, just before Annalise was born.

"I'm okay."

"You sure about that?"

"Yeah." A quick glance at Heinz found him still engaged in quiet conversation. "Who's he talking to?"

"Some salesman trying to convince him he needs to invest in a lot of new equipment."

He glanced about the place. "Nothing wrong with the stuff he's got."

She chortled. "Have you tried to light our stove lately?"

"Well, maybe he needs to replace a few things."

"He does, but he won't."

Luke knew she was right. Heinz was as tight with his wallet as an over-wound watch. Besides, chances were good he wouldn't stay around much longer, although he wouldn't mention that fact to Hazel. Luke wasn't sure how much she knew. Stefan and Erich had been talking about pulling out of the restaurant business altogether, but Heinz was dragging his feet. "It is all I know, this restaurant" he'd told Luke in his heavily accented voice a couple of weeks ago. "But if my boys insist, I will follow them. They are all I have left."

"What would you do?" Luke had asked.

He'd shrugged, forehead furrowed. "My boys seem to think they could start an insurance company."

"What do they know about insurance?"

"Not much, but they are resourceful. They will learn. More and more folks are investing in insurance. It is the smart way to go."

"I'd hate to see you walk away from the restaurant, Heinz." Even more, he'd hate for Heinz to close the doors to the setting of his own special memories. Where else would he go to feel close to Annalise? Some people visited gravesites to get a sense of closeness, but nowhere else did he feel her presence as strongly as within these walls. He could almost hear the sweet sound of her laughter above the lunch and supper crowds; he envisioned her lithe body flitting around the room while he waited at a corner table for her to finish work.

"I did not see you come in," Heinz said.

Luke swiveled in his bar stool. "I've been here a few minutes."

Hazel took up a cloth and started wiping down the counter just as the bell above the door jingled to signal incoming customers. She smiled and waved in her usual manner, set down her rag, and went over to greet them, hauling her coffeepot along.

Out the corner of his eye, Luke looked to the rear of the establishment, watching as the salesman gathered the last of his papers and stuffed them into his attaché case. Once done, he shoved it under his arm and disappeared out the back door.

"I hear that fellow tried to sell you a new kitchen," Luke said, his long fingers wrapped around the nearly empty Coca-Cola bottle. He brought it to his lips and drained the final drops.

"Pfff. He would just as soon turn my pockets inside out!"

Luke chuckled. "He's trying to make a living like everybody else."

Heinz sat down on the stool beside Luke and pulled out his trusty pipe. A book of matches lay tucked under a sugar bowl. He struck a match and took a couple of drags off the stem while lighting the bowl of his pipe. Smoke circled the air over their heads. Luke had never quite figured out the benefits of smoking tobacco, but many enjoyed it, and there was something comforting about watching Heinz relax with his long-stemmed pipe, a family heirloom that had been passed down from his father's father. He wondered when he planned to pass it down to Stefan, the older of his sons.

"Your aunt left you a good settlement, no?"

"I still have to work—to stay busy."

"Ah, yes, keeping busy does help the mind and body."

The two sat in comfortable silence, eavesdropping on the few customers who'd wandered in. Luke rolled the empty bottle between his hands. "Owen Perry forced me into a three-month leave from the paper," he finally blurted out. "He thinks I'm losing my mind."

Heinz removed his pipe and stared at Luke, who fastened his eyes on the *Hamburg Amerika Line*, particularly the waves sweeping up on either side of the hull and the sun breaking through an array of white, puffy clouds—anything to avoid the sharp eyes of Heinz Engel, who did have a way of seeing clear to his soul.

"What will you do?"

"He's got me going to some orphanage on the Upper East Side. Wants me to do a human interest piece on street Arabs."

"Ah, it is a problem, the little lost ones. A story would be good, no?"

"You think so?" Luke valued the opinion of Heinz Engel more than he realized. He had looked forward to joining the family ranks, despite the good-natured verbal whippings he took from Stefan and Erich. No man would ever be good enough for their baby sister, and they let him know it at every turn. Ever since the deaths of Zelda and Annalise, though, the teasing had ceased, as had most of their buoyant conversations. The truth was, Luke had a strong sense that the brothers didn't want him around anymore, perhaps due to the memories stirred up by his presence. Thankfully, Heinz never questioned his visits, nor did he ever seem unhappy to see him.

"It is always good to open the eyes to injustice."

"He's pulled me off the *General Slocum* case. Where's the justice in that? I have files full of evidence to prove all sorts of negligence."

"It is done, Luke. You must give up your quest to lay blame. Let those in authority do their jobs."

"That's what Perry said. Are you two in cahoots?"

The curled, waxed ends of Heinz's grey mustache trembled with a slight smile when Luke turned to look at him. "I do not know this man, but I am sure he is concerned for you."

Owen and Ila Perry were good people, it was true, and while Owen referred to Luke as "kid" more often than not—probably because he'd hired him straight from college—he seemed to take a liking to Luke in his own gruff way. And the feelings were mutual.

"And this article—it will take three months to write?"

Luke didn't want to talk about the orphanage with Heinz, but getting it out in the open had him thinking about it. He'd avoided returning there after his initial visit because the stories he'd heard still gnawed at his already brittle heart. "I doubt it, but Perry doesn't want me around in the shape I'm in, so I'll do what I can to stay busy—maybe do some traveling. I might even take a ride on the train next month when they ship the orphans west in search of new homes. I don't know, it could prove interesting research." Put that way, it sounded half reasonable.

Heinz studied him as he might a specimen in a jar, his gray eyes narrowed pensively. "It is good that you do this. Your mind is too—how do you say it?—*preoccupied* with the past. It is time you look ahead. You are young, Luke. You will survive this—this loss."

His words stung him to the core. "And you?"

He sighed. "I have my family. And my God."

The Engels were a religious bunch. It had been the only thing standing between Annalise and Luke, his lack of zeal for the God she so ardently adored. And despite their difference, she'd agreed to marry him, appeased by his promises not to interfere with her faith and to attend Sunday services with her. Of course, since her passing, he'd forgotten his promise about church attendance. He saw no point in praying or singing to a God who evidently held little compassion for his pain.

"The woman who runs the place expects me to stay in a spare room on the third floor, where they house a bunch of boys."

"This is good then, no? Always, when you focus on another's needs, it takes the attention from your own. You should give this orphanage article your full attention. It will be an excellent piece, I'm sure of it. Perhaps award-winning, no?"

Luke chuckled at the way Heinz often ended his sentences with "no?", his German accent still as strong as the day he'd met him two years ago. He shook his head and smiled glumly. "I think that's a bit far-fetched, sir, but thanks for your confidence in me."

Another wave of silence swept over them. Luke straightened his back, flexing sore muscles. Lack of sleep truly wreaked havoc on the body. "I won't be able to come by as much."

"I understand."

Luke slid off the stool, so Heinz followed suit. Hazel flitted by, coffeepot still in hand, oblivious to their conversation.

"Let me know if—what you decide to do with the restaurant."

"No hasty decisions will be made, much as my sons might like. I'll keep you informed."

Heinz followed him to the door, where Luke paused for a brief moment, his hand on the knob, and looked absently out at the street. "I miss her, you know."

"I know," Heinz murmured in return, patting his shoulder.

Since there was nothing more to say, Luke gave a quick nod, then slid out the door. Outside, a flock of birds flew overhead, settling en masse atop the roof of Harvey's Fish House.

There was no telling how long he'd stay at Sheltering Arms Refuge, but in his mind, he determined not to stay a day longer than was necessary. The moment his research was complete, he'd be out of there.

As he stepped off the sidewalk to cross the road, he kicked a pebble out of his way and wondered who would leave first—him or that innocent little miss from Michigan.

Chapter Seven

Sunday dinner proved to be a rather lively affair, with all the children except the infants gathered around the dining room table, extended to its maximum length by several extra leaves. It was the only meal they all ate together all week, Mrs. Bingham told Maggie, so it required extra planning, particularly since Sundays saw no outside volunteers. Children arranged themselves around the massive table so that the older ones could assist the young ones in cutting their pieces of chicken and scooping portions of mashed potatoes onto their plates. When the gravy bowl came around, the older ones ladled it out, and when the basket of rolls came along, they did the buttering. Maggie enjoyed the sense of community at Sheltering Arms, the selfless way the children cared for one another.

During dinner, Maggie assisted Mrs. Bingham in the kitchen, rinsing soiled pots and pans, replenishing empty serving bowls, filling water pitchers, and wiping up spills. The heat from the stove and ovens permeated the large kitchen, causing beads of perspiration to form on Maggie's forehead, much to her dismay. Worse, she feared the powder she'd sprinkled on her underarms that morning was failing miserably at absorbing any odor. To date, her job at the orphanage entailed everything from dusting to cooking, pulling weeds to changing diapers, and washing windows to reading to the younger children before they went to bed at eight o'clock sharp.

And she loved every minute of it. Yes, she missed her family and continually wondered what they were doing back in Sandy Shores, but Sheltering Arms was her home now, its residents her family, and she found herself thanking the Lord daily for opening the doors of opportunity to her.

At exactly 1:15, each child dutifully filed into the kitchen, plate and silverware in hand. At the waste barrel, the children scraped off their plates then carefully handed them over to fourteen-year-old Jenny Pelton, one of the assigned dishwashers, before heading upstairs for two hours of quiet time. Little Dag Haskell and brothers Gilbert and Samuel Garrison also had Sunday kitchen duty, which entailed carrying the serving dishes from the dining room to the kitchen, scraping the leftovers into the waste can, and then rinsing and stacking them. After that, one would wash, one would rinse, one would dry, and one would put away, all under Mrs. Bingham's strict supervision. Anyone on kitchen duty knew that she had eagle eyes when it came to inspecting dishes for spots, and woe to the child who carelessly handed off a dish to be dried if a speck of food remained on it. Before meeting Mrs. Bingham, Maggie had considered Grandmother Kane the biggest stickler when it came to cleanliness, but now she wondered if Grandmother hadn't met her match.

Since her arrival last Tuesday, Maggie had learned all of the children's names and ages, along with a few of their stories—everything from abuse to desertion to the death of one or both parents. Each account gripped her heart in a new place until she thought it might burst open with pain and compassion. Mrs. Bingham told her that she must try to put the children's yesterdays behind her, as many of them had done, and focus instead on their promising futures.

"What did you think about the preacher's sermon today?" Mrs. Bingham asked as Maggie wiped down the stovetop while the children worked at the sink. The older woman was helping little Dag put away the plates and silverware, and the other three were washing and drying dishes, thirteen-year-old Gilbert and ten-year-old Samuel whipping each other with their towels when she wasn't looking.

"I thought it was excellent," Maggie replied. "The people there were so warm and friendly, and I felt very welcomed."

"Yes, the reverend delivers fine messages. Only thing is, they always seem to hit me right here." She pressed a hand to her bosom and shook her head in disbelief. "I don't know how he does it."

Maggie laughed. "I thought he was preaching right to me this morning, especially with that part about taking all our cares and worries to the Lord. I sometimes like to hang onto my fears."

"Oh, I think we all do that, dear, probably because we forget how very capable the Lord is of handling things for us—if we would just learn to let go of them."

"You make it sound so simple," Maggie said, crossing in front of Jenny to ring out a damp cloth before hanging it on a hook above the sink. The children carried on with their private banter, the Garrison brothers still waging their towel war and Jenny trying to discourage them, giggling all the while at their antics.

Mrs. Bingham cast them all a warning look, which they heeded until she turned her back to lift a platter to a high shelf.

"Not simple," she answered, stretching to her full height. She came down on her heels again, then turned and smiled at Maggie. "But God lends us the strength and might to carry out His plans. You discover that the longer you stay at Sheltering Arms."

Maggie chewed on her lip. "Many of the children haven't warmed up to me quite yet," she confided in Mrs. Bingham.

The woman flicked her wrist. "Don't worry! They'll come around. They're always cautious with newcomers." Giving the youngsters at the sink one last look, she said, "You ragamuffins finish your jobs so you can head up to your rooms for a period of rest. Dag, you may be excused." The young man gave a full-faced grin, as if he'd just been exonerated of a petty crime, and made a beeline for the stairs. She chuckled as he scurried from the room.

Just then, a racket in the front room stole their attention, Mrs. Bingham leaving the kitchen and Maggie following after. Vivian Pelton, Jenny's sixteen-year-old sister, and Maxine Ward had taken to arguing over whose turn it was to hold baby Christina. Their arguing had reached the squalling stage, exciting the baby into a screaming fit of her own.

"Girls!" Mrs. Bingham said with controlled severity. "Give the child to me. For mercy's sake, you would think Christina was a coveted toy, the way you're carrying on."

"I had her first," Maxine said.

"Yeah, for the last half hour," Vivian complained. "But now, it's time for her bottle, and Mrs. Bingham told me I was t' give it to her."

"That's true, Maxine." Mrs. Bingham lightly rocked the infant back and forth until she settled down. "Why don't you go check on little Emily, Maxine? Dr. Hesselbart said her cough is improving, but I'm sure she's growing weary of not feeling well. Why not go keep her company? You know how she enjoys that. Perhaps you could read a book to her?"

Maggie saw the girl give the matter a moment of serious thought, but rather than accept it, she headed for the door.

"Maxine, you may either spend time with Emily or go upstairs. You know the Sunday afternoon rules," Mrs. Bingham said, but the door slammed before she had finished her sentence.

Just then, Mr. Bingham emerged from the library. "I'll go talk to her."

"Would you, Henry?" Mrs. Bingham asked. To Maggie, she added, "Sundays are always like this, I'm afraid, starting with having to go to church."

"I noticed how Maxine balked at getting up this morning."

"Maxine hates to be told to do anything," Vivian volunteered, taking the baby from Mrs. Bingham's arms. She moved to the adjoining parlor and settled into a rocking chair by the brick hearth, propping the baby on her arm and bringing the bottle to meet her eager mouth.

Mrs. Bingham approached the front window and gazed out. "Henry's good with her. He'll have her calmed down in no time."

Maggie came up beside her. Mr. Bingham appeared to be keeping his distance from Maxine and speaking in low tones. A couple of bicyclists, a man and woman out for an afternoon spin, passed at a slow speed, the woman doing what she could to keep her skirt away from the spokes and to hold her hat in place. The man coasted along at a bike's length behind her. Overhead, bright sunlight poked through leafy oak branches, casting shadows across the lush front lawn. Encircled by the drive was a large garden of day lilies, roses, daisies, and an array of other colorful blooms swaying gently in the August breeze.

Mrs. Bingham sighed. "I sometimes worry that Maxine won't stay with us."

"What do you mean?" Maggie asked.

"She's restless. Yes, she escaped that awful house of ill repute, but she's not happy here, either. She's a child who's never known love and has no idea how to receive it. She believes she has no value."

"Oh, but she has so much. In God's eyes, she's a precious gem."

"You and I know that, but it will take a great deal of convincing to make her believe it."

Maggie inhaled deeply, feeling the air rush into her lungs. "Then I shall do everything in my power to convince her."

Mrs. Bingham smiled and patted Maggie on the arm. "I believe you will, child."

They started toward the kitchen, but the sounds of clattering hooves and rumbling carriage wheels quickly drew them back to the window. "Well, what do you know?" Mrs. Bingham muttered under her breath, her nose practically pressed against the window.

"What is it?"

"It's that young man from the *World*—Luke Madison."

Maggie was surprised to feel her heart skip a beat. *The handsome reporter.* She'd thought they'd seen the last of him.

"I was beginning to think Henry was right—that we had scared him off. Look there." Mrs. Bingham drew the curtain away from the window to get a better view. "He has a valise in hand. Well, glory be! It looks like we may have an extra boarder."

𝒦

Luke paid the driver his fare and stepped down into the center of the driveway, his suitcase hanging at his side, and again studied the massive house. This time, however, he looked through slightly different eyes. It was not his home, per se, but his temporary quarters—and he mentally under-scored the word *temporary*. A curtain fluttered, and a few seconds later, the front door opened wide, revealing Mrs. Bingham in the archway, bearing a bright smile. To prove her excitement, Virginia Bingham bounded down the front steps with the energy of a child, holding her skirts above her ankles to keep from tripping over her boots, and skittered across the lawn to greet him. Henry Bingham waved and joined his wife, an unsmiling young lady trailing on his heel. Over Virginia Bingham's shoulder, he caught sight of someone else observ-ing the action. She hovered in the doorway, her slender body slanted against the doorframe, her arms folded across her front, and her perfectly sculpted face an expression of wari-ness. *So, the prim little miss from Michigan hasn't left yet.*

"Mr. Madison, you came back!" Mrs. Bingham gushed. "You had me a bit worried there. Henry says I always go over-board with my welcomes, so I thought maybe I'd scared you off. I suppose I can be somewhat overbearing, at times." The woman yanked his free hand from his side and started pump-ing it. "My, you're looking famished. When did you last eat, young man?"

"I—."

"Well, come in and have some lemonade, at least. After that, I'll get you situated in your room, and then we can talk about supper."

Luke thought she'd never drop his hand, and when she finally did, he stuffed it in his pocket. Over the past few months, he'd taken care to avoid social contact as much as possible, but something told him Mrs. Bingham would have none of that. The young girl standing next to Mr. Bingham eyed him with suspicion. Her long brown hair, coming loose from her braids, blew in front of her eyes. She swept a hand across her face and tucked the rebellious strands behind her ears, all the while giving him a frown the size of a city block. She stuck out her chin defiantly. As young as she appeared, he didn't think he'd want a run-in with her. She looked like she'd been around the world and back again.

"Good to see you again, Luke," Mr. Bingham said, touching his elbow.

Luke nodded and forced a smile. "Thank you, sir—and ma'am. I decided I'd better write that article, after all. I appreciate your willingness to let me stay here a spell. I think that in the end, it'll be more convenient for me. I'll be doing a bit of research, so I'll appreciate having a room to come back to. I trust I'll be able to work here with only minor interruptions."

Mrs. Bingham chuckled. "Well, we shall certainly hope for that, but with a houseful of children, Henry and I don't make any promises, do we, Henry? But don't worry. There'll be plenty of time for writing your article once everyone goes to bed. In fact, you can use Henry's Underwood typewriter, if you desire."

"I appreciate that. I write most of my research and my first draft in longhand, then finish on the typewriter, so I may have a need for it later."

He was still mulling over what she'd said about his working after everyone had gone to bed when the girl standing alongside Mr. Bingham tipped her chin up and shot him a narrow-eyed glare. "What kind o' article you writin', mister?"

"This is Mr. Madison from the *New York World*, Maxine," Mrs. Bingham announced. "He's a news reporter. Isn't that exciting? Mr. Madison, meet Maxine Ward."

Maxine. The girl they'd mentioned having come from the brothel? His stomach squeezed into a tight knot. He set the heavy suitcase down. "Hello there, Maxine Ward," he said, stretching out a hand but knowing she probably wouldn't take it. Sure enough, she looked at it disdainfully, so he tucked it back in his pocket. Something about this girl fascinated him—the anger boiling under her skin, those eyes narrowed with skepticism, the stubborn set to her jaw, that cynical twist to her mouth—and now he knew what it was. She mirrored *him*—at least when it came to inner rage. As a matter of fact, he could almost guarantee they would relate to each other on some level, not that he planned to make it his mission to find out. His mission from this day forward consisted of zipping back to the *New York World* and his eight-to-seven job just as soon as Owen Perry opened the doors to him. But for now, something else took precedence. He had to finish this silly orphan article, then convince his boss he had the brainpower, the stamina, and the mental stability to return to his *real* job.

"What's he doin' here?" the girl asked.

"Maxine…," Mr. Bingham said with a warning tone.

"That's fine," Luke said, somehow understanding her leeriness. "I plan to write about Sheltering Arms," he told her. "It's what you'd call a human interest story. Maybe you could help me with it."

She pulled her brow into an affronted frown and sneered. "I doubt it. And don't go gettin' any ideas about mentionin' my name, either—or expect me t' answer any questions."

More went into her words than anger and bitterness. He thought he detected shades of fear in her face—a face that would almost certainly be pretty after she had passed through the awkward stage of puberty, leaving behind the sprinkling of pimples that peppered her forehead. Just what had happened to her at Miss Violet's Saloon? As much as he didn't like the idea, he knew he wouldn't rest until he had done some serious investigating. If he were going to write this article, it would be the best doggone article ever written on street urchins.

"I wouldn't expect you to tell me anything that made you feel uncomfortable," Luke said to Maxine. "I'll let you read my article after it's written, and if there's anything you want to add, anything important you think I may have missed, you can tell me then."

"Fine." Her half smile didn't come close to reaching her eyes. "But just so you know, I don't plan to tell you anythin'."

Mr. Bingham inhaled a loud breath and shifted his weight. "Maxine, why don't you go back in the house now?"

She turned on her heel with an insolent scowl. "I'll go check on Emily."

"Oh, that will be a great help to me," Mrs. Bingham called after her. "She loves when you visit her, you know. Please come back and tell me if she's taken a turn for the worse."

Maxine marched toward the house without acknowledging Mrs. Bingham's remarks. Out of earshot, the Binghams gave a simultaneous sigh.

"Does she give you a lot of problems?" Luke asked, noting the lovely Miss Kane's sudden departure from the doorway and wondering where she'd gone.

"Enough, although we've had others who have created far more. She's a little lost soul, that one, with a very low opinion of herself." Mr. Bingham pulled on his mustache while mulling over his own words.

"She doesn't get on well with the other children her age or older," Mrs. Bingham elaborated. "But she's wonderful with the younger ones. She takes them under her wing as if they were her own. 'Course, I don't expect her to do the job of carin' for the babes, but it does her good to pour her energies into their care—gives her a sense of purpose, you know, not to mention lightens my load and Charlotte's. Under that tough façade of hers is a soft, moldable heart. I'm convinced of that."

"And who is Charlotte?" he asked.

"Oh, you haven't met her yet. She's a young lady who takes responsibility for the babies on the main floor. She's been away for a while, but we expect her back sometime tomorrow. I know she and Maggie will become fast friends." Luke nodded and sniffed the fragrant air. Flowers in full bloom lined the driveway, casting their scents in his direction. He took another gander at the massive house. Mr. Bingham seemed to sense his curiosity about the edifice.

"Ginny inherited the place from her grandfather. Don't recall if we told you that. It's got somewhere around eighteen to twenty rooms. I lose track myself." He chuckled. "'Course, you saw all the rooms the other day when I give you that grand tour. A person could hide out for days in some nook 'r cranny, and I daresay, plenty o' younguns have tried it over the years. Ginny here knows all the hiding places, though." He grinned and hooked his thumbs in his suspenders, gazing up at the house with Luke. "Yep, it's a grand ol' house, all right, but that's all it is—a house with a bunch of walls and space.

Ginny and I dedicated it to the Lord soon's we took possession of it, so we consider it more His than ours. Because of that, anyone who walks through the doors is welcome to call it home, including you."

Some kind of dormant emotion stirred, but Luke stifled it. He had no room in his heart for friendly, caring people such as these, much as he could use a few more friends, especially in his present condition. But the truth was, he didn't have the energy it took to invest in true friendships. No siree, his main focus was to complete his research, write that silly orphan article, return it to Owen Perry for his approval, and then hope for a hasty welcome back to the office.

Chapter Eight

Maggie lingered in the library as the Binghams ushered Luke into the house. He set his suitcase down by the door and walked across the Persian rug to a velvet wingback chair, and Maggie managed to stay hidden behind the tall potted fern while she followed him with her eyes. In the next room, connected by a pair of French doors, Vivian was still rocking baby Christina.

"I'll get us some lemonade," Mrs. Bingham said. Then, she turned with a start. "Or would you prefer a cup of tea? We have both."

"Lemonade will be fine, and, please, don't feel you have to wait on me."

"Nonsense. I enjoy it. Besides, after today, you'll be on your own."

She left the room, speaking in a low voice to several children who were just finishing up their kitchen chores and preparing to go upstairs.

"You'll learn to make yourself at home here," Mr. Bingham said. "When you have need of something from the kitchen, you help yourself or go without."

"Does that go for the children, too?"

"My, no! If we gave them free reign in the kitchen, there'd be nothing left by the end of the week, specially as far as the bigger boys are concerned. Ginny can hardly fix enough to keep their stomachs satisfied." Mr. Bingham took a chair adjacent to Luke. "They get plenty, though, those boys. More than they had before coming to us. Matter of fact, nobody here at Sheltering Arms goes hungry, no indeed."

Luke removed a small pad and pencil from a pocket inside his dress jacket. "I may as well start taking some notes, if you don't mind."

"Not at all. Got my doubts about saying anything noteworthy, though."

Luke gave a light laugh, and the sound fairly resonated off the walls. Maggie adjusted her position behind the fern, parting a few fronds to improve her view. "Well, what say I ask the questions, you answer them, and I'll decide what's noteworthy?"

"Sounds reasonable. Ask away."

"Okay. For starters, how did you and Mrs., er, Virginia, get the idea for opening your home to orphans?"

Mr. Bingham chuckled. "You would start with a question that required a detailed answer."

"I can answer that," said Mrs. Bingham, rounding the corner with a tray carrying a pitcher and four glasses. "But first—where is Maggie Rose? She should join us."

At the mention of her name, Maggie let go of the fern frond she'd been holding, causing it to snap back with a noisy rustle. To worsen things, she tripped on Mr. Bingham's slippers as she stepped back from the plant, inadvertently knocking over an oil lantern in the process. The shattered piece drooled oil down the narrow table leg and onto

Mrs. Bingham's wool rug, creating the worst mess possible. Horrified, Maggie hastened to snatch a rag from her apron pocket to start wiping up the oil.

"Well, my stars in Stratford!" Mrs. Bingham said, rushing around the corner, tray still in hand. "I didn't know you were in here, child."

Maggie looked up from her stooped position. "I'm sorry. I tripped on those slippers."

"Don't apologize for that, my dear," Mrs. Bingham said. "Henry is always leaving those things lying around. Henry!" Mr. Bingham hurried into the room and gawked at the mess.

"Go get us a proper cleaning cloth, would you?"

He disappeared to the kitchen before Maggie had a chance to protest. Goodness, what an awkward situation. This had nothing to do with Mr. Bingham's slippers and everything to do with her spying through the fern!

"I've ruined your beautiful rug," Maggie lamented.

"Nonsense. It's just an old rug from Austria."

"From Austria?" Maggie nearly choked.

"Or maybe Hungary; I'm not sure. It came over on the boat with my great-grandfather, but the truth is, I've never liked the thing. It's dark and morose."

"Dark and—but it's an heirloom!"

"My dear, heirlooms or not, things are far less important than people. Haven't you learned that yet?" With each day, Maggie had come to view Virginia Bingham as a most selfless, outstanding, and benevolent woman. Why, she wasn't even sure Grandmother Kane would have reacted in so charitable a manner, had someone spilled oil on one of her fine rugs. "Henry's coming with a better wiping cloth. We'll work on this spot while you tend to our guest."

"What? Oh, but I don't know what to say to him."

Mrs. Bingham nodded toward the tray holding the pitcher and glasses. "Go serve him some lemonade."

"You ladies need any help?" Luke called from the other room.

"We're just fine, Mr. Madison. Be with you in a moment."

Maggie slowly rose to her feet and left the room, taking the tray with her. She forced a cordial smile. "Hello again, Mr. Madison." She hated that her voice came out sounding sheepish.

Luke jumped to his feet and tucked his notepad and pencil back in his pocket, giving her a cursory nod. My, but he was even better-looking than she remembered. And tall. Yes, taller than she recalled. She found herself craning her neck.

"Miss Kane." He gave her a rapid scan, and icy heat prickled down her spine. "Do you conduct frequent espionage from behind overgrown houseplants?"

"Excuse me? I—." She clutched her throat, where a knot had formed. "I wasn't spying," she fibbed. How terribly humiliating! If only the floor would open up and swallow her whole.

A flash of amusement crossed his face as one thick eyebrow arched in a curious fashion, and he rocked on the balls of his feet. Leaning forward, he whispered, "I saw you, so there's no use denying it."

"Oh." She felt her shoulders drop and the air go out of her. How had he spotted her when she'd been so careful to hide herself?

He laughed. "I'm a reporter, remember? I don't miss much." He eyed the tray she was holding. "Did you want to set that down before you spill it, as well?"

Flustered, she turned her back to him and set the tray on the tea table in front of the sofa. She picked up the pitcher and filled two glasses, trying to regain her composure. "Tell me, Miss Kane, how do you like it here at Sheltering Arms? I rather thought you'd have gone back to Michigan by now."

She gritted her teeth, swallowed hard, and turned to hand one of the glasses to him. He nodded his gratitude and took a long swig, eyes focused on her as he drank.

She leveled him a steady gaze. "I am enjoying it immensely, Mr. Madison, and particularly because I know I am exactly where God wants me to be." She measured out each word, punctuating as needed.

A slight tip of the chin and a glimmer in his charcoal eyes reflected a morsel of resignation. "Fair enough." He removed his pad and pencil from his pocket. "Mind if I ask you a few questions, seeing as you're Sheltering Arms' newest employee?"

She took a sip from her glass. "I'm not sure I can be of much help, but you are free to ask me anything."

His dark eyes narrowed speculatively. "Good. First off, what would prompt a young, sheltered thing like you to come to the ruthless jungles of New York?"

"Young, shel—I'll have you know that I'm twenty years old!"

He tipped back on the balls of his feet. "No. That old?"

"And I'm here because the Lord called me. Therefore, I shall rely on His strength and wisdom to direct me through this 'jungle,' as you refer to it."

He scribbled something on his pad. "A call from God, you say? Was this an audible voice you heard?" Distinct cynicism rang in his tone as he continued to write. Now was not the time to allow her temper free reign.

"It was more a deep sense of conviction, Mr. Madison—a sense that if I walked away from this opportunity, I might miss out on something wonderful. There is a great deal of peace to be found in simply obeying God's gentle nudging."

His hand ceased its scrawling, and he snapped the notebook shut. Clearly, she'd hit a raw nerve.

Just then, the back door squeaked open, and Stanley appeared in the doorway between the kitchen and dining room. "Hey, I thought I heard a driver pull up a while ago. Good to see you again, Mr. Madison."

Despite its being the Sabbath—a day of rest, for most— there were still plenty of barn chores to do, and Stanley's grimy overalls, smudged face, and tattered straw hat proved it. At the sight of their guest, he removed his hat and strode across the room, smiling warmly.

"Unfortunately, I don't look any better today than I did a few days ago when Henry introduced us." A light chuckle bubbled up from his diaphragm. "Sorry 'bout that." He wiped his hand on the side of his overalls before extending it.

Luke stepped forward to receive the handshake. "No problem. Good to see you again. And please, call me Luke." Maggie pushed down the twinge of resentment that he hadn't requested the same of her.

"Then you'll call me Stanley—or Stan, whichever comes natural. You planning to spend some time with us? I could sure use the help with those rowdy boys of mine."

"He sure is," Mrs. Bingham answered for him, stuffing her wiping cloth in an apron pocket as she stepped from the library. Mr. Bingham busied himself putting the side table back in its proper place. "He's goin' to be working on writing the best human interest story the *World*'s ever published.

Matter of fact, I can hardly wait to read it. I know it will give a whole new perspective on the plight of these children. God knows it's time the city opened its eyes *and* its pockets."

Stanley clasped his hands behind his back and gave his head a thoughtful toss. "There'll be plenty to write about, that's for sure. Let's hope your article serves its purpose well."

Luke shifted his weight from one foot to the other, looking half embarrassed by the attention. "I certainly can't predict how it will turn out, but I'll give it my best effort."

Mr. Bingham stood in the opening between the library and living room, twirling one end of his mustache between two fingers. "Stanley here could give you a good deal of history, considering he's been with Ginny and me for years, right, Stan? He's like our son."

Stanley's face fairly gleamed. "They took me in when I had no place else to go. God has surely used them over the years, and I'll be the first to testify to that. 'Course, I'm not the only one whose life they've touched. There have been countless success stories of others who've come and gone from here."

"Well, now, God's done most of the work," Mrs. Bingham put in. "Without His divine guidance and strength, not to mention financial provisions, Henry and I might well have given up a while back. God just has a way of coming through at the last minute." She chuckled to herself. "It's a simple test of our faith, sometimes."

Out in the hallway, a door closed; seconds later, Maxine appeared, little Emily in tow. "Emily's feelin' good," she announced, her usual scowl somewhat mitigated. "I'm bringin' her up to my room, if that's okay."

"That's a fine idea, Maxine," Mrs. Bingham said. "Come here, little one. Let me feel your forehead." Emily left Maxine's side. She was still pale in appearance, but her eyes showed a bit more spark than usual. Maggie had yet to see the child fully healthy.

Mrs. Bingham placed her palm on the brow of Emily's oval face and smiled. "No fever that I can detect. Maxine is good medicine, isn't she, pumpkin?"

Emily gave a bashful nod and toddled back to Maxine, taking hold of the bigger girl's hand. The pair started for the stairs, but at the door to the kitchen, Maxine paused and turned, one lifeless braid dangling down her front. "I heard you talkin' 'bout that newspaper article again," she said, directing her statement at Luke. "Don't forget, you promised I could read it 'fore you print it."

Luke produced a smile that was genuine, albeit minuscule. "I don't break my promises," he assured her.

Rather than linger, Maxine gave a curt nod, then vanished around the corner with Emily.

With the sounds of feet padding up the stairway, Stanley murmured, "She carries quite a chip, that one. But she'll come around once she gets to know you. I assume Henry and Ginny told you her story."

Luke's square jaw tensed. "Only that she came from a house of prosti—."

"Vivian!" Mrs. Bingham stepped forward as the girl entered the room, empty bottle in hand, sleeping babe in her arms. "Why don't you go put Christina in her crib now? Cora and Lillian are both sleeping in the nursery, so try not to wake them." Vivian nodded, giving Luke a curious appraisal before leaving the room and heading for the nursery at the end of the long hallway. Mrs. Bingham sighed, watching the girl go.

"I'm not sure how much the rest of the children know about Maxine's plight," she whispered.

"Oh, I see," Luke said. "I'm sorry if I...."

"No, no, it's my fault," Stanley said. "I should have thought to look around before I commented about Maxine. I didn't know Viv was in the parlor."

"Well, never mind," Mrs. Bingham said, flapping her wrist. "No harm done."

Luke nodded, his brow crumpled with uncertainty. "Miss Violet's Saloon, was it?" he asked in a hushed tone. "Over on 65th Street?"

Stanley nodded, solemn-faced. "That's the one. As far as I can tell, she escaped with little time to spare. She left behind her best friend, a girl by the name of Clara Warner. Afraid I don't know much about the girl, though. Maxine's pretty tight-lipped whenever I press her for particulars. Deep down, I'm convinced she wants to talk, but the notion of it creates an awful terror in her."

Luke's face took on a thoughtful expression. "Clara Warner? Any idea how old she might be?" He hastily scribbled something in his tablet.

"I'm thinking around Maxine's age. She said they bunked together in a tiny room when they weren't, um, working. She worries about her, I know."

"Oh, my goodness," Maggie murmured. The mere mention of the word "working" set off a whole string of abhorrent mental images. Mrs. Bingham came over to put a hand on her arm, patting it gently. "There must be something we can do."

"I could scope the place out, see if I can get a glimpse of this girl—or any other young girls, for that matter," Luke offered.

"That could be dangerous, son," Mr. Bingham spoke, pulling himself away from the doorjamb and moving into the room. "That's a bad neighborhood. I wouldn't want you—."

Luke harrumphed as an air of self-composure passed over his face. "Writing a human interest piece often requires digging—sometimes in sinister places others haven't mustered the pluck to explore." That dark brow of his crinkled even deeper, captivating Maggie more than she liked to admit. In fact, she found her eyes quite fixed on his profile. "Any idea how thorough an investigation the police conducted?"

Mr. Bingham shrugged. "Not very thorough, I suspect. These kinds of places dot the city like fireflies on a summer night. They're everywhere, but the police claim they haven't spotted any illegal actions. My guess is, they're swamped with similar complaints and don't have the manpower or time to investigate."

Maggie gasped. "That's plain awful. I would think a matter of this magnitude would be their highest priority."

She felt the eyes of Luke Madison come to rest on her face. Their gazes locked for mere seconds until his expression turned into a cynical smile. "Welcome to our fair city, Miss Kane."

K

Maxine walked Emily down the hallway to the room she shared with sisters Julia and Sofia Zielinski. She couldn't explain the sudden swirl of anger and worry stirring in her stomach, but for certain, it had to do with that reporter downstairs and all that talk about writing some article about Sheltering Arms for the *New York World*.

Suppose *they* read it, those hideous people down at Violet's place, and then somehow figured out where she was hiding? Sure, that fellow promised she could read his article, but what guarantee did she have that he wouldn't add stuff to it after she had read it? For all she knew he could be one of *them*, spying on Sheltering Arms so he could report his findings back to those creeps working for Violet. Maybe they were paying him to find her. Maybe this whole newspaper business was nothing but a big front, a way for him to wheedle his way inside Sheltering Arms and reveal secrets—*her* secrets. She rebuked herself for having told Stanley as much as she had, even though he seemed a trustworthy guy. The truth was, she couldn't trust him or anybody else—and especially not that new guy. And what about that woman, Maggie Rose Kane? Sure, everyone raved about how pretty and sweet she was, but what did anyone really know about her? In her thirteen years, Maxine had learned two mightily important lessons: one, be careful whom you trust, and two, hold tight to your heart.

Her head ached, her chest burned, and her throat felt parched. She felt that she should probably leave Sheltering Arms, but where would she go if she did? She couldn't go back *there*—even though poor Clara probably missed her almost to death. Oh, why had she refused to come with her when she'd climbed out that upper story window?

"I'll fall and break my arm, I just know it!" she'd wailed.

"No, you won't, Clara. I'll help you," Maxine had coaxed, extending her hand.

"I—I can't. They'll find us and drag us back here anyway!"

"I won't let them," Maxine had said.

"You go without me. Remember, it's called Sheltering Arms Refuge. Ask someone the way if you have to, but go there. I heard it's a good place."

"Come with me."

The two had stared at each other for scant seconds, Clara trying to drum up the courage, when the familiar click-clack of ol' Violet's high heels sounded on the weary wood floor outside their room, drawing nearer, nearer. "You little ladies hurry on outta here this instant, you hear me? Someone's a waitin' on ya', and they ain't got all night."

"Come on, Clara," Maxine had pleaded one last time as she hung halfway out the window, one foot dangling in midair, the other barely touching the shingled roof. Clara was a frail thing, but Maxine couldn't force her to do something she refused to do. That's why she'd made the decision to go on without her. What choice did she have?

But even now, weeks later, her conscience felt burdened whenever she thought about Clara and pictured her standing there pale, terrified, alone. To appease her guilt, she tended tirelessly to little Emily, Millie, Audrey, and Rose Marie. The bigger girls could take care of themselves, but the younger ones—they were helpless. What if those horrid men broke into Sheltering Arms and took them? That ugly monster named Byron, in particular. The very idea of it made her Sunday dinner churn uncomfortably in her stomach. She swallowed down a hard, sour lump.

The sound of conversation coming from Vivian Pelton's room brought her steps to a halt.

"Who is he?"

"I don't know exactly, but he's writing some sort of news piece about Sheltering Arms," Vivian was saying.

"Are we gonna get our picture in the paper?" Maxine recognized the squeaky voice as that of nine-year-old Sofia Zielinski. "Maybe folks will come and adopt us if they see our pictures."

"If they see my picture, I'll never get took, 'cause I'm too fat." This had to be Julia, Sofia's older sister by two years.

"That's 'cause you always takin' seconds and sneakin' extra cookies," said Millie Sargent.

"You aren't fat," said Vivian. "Just slightly chubby."

"Thanks."

"Anyway, some of us will be riding on a train in a few weeks," Vivian said. "I overheard Mr. Bingham talking to the reverend at church last Sunday how they're getting all the arrangements put together."

"Why we riding a train?" Audrey Wilson asked. It seemed nearly every girl on the floor had gathered in Vivian's room to hear her talk about the reporter.

"To find homes, silly."

Maxine couldn't make out Audrey's whiny, muffled reply, so she tugged Emily away from the door, a trifle guilt-ridden for eavesdropping.

On the way to her own room, she mused about the whole notion of riding that train. It would be her ticket away from that battle-ax Violet and the thugs who worked for her. But then Clara Warner's face came into view. Somehow, she had to figure out a way to free her from that dreadful place before she gave another thought about going anywhere. She could not—she would not—leave Clara behind. Emily padded alongside her like a lost pup, still fragile from her nasty cough, and Maxine put a protective hand on her shoulder.

At the end of the hall, a ray of sunshine shone through the window, and a gentle breeze ruffled the long lace curtain, giving the appearance that all was well with the world.

Too bad it couldn't be that simple.

Chapter Nine

Luke awoke in his tiny bed—in a room that wasn't much larger—to the sounds of squalling boys, spurts of laughter, and the occasional slamming of a door followed by thundering feet running up and down the hallway. He squinted to read the small walnut bracket clock on the nightstand and discovered the time to be just past 7:30. *Where do those boys get so much energy at such an early hour?* he wondered, running a hand over his day-old beard and drawing back the lone sheet that covered him. Sunlight peeked through the branches outside the window of his third-story room, promising another clear day.

"Hey, I'm next in there," chimed some young lad's voice.

"I gotta go worse than you!"

"Stan-leeey!" the boy wailed. "Noah cut!"

"Hey, hey, pipe down, Ricky. Our guest is sleeping. Go use the outhouse," Stanley said, his voice coming from a distance, probably his room. "You know very well that whoever uses that pot is going to have to empty it."

More murmuring and skirmishing had Luke shaking his head as he stood up and stretched his arms toward the ceiling. How did eleven boys go about sharing one washroom? He told himself that from now on, he'd rise ahead of them and thereby miss the hubbub. Of course, if he played his cards right, he'd be out of here in a couple of weeks and spend the remainder of his time doing…what? Owen Perry didn't expect to see him back at the *World* for three months, which would bring him to the first of December. He didn't know how anyone could expect him to while away his time at an orphanage, but he also wondered what else he would do with himself if he wasn't at Sheltering Arms. Even he knew he wasn't worth much stuck alone in his big apartment. He figured he might as well try to make the best of a poor situation.

"I don't wanna run all the way out there," Ricky clamored, not piping down one iota.

Somebody paraded past Luke's door and bounded down the stairs, running at full tilt. Unfortunately, his room just happened to be situated at the end of the hall, where the staircase began; thus, every sound echoed up through the floorboards like a volley of cannon fire. He rubbed his eyes and moaned. Two weeks ago, he wouldn't have dreamed he'd be in this position.

"Hey, Stanley, you gettin' anxious?" someone asked, probably an older boy, judging by the sound of his cracking voice.

"For what?" Stanley asked, footsteps drawing nearer.

The boy laughed. "You know for what. She's coming back today, ain't she? You gonna give her a kiss?"

"Stanley and Charlotte, sittin' in a tree, K-I-S-S-I-N-G!" someone else chanted in a singsong voice.

"Hush up. No, I'm not going to give her a kiss."

"Why not? She's your sweetheart, ain't she?"

"Don't say 'ain't.' And what makes you think she's my sweetheart?"

"Who's sittin' in a tree?" some new voice asked, apparently just emerging on the scene.

"Stanley and Charlotte is," said another.

"I can tell by the eyes you make at her. Woo-hoo," he teased.

"I don't make eyes at her," Stanley said firmly.

"Hey, hurry up in there!" Ricky pounded on the bathroom door. "What you doin', sleepin' on the p—?"

"Ricky, be quiet," Stan commanded him sternly.

Luke remembered Virginia Bingham telling him about a woman named Charlotte who cared for the babies and toddlers. Apparently, Stanley carried some sort of torch for her, or the boys wouldn't be teasing him so. Downstairs, the shrill shrieks of a baby reached to the rafters, no doubt the demands of one hungry for food and attention.

Argh! He wriggled into the pants and shirt he'd laid out the night before, frowning at the number of wrinkles in them but not caring enough to press them out with a hand iron. Something told him the people in this house had other things to worry about besides his disheveled appearance—that young ragamuffin Maxine Ward, for one. He had half a mind to go to Miss Violet's Saloon tonight and sniff around, but common sense told him he needed to come up with a strategy first. One didn't just walk into a brothel without a plan.

Outside his window, a squirrel made a running leap from one oak branch to the next while two blue jays puffed up their feathers and gave the creature a good dressing-down, their jeers as scolding as the rusty voice of a crotchety schoolmarm. Luke watched in fascination, trying to remember the last time he'd marveled at the everyday wonders of nature.

"Well, it's about time," came Ricky's voice again, followed by the sharp sound of a door slamming shut.

Luke buttoned his shirt, then surveyed his appearance in the mirror situated over a marble stand that held a wash jug and a large bowl. He yanked open the top chest drawer and nabbed his shaving kit. The least he could do was freshen up and eliminate his scruffy whiskers.

K

At the breakfast table, he somehow found himself sitting next to Miss Kane, her citrus scent mingling with the aromas of bacon, eggs, and pancakes. All in all, he didn't object to her proximity, but he didn't intend to go out of his way making conversation with the naïve little lady, either. Also seated at the table were brothers Stuart and Ricky Campbell, Ricky temporarily quiet now that he had food in front of him, Peter Kramer, Maxine Ward, a few others whose names he hadn't learned, and lastly, Virginia, with baby Christina in her lap, having stopped howling.

He figured the rest of the residents must have eaten earlier. Stanley and Henry, for example, had already left for the city to get supplies, and he'd seen a few of the older children heading out to the barn to start the morning chores. He could only surmise where everyone else had gone—some to the garden, others to the playground, some to the chicken coop to gather eggs, and others to their rooms to finish making their beds. One of the first things he'd learned was that Virginia Bingham did not abide unmade beds or cluttered rooms. He then made a mental note to make his own bed before she noticed.

The conversation around the table ran the gamut from an older boy's comment that Alton B. Parker didn't stand a ghost's chance of winning the presidency against the popular Theodore Roosevelt to little Rose Marie Kring's assertion that butterflies were hatched, not "borned." He listened with moderate interest, even catching himself making a smile or two between chews, but he sobered up when Maggie and Virginia laughed aloud over Ricky Campbell's claim that he'd recently seen an ad in the *New York World* that read, "For Sale: an antique desk suitable for lady with thick legs and large drawers."

"Are you sure you read that in the *World*?" Luke asked. "That sounds more like something you'd read in the *Times*."

Ricky laughed. "You're just sore 'cause I'm pokin' fun at your paper."

Smart aleck. "No, I'm just saying someone would have caught a mistake like that before printing it."

"So, you're sayin' the *Times* has more idiots working for it?"

He didn't think he liked Ricky very much. "That's not what I said."

Ricky's annoying chuckle did what he'd intended it to—irritated Luke. He told himself that only a fool would allow a mere child to goad him, so he forced out a tight-lipped grin. He glanced at Miss Kane, further irritated to discover she was still laughing quietly with a dainty hand pressed to her mouth to cover her growing smile. Even Virginia hadn't stopping smiling, but she pretended it was because of the baby in her arms.

Around the table, the younger children appeared more interested in cleaning their plates than in sharing in the joviality. Maxine Ward picked at her pancake, apparently indifferent about the conversation. Her face bore a bland expression, and the discovery that she probably rarely found anything to smile about hit him with a force. Not that he was any barrel of laughs right now, but before the *Slocum* went down, and Annalise and he had firm wedding plans in place, life could not have been better. He'd found something to laugh about every single day back then.

When, if ever, had life been pleasurable for Maxine—or for any of these children, for that matter? No doubt, even Ricky had a sad history, and Luke suddenly didn't want to know it, which would make researching his article a trifle difficult, he realized. He told himself he needed to work on remaining objective, indifferent. In other words, he needed to get the job done and get out of here.

Sympathy and kindness just weren't in his vocabulary right now.

K

In the mid afternoon, Maggie was just sitting down to take her turn rocking baby Christina when a young woman came through the door. She swept inside like a warm breeze, skirts flaring, all smiles and cheer, set down her two small suitcases, and opened her arms. Every child present—Rose Marie, two-year-old Cora, toddling Lillian, Jenny Pelton, and Millie Sargent—all ran to her like subjects to the beloved queen of some faraway country, shrieking with joy and jumping up and down.

"Miss Charlotte!" Jenny cried. "You're back! We've been wondering when you'd get here."

"Did you bring us somethin'?" Millie asked, her voice pitched high as the stars.

Ah, the famed Charlotte Decker had come home at last. Maggie watched, still rocking the baby as she suckled her bottle, and waited for a proper introduction, not wanting to interrupt the excited circle of young girls all vying for Charlotte's attention and pressing for hugs. Charlotte smiled warmly at each eager face, tweaking noses, pinching rosy cheeks, and ruffling hair.

"Oh, I've missed you all so much!" she exclaimed. "And of course, I brought you something. Nothing big, mind you, but tasty."

"What? What?" they all shrieked at once.

"You'll see," she said. "But if you persist in begging, I'll make you wait clear into tomorrow. How would that be?"

That hushed the group.

Charlotte stood and looked over the heads of the clamorous children, spotting Maggie in the rocker on the other side of the room. "Oh, my goodness, forgive my manners. You must be Maggie, and I daresay, you're even prettier than I'd imagined. And look there, you're taking lovely care of my precious Christina." She glided across the room, tossing her hat on a chair. Immediately, Millie snatched it up and plopped it on her head, trailing behind her with the rest of the children.

As Charlotte approached, her smile broadened, and in that instant, Maggie knew she'd found a friend in Charlotte Decker.

For the next few minutes, the ladies grew acquainted, Maggie answering questions about the home and family she'd left behind in Michigan and Charlotte explaining her weeklong absence. She had attended a great aunt's funeral, visited family and friends in Baltimore, and traveled by train to Boston, where she and her long-standing male companion spent a few days visiting museums and taking strolls through the park.

"What's your beau look like?" Jenny asked during a short pause in the conversation. She had dropped to the floor at Charlotte's feet, her adoring eyes fixed on the woman's every move. Millie sat beside her, still wearing Charlotte's flowery hat, and Rose Marie nestled in Millie's lap. Across the room, the other children had succeeded in emptying the toy box, spreading an array of wooden objects about the room. Baby Christina dozed peacefully in Maggie's arms.

"My—beau?" Charlotte's brow wrinkled slightly. "Well, he's more like an old family friend."

Maggie hated to admit her own curiosity. She'd never had a beau, or even a gentleman caller, for that matter, so the whole notion struck her as foreign yet fascinating.

"Ain't you gonna marry 'im?" Millie asked, clear disappointment in her tone. "You was gone a whole week."

Charlotte's laughter fairly floated across the room. "Millie Sargent, you don't just come out and ask someone such a question. Besides, I visited many people over the past several days."

"Miss Charlotte's right," Jenny said. "If she wants to tell us her personal stuff—like what her beau looks like…."

"He's not my b—." But before Charlotte could say another word, the back door opened and the voices of Mr. and Mrs. Bingham, Luke, and Stanley filled the kitchen.

"Hey, come and see who's here!" shouted Jenny, startling baby Christina with her yelp so that the infant screwed up her little mouth in a pout and let out an earsplitting scream. Maggie set to bouncing her, but to no avail, so Charlotte swept her up and quieted her instantly. Moments like these made Maggie wonder if she'd ever get the knack of handling babies.

Stanley shot around the corner first, and in the flick of an instant, Maggie caught the hopeful glimmer in his eyes when he spotted Charlotte. She turned her gaze to Charlotte, but nothing about her countenance looked particularly different.

Mrs. Bingham was next to run into the living room, wringing her hands on her soiled apron and twittering like a bird, while her husband smiled from the doorway. Luke stood beside Mr. Bingham, his lanky body leaning against the doorframe, arms folded in front of him. The bright afternoon sun behind him left his face in a shadow, veiling his hard-to-read expression. Maggie wished he didn't intrigue her so. Just when she meant to tear her eyes off him, he sank his own into her, and her heart thumped in a ridiculous manner, warming her cheeks.

"Oh, my soul, it's good to have you back," Mrs. Bingham cooed, wrapping her arms around Charlotte and the baby.

"Indeed," Mr. Bingham said. "Some of us around here can hardly function without you." His eyes twinkled as they moved from the children to his wife and finally to Stanley. Was he implying what Maggie sensed he was? He fingered the ends of his mustache, looking thoughtful.

Stanley shifted his weight and smiled. "Welcome back, Char," he managed in a somewhat croaky voice.

"Thank you," she said, passing the baby to Mrs. Bingham's outstretched arms.

"My, my, so much has happened in the past week," Mrs. Bingham said. "I see you've met our dear, sweet Maggie."

"Yes, I was so eager to! We're fortunate to have her here." Charlotte smiled, and for the first time, Maggie noticed the tiny dimple in her chin. Warmhearted described her better than beautiful, but she was attractive in a wholesome, home-spun sort of way with her brown hair swept back in a bun, her blue eyes pretty but not striking, and her bright, round face peppered with a few freckles. Her pale blue dress, cinched at her slightly plump waistline, bore wrinkles, no doubt from the hours she had spent riding to her destination.

"And this is Luke Madison from the *New York World*," Mrs. Bingham said, gesturing behind her as she swayed slightly to still the fussy baby. "I believe I may have mentioned him just before you set off on your journey. He's to write an article about Sheltering Arms."

"Yes, of course. I do remember. Hello, Mr. Madison."

"And Mr. Madison, this is Charlotte Decker, the house-mother for our children four and under. I'm sure you heard us mention her."

At the introduction, the man stepped all the way into the room and waited appropriately to see if Charlotte would extend her hand. When she did, he graciously took it, his expression friendly. "Nice to make your acquaintance. And, please, no need for formalities. Call me Luke." Again, resent-ment reared its head in Maggie's heart that Luke Madison could be so downright amiable to everyone but her. Right from the start, he'd treated her like some kind of sour morsel.

After the introductions and a bit of small talk, Charlotte yawned.

"Gracious me, you're tired, Char," Mrs. Bingham said. "Why not go lie down for a while? We'll manage just fine, as much as Henry here seems to think we can't function another minute without you." Her eyes glittered with amuse-ment, spurring Mr. Bingham into quiet laughter. Stanley stood mutely.

"That does sound nice, if for only a few minutes. I'll just take my suitcases to my room."

She moved to the doorway, where she'd set down her luggage.

Mr. Bingham cleared his throat loudly, and at the blatant hint, Stanley jumped into action. "Please, allow me."

Well, isn't this engrossing? Maggie mulled to herself. *Stanley performed like the perfect gentleman when he picked me up at the station—he was self-assured, funny, and talkative—but since Charlotte's return, he can't seem to put more than two words together.*

It would seem Charlotte Decker had quite a hold on Stanley Barrett.

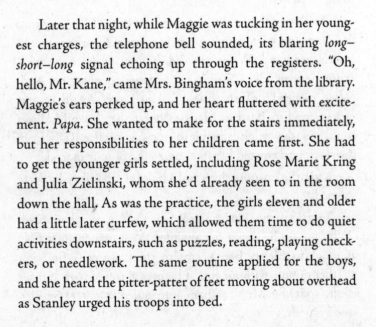

Later that night, while Maggie was tucking in her youngest charges, the telephone bell sounded, its blaring *long–short–long* signal echoing up through the registers. "Oh, hello, Mr. Kane," came Mrs. Bingham's voice from the library. Maggie's ears perked up, and her heart fluttered with excitement. *Papa.* She wanted to make for the stairs immediately, but her responsibilities to her children came first. She had to get the younger girls settled, including Rose Marie Kring and Julia Zielinski, whom she'd already seen to in the room down the hall. As was the practice, the girls eleven and older had a little later curfew, which allowed them time to do quiet activities downstairs, such as puzzles, reading, playing checkers, or needlework. The same routine applied for the boys, and she heard the pitter-patter of feet moving about overhead as Stanley urged his troops into bed.

"Yes, she's settled in nicely," Mrs. Bingham was saying. "Uh-huh. What's that, sir?...Oh, absolutely—she's the perfect addition to our staff."

Virginia Bingham had the type of voice that carried great distances without effort. Of course, these newfangled telephones did not allow one to speak quietly. Even though the Bell System had installed phones in millions of American households, the contraptions made conversing difficult what with all the static and constant cutting in and out.

"Yes, yes, I'll get her straightaway. One moment."

Audrey Wilson's whistling snores had already begun when Maggie pulled the cotton blanket up under her chin and bent to put a feathery kiss to her forehead. On the bunk above her, Millie lay on her side and watched Maggie, her big, round eyes visible in the dusky glow.

"You best go to sleep, too, pumpkin," Maggie told her, brushing her hand over the child's forehead. "Morning comes quickly."

Millie sighed. "I gots the bathroom chore tomorrow. I hate that job of cleanin' out that stinkin' room."

Maggie tempered her smile. "I don't blame you, but please don't lose any sleep over it. If I have time, I'll help you. How's that?"

Millie grinned, revealing the toothless gap in her upper gums, and flipped to her other side to face the wall. "I like havin' you at Shelterin' Arms."

Maggie patted the child's bony shoulder. "I like being here," she whispered back.

Once she was downstairs, she eagerly accepted the telephone receiver from Mrs. Bingham. The line cracked and hummed with static as Maggie struggled to make out Papa's garbled words. "We miss you, M__ie. Gra__other sends her l_ve."

"PAPA, SEND GRANDMOTHER MY LOVE, AS WELL!" she shrieked into the receiver, embarrassed at being compelled to yell.

"Are you g__ng along all r__? We had quite a __...Sandy Shores," Papa said.

"YOUR VOICE IS CRACKLING. THINGS ARE LOVELY HERE. THE WEATHER HAS BEEN NICE. I HOPE YOU CAN COME VISIT SOMETIME. I MISS YOU, PAPA."

"We m_ss you, too! Folks around here__. They say __ funny, but I don't __. ...at the Whatnot."

"WHAT DID YOU SAY?" For some reason, he'd worked the family's general store into the conversation, but she had no notion why.

He rattled on. "...can't decide. Your grandmother __ wouldn't, but I told her __. Isn't that funny?"

Oh, mercy, something funny had happened back home, and she had missed the entire tale.

"PAPA, YOU'LL HAVE TO PUT IT IN A LETTER!"

Sheer frustration at having to shout into the silly apparatus made her temples hot. After all, the children were trying to sleep, Henry and Virginia were reading their Bibles in the front parlor, and the older children were playing quietly in the adjoining living room. To make matters worse, Luke kept peering at her over the top of a *Life* magazine. It annoyed her that he hadn't left the library when she'd walked in.

Papa continued. "Hannah, Gabe, and Jesse __ go __ Colum__. They're going to celebrate __ bir—." Several more crackles, spits, and sputters followed, ending with a block of silence.

"ARE YOU THERE? PAPA?"

"Maggie, can you hear me?"

"PAPA?"

Nothing but empty silence answered her, followed by a tedious click. She frowned and put the receiver back in its cradle.

"Wearisome gadgets, aren't they?" Luke said, surprising her by speaking first.

She dabbed at a silly, unexpected tear. Her father's voice, garbled as it was, had created an awful ache in her heart. "I hate them. They'll be forever useless until someone comes up with a way to stop all that static."

"I couldn't agree more."

Chapter Ten

Blast if he didn't feel sorry for the girl! She'd hotfooted it down the stairs, unable to hide her enthusiasm, grabbed the receiver from Mrs. Bingham's hand, and pressed it tightly to her petite ear, only to have to shriek into the mouthpiece. If that wasn't enough, the worthless device cut out on her midway through their none-too-private conversation, and now she looked devastated, wiping a tear from her cherubic cheek.

And he hated that he'd noticed.

After hanging up the phone, she had stood staring down at the thing as if willing it to die a slow death. Finally, she turned her gaze on him. As much as he'd have liked to pay her no heed, he put down the magazine he'd been skimming and asked, "Your father, I take it?"

She nodded glumly. "I haven't spoken to him since I left home a week ago."

He returned a slow nod. "And you miss him," he said, studying her model-like face framed by loose tendrils of shimmery gold hair. Her finely sculpted cheekbones, exquisite nose, and faintly rosy mouth, now drawn into a droopy pout, struck him, making him wonder if she more resembled her mother or her father. He also wondered how she could feel so strongly that the very voice of God had told her to leave her family in Michigan for a bunch of dispossessed orphans in New York. And Stan and Charlotte—what kept them here, living lives of such sacrifice? Perhaps, in the course of his research, he would place some emphasis on the people who devoted themselves to the work at Sheltering Arms— the Binghams, at the very least.

"Yes, and my sisters and grandmother. We're a very close family."

"Hmm," he said with a nod. "Your sisters all look like you?" He didn't particularly feel like talking, but he'd started the conversation, after all.

She laughed like a youthful sprite. The sound reminded him of wind chimes tinkling in the breeze, and his soul lurched in a painful way. "Hardly. Every one of us is different as night and day—except for our personalities, I suppose. Those have some similarities. And people say our voices sound alike." It seemed that her melancholy mood had lifted, judging by her sudden proclivity for chatter. "My oldest sister just got married to our town's new sheriff this past spring." She stepped up to the fireplace and looked down at him, her blue button eyes creasing softly at the corners. "That was a fast courtship. Once they fell in love and he proposed, my grandmother's planning wheels went into action. They have an adopted son, Jesse. He was an orphan, but, oh my, that's a whole different story, and I don't want to bore you."

If she was fishing for an invitation to continue, she wasn't getting it. He set his magazine down on a nearby tea table and thought about standing up, but just then, Maggie lowered herself to the wingback chair opposite his own on the other side of the fireplace, and he felt getting up would be rude.

"Do you have family nearby?" she suddenly asked. It was an innocent question, and yet his jaw and shoulders tensed. "I don't mean to pry, but—I remember Ginny saying something about you having an apartment on the Lower East Side. I just wondered if—well, if your parents or siblings might—."

"It's only me."

"Oh. You mean, you live by yourself?"

"Exactly."

She steepled her fingers under her pert chin and pondered his laconic response. He could almost see the wheels of thought spinning a wild web under that pretty head of thick, blonde hair. "So, your family...."

"I just said, it's only me."

"You have no family—at all?" Her jaw dropped, then quickly clamped shut again.

"I'm an only child. My parents died when I was a little tyke, and my aunt raised me."

"Oh. I'm so—sorry—about your parents. I lost my mother when I was young, so our grandmother helped our father to raise us girls. I know he appreciated her help." She snagged a breath and crimped her brow. "So, your aunt...."

"Died recently," he finished abruptly. "As did my fiancée and her mother." Daunted and confused, her mouth fell again, and this time it stayed that way. Out in the parlor room, Mr. and Mrs. Bingham could be heard rising from their chairs and instructing the children in the living room to put away their things. He didn't think they'd heard any of the exchange between him and the little Michigander, but then again, that could be the very reason for their hasty exit.

Maggie fumbled with the folds of her skirt, balling up some of the fabric in her fist as she waited for him to go on.

He rather enjoyed watching the impact of shock on her lovely face, and though he felt like a scoundrel, he figured that was what she got for prying.

"So...what...how...?" Her voice cracked like thawing ice.

Cold waves of revulsion swept over him at her curiosity, yet a fiendish compulsion drove him to retell the sordid tale expressly to cause her pain. "You ever hear about the *General Slocum* disaster?"

She breathed deep and pinched the skin beneath her chin, her pale face taking on a whiter sheen as she adjusted her slender body. "Y-yes. I read about it—a terrible boat fire back in mid-June and hundreds of lives lost. Why?"

"Well, they were all on the *Slocum*—my aunt, my fiancée, Annalise, and her mother—heading up the East River to Long Island's Locust Grove for a church picnic."

"Oh, no!"

He shifted his gaze to a painting on the wall, a picture of angels hovering over a child kneeling at his bedside, when she gasped sharply. Around the corner, Mr. and Mrs. Bingham were corralling the children. He heard books snapping shut, game box lids closing, and a few whiney complaints, followed by the rustling and shuffling of soft-soled shoes on the hardwood stairs. Tense seconds pulsed by; the chill black of silence engulfed the two of them after everyone else had left.

"There were some 1300 people on the boat that day when the fire broke out—'bout the same time the captain was maneuvering through the East River's tricky passage at Hell Gate." He let out a sick chuckle. "Ironic, huh? Hell Gate. Some picnic for the faithful people of St. Mark's Lutheran Church."

She gave no response. Good. He'd shocked the woman into a speechless state.

"More than a thousand people, mostly women and children, lost their lives that day," he murmured, shifting forward in his chair to rest his elbows on his knees. He clasped his hands together and stared at the floor between his shoes, noting a seasoned gouge in the wood. "They found Annalise and her mother clinging to each other under a fallen plank. My aunt had jumped overboard, probably hoping someone would save her before she sank. Her body washed up on a bank that same evening."

A whiff of air came from Maggie's throat, but she refrained from speaking, so he used the lull to continue his horrific story. "That infernal paddleboat was a veritable deathtrap—nothing but tinder and fresh paint and crumbling life preservers, not to mention the cheapest fire hoses her owners could buy. Darn thing hadn't had a decent inspection in years. I know, because I've done thorough research." He cussed under his breath, not caring what she thought of him. "Crew never had as much as one fire drill."

At last, he had run out of words. He hadn't talked this much about the tragedy since a few days after it'd happened. One funeral after another had taken its toll on him, and to get through them, he had kept his grief locked up tight. Instead, he focused on the circumstances surrounding the tragedy—cold, hard facts to fill in the details for a newspaper piece. What he had discovered fueled his anger, masking the immeasurably deep emotional wounds. Even now, fresh rage boiled to the surface, creating an awful urge to retch. To push the feeling back down, he waved his hand in a dismissive gesture, thinking to end the evening.

But then her sniffling began.

K

And to think she'd let his petulance get to her. She wiped away a stream of tears; his heartrending story, though told with surprising matter-of-factness, had struck her at the core of her emotions. Moreover, it grieved her that she'd been so nosy about the reasons for his bitterness.

She fought to get a grip on herself before speaking, but all attempts failed. "I'm ever so—sorry to—hear—about your losses," she sputtered in between sobs.

From the corner of her eye, she saw Luke jolt back and grip the arms of the chair. For mercy's sake, he probably had no notion what to do with a sniveling female. She wondered if he'd ever had to deal with his fiancée's crying spells. She imagined him comforting her, whispering in her ear that everything would be all right.

Feet padded overhead. Maggie knew she should excuse herself and tend to her girls, but she couldn't bring herself to stand. Her legs had turned too jellylike to hold her weight.

"Uh—I guess I shouldn't have told you all that."

She shook her head, unable to respond for her running nose and dripping eyes, then dug in her pockets for a handkerchief. When she came up short, Luke produced one himself, spanning the distance between them with an outstretched arm. She gladly took it, despite its wrinkled condition, and blew her nose. He looked at the ceiling, then the floor, then back at the ceiling.

"Sorry about that," he murmured.

"No, no, it's—I'm glad you told me," she managed, giving her nose another good blow and gathering her wits. "I'm just so—sorry for you."

Fierce pride glittered in his currant-black eyes. "I don't need your sympathy," he enunciated clearly.

"No, I don't mean that in a negative way. I'll rephrase. I'm sorry about the entire situation—for all the families involved." She shuddered at the sudden chill she felt. "It's such a terrible thing. I—don't even know what to say."

"Say nothing. It happened, it's over, and hopefully, someday, justice will prevail. A lot of people are to blame—Captain Van Schaick, for one. He made a very bad choice in not turning back, or in not at least running the ship aground at the nearest bank. Instead, he sped up his course and fanned the flames in the process."

A loathsome tone rang through his words, and she remembered his comment about having researched the event thoroughly. Naturally, he would want to find out as much as he could, having lost the people dearest to him. But would knowledge bring him any closer to feeling whole again? She detected his resentment, if not hatred, toward the people presumably responsible, and so she issued a silent prayer for the obvious ache in his heart. She wondered about his spiritual condition—did he know about the power of Christ to bring strength, peace, and healing into a life? She decided now wasn't the right time to probe him about spirituality, however.

The mahogany clock on the fireplace mantle chimed nine-thirty. Maggie sniffed once more and wiped the cloth across her face, slightly embarrassed. "I've always been quick to cry. Papa always says my heart is as soft as a down pillow."

The slightest hint of a smile skipped across his face.

She held up the handkerchief before tucking it in her pocket. "I'll wash this and get it back to you."

"No hurry."

After a moment's hesitation, they rose simultaneously, each turning down a low-burning lamp and heading for the stairs by way of the kitchen. "I think I need a drink of water," Maggie said, veering toward the sink.

"Let me."

Stepping in front of her, he took a glass from the cupboard and proceeded to fill it from the spigot. She watched, admiring his long fingers and their swift efficiency, and she was touched by his offer to serve her.

"Thank you," she said when he handed her the full glass. Greedy as a parched pup, she gulped it down in what probably seemed an unladylike fashion and, when done, set it down a trifle harder than necessary.

He actually chortled. "You guzzled that like a sailor guzzles ale. I'm impressed."

She couldn't help smiling, despite her slight embarrassment. "There's nothing like a cold glass of water after a good cry."

He gave a simple nod.

Just outside the back door, two cats were tussling. Hearing the scuttle, a dog barked in the distance. Upstairs, a floorboard squeaked, and someone coughed.

Maggie breathed deep, expelling one last sigh. She had to tilt her head to see into Luke's raven-like eyes. "Well, good night, then."

Rather than turn with her toward the stairs, he cleared his throat and kept his feet squarely anchored. "Good night."

At the bottom of the stairs, she paused and turned. "Thank you for—telling me about what happened, Mr. Madison. Perhaps someday, you'll tell me about Annalise. I'm sure she was lovely." At the mention of her name, something blazed across his face, and she identified it as razor-sharp pain. Quickly, she added, "If you want to, that is."

A muscle tensed in his jaw and then relaxed. "Call me Luke."

In the backyard, the cat skirmish continued. "All right. And you must call me Maggie." That said, she turned, picked up her skirts, and hurried up the stairs.

Chapter Eleven

There was a kind of comfort in the routine existence at Sheltering Arms Refuge, beginning with breakfast and the assignment of chores to the noon and evening meals and the extracurricular activities interspersed throughout the day. For the girls, there was needlecraft, laundry, cooking and baking, household cleaning, and gardening; for the boys, there was everything from fence repair to painting to woodworking to small building projects. Boys and girls alike chipped in with barn chores and kitchen duties, and each child was responsible for keeping his or her own area neat and tidy. As far as Luke could tell, except for the very small, they all had tasks to do, and he couldn't very well sit back and do nothing.

Some days, he worked alongside Stanley, mucking stalls and milking the cows—two jobs he never dreamed he'd have to learn. Other days, he painted fences with Gilbert Garrison and Bernard Munson, chopped wood with Allen Kramer, hauled coal to the furnace room with Billy Harper, or helped Mr. Bingham mow the lawn. None of these things had he done before. Shoot, he could count on one hand the number of jobs he'd accomplished in his lifetime that required muscle and grit and produced a healthy sweat, and, frankly, he felt cheated. Having always lived in swanky city apartments with maid and butler service, to boot, he'd barely had to lift a finger. Aunt Fran never wanted him doing anything meant for hired help, and she'd often scolded him for making himself snacks in the kitchen when he could have simply rung Mrs. Jennings in her quarters. "I don't like bothering her for something I can do myself," he'd argue.

"Nonsense," Aunt Fran would chide. "I pay her a good wage to see to our needs. If you start taking up her responsibilities, she might grow lazy on us."

Of course, Irish-born Doreen Jennings didn't know the meaning of laziness, but try to convince his aunt of that.

He'd been at Sheltering Arms more than a week when it occurred to him that he hadn't written a single word of his article. Oh, he'd done research, but most of it he'd scrawled across the pages of his journal in a haphazard fashion before throwing himself on his narrow bed every night, too exhausted to think beyond that. Every day, he told himself he'd start the blasted thing tomorrow, but tomorrow would come, and he'd find himself out tossing hay, stacking wood, or, if he had time, tossing a baseball back and forth with one of the boys, joining in a game of football, or rubbing down a horse. He found pleasure in keeping busy, especially with manual tasks, as it helped to dull the ache of his loss.

One warm afternoon, while Luke was feeding oats to a trusty old mare that had just returned from a jaunt to a city market, Ricky Campbell sauntered through the big double doors of the barn, his saggy britches soiled at the knees, his short-sleeved shirt bearing a hole or two in the front and missing a button. His straw hat, perched at an angle, blended in with his straggly, sand-colored hair.

Across the room, Stanley was bent over a vise at the work-table, repairing a tool. When the boy entered, he glanced up. "Hey, Ricky."

"Hey." The boy stole Luke a humorless glance. So far, no warm feelings flitted between them. Of course, Luke realized, he had done little to remedy that. Even now, it took effort to dredge up a smile.

"You done with your chores?" Stanley asked in a casual tone.

"I been done for an hour."

"That's good. You want to help me, then?"

"Not especially."

"Suit yourself."

He sauntered further into the barn, thumbs tucked under his suspenders, boots kicking up dust. Luke watched him out the corner of his eye while Rhoda, the mare, finished off the last of the oats in the pail he was holding for her. Ricky stopped at the stall, his eyes boring into Luke's every move, not saying a word. Luke set down the pail and picked up the horse brush, slipping his fingers through the hand strap and then laying it to the horse's withers.

"You're s'posed to use the currycomb first."

"What's that?"

"The curry. You're using the wrong brush. You're using the dandy. Curry, dandy, soft. In that order."

Luke looked down at the brush fitted in his hand. "Oh." No one had told him there was a particular order to this horse-grooming process. The fact was, he hadn't had a single lesson. Mr. Bingham had simply put a brush in his hand a few days ago and said, "Here, brush 'er down." How was he supposed to know the difference between a curry and a—a—dandy?

He'd never brushed a blasted horse in his life since his aunt had always hired drivers to take them everywhere. If they had the means, most city folk hired drivers to avoid having to navigate the heavy traffic, and he was no exception. Of course, most days, he preferred to walk to work, needing the outlet the exertion provided.

"The dandy's bristles are too hard," Ricky was saying. "The curry gets down deep and digs out the gook. You run that over all the bad spots first. Then, use the dandy all over her to brush away the loose stuff, and then finish off with the soft-bristled brush. That's what'll give ol' Rhoda a nice shine."

"Ah." He'd be lying to say he didn't feel a little silly having a smart-aleck boy set him straight. He put down the brush and looked in the crate, bending to retrieve the curry and start again.

But halfway through his first stroke, Ricky cut in, "Don't you know anything about groomin' horses? You're s'posed to start at the top of 'er neck, not the side of 'er belly, and work your way to her rear, then switch sides."

"Oh. Got it." Luke took a few deep, calming breaths and moved to the neck area. Patient Rhoda nickered and gave her head a gentle toss. He could use a little of her patience about now.

"How you gonna get the dirt off 'er coat with them straight sweeping motions?"

"What?"

"You don't do the straight sweeps till you use the dandy brush. You look like you're sweepin' the floor. You do circles with the curry. Like this." Ricky made circular motions with his hand to demonstrate. Over Ricky's shoulder, Luke glimpsed Stanley shaking his head and laughing quietly to himself.

"Circular. Like this?" Luke put the comb to work in the manner in which he thought Ricky meant.

"Not so big. And go deeper."

He made the circles smaller, deeper. Rhoda whinnied and sidestepped.

"Not that hard!"

Luke stopped and dropped his head. "One, two, three, four, five, si—."

"What are you doing?"

"What does it sound like I'm doing? I'm counting. Don't interrupt me."

"Why you counting?"

Luke rubbed his forehead and snagged another cavernous gulp of air before regarding the boy for several moments. "To keep from strangling you."

"Oh."

More seconds ticked by, all in silence, save for the muffled chuckles coming from Stanley's corner. Luke scratched the back of his neck. "Look, why don't you come inside and show me the proper way to groom this critter?"

"You bet." Rather than come through the stall entry, Ricky bounded over the gate like a monkey, nabbed the comb from Luke, and proceeded to prove his skill at horse grooming.

Later, Luke walked back to the house with Stanley. "So, what's Ricky and Stuart's story? How long have they been here?" he asked as they ambled along the flower-strewn pathway.

"Ah, the Campbell brothers. They came to us a couple of years ago, right after their mama died from some coughing ailment, probably pneumonia. They'd been living on the street pretty much, begging off strangers and sleeping under bridges and on benches in Central Park. Ricky's a lot scrappier than Stu, probably because he's older and has spent a good share of his life looking out for his younger brother."

"He's downright contrary, if you ask me."

Stanley chuckled. "He did a pretty good job of gettin' your goat in the barn with those horse-grooming lessons of his. He likes to get a rise out of folks, especially someone he doesn't know and trust yet."

"Or *like*," Luke added.

"He's had a rough go of it. A person's got to earn his friendship. To tell you the truth, I'm not sure where I stand on his list of possible friends. Henry's probably okay in his book."

Guilt squeezed Luke for having been hard on the boy. "It's too bad about their mother."

"Yeah. From what Ricky's told us about her, besides being physically ill, I think she went plain off her noodle toward the end." Stanley pointed at his temple. "She thought the park had elephants, and she was forever leaving peanuts sprinkled around on the ground for them. Ricky told us he and Stu got so hungry one night that after their mama went to sleep on a bench, they went and picked up all the stray peanuts. Apparently, the next morning, she said, 'See, that proves it. Them peanuts is all gone!'"

Luke shook his head and chuckled at the absurdity of it, kicking a long stick out of his path, which sent a frightened chipmunk scampering up a tree.

"Where's their pa?" he asked.

Stanley shrugged. "Ricky said they never did learn his name. If the man cared at all, he never lifted a hand to show it. My guess is, he stayed with their mother till after Stuart was born and then skipped out. It happens a lot. Or, it might even be the boys have different pas. They don't look much alike. Anyway, after their mama died, the authorities discovered them draped over her body in Central Park. From there, they saw to her burial and then brought the boys to us. That's mostly how we get these waifs, you know. The cops find them wandering the streets, digging through garbage, begging in front of hotels, huddled in dark corners—you name it. Or, sometimes, the bigger orphanages downtown get overcrowded, so we take the overflow."

The hair on the back of Luke's neck stood up. Overhead, a blue jay called down to them, then darted from one tree to the next. "Can't the Binghams find homes for them?"

"Well, there's the train that takes orphans west. Last spring, we set off with seventeen children and came back with seven, the Campbell boys being two of them. Not many folks want more than one, and unlike other agencies, we insist that siblings stay together. I'm hoping someone will offer to take Ricky and Stu on the next trip. We're heading out in about ten days. You riding along?"

Mrs. Bingham had been talking about the trip yesterday while Luke was preparing to accompany Mr. Bingham into the city to pick up some shingles for a shed roof repair. She'd said he would find the experience interesting. The adults going were Charlotte, Maggie Rose, and Stanley; the Binghams always stayed behind to receive any incoming children, as well as to look after those not taking the trip.

"I expect I will," he heard himself say.

"Good, that's good." Stanley slapped him on the shoulder. "I'm sure we'll be able to use your help in managing the children."

It was hard for Luke to anticipate what the trip would entail, but if nothing else, it would surely provide ample writing material.

They entered the kitchen to find Mrs. Bingham flipping the page on the wall calendar. "It doesn't seem possible that summer could be almost over. Here it is, September already," she muttered to herself. Mr. Bingham stood in the doorway between the kitchen and dining room, sipping a cool drink. Two women who volunteered their services at Sheltering Arms twice a week hovered over the sink, peeling potatoes faster than a steam turbine, and they looked up for a scant second. At the big wood-burning iron cookstove, Maggie stirred a steaming kettle from which wafted some kind of delicious, meaty aroma. Luke's stomach growled. He hadn't eaten this well since Mrs. Jennings' fine cooking. Not long after he had let her go, he realized it was a big mistake. He couldn't even fry an egg without turning it black. But when he was considering rehiring her, he learned that she'd taken another job in New Jersey, closer to her daughter.

Maggie raised her head when they entered and smiled at Luke, who returned the gesture. Ever since the night when he'd brought her to tears by spilling the entire wretched story of the *General Slocum*'s burning, they'd exchanged hardly three sentences. Whether the reason was her feelings of embarrassment or his own stubborn will, he couldn't say. Regardless, the idea of rehashing that night or inviting more questions about the boat fire didn't set well with Luke. Maggie had expressed a desire to know more about Annalise, and quite frankly, he didn't want to talk about her. Not now. Not ever.

⌒𝒦⌒

My, but it did seem to Maggie that Luke·Madison grew more and more handsome on a daily basis. She turned back to her stirring chore at the stove and tried to appear unaffected when he and Stanley moseyed through the kitchen. It irked her no limit that a simple little matter of a smile should mean so much, and she admonished herself for thinking so. Mercy! Such musings weren't proper for a lady who was pursuing mission work. Her focus needed to remain on the children.

Since the evening when he'd poured out the events of the *General Slocum* disaster, and she'd blubbered like a baby, their communication had dwindled back to where it had been before—next to nothing. Not that she blamed him for it; most men didn't handle women's wails with much finesse. She thought about her poor father, who'd had to endure living under the same roof with four emotional women, all of whom found various reasons to shed tears on sporadic occasions throughout each month. Usually, he did what he could to fix matters, but when his attempts failed, he did the next logical thing—retreat. And she suspected Luke Madison had retreat on his mind this very moment, if the manner in which he stood there shifting his weight warily were any indication.

"You say it's September already?" Stanley asked. "When did that happen?"

"Three days ago," Mrs. Bingham answered, looking up at the two arrivals. "You boys look as thirsty as a team of horses pulling a two-ton wagon."

Stanley laughed and walked across the room to plant a kiss on Mrs. Bingham's cheek. "That's one way to put it.

Nothing quenches the thirst quite like cool, clear water, right, Luke?"

Feigning focus on her stew, Maggie watched out of the corner of her eye. "Water suits me fine," Luke said.

Stanley filled two glasses and handed one to Luke. They pulled out chairs and sat down at the table, and Mr. Bingham decided to join them. His wife walked over to the tall, white porcelain cabinet, reached behind a pot of fresh flowers on the middle shelf, and produced a large cookie canister. She removed the lid and advanced to the table, setting down the container in the center. "Fresh-baked snickerdoodles," she announced with a hint of pride. "Maggie and I baked 'em after lunch today."

"Hmm." Mr. Bingham helped himself first. "Ginny's snickerdoodles have always been mouthwatering, but now, I imagine that with Maggie's hand in the baking, they're regular prize-winners."

Maggie glanced around. "Why, thank you, Henry, but I can't take credit. All I did was sift the flour and crack the eggs." Luke granted her a look, his dark eyes hard to read. Quickly, she turned back to her stew.

"And stir the batter, my dear," Mrs. Bingham added, "for which these arthritic hands thank you very much!"

Lighthearted banter continued for the next several minutes, the men chewing one cookie after another until Mrs. Bingham finally removed the jar from the table, claiming they'd be no good for supper. The volunteers peeled the last of the potatoes, dropping them in a large pan of water to be boiled later for potato salad. When they had cleaned away the remains of their chore, they went about mixing bread dough, chiming in every so often on the conversation. Maggie placed a lid over the kettle of stew, tonight's meal, and moved it onto a flaming burner that emitted less intense heat. Then, she set about washing a few dishes, content to listen to the group's chitchat while she wiped crumbs from the counter.

Charlotte sauntered in with a wiggling baby Christina in her arms and two toddlers hanging onto her skirts. Sixteen-month-old Lillian Reese had her thumb in its usual spot, stuck between her pouting lips. Maggie didn't know how Charlotte did it—cared for all those little ones with such ease and confidence. She longed to have children of her own some-day, and she hoped to learn a thing or two from Charlotte about handling babies. Of course, one needed a husband for such things as child rearing, and since she didn't see that in her near future, she pushed aside the illusive dream.

Two-year-old Cora Van Sanden let out a squeal of delight at the first glimpse of Stanley, and as quick as her chubby body allowed, she left Charlotte's side to toddle over to him. He grinned and hauled her up on his lap. "Hey, little one," he said, scooting backward to allow for more room.

"I swear, that child's in love with you," one of the kitchen volunteers said while covering a ball of bread dough with a piece of oil cloth. "Every time she sees you, those little eyes light up like the mornin' sun."

Stanley chuckled and bounced the child on his knee. "That's because I'm so irresistible, Mrs. Ormston."

At that, Maggie glanced at Charlotte and thought she detected the faintest gleam of awareness, although the young woman kept her eyes set firmly on baby Christina. Others replied with good-natured jabs and laughter.

When the chuckling died down, the topic turned to the train and its upcoming departure. Mrs. Bingham said,

"Henry and I've decided to keep Emily and her brother with us till next spring, what with Emily's health still a bit unstable. Millie, of course, being dark-skinned, doesn't stand much of a chance for adoption unless some childless couple comes knocking on our door, so she'll have to stay back. As for the rest, Reverend Miles says there's been a lot of interest in response to the advertisements he's placed in the local newspapers of the towns where the train'll be stopping off—Columbus, Springfield, and Lincoln."

Maggie's heart clenched to think how Millie would feel to be left behind. How unfair that the color of her skin should determine whether or not she found a permanent home! "Will they all find homes?" she asked, turning around and leaning back against the cupboard, damp cloth still in hand. Her eyes met Luke's, and she couldn't help the tiny shiver that scampered up her spine. Hastily, she averted her gaze.

"We can only hope," Mr. Bingham said. "Often, the older boys go to farmers wanting help in the fields, while the older girls go to homes where the wives need help caring for young children. You never can tell, though; sometimes, a childless couple comes along just wanting a youngster or two out of a sheer desire to nurture them."

"It seems an odd way to acquire a family—almost like picking them off an auction block," Maggie mused. "Isn't it a gamble?"

"In some ways," Mrs. Bingham replied. "That's why we pray so fervently that the right folks will present themselves. These children deserve a proper chance at life."

"But don't they have that here—now?"

"Unfortunately, Sheltering Arms can provide only temporary housing," Mrs. Bingham answered with a plaintive tone.

"I am one of the blessed few who got to stay," Stanley said.

Mrs. Bingham nodded and smiled. "Because you were so irresistible." That brought about a few more chuckles. Mrs. Bingham sobered. "Our main goal has always been getting these children into permanent Christian family settings. Just this morning, I spoke with Mrs. Farmington from the Children's Aid Society, and she said they have an overflow of children right now. Plus, with colder weather moving in, there's sure to be an even greater number needing housing. The plan is to give them some relief once we get our younglings placed out next week. The Children's Aid Society is planning a placing out, but that won't happen till late February. So, when you return from your train travels, you should find a whole new batch of youngsters awaiting your care."

"Just so you know, I ain't ridin' that train."

All heads turned to see Maxine Ward emerge from the dining room, a frown pasted across her pursed lips. One strap of her plaid jumper was falling off her shoulder, and her long braids were matted for lack of plaiting them that day. "I'll run away first."

Chapter Twelve

Maxine—." Mrs. Bingham moved toward the girl, but Maxine quickly flitted away from the woman's outstretched arms.

"I been listenin', and there's no way I'm leaving New York without—." She clamped her mouth shut and stared daggers at each of them.

Finally, Mrs. Bingham cleared her throat. "Maxine, if you're talking about Emily, it's best for her to stay back until she's fully recovered."

"I know that," she shot back. "I was talkin' 'bout someone else."

"Oh."

Rather than say more, the girl spun on her heel and ran toward the front door, braids flying. As soon as it slammed shut, nearly rocking the house off its foundation, the room came to life.

"Well, mercy, I had no idea she was in the room," Mrs. Bingham said. "I wonder how long...."

"Poor thing," said Charlotte. "She's so confused and unhappy."

"I should go try to talk to her," said Mrs. Bingham.

"I could probably go out there," said Stanley. "I know where she's coming from. She's got that Clara girl on her mind and can't think of leaving her behind."

"I'd let her be for now," said Mr. Bingham. "She'll cool off. Much as I'd like to help that girl, we just can't be responsible for her and every other displaced child in the city. We have our hands full enough right now."

"You're probably right," Mrs. Bingham said, chewing her lower lip. "The Lord knows we're doing everything we can for the ones we have under our roof without chasing down more. You're always so practical, Henry."

Maggie laid the dishcloth on the counter. "I think I'll go try to talk to her. So far, we haven't established much in the way of common ground, but we are both women, so that should count for something. Maybe I can come up with a few words of encouragement."

Mrs. Bingham's breath whistled past her lips. "You have my sincerest blessing for trying."

After searching the entire front property, Maggie finally found the girl out back, behind the barn. She was standing on the second rail of the wood fence of the horses' corral, braids dangling in front of her. Maggie stood in the shadows and prayed a quick prayer, then quietly approached, deciding to climb up on the fence beside her. If Maxine intended to bolt, she gave no hint of it; she merely stared ahead, watching as the horses grazed and a rooster scooted across the field after a squawking hen.

Maggie refrained from saying anything, choosing to wait the matter out. In the corral, two horses took up a game of tag, one nipping at the other's backside and prompting it to whinny unappreciatively. A third joined in, throwing its head to the skies and neighing before breaking into a gallop, kicking up the dirt with dancing hind legs to make an impressive cloud of dust.

"Show-offs," Maxine muttered.

Maggie knew little about horses. Back home, her father kept a horse and wagon at the local livery, but because of the close proximity of their house to the center of town, most everything, including Kane's Whatnot, the Third Street Church, the bank, the post office, and the train station were all within walking range. Seldom did her father ride his mare, except in cases where he had to pay a call on one of his insurance clients, and for these trips, he usually took his rig. If there was a rider in the family, it was Abbie Ann, and only because she often visited her best friend, Katrina, who lived on a farm with her husband a few miles out of Sandy Shores' city limits.

Still, despite her scant knowledge about horses, Maggie certainly derived a great deal of pleasure from watching their graceful movements. "They do put on a lovely show, don't they? Do you think they're performing for us?"

Maxine sniffed, taking care to keep her defenses high. "Sure. And they're hopin' it'll earn them a treat."

"Oh." Maggie felt around in her pockets, but they were empty. "I did have some hard candy earlier, but I gave it to Millie and Audrey for tidying their spaces."

Maxine reached into her pocket and brought out an orange. She gave an almost sheepish look. "I always have one handy."

"Ah, good idea."

She proceeded to peel the thing, and Maggie wondered how long it would take the horses to detect the scent of citrus.

Apparently, not long, for as soon as the first peel hit the ground, they hoofed it over to the fence. Maxine ripped out a segment and handed it to the first one that had nudged in the closest, a monstrous black Morgan named Beauty, after the famous book, no doubt.

Maxine carefully separated a section at a time for each patient horse until she'd finished the fruit. "That's all," she said, rubbing her hands together.

The chestnut-colored one gave his head a mighty shake, then nuzzled Maxine's arm for more. She reached up and caressed the white diamond-shaped marking on his head, which seemed to ease his disappointment. As she watched the girl, Maggie determined one thing: Maxine Ward did not have an impenetrable heart.

"You seem to have a knack with horses, almost like you speak their language," she ventured to say.

"I like most animals," she replied, moving her hand down the horse's velvet nose. "But horses especially, 'cause even though they're big ol' giants, they need a lot of care."

"And you're very good at caring for them, just as you are at looking after the younger children. I've watched you with Emily, in particular. You seem to have an eye out for anyone needing help or protection. That's a gift, you know."

"A gift?"

"Yes. Not everyone is as compassionate about the needs of others, but to you, compassion seems to come naturally."

Maxine sniffed and stepped down from the fence rail, so Maggie hopped off, too. She worried that she'd said too much and that the girl would make a dash for it, but instead, she put her back to the fence and looked out over the yard, breathing in the fresh September air. A faint smile played across Maxine's face to see a batch of kittens following their mother across the yard. "They're seven weeks old now. They was born on July 10."

"You remember the date?"

"Sure. It was exactly a week after I—."

"After you…?"

"Came here." She whipped back around to look at the horses, draping her arms over the top rail of the fence. Maggie turned with her.

"It was a very brave thing you did, escaping Miss Violet's Saloon."

Maxine's head jerked back, as sharp assessing eyes lit on her. "You knew about that?"

"Mrs. Bingham told me. I'm sure you were terrified. I don't know if I could have done it."

"It wasn't nothin', really. I jus' crawled out on the roof, made a leap to a tree branch, took hold like a monkey, and made my way down. Good thing for me our room faced the back alley. Otherwise, there wouldn'ta been a tree. Scratched myself up pretty bad, but that was okay. At least I made it."

Maggie shivered and hugged herself. "My goodness, you are a brave young lady."

She turned her gaze on Charlie, the brown, droopy-eared dog. No one quite knew his age because he'd wandered onto the property five years ago, an orphan himself, and had never left. He sauntered past the cats and plopped down in a patch of sunlight near a rope swing.

Maggie sighed, smelling the heavy scents of dust and manure. "I'm sure you miss her."

"Who?"

"Your friend who stayed behind."

Again, Maxine's neck snapped. "How you know 'bout her?"

"Stanley mentioned her."

She squeezed her lips together, and Maggie worried she'd drained the girl of all talk. She decided to tread more lightly. "I have a couple of friends back home whom I dearly miss, along with my sisters. You name it, we did it: played dress up, walked to Maria's Ice Cream Shop for sundaes, jumped rope, swam in the Big Lake, climbed sand dunes...."

"What's the Big Lake?"

"Why, Lake Michigan, of course. From the shoreline, it looks exactly like the ocean, big waves and all. Of course, there's no salt, which makes swimming in it most lovely."

"You can't see across it?"

"Goodness, no."

Several blocks of silence followed, and then, "Clara is my best friend."

"I suspected so. I'm sure she's a lovely person."

"She's kind of shy. I think it comes from livin' in all sorts of places and not findin' anywhere to belong. Her mama left her with her aunt when she was a baby, but her aunt got to drinkin' lots of booze and said that Clara was costin' her too much, so she sent her to live with a real old lady who lived down the street from her aunt. But then the old lady up and died after a few years. Clara says she found her lyin' in her bed starin' at the ceiling one morning, 'cept she wasn't really starin'. 'Course, by then, she didn't even know where her aunt had took off to."

"Oh dear, that's awful."

"After that, Clara went out on the street lookin' for a way to make some money so she could find some food, and a fellow started givin' her handouts and lettin' her stay in his big house. Least, that's how she explains it. She thought he was tryin' to help her, but turns out he jus' wanted to bring her to Violet's place. Clara says she saw Violet pay him money."

Maggie's stomach roiled with anger and despair, but then she was overwhelmed with a sense of awe at what the girl had divulged. Could it be that she'd earned a place of trust in Maxine's skittish heart? "Did she ever see that man again?"

"Naw. There's all kinds of men what come into Violet's, and most of 'em we know by name, but that feller never did come back."

"I'm so sorry about your friend. Thank you for sharing her story with me."

"I ain't leavin' on that train, you know. I can't leave Clara."

"I understand that, I do. But Maxine, the train leaves next week, and if you don't go, you might miss out on an opportunity to find a good family."

"I said I ain't going!" In a huff, she whirled around and then gasped to find herself face-to-face with Luke. "What—what're *you* doin' here?" she asked. Maggie wanted to ask the same thing. So engrossed had she been in her dialogue with Maxine that she hadn't heard his approach.

"You best not write any of that stuff I just said in your article, you—you—eavesdropper, you!"

He chuckled low in his throat. "I wasn't eavesdropping. You simply didn't hear me coming. Besides, didn't I tell you I'd let you in on the article before I gave it to my boss?"

"I guess."

He turned his face to one side, narrowing his penetrating gaze on her. "What if I told you I might be able to get your friend out of that place?"

"Huh? You'd go get Clara? How you think you're gonna do that? You'd not be able to get her past the door."

"It might take me a couple of tries." Maxine's mouth dropped. "You'd have to give me some information. I'd need to know everything you can tell me about her, like her size, hair and eye colors, and any other physical traits you can think of." Guarded, wary eyes blinked hard as she pondered his words. "And you'd have to trust me."

K

Luke could not believe he was doing this—strategizing the kidnapping of Clara Warner from Miss Violet's Saloon. First off, he'd never been much for hanging around saloons, most of them dark, dank places with a depressing atmosphere; and second, since when did he volunteer to risk life and limb for the job? He was a reporter, for crying out loud—not some martyr out to save the world. *But this is not the world*, he reminded himself. This was one helpless, innocent young girl needing someone to stand up for her rights, to snatch her out of that filthy environment she'd landed herself in through no fault of her own. As much as he resisted the notion, since he had taken up residence at Sheltering Arms Refuge, his heart had started to soften.

He'd spent the better share of the last two days planning how to go about this rescue and figured it was time to take action. Mr. Bingham loaned him the rig for the evening, promising to pray for his safe return and for that of the girl. For once, he didn't balk at the mention of prayer but rather welcomed it. Maxine turned into his shadow, giving him final pointers about what to say to Clara to convince her he wasn't the enemy. "Be sure to tell her you're from Sheltering Arms. She knows about the place. Oh, and give her this," she said, pulling a hanky from her pocket. "She'll recognize it as comin' from me. She gave it to me last year for my birthday."

Luke shoved the lacy cloth into his hip pocket and gazed down at the girl who had taken on a new spark in the past two days. He tried to determine what it was, finally identifying it as hope. Mrs. Bingham had noticed it, too, saying she looked and acted like a different girl.

Speaking of Mrs. Bingham, she seemed to be wringing her hands a lot lately and lecturing him at every turn. "I don't know, Luke. You came here to do research for an article, not to perform some heroic feat," she'd said to him the day before as he was heading out to help Mr. Bingham with a house repair. "If anything happens to you, I won't be able to forgive myself. After all, I'm the one who talked you into coming here. Not only that, but what if that young girl refuses to leave with you? You'll have risked your safety for nothing."

About that time, Maggie walked through the door, hearing the last of Mrs. Bingham's argument. "She's right. In Clara's mind, you could well be an even worse threat to her well-being."

"Or, she just may have reached the point of not caring, and I'd just as soon get her out of there before she loses her will to care. Besides, you heard Maxine. She won't get on that train next week without Clara."

That ended the discussion, particularly when three youngsters came bounding through the door in need of a drink.

By 7 p.m., supper and cleanup had ended, and most of the children had gone outside, the older ones supervising the younger ones as they played in the backyard. Others had retreated to their rooms. Luke tried to slip out the door unnoticed, but Stanley would have none of it. "You sure you don't want me to come along?"

"And have you standing out like a white dog in a mud hole?" Luke retorted playfully. Stanley did not look the part of bar patron. He couldn't say he did, either, but at least his two-day beard growth helped give him a worldly-wise appearance—that, and his sagging, soiled clothes.

"You got a plan of action?"

"Yeah. Instinct."

"That's it?"

Luke chuckled. "Don't look so worried. I'm hoping my years of experience in investigative reporting will pay off tonight. I'm pretty good at reading people. If I detect a problem brewing, I'll scram."

Stanley placed a hand on his shoulder and nodded gravely. "You do that."

Charlotte and Mrs. Bingham emerged from the nursery toting babies on their hips. "We'll be praying for you and watching out the window for your return."

Luke lifted his eyebrows. "It could be a long wait."

"Trust the Lord. He will go before you," Stanley said. "I'm confident of that."

"That's something my aunt would have said. She could be pretty crusty at times, but she had a strong faith, and she didn't make any bones about it."

"She sounds like a fine person. I'm sure she'd be proud to know what you're doing tonight."

The rig stood out front with Mr. Bingham's best horse, Beauty, hitched to the front. "You sure about this?" he asked Luke, concern etching his face.

Luke tried to make his smile appear carefree while he jumped onboard, rocking the weary springs in the process. "I'll be fine." He picked up the reins and nodded at Mr. Bingham before clicking the horse into action. Beauty quickly gained a comfortable gait, trotted to the end of the circular drive, and headed north. The horse had made the trek into the city a hundred times before and seemed to possess confidence enough for both of them. Luke hadn't seen Maggie Rose at the dinner table, and he figured it was because she'd gotten involved with her charges upstairs. He had no idea why it bothered him that she hadn't even come down to wish him well.

It took a good fifteen minutes to traverse the distance between 65th and 74th, what with folks heading home after the workday and others coming into the city for various reasons. Horses, rigs, streetcars, and gas-powered horseless carriages crowding the road. Stop. Start. Stop. Start. He swore he'd move out of this wretched busy place someday. When he approached the intersection, he jolted with shock when the blanket behind him unfolded and out crawled Maggie Rose Kane.

"What—in—the—?" His heart thundered in his chest. "What are you doing here?"

"What does it look like?" She asked, climbing over the seat and sitting herself down beside him. She brushed a few pieces of lint from her skirt and looked straight ahead. "You hit nearly every pothole on the road back there, I'll have you know. Are you accustomed to driving horse wagons?"

"You haven't answered my question. I don't want you with me."

"That's exactly why I kept myself hidden until now." The wagon tipped and jostled, making her bump against him. She straightened hastily, grabbing hold of the seat and setting her eyes on the road.

He set his penetrating gaze on her. "I can turn around." He pulled back on the reins, intending to do just that, but the fellow directly behind him yelled out a few choice words. Luke looked both ways and begrudgingly veered Beauty onto East 74th. When it was safe, he directed the horse to the side of the road and stopped the rig. "Explain yourself."

He would say that.

"That girl is going to be frightened to death when you haul her out of that wicked place."

"Yes?"

"And she'll need a woman to lend her comfort."

Mercy! He looked mad enough to bite a snake.

"What am I supposed to do with you? You can't follow me into the saloon."

"Well, of course I can't. I'll just sit in the wagon and wait for you."

"I don't know how long I'll be in there."

"I don't mind waiting."

He opened his mouth, but nothing came out, so he huffed a loud breath instead and narrowed his eyes. After a few sharp gulps of air, he said, "You are making this mission harder for me, you know that?"

"I don't know why you'd say that. It's not like I'll be in your way."

He blinked at her. "Most likely Miss Violet's Saloon isn't located in the nicest of neighborhoods. You think you can just sit on this wagon seat and escape the notice of every bum who walks by?"

"I'll go back under the blanket, if it'll make you happy."

"And stay there!" He sounded like a stern schoolmaster scolding a wayward student. "And if you don't promise me here and now you'll do just that, then I will turn around."

"For goodness' sake, you don't have to be so—so ornery about it."

He pursed his lips and gave his head a brisk shake, then looked out at the road ahead, holding the reins loosely with his elbow resting on a propped up knee. He was a tall, lanky man, not especially muscular like her brother-in-law, Gabriel Devlin, but every bit as masculine with his square jaw, whiskery face, and dark wisps of thick hair falling forward. The truth was, he fascinated her, but she questioned his faith in Christ and was troubled by its probable absence. She could never love a man who didn't love God first. Not that he would ever give her a second glance, anyway—particularly since his anger now revealed anything but attraction to her.

"Does Ginny know about this? You stowing away in the back of my wagon?"

"Goodness, no. Although she might by now."

He slumped. "Great. Now I have to turn around for sure."

"No, you don't. Charlotte knows, and she promised to explain my position to Ginny—how I feel very strongly that Clara will need the support of a woman when she gets on this wagon, not to mention a great deal of convincing that we don't mean to harm her. Had you thought what you might do if the girl simply jumps off and runs away once you've abducted her?" His confounded expression said he hadn't. "You can't assume she'll cheerfully follow you out the door, you know— or however you plan to get her out of that cesspool. My being here to hold her hand will be a comfort, you'll see. Not only that, but Maxine has given me some ideas of what to say to her, things that will prove we're not her enemies."

Mild interest sneaked into his expression. "Such as?"

"For one thing, she gave me a little poem to say that only Maxine and Clara know about, and it goes like this: On some clear and sunny day, we will pick a fine bouquet. One for you and one for me. Then we'll have a cup of tea."

He gave a simple nod and reached in his pocket, drawing out a piece of frilly white cloth. "Maxine gave me this handkerchief, a gift from Clara. I'm to show it to her as proof that we're friends."

"That should help."

They sat side by side, the chill fall breeze reaching their bones. "Will you promise to stay put?" he asked, the sternness returned.

"I told you I'd go back under the blanket."

"Good. Then go."

"Now?"

"I'll not move until you do. We're only a few blocks away, and I don't want you scrambling back there after I've parked the rig. Someone is sure to spot you and wonder what gives."

"Oh." She hadn't thought of that. "Well, can you at least tell me your plan while we're riding?"

"And make it look like I'm talking to myself?"

"People do it all the time."

He shot her a paltry grin and studied her for a full five seconds before speaking. "I hadn't figured you for being the adventurous type, Miss Kane."

"I came here all the way from Michigan by myself, didn't I, Mr. Madison?"

He chuckled. "I'll give you that, but hiding under a blanket, knowing we could be riding into a dangerous situation? Do you understand your safety could be in jeopardy?"

She straightened her shoulders. "Yes, I do. And for your information, I did not go into this halfheartedly. In fact, I'm praying about it this very moment."

"While you talk to me," he stated with evident disbelief.

"Absolutely. God knows what lies ahead for us, and I'm persuaded He'll grant us His protection. I'm not afraid, and furthermore, I'm not some prissy pants, much as I'm sure you'd like to think of me as such."

This provoked a hearty chuckle—a rare sound from Luke Madison as of late. A scrawny dog darted across their path with a large bone clamped in its teeth. Up the street stood a rundown barbershop, a meat market, a bicycle repair shop, a restaurant, and a dingy-looking barroom. And on the sidewalk, three men were involved in some sort of loud verbal scuffle.

He quickly sobered. "I want you under that blanket *now*."

"All right, all right, I'm going." Turning around, Maggie stepped up on the seat, lifted her skirts to just below her knees, and hopped to the back, certain she'd made a grand spectacle of herself. Once situated in the back, she pulled the wool blanket over her body and hissed, "Now, if you don't mind, would you please tell me how you plan to go about rescuing Clara?"

Chapter Thirteen

It was a stinking place, reeking with thick smoke and spilled liquor. Loud, boisterous piano music assaulted his ears, not to mention the off-pitch singing coming from an overly made-up tart standing on a makeshift stage. The room was dark and grungy, peppered with patrons—mostly men, but a few female patrons, too, all painted up with bright red lips, rouged cheeks, and coal-black eyebrows, dripping with gaudy jewelry and hanging on their men. Here and there, scantily dressed women, also painted up to impress, were carrying trays of food and drinks. He wondered how many of them used their table-waiting jobs as cover-ups for what they really did upstairs. At circular tables scattered around the space, men held women in their laps while they played cards, smoked cheap-smelling cigars, and let out hoots of raucous laughter.

Luke weaved his way through the crowded room toward the bar, where he saw a single vacant stool. He felt several pairs of eyes following him, so he took great care to act the part of slipshod drifter, wearing his hat low and walking with a kind of swagger.

As soon as he had situated himself on the stool, a hard-looking woman approached from the other side of the bar.

She looked to be in her mid-forties or early fifties, her face worn, wrinkled, and covered with rouge, and fake eyelashes batted over eyes narrowed in assessment. She leaned across the counter in a seductive fashion, practically coming nose to nose with him and brushed his cheek with her forefinger. It took every ounce of willpower he could muster not to shrink back from her strong stench, a mix of potent perfume and whiskey-scented breath.

"Well now, who do we have here? I'd remember a face as fine as yours," she said in a gravelly voice, smile oozing with insincerity.

"Give me a brandy and I might tell you," he said. He meant to keep his wits about him, so he had no intention of drinking one drop of brew, but it remained that he had a part to play.

She raised a sculpted eyebrow and snapped her fingers behind her. "Give this gentleman a brandy," she called out, eyes scanning every inch of his face as she issued the order. In less than a blink, a hefty man plopped the drink in front of him. Madame Hussy kept up her quiet assessment. Luke lifted the glass to his lips and pretended to take a sip. The smell alone was enough to make him gag, but he didn't let on.

"Name's Rusty," he lied, setting the glass down. "I been workin' on the subway system, but my job'll be done there in another month or so. After that, I 'spect I'll be movin' on."

"That right? Where to?"

He had to think fast. "I'm from Ohio. Might be I'll head back thataway. I ain't makin' any fast decisions, you see. Never can tell what might crop up for me in these here parts."

The woman on stage finished her song and stepped down, but the man at the piano continued to play, pounding out his own rendition of "A Hot Time in the Old Town Tonight."

At a table near the stage, an inebriated group attempted to sing the lyrics but couldn't get past the first line, so they kept repeating it. Out the corner of his eye, he saw three couples saunter up the stairs, the women leading the way.

"What line o' work you interested in?" she asked.

He shrugged and grinned. "Ain't decided, but one thing's for sure—wherever there's booze and women, that's where you'll find me."

"Ha!" She tossed her head back and laughed. "You sound like my kind o' fellow. You want booze and women? We got it all right here."

"Oh, yeah? What you got t' offer?" He glanced around the room. "'Bout all I see're women who look pretty used up."

She tipped her face to one side and reduced her eyes to mere slits, her thick, spurious lashes nearly blinding her, as far as he could tell. "What you got in mind?"

"Humph, someone a lot younger and—."

Red lips turned up. "And?"

He chortled. "Innocent? You got any innocents hidin' 'round here?"

Her smile gently faded as she pulled back. "This here's a saloon, mister, nothin' more. The women here'll be happy t' sit on your lap, but you'll have to look elsewheres if you want more than that."

"That right?" He picked up his glass and pretended to sip again, then licked his lips. "What about all that booze and women talk you was givin' me? You weren't just feedin' me a line, were you?"

He reached into his hip pocket and brought out a stack of bills. Aunt Frances would roll over in her casket if she had an inkling he was waving her money around in such an uncouth place. He hoped he'd get out of here without having to part with all of it. In a fleeting instant, he made a promise to stick the entire wad into the offering basket next Sunday if he made it out the door with the money and Clara Warner. In fact, he'd personally do the honors, which said a lot, seeing as he hadn't set foot in a church since Annalise had died.

Her mouth gaped at the thick sheaf of bills. "What'd you say your name is again?"

He had to think for a second, but he covered the moment with as poised a grin as he could rally. He laid a hand on her wrist and found it cool. "I'm disappointed you have to ask. I thought you told me I was memorable." He set to rubbing her clammy skin. Her demeanor softened around the edges, especially when he leaned into her. "Rusty's the name. And yours is?"

Pencil-drawn eyebrows slowly arched. "This here's my place. That give you any clue?"

His pulse quickened for a mere instant. So, this was Miss Violet herself. He wanted to lambaste her on the spot. Where was Clara? "Well, that so? I'm impressed and flattered that the proprietress herself would pay me a second's notice."

"It'd be hard not to, darlin'," she said, batting her lashes. "Most of what wanders in here can't hold a candle to you. Why, you even got straight, clean teeth, not to mention a mouth full of 'em." He hoped that particular feature wouldn't make her suspicious of his otherwise unkempt appearance.

High-pitched laughter impelled him to turn his body. Across the room at a gambling table sat a middle-aged man, dressed quite nattily in a white shirt, bow tie, and business suit. He looked vaguely familiar, but Luke couldn't place him. Behind him stood two bulldog-like characters in black suits, feet parted, hands clasped in front of them. Something about the threesome nettled him. A scantily clad woman, too made up to judge her age, perched on the guy's lap, her ample bosom bulging out of her low-cut dress. At the exact moment Luke noticed him, the fellow eyeballed him in return, gave a slow, measured nod, and then lowered his gaze. Luke quickly swiveled back around, not wanting to blow his cover. "Who's he?" he asked, gesturing with a hooked thumb.

Violet glanced over his head. "Him?" She laid a flat palm to Luke's cheek and massaged it, letting go a low-throated chortle. "Nobody you'd know, darlin'."

He lifted his glass and feigned another swallow, then wiped his mouth. "Yeah? He somebody important?"

"Might be. Lots of men come through my doors, every color and class. Why do you care, anyway?"

"I don't. Just curious, is all. Thought you said most of what wanders through here is scum. Leastways, that's what you hinted at. He don't look too bad off, if y' ask me."

She cackled. "I suppose not, but then, what difference would that make to you, honey?"

"None whatsoever," he fibbed with a forced chuckle. But what was he thinking? He had a job to do, and it did not include identifying some mystery customer.

"So, you like your ladies young, do you?" Her sour breath just about knocked him over.

He winked. "And innocent, don't forget."

She licked her lips and eyed his wad of cash. "Ain't that a lot of dough for a railroad man?"

He weighed his next words, even saying a quick prayer that they'd come out sounding believable. He hoped God listened to sinners. He touched her hand in a brief caress. "They pay us decent money. Workin' underground day in, day out ain't the most pleasant of jobs. I live cheap, so most of what I make goes straight in my pocket."

"You got a pretty deep pocket, I see." Gray-green eyes glistened with greed. He sensed her walls of reservation caving in.

He removed several bills from his stash and waved them under her nose. "Man goes by the name o' Clayton tol' me about a fine little whelp you keep upstairs. I think her name was Clara Waters, Walker—Warner? Warner, that's it."

Silently, he thanked the Lord he remembered the name Maxine had given him of one of Violet's former clients. One night, in a drunken stupor, he'd slapped up Clara, and Violet had kicked him out with orders not to return, claiming no one wanted bruised goods. The account had nearly ripped Luke's gut in two. Even now, he could easily tear into this woman responsible for wreaking havoc on innocent girls.

"Pfff, that good-for-nothing fool."

"So." Luke reached for Violet's hand and drew it to his chest. "What do you say? Can you provide me with a little entertainment for the night?"

She made a clicking sound with her tongue and whispered across the counter. "Clara's awful lackin' in experience. Now, I got me some honeys upstairs who'd...."

"I got my heart set on Clara."

She shrugged. "There's a fox goes by the name o' Clarissa who'd...."

He stuffed his money back in his pockets and started to turn. Swiftly, she nabbed him by the arm. "Oh, all right, mister, but I can't guarantee your satisfaction."

He drummed up an alluring smile. "You let me worry 'bout that. I pay you or her?"

"I take my three-quarters and you pay the girl the balance."

"You get a full 75 percent? Ain't that a bit stiff?"

"My girls do all right for themselves. Plus, I give 'em room and board."

He wanted to string her up, but instead brought out his wad again and fanned it under her nose, watching as she greedily yanked her portion from the stack and tucked the bills daintily down her bulging bodice. "My, my, if I was a few years younger…," she ogled him.

"And I a few years older. It's a cryin' shame, ain't it?"

She actually blushed, and he had to drive down the need to gag.

He glanced off to collect himself and noted the fashionable gambler escorting the well-endowed woman upstairs. Halfway up, the guy glanced down at Luke, a thin-lipped, satanic smile spreading across his mouth. Some kind of spark triggered in his brain, but not big enough to light a fire of recognition.

"Byron!" Violet called out in a raspy voice, forcing his attentions away from the gambler. She trained her eyes on Luke's face. "Get yerself over here. I got someone here who needs an escort upstairs."

K

What was taking Luke so long? Maggie made a minor adjustment under the itchy wool blanket, eager for a fresh breath of air, not fully understanding the reasons behind her need for staying put. My, but that man had a testy side. She wished she'd had one of those new Kodak Brownie cameras on her so she could have captured his expression when she'd emerged from the back of the wagon. Why, he'd looked about as shocked as a bear in a trap! Even now, she giggled, then quickly stifled her laughter for fear someone would hear.

Beyond her dark hiding place, a whir of activity buzzed, everything from men chatting up about the November presidential elections to the clatter of a squawking chicken. A chicken on the street? She fought down the urge to take a tiny peek when she heard a cat yowl, saloon tunes ring, a door slam, a horse snort, and countless wagons pass by, some with squeaky wheels. Oh, how sounds seemed amplified when one was deprived of sight.

She stretched her leg to prevent an impending cramp, sighed, and then surrendered to the situation at hand, knowing she could very well be here for some time to come. It was best to take advantage of the moment, she decided, by praying for Luke's safety and that of dear Clara Warner.

Yes, that is exactly what she needed to do. Pray.

K

The big lug named Byron led Luke down a dimly lit hallway, long and narrow, with numerous closed doors on either side. His heart thrummed with dread and expectancy, then with downright anxiety. What on earth had he gotten himself into, and what made him think he could get the girl and himself out in one piece? *Lord, I could use some guidance here,* he silently prayed, much to his own surprise.

Even greater a surprise was the response. *Have a little faith, My son. I have never left you, and I remain at your side, even now. Be of good courage. I will help you.*

The clear insight nearly stopped him in his tracks; in fact, he unknowingly halted so that Byron turned and looked at him. "Somethin' wrong with you? Don't go thinkin' you can get your money back now. Miss Violet don't never return fees, not even when the customer ain't a hundred percent satisfied with the goods."

He swallowed bile and shoved back the awful urge to put his hands to Byron's thick, meaty throat and squeeze. *I could also use some self-control, Lord.* "No, I'm just...."

Byron sneered and lifted a graying brow. "Anxious, are ya? Don't go gettin' yer hopes too high. Clara's a young thing, and she ain't got a lot of knowledge 'bout the ways o' the world." His voice dipped low while his shaggy eyebrow shot higher. "You know what I mean, bub?" Luke did know what he meant, and the knowledge only increased his desire to clobber the man for being so crass. "'Course, Miss Violet says that's what yer lookin' for—the quiet, innocent type. She ain't entirely innocent, mind you, but she's pert near close as you can get."

Luke had had enough. "Why don't you just shut up and take me to 'er room?"

"Fine, fine. You don't need to get all bent like a green twig. Follow me."

Rage burned like fire in his gut as he followed the sad excuse for a human down the hall. Two doors from the end, Byron stopped and rapped on the door. "Hey, little girl, you best open up. You got yerself a visitor."

A slight stirring inside the room had Luke's heart pounding fast and hard. "I'll take it from here," he said, pulling back his shoulders.

"You sure?" Byron asked. "You might need some help gettin' 'er t' cooperate."

Luke pulled his mouth into an ice-cold smile and stared deep into the beefy man's eyes. "You think I ain't done this before? I work best when left to my own devices. Now, get!"

His tone put the fellow back a bit. "All right, all right, I'm goin', but you jus' call downstairs if you need anythin'.'" He laughed to himself and turned away, whistling under his breath. Boisterous yelling and carrying on downstairs soon drowned out the dope's grating tune as he sauntered down the hall and around the corner.

Luke tapped on the door. "Clara, let me in. I'm not going to hurt you." This he whispered through his teeth, mouth nearly touching the crack in the door. He turned the knob, but as suspected, she'd locked it tight as a drum. "Clara, listen to me. I want to help you. You hear me? I promise I'll not hurt you."

The door across the hall opened, and a middle-aged man emerged, a glowing cigarette hanging from his mouth. He gave Luke the smallest glance before heading down the hall-way, tucking his shirt in as he went, his boot heels clicking. Luke closed his eyes and rested his forehead against the door. "Clara," he hissed again.

"Why don't you just leave her be?" came a hoarse female voice. He whirled on his heel, taken aback. In the doorway the man had just exited stood a dolled-up woman wearing a belted, satin robe several sizes too small for her abundant figure. She looked twice his age, if he had to guess, her mousy brown hair peppered with white, her face pock-marked and sagging. Still, despite that tough-looking exterior, some unspecified emotion skipped across her face. "You want a good time, I'll show you one." She crooked an index finger at him.

His stomach rolled over. "No, thanks."

He turned and knocked again on Clara's door.

"She's not available, mister."

"What? But I just paid...."

"I been takin' 'er business. You want to give 'er the money, fine. Slip it under the door. That's what the feller before you did."

"You mean—." He could not believe his ears. "You're covering for her?"

"Whenever I can, yeah." She started to open her robe.

"Stop." He stretched out his hand in a halting fashion, quickly averting his eyes. "I'm not—I don't *need* your services."

She made a clicking sound with her tongue. "It ain't often I get turned down, darlin'. If you're worried I won't make it worth your while, you can jus' put that right out of your head. I can...."

"Why do you do it? Why do you take her clients? Does Violet know?"

She cursed a good one. "'Course not, and my customers know enough not to tell her, too. I show 'em a far better time than Clara ever could. Only stipulation is, they have t' put the money under her door."

"Which means you take nothing."

"Not for her jobs, but that's okay. I get plenty o' my own business. That little girl's had enough bad stuff in 'er life. Somebody's got t' look out for 'er. It sure ain't goin' to be that ol' bag, Violet. That woman's nothin' but a—."

"Why don't you just leave?" he cut in, trying not to give himself away, but too curious to keep entirely quiet. For all he knew, she could be playing him for a giant fool, setting up the perfect trap. After all, he hadn't even seen Clara yet. How could he even be sure Byron had led him to the right room? He realized he had to watch his step.

Her laughter came out hard and cynical. "And do what? Honey, I been doin' this business most o' my life. It's all I know how t' do."

"Most of your life?"

"That's right. Had no place else t' go, no money in my pocket, and no food in my belly. When I was barely eleven, my parents came over on a boat with high hopes for makin' a good livin', 'cept Mama got sick an' died just shortly after arrivin', leavin' me an' several brothers and sisters with my Pa. He tried hard to find work, but there was nothin' to be had, and everyone he came across was in just as bad a straits. We was plain starvin', so he had no choice but to send us out beggin'. Couple of my brothers refused and ran away, one of my sisters caught that same dreaded thing Mama had and died, and my oldest sister jumped on a ship and went back to Europe. Never did hear if she arrived safe or not. Weren't even two months later Pa got kilt in a fight—got a gunshot to his heart in front of a barroom down on East 23rd Street. I guess you figured out by now that left jus' little ol' me. Somebody found me wandering the streets when I was 'bout twelve or thirteen and promised to take me 'home.'" She cut loose a hoarse chuckle. "How could I have known his idea of home wasn't what I dreamt it'd be? Since then, I been in jus' about every bordello in this stinkin' city. Finally settled here 'bout five years ago, and this is probably where I'll die."

Luke hardly knew what to say. He'd never put a real face to a lady of the night before, never even thought about the pain that drove these women to their places of utter despair. For the first time in a long while, he had an ache in his heart for another human being. Strange how casting off his own despondency, if for only a moment, made room in his heart to care about another's sadness. It occurred to him he had to keep his wits about him, though—he couldn't dwell on this woman's sorry state if he were going to complete his mission.

"About the girl," he said, eyeing the closed door.

"I already told y', she ain't available."

He sent up a prayer that his next words would not be his demise. "I want to rescue her from this place, not do her harm, nor to avail myself of her services. A young lady by the name of Maxine Ward told me about Clara."

The woman's mouth dropped nearly to her waist. "Maxine's safe? Where is she? You spoofin' me? I don't know as I can believe a word you're sayin'."

He actually chortled. "I've been thinking the same about you."

"What's your connection to Maxine? So help me, if you're runnin' your own joint somewheres and you intend to haul little Clara off to…."

"No! Listen." He lowered his voice to a whisper. "Maxine's fine. A rapscallion, mind you, but she's healthy and in good hands at, well, at Sheltering Arms Refuge. I'm working as—I'm one of the volunteers there. There's a train of orphans heading west next week, and Maxine refuses to get on it without Clara."

"I heard o' them trains when I was a youngster, but the opportunity to jump aboard one passed me by." She folded her arms and straightened. "Well, I'll help you then, but be aware, Miss Violet ain't goin' t' be happy. Far as she's concerned, she owns the ladies what work here—includin' me. She ever finds out where you took Clara, you'll be in deep trouble. Matter o' fact, I wouldn't doubt they been lookin' for Maxine." She stepped across the hall and gave Clara's door a gentle rap. "Honey, open the door. Everythin's gonna be all right."

Chapter Fourteen

How long did it take to walk inside a saloon, hand over a roll of money to the madam, and convince Clara to climb out the same window Maxine had when making her escape? Surely, by now, Luke had had plenty of time to persuade the girl that he knew Maxine and that her friend was waiting for her arrival at Sheltering Arms. She prayed his plan hadn't gone awry, that he and Clara remained safe.

Maggie squirmed under the scratchy wool blanket, glad for the warmth it provided as the sun disappeared entirely and night settled in. Still, she desired a good stretch to work the kinks out of her muscles. She peeked out from under a corner of the blanket and observed a few passersby through a large crack in the side of the rig; mostly of them were shabbily dressed men with cigars hanging out their mouths. Some loitered at the door of the saloon, gabbing about this and that, and, every so often, a formally dressed gentleman would enter through the doors. Looking for a way to shuck off a day's worth of stress with a drink, was he? Or, worse, seeking a woman to satisfy his lustful desires? Maggie's stomach lurched with queasiness. How could such an evil establishment exist mere blocks from Sheltering Arms? She breathed a prayer of thanks that Maxine had known enough to seek refuge at the home.

She lifted up the blanket another notch for a better view, thinking she might spot Luke inside the saloon, but her view was blocked by the frosted glass windows. The stench of smoke billowed out of the place, beating a path to her nostrils. The woman who couldn't sing worth spit started another tune, this one "The Sidewalks of New York." Maggie had half a mind to march inside, stand up on that stage, and sing "Amazing Grace" at full lung capacity. That ought to wake up a few sleeping souls. Not that her voice outshone the woman's by a long shot; according to her sisters, the world would be a better place if she took up, say, quilting, and left the singing business to those with actual talent. Of course, their jesting always got her dander up enough so that she would sing the louder just to spite them. She had yet to muster the courage to try out her musical skills at Sheltering Arms, and she wondered if the children would be more inclined to appreciate her potential.

A big, mangy brown dog meandered up to the wagon. Would it detect her presence under the blanket? She heard it sniffing as it investigated the wheel, then proceeded to relieve itself. She held her breath, hoping the canine would move on, then let it out when it sauntered away none the wiser. Raucous laughter, neighing horses, the clip-clop of hooves, and loud, boisterous talk filled the air. Someone spewed a deafening curse, and she resisted the urge to rise up and give the offender a piece of her mind. How dare anyone take her loving Lord's name in vain?

Wincing at the tingling pain of a foot that had fallen asleep, she adjusted it carefully, curling and stretching her toes inside her boot. Boredom was setting in, so she took to praying for Luke and Clara again. But that only led to fretting. Had he stumbled upon a problem that put a snag in his plans? What if he didn't return for hours? Just how long could she remain in this prone, awkward position? *Lord, I do believe You prodded me to jump on this wagon, did You not?* A tiny frown pulled at her brow. More likely, He had done nothing of the kind. And the more she thought about it, the more she berated herself for her foolish thinking. She should have left the job of rescuing Clara Warner entirely up to Luke.

A chilly breeze picked up, so she tucked her head back under the blanket and pulled it more tightly around herself, but a frayed piece of yarn brushed the tip of her nose in the process and tickled her. It tickled so bad, in fact, that her eyes welled up with tears, and that horrid feeling that comes before an explosive sneeze overwhelmed her senses. Squeezing her eyes shut, she did everything within her power to hold back the awful urge, pressing her lips tight, wrinkling her nose, holding her breath—but it made no difference. When a person's got to sneeze, a person's got to sneeze, and there's generally no quiet way to go about it. "A-CHOO!"

Afterward, she wondered if anyone had heard, but she needn't have wondered long. For in less time than it would take a hen to lay an egg, someone swept the blanket off her outstretched body. When she dared turn her head, she looked up into a smudged, bug-eyed face bearing a toothless, greedy grin. "Well, lookie here," the man said. "I found me a prize."

K

It took some fast talking on the part of the woman who went by the name of Floretta, but at last, Clara opened her door a crack, enough to reveal one big, sky-blue eye peeking through the slit. She scanned Luke warily from top to bottom. Without a peep, she kept up her silent perusal.

"Open up, dearie," Floretta urged her. "This man don't mean y' no harm. Matter of fact, he's goin' to get you outta here. Ain't that good news? Remember how I tol' y' I don't want you wastin' your life the way I did? Now's your chance, sweetie."

The door remained firmly in place. "What about Miss Violet?" Clara asked, her voice not much stronger than a sparrow's warble. "She'll be mad at me."

"You let me worry 'bout her. She won't know you're gone till mornin', if we do this right. But you'll have to let this man inside so he can tell you the plan."

"It's pretty simple, Clara, but you'll have to trust me," Luke said. "You remember how Maxine climbed out your window and down that tree limb?"

"Maxine?" The door eased open another inch. "How you know her?"

"She's at the Sheltering Arms Refuge—where I want to take you. She's anxious to see you."

"She made it there, then?" she burst out. "I tol' her to go there."

"She made it fine." Luke glanced at Floretta. "She told me to show you this." He withdrew the frilly handkerchief from his pocket.

"I gave that to Maxine."

"I know. She said you'd recognize it."

"I wish I could climb down that tree, but I can't."

"Why don't you let me have a look?"

At last, she stepped back and the door drifted open. He stepped inside, and Floretta followed. Someone had nailed two thick boards across the window, making it impossible to escape. "I see what you mean," Luke said. Anger boiled in his gut. They'd made a prisoner out of the child.

"That Violet is nothin' but a—." Floretta's aptly spoken curse was mostly drowned in some sort of commotion happening on the first floor, a woman screaming like a banshee, probably a drunken hussy. He tried to ignore it.

"Come have a look out my window," Floretta said. "I've got a sloped roof facin' a back alley. She could climb onto that, and if you could back your wagon up to the side o' the building, she could maybe jump down onto it." Luke didn't like the sound of that plan, but what other options did they have? He couldn't very well walk out the front door with her.

They walked across the hall, Clara following like a scrawny lost pup, and entered Floretta's room. Meanwhile, the upheaval downstairs intensified. He avoided looking too closely at the mussed bed, dark floral wallpaper, walnut dresser, and velvet high-back chair. Floretta swept the blood-red drapery to one side, revealing a window that was opened a crack. Bending down, she pulled it up to open it the rest of the way.

Luke stepped forward to have a look. "That'd be a big leap."

"You can use the blanket t' help cushion 'er fall."

Luke looked at Clara, scruffy in appearance from lack of hygiene, downright bony beneath her holey nightgown. Her big-as-the-moon eyes stared at him as if he were a mirage, holding in their depths a glimmer of something like hope. He couldn't possibly leave her here another day—or night.

He sucked in a cavernous breath, then slowly let it out. "You think you can do this? Jump down to my wagon?"

"I shoulda gone with Maxine, but I was too chicken." She swallowed an even louder breath. "But I don't wanna stay here, so I'll do it."

He nodded and looked from Clara to Floretta. "It might take me a few minutes to maneuver my rig back around unnoticed."

"You can drive down t' Crocker Street, which is a block south o' here, take a left, and veer onto the alley from that end," Floretta explained. "It'll be dark, but that's good. You'll see the back o' the saloon and the door to the kitchen. Look for a blanket hangin' from the roof. If anyone's standin' out there, though, it might hold up the works. We'd have to wait for 'em to move on, and y' might have to circle 'round again. But don't worry; most customers don't congregate out there, 'cause there ain't no back entrance for the public to use."

Another loud shriek peeled up though the floorboards. "What is going on down there, anyway? It sounds like some-one's gettin' tortured," Luke said.

Floretta shrugged as if the sound meant nothing to her. "There's always some kind o' hullabaloo 'round here. Women are always askin' for trouble when they step through these doors."

A most foreboding sensation crept along his skin. Surely, that exasperating Maggie Rose Kane would have stayed put, as she'd been instructed. What with his ploy to rescue Clara Warner, he'd had little time to think about the woman hiding under a blanket on the floor of Mr. Bingham's rig. He stepped into the hallway and started toward the stairs.

"You get your filthy hands off me, you big galoot!" came the rasping order. The voice was familiar, and Luke's heart dropped clear to his shoes. Good grief! What had possessed Maggie to come inside, and, worse, what were they doing to her?

Panicked, he ran back to Floretta's room. "I got me a heap of trouble downstairs. I have to go. Can you—?"

Another scream rattled the floorboards.

Floretta nodded. "I'll help 'er onto the roof, but you better make it snappy. I never know when I might get me a customer. Things could get complicated."

Luke's mind started racing while his blood turned to lava. "Just—get her out there and I'll do the rest." He took off on a run, then halted and turned, a sense of wistfulness mixed with angst running through his veins. "You could always jump down there, too, you know."

Floretta shook her head. "I'd break every bone in my body if I tried that. 'Sides, I'll be fine. You jus' get this youngun out o' here and I'll be happy."

He only had time for one last look at the pair. "Thanks," he managed before turning and bolting toward the stairs.

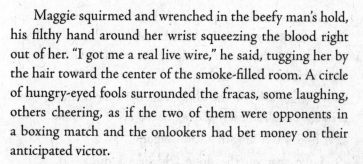

Maggie squirmed and wrenched in the beefy man's hold, his filthy hand around her wrist squeezing the blood right out of her. "I got me a real live wire," he said, tugging her by the hair toward the center of the smoke-filled room. A circle of hungry-eyed fools surrounded the fracas, some laughing, others cheering, as if the two of them were opponents in a boxing match and the onlookers had bet money on their anticipated victor.

She let out another loud shriek, lurched forward, and managed to bite her captor on the forearm and then kick him square in the shin. "Yow!" he yelped. Wild, ear-splitting hilarity erupted all around.

"Why, you little saucebox!" he shouted, wincing in pain.

"She ain't takin' no guff from you, Grayson. Ain't you gonna show 'er who's boss?"

"Sure as shootin', I am." The fellow raised a hand in preparation to strike her.

Maggie ducked, waiting for the pinging blow to her jaw, but the blast of a gunshot stopped the brute's progress.

"Unhand her this instant!"

The deep, resonant voice of Luke Madison caught the attention of everyone present, but Maggie was especially astounded. She had no idea he could speak with such authority—or that he'd had a gun on his person, for goodness' sake! He didn't look like the gun-toting type—or did he? Right now, something about his demeanor made her think of a hissing rattler. Unfortunately, Mr. Grubby Face kept a tight hold on her arm with one hand and clenched a wad of her hair in the other, despite the gun aimed at his forehead.

"Who are you?" her assailant spat at Luke.

"The lady's husband."

Maggie jolted, prepared to deny the ridiculous claim until she got a warning look from Luke fit to scare a bull out of its skin. "What—are you doing here?" she asked, pretending shock, her voice wobbly.

"I might ask you the same." She noted he hadn't yet lowered the pistol, and it made her heart race out of time.

"I—I was hiding in y-your wagon."

Luke spat on the floor. "Spyin' on me again, was y', woman?"

Now, the room took on a different tone as the focus shifted from Maggie and the dirty bully to Maggie and Luke, who obviously wanted her to play along. Trouble was, she had no idea where this playacting would lead.

"He been havin' hisself a good time upstairs, li'l lady. That bother you?" This came from some bearish fellow who was standing behind the bar mixing a drink. "I ought t' know. I give 'im a personal escort to the little tart's room." Beside him stood a middle-aged woman, excessively painted up and wearing a devious smile.

"Why, ain't you the crafty one?" she said, shifting her weight. "Here you had me believin' you was unattached, the way you was inquirin' about my girls. Now, I find you got yourself a wife? You nasty buzzard, you." At this, she cackled so loud she had the whole room laughing along.

"You—what?" Maggie shrieked. "Why, I ought to—to divorce you! And I would—if it weren't for ar'—ar' brood." Now, where had that come from?

To her great relief, the big ox released her hair and dropped her arm like it was a sizzling, red-hot piece of coal. "You got younguns?"

She gave a slow nod. It felt dreadful to lie, but what could she do? Oh, she could just kick Luke for putting her in this position. *My child, who are you to place blame? Did you not jump on that wagon of your own accord because you did not trust that I could handle matters without your help?* Whether the inner voice came from her conscience or directly from God Himself, it gave her pause.

Forgive me, Lord. It seems I've made a mess of things. Please protect us, and above all, keep Clara safe—wherever she is. She rubbed her forearm and plastered a frown on her face, taking a giant step away from the creep and toward Luke. He snagged her by the arm and yanked her to his side, fairly jarring her senses. Did he have to be so harsh? Even Mr. Grubby Face hadn't handled her with quite the same force.

"Come on, woman. I'm about to teach you a lesson!" he growled, stuffing his pistol back in his belt and hauling her toward the door.

Behind them, a rousing cheer shook the walls of Miss Violet's Saloon.

"What exactly did you think you were doing in there?" Luke hissed under his breath, truly sounding like a snake now.

"Me! What about you?" she returned.

"You could have gotten us both killed."

"You were the one with the gun, Mr. Madison, not I!" she argued. "Where did you get a gun, anyway? And where is Clara? Did you see her?"

"It's Henry's gun, and yes, I saw Clara. Now, hush!"

Neglecting to help her up to the wagon seat or to wait till she had situated herself, he grabbed ahold of the reins and slapped the horse into action. The sudden lurch of the rig had Maggie scrambling for something to hold on to lest she fly backwards. She chose the bar next to the seat.

"Why are you going this way?"

"I told you to be quiet."

She could hold her silence only so long. "Where are we going?" He ignored her, whizzing past one storefront after another, the horse's hooves creating a whirl of dust so thick that she felt that old tickle in her nostrils again. She pressed a finger to her nose.

"What possessed you to come inside, anyway?" Luke finally demanded. "I thought I told you to stay put under that blanket."

"I sneezed. Where is Clara?"

"You—what?"

"I sneezed...just like...I'm about to do...again...a-CHOO!" Out it came, even giving the horse a start. Beauty's ears tilted back, and his head twisted to one side.

"You sneezed," he said matter-of-factly. "And...?"

"And that old fool heard it, ripped the blanket off me, and he hauled me inside."

Momentary silence followed her confession. "Are you okay?"

"Well, thank you for asking. I didn't know you cared. Yes, I'm fine."

"I told you that you shouldn't have come."

Oh, how she hated I-told-you-so's. Growing up, her younger sister, Abbie, had been famous for them. She felt her shoulders go up in a shrug. What was the use in arguing when he was clearly right? Instead, she folded her hands in her lap and watched the stores blur by. They slowed at the corner and made a left turn. She had no idea where Luke was taking them, much less if she had a right to know. He drove the rig only a short distance before making another turn, this time onto a dark, narrow alley.

"Keep your eyes peeled for the back of the saloon," he whispered.

"May I ask what you're planning to do?"

"There should be a blanket hanging from the roof."

"A blank—oh, I see it!"

"Where?"

"There." She pointed straight ahead. Barely visible in the shadows, a blanket dangled from the roof like a tattered flag, the moon's glow providing just enough light to make it visible.

Luke reined in the horse and maneuvered the wagon so it was parallel to the building. He stopped it just under the blanket. "Jump in back."

"What?"

"Get in back and be ready to help break Clara's fall." He leaped to the ground from his seat as he issued the order. "Clara!" he whispered toward the roof, hands cupped around his mouth. "You up there?"

Maggie stepped over the seat to the back, but a niggling worry about the distance from the roof and the rig had her wondering about the safety of this mission. The poor girl could wind up with a broken bone or two.

"She's here." A woman in a long, flowing robe came to the edge of the roof and looked over, training her eyes on Maggie. "She the one causing the big stir downstairs?"

"She is."

"My, my. Well, you might better thank her later for taking the attention off'n you and this whole escape thing."

"Where's Clara?" Luke asked, passing right over her remark. "We need to move fast."

The woman reached behind her and ushered forth a mite of a girl. She drew the child close and whispered something in her ear, then inched her forward. "It—it's too far down," Clara stammered.

The woman bent to release the blanket, and down it came. Maggie spread it out on the wagon floor.

"You can do it, Clara," Luke urged. He jumped up on the rig, rocking the springs with his weight, and stretched his long, sturdy arms upward, shortening the span between the roof and the rig. "Come on." Maggie swore his arms looked so inviting that if it were she standing on that roof, she'd leap without a moment's thought.

Brushing off the silly notion, she braced her footing alongside Luke and lifted her arms. "Maxine's waiting for you back at the house, Clara. You don't want to disappoint her."

"I promise we'll catch you," said Luke.

"You sure?" Clara asked.

"Positive."

Heart pounding through her cape, Maggie whispered an audible prayer that God would grant the girl courage, but still she didn't move. Suddenly, the back door to the saloon flew open. "What's goin' on out here?" came a gruff-sounding voice.

Chapter Fifteen

J ump, Clara!" Luke shouted.

Maybe it was Floretta's tiny push that had the girl hurling downward with a screeching wail and landing with a thud in Luke's arms, setting him briefly off balance so that he fell sideways before rapidly righting himself and leaping into the driver's seat to take up the reins. Or maybe Clara simply saw it as her very last chance for survival. At any rate, there they both were, Maggie and Clara, lying on the floor of the rig, two bear-sized men charging off the back steps and running in their direction.

"Hurry!" Floretta bellowed. "Go!" Had there been more time, Luke would have tried to convince her to come along, but time was not on their side. He slapped the horse into action, nearly running down the big oaf named Byron.

"You!" Byron hollered, diving into a waste heap to avoid being hit. Several curse words spewed from his mouth. The other fellow, big and brawny like Byron, glared daggers through Luke when the wagon whizzed past him. As he prepared to take the bend, the last things he heard were fighting words. "Floretta, you're goin' t' pay big for this."

And his heart sank.

The unlikely pair sitting behind him had little to say on the way back to the house—perhaps they both were reflecting on the events of the evening. Apparently, though, Maggie had won the girl's trust, for as they bounced along the gravel street, Clara rested her sleepy head on Maggie's shoulder. Maggie drew the blanket over both of them and started humming the hymn *Blessed Assurance*, albeit out of tune, but the sound was strangely comforting to Luke's ears.

It occurred to him that he, too, was keeping silent, his eyes trained on the road ahead. He glanced around every so often to be certain that no one was trailing them, even as he encouraged the horse along at a pace faster than normal. No one was following, and chances were good that he'd have lost them in the traffic anyway, given his decent head start. Still, he couldn't take any chances, so he weaved his way up and down a few side streets before taking 1st Avenue for one block south and then turning west on 65th.

"Almost there," he said, glancing behind him.

Maggie put a finger to her mouth, indicating the girl had drifted to sleep. Amazing! They'd come through the escapade relatively unscathed; every last detail, save for the two thugs who showed up at the last minute, had worked out fine. And the girl had even fallen asleep! Who'd have thought that would happen, especially when he'd pictured a little wild thing fighting him all the way back? Even Maggie's unexpected company wound up working in his favor, little as he wanted to admit it. Floretta had been right. Maggie had made a nice decoy. A tiny spot of appreciation for her bravery nestled in his mind.

He looked at her again. "Are you all right?" he asked.

She nodded and smiled, and again, he noted what a pleasant face she had—well, more than pleasant, actually.

Downright pretty described it better. But now was not the time for such thoughts, and he silently admonished himself.

"She's a dear," Maggie whispered.

He looked at the girl, then back at her. "Yeah," he confessed.

Turning back around, he veered the horse onto Dover Street. Sheltering Arms Refuge lay in wait, its front light aglow, as if beckoning them back to safety, welcoming them home.

Strangely enough, it felt like coming home to him.

K

Maggie could barely open her eyes the next morning, but open them she did—at 6:30 on the dot. The hallway remained quiet, but the clatter of pots and pans in the kitchen reminded her about her duties, so she rose with a sense of expectancy, despite her utter fatigue. What a night it had been!

Upon their return to Sheltering Arms the night before, Maxine had been the first to greet them, her precious, unadulterated smile reward enough for undertaking the rescue of Clara Warner. The girls had squeezed each other breathless.

Then, Mrs. Bingham had stepped forward and cleared her throat. "My dear, if your father ever found out about you sneaking off like that, why, he'd have you shipped back to Michigan so fast your head would spin." The room had grown quiet at the woman's unnaturally severe tone—until her face broke into a smile. "But I can keep a secret as good as the next person." Relief had washed over Maggie as she fell into Mrs. Bingham's warm embrace.

Soon, Mr. Bingham had stepped in, first shaking Luke's hand and then giving Maggie a quick hug. After him had come Stanley, Charlotte, and several of the older children, who had gathered around like a herd of curious sheep, eyes fixed with interest on the new girl.

"Meet Clara Warner," Luke had announced, eyes shining with something like pride; not the haughty kind, mind you, but the kind that comes after you accomplish something you weren't quite sure you could do. Maggie's heart had danced a little jig when their gazes briefly caught hold in the midst of the fuss. She'd forgotten to thank him for saving her from that awful man in the saloon, and she decided that she must do that today.

As she lay in her bed, it happened again—that little churn in her stomach. She had to admit it: she was falling for Luke Madison. Shoving aside the realization, she hurriedly dressed and brushed her hair, pulling it back at the sides with two combs, then set about pouring water from the pitcher into the large bowl on the washstand. Perusing her appearance in the oval mirror, she frowned to see how the skin beneath her blue eyes was puffy from lack of sleep. How utterly ridiculous to think one as handsome as Luke Madison should give her a second glance. Of course, what did it matter anyway, considering his apparent apathy toward all things spiritual? She gave her head a tiny shake of disapproval, then quickly washed and dried her face. Finally, she donned her wool cape in preparation for her walk to the necessary.

Indoor plumbing hadn't quite caught on in many places. While Maggie's father had paid to have it installed in their home and at Kane's Whatnot a couple of years ago, a considerable share of Sandy Shores residents still went without. And it would seem the same rang true in New York City, particularly in antiquated estates.

There were two "necessaries," as Maggie chose to call them: one for the girls and, some thirty feet away, another one for the boys. The girls' "house" had four little stall-like areas, allowing it to accommodate four at a time. Still, she always hoped she'd be the only one in need of it at any given time, being that the holes were separated by boards a mere eighteen inches tall. These separators were meant to offer privacy, but they fell short of their purpose, in Maggie's opinion. And she didn't particularly cotton to people watching her go to and from the place, either. That was why, when she found herself on the single path leading out to both buildings with Luke Madison at her side, her face and neck went hot as a poker stick, no matter the morning's chill.

How it happened, she couldn't quite say. She'd come through the kitchen at precisely the same time as he, she supposed, and rather than linger with Mrs. Bingham and wait for him to go ahead of her, she scooted out the back door, thinking he'd do the polite thing and wait. Trouble was, he didn't. Now, she felt at a loss for words as they sauntered along side by side.

"Nice morning," he said.

"Yes. Chilly, though." She drew her cape up to her sweating neck.

"You sleep well?"

"What? Yes. You?"

"Not really."

"Oh."

She might have asked him why that was, but that would have stalled their progress, and who could stop and carry on a decent conversation in front of the necessaries?

At the fork in the path, they went their separate ways, but just as she grabbed hold of the door handle, he called out, "You did a good job last night. I meant to tell you that."

She paused, her hand on the door. "I did?" Then, she dared look at him. How strange, both standing at their respective outhouse doors, staring at each other. "You saved my life. I meant to thank you."

Even through the heavy morning mist, she saw a smile sneak out and heard the hint of a chuckle. "You weren't having any of that fellow's monkey business, biting him in the arm like you did and giving him a boot in the leg. Something tells me that even without my help, you would've figured a way out of your...er, predicament."

"Well, I don't know. Maybe. But that gunshot helped."

"Ah, the gun. Henry gave me a quick lesson before I left. Said I might need to protect myself. Funny thing is, I forgot everything he taught me. The gun went off quite by accident, but once it did, I tried to act like I planned it."

She couldn't help giggling. "You looked downright sure of yourself, if you ask me. You got everyone's attention, including mine."

He stared at her, the smile still playing at his lips. "I did, huh?"

"Well, I mean...."

"I'd say most of the attention fell to you, with your threatening to divorce me and all."

"Oh, that." Good thing the sun hadn't shown its entire face yet. He'd have surely seen the flush of her cheeks. "I don't know where that came from, exactly."

He laughed heartily now. *What a lovely sound*, she thought—the way it echoed through the trees, waking the birds. "You're a corker, Maggie Rose Kane. I'm finding that out."

And just like that, he opened the door to his "house" and went inside, leaving her no choice but to do the same.

K

Maxine could hardly believe it. She and Clara. Reunited. She'd prayed it would happen, but she had never imagined God actually answering her prayers. Perhaps she ought to give Him more attention. Maybe He truly did care about the weak and helpless of this world. Until now, she'd thought of God as impersonal and distant, even though the Binghams and Stanley and Charlotte always told her otherwise. Even Reverend Miles' words of two weeks ago still rang like a bell in her thoughts: *"God hears the prayer of a surrendered heart."*

Surrendered. What would it mean to surrender her heart and life to God? Mrs. Bingham claimed He could help her with her unwarranted outbursts of temper. This discussion had come after she'd thrown a particularly unladylike fit at the lunch table one day over who got to take the last slice of watermelon, her or Peter Kramer. Naturally, she thought it should go to her, no matter that she'd already had two slices and Peter hadn't had even one. How irrational she'd been to think she deserved the last slice. Now that she took a moment to reflect, she saw the unpleasant ways she treated others.

On the bunk beneath hers, Clara stirred, shifted in her bed, and released a little yawn. Maxine quickly rolled over and poked her head over the side. "You awake?" she whispered. Across the room in their own set of bunks, sisters Julia and Sofia Zielinski still slept as soundly as two pups.

An instant smile erupted on Clara's perfect face—perfect, as far as Maxine was concerned, especially now that it'd been washed. One of the first things Mrs. Bingham had done last night upon Clara's arrival was to draw her a bath. Clara had never had a bath in a claw-footed tub; their only means of bathing at Miss Violet's had been in an old tin tub they kept stored in a corner of their tiny room. Before that, Maxine wasn't sure Clara had ever had a bath, period.

"Am I really here?" Clara asked.

"You really are."

"It's like a dream."

"That's what I was jus' thinkin'."

With Maxine's head still hanging over the edge, the girls stared at each other. "You believe in God?" Maxine asked quite without thinking.

"'Course I do. Don't you?" Clara shot back.

"I guess."

"I'm here, aren't I? God must've had somethin' to do with that."

"They talk a lot about praying and reading your Bible here at Shelterin' Arms," Maxine informed her. "Do you pray?"

Clara's forehead wrinkled in thought. "Sure. I used to pray special hard when them men, you know...."

Maxine winced. It was one thing to have endured the abuse herself, but quite another to think of little Clara having to suffer through it. Would those bad pictures ever get out of her head? Is that something God could help her do—forget her painful past?

She studied Clara carefully—quiet, gentle, sweet Clara. She didn't have a mean bone in her. "How come you never scream and yell? I never knew you to get mad. Not even when them awful things was takin' place."

The girl chewed her lip thoughtfully before answering. "Maybe 'cause I knew it wasn't me who was bein' so evil; it was them. God always helped me see flowers in my head, pink and yellow and blue ones. I asked Him t' forgive me all my sins, and He did, but He also told me it wasn't me who was doin' the sinnin'."

"He did? How'd He do that when He can't talk?"

Clara's eyes popped wide open. "'Course He can talk, Maxine Ward, but y' gotta have the kind o' ears that hear 'im when He speaks. If you spend all your time bein' mad and hateful, your ears won't work. But if you sit still and ask Him to talk to you, you'll start hearin' stuff you never imagined."

"Like what?"

"I dunno…like, well, love messages. I never had no papa to speak of, but something deep in here"—she pointed to her heart—"tol' me God wanted to be my substitute Papa. As soon as I started thinkin' 'bout Him that way, why, it was like a miracle. Life started takin' a big turn. I started rememberin' this church some woman took me to when I was only 'bout five or six, and the songs they used to sing, and some of the Bible verses what got taught to me. Like, '*God so loved the world, that he gave his only begotten Son, that whosoever believeth in him should not perish, but have everlasting life.*' That's John 3:16, by the way. Oh, and guess what else? You know Miss Floretta?" Maxine nodded, fascinated. "She started takin' all my customers."

"She didn't!"

"Did, too. In fact, she made me keep my door locked all the time, tol' me not to open it for nobody, said she was plain sick to 'er stomach that Miss Violet would keep me locked up like I was a slave. I know God was protectin' me. All along, He's been protectin' me—and you, too, Maxine. Why, look how you found Shelterin' Arms."

"How'd you know about this place, anyway?"

"One day, I got to go out with Miss Violet to get me a new dress—she said it was time I started lookin' prettier—and I saw a couple signs on some windows. I think they must post them up in places so's kids can know where t' go if they need help. I memorized the name and address."

"That was good."

"Take away a letter, Maxine. That was *God*."

Chapter Sixteen

Dear Maggie Rose,

I have finally found some time to sit down and write you a letter. Jesse and Gabriel are in the backyard. Gabe said they were going to start digging a new hole for the outhouse, but from the sounds of Jesse's laughter and Dusty's wild barking, I think they've decided to play a while instead. Who wants to dig an old hole, anyway? Gabe says he intends to install indoor plumbing before cold weather sets in. I am certainly in favor of this idea, as I don't cotton to the notion of freezing my bottom to an outhouse seat in January!

The Whatnot is a busy place, especially since you left me in the lurch. (I'm just joking, dear sister.) Abbie Ann is not much help, I'm afraid. Her heart is not in Kane's Whatnot. Actually, I'm not sure where her heart is, exactly. She can't quite decide what she wants to do with her life, whether move on to college to pursue a career or to take a job locally. I think your leaving and my getting married have turned her mind toward more serious matters. Oh, and her best friend, Katrina, is with child—

due around Christmas, I believe—and perhaps that has sobered her the more. Just the other day, she was complaining that Katrina and Micah are so absorbed in each other that Katrina hardly has time for her. I laughed and said, "That is the way of it with young married couples." It certainly is where Gabe and I are concerned. Well, enough of that.

Things are not quite the same around Sandy Shores without you. Everyone says so. Old Mr. Fisher came into the store yesterday, carrying his cane, as usual, and a sack of books. It is hard to keep him in books. I have ordered some new titles from the Grand Rapids library, which should keep him busy for a few weeks. Mr. Fisher asked after you, by the way. He says he misses hearing you sing "Amazing Grace" clear up to the rafters. (I am giggling as I write this.)

I pray for you daily, my darling sister, as do Gabe and Jesse. Last night, Jesse asked the Lord to please change His mind about sending you to New York City. Gabe told him that was not an appropriate way to pray, and that since God had called you into mission work, particularly to Sheltering Arms Refuge, he should pray instead for your protection. I will let you know which direction his prayers take tonight.

Your loving sister,
Hannah Grace

PS: Has that news reporter's disposition improved? Perhaps you should try telling him one of Abbie Ann's jokes.

Maggie gave a small smile at her sister's postscript, folded up the letter, and placed it in the drawer with her stationery items.

Today was washday. Everyone dutifully carried his or her soiled clothes to the laundry room off the kitchen and dropped them in the appropriate piles. There was one for overalls and dark shirts, one for bedding and towels, one for the girls' underclothes and another for the boys', and several other piles for various colors of wash.

On washdays, Mrs. Bingham showed her terribly serious side. Everyone knew not to cross her, for she had a system, and woe to the person who interfered with it. Assignments went as such: older boys manned the drying process, pushing wet clothes through the mangle, the wooden roller above the washing tub used to remove excess water. Girls handled the wash portion. And everyone worked at carting baskets of wet clothes to the rows of clotheslines, where they carefully pinned up each piece to dry. Since washday was a daylong process, everyone worked in shifts, Mrs. Bingham delivering a series of lectures regarding keeping fingers clear of the rollers and not making a fuss as to exactly whose clothes you were handling. Some boys had a tendency to make the "ewww!" sound, particularly if they happened upon someone's petticoat.

Today, Maggie's job consisted of supervising the girls and, somehow, Luke had been assigned to the boys. Allen Kramer and Benny DeLuca worked the mangles while Maxine, Clara, and Jenny handled dipping the soiled clothes into buckets of water, using scrub boards to help remove any stains before dropping them into the big tub on wheels. Rather than complain about her task, Maxine jumped in with zeal such as Maggie had never seen, and she figured Clara's presence had everything to do with it. Clara, on the other hand, watched the process with awe and wonder, mimicking Maxine and Jenny's every move but acting completely out of her element. Had she ever even taken part in a washday experience before? Moreover, where had the little waif been before landing at Miss Violet's Saloon? Not for the first time, Maggie prayed for the woman named Floretta who'd assisted in Clara's escape, wondering what, if anything, had happened to her after Luke had made his swift getaway.

"We should sing a song while we work," Jenny suggested, dropping two shirts into the big washtub.

"You start singin', Jenny Pelton, and I'm leavin' my responsibilities to Allen," said Benny. "I've heard you sing before, and it hurt my ears."

"Be nice," said Luke, pulling a pair of trousers from the wringer mangle and dropping it into the wicker basket, which was filling fast with damp clothes. He, too, looked a trifle out of his element, Maggie decided, stifling the urge to giggle while watching him handle the garment. She and her sisters had been helping Grandmother Kane on washdays for as long as she could remember. Somehow, she doubted the chore had ever fallen to Luke Madison. Gilbert Garrison stood at the ready behind Luke, waiting for a few more pieces of clothing to go into the basket before hefting it up to take to the backyard. He looked about as happy as a hare on the open prairie.

"He can't be nice. He's a boy," said Maxine.

"Girls is what's the pain," Benny retorted.

"Depends on what girl you're talkin' about," Allen chimed.

"Yeah, he thinks the sun rises every morning just for my sister," Jenny said, grinning across the washing machine at Allen.

He blushed. It was clear to everyone at Sheltering Arms that Allen Kramer had a very serious crush on Vivian Pelton.

"I think Jenny had a good idea. What say we all sing—boys included?" Maggie suggested.

"I don't know no songs," Benny said. "Wait! I know one called 'Johnny, Get Your Gun.'"

"That's an old, stupid song," Jenny said.

"It ain't neither—stupid, that is."

"I was thinkin' more along the lines of a nice hymn," Maggie put in.

"Hymns is strictly for church." Allen argued.

"No, they're not, dummy," Maxine said. "You can sing hymns anywhere you like." Maggie had never known Maxine to rule in favor of anything church-related. "Which one should we sing, Maggie?"

"How about 'Showers of Blessings'?"

"How's it go?" three voices asked at once.

"You don't know? Oh, mercy, it's—a lively tune. Do you know it, Luke?"

He issued a grin. "You're on your own, young lady. In fact, why don't you sing it for us?"

"Me? Well, all right, then, I'll give it a whirl." Without hesitation, she burst into the verse and chorus.

> "There shall be showers of blessing;
>
> This is the promise of love.
>
> There shall be seasons refreshing,
>
> sent from the Savior above.
>
> Showers of blessing, showers of blessing we need.

Mercy drops round us are falling,

but for the showers we plead...."

For some reason, everyone ceased working and took on wide-eyed stares, some dropping their mouths agape. Even Mrs. Bingham and the volunteer ladies who'd showed up for the day stood stock-still. She sounded either very, very good or—completely horrid. Perhaps even earsplitting. Why, she recognized those looks from ones she'd received from the folks back home. "You want to hear the next verse?" she ventured.

"Uh, you got a different song?" Allen asked.

"Let's see." She gave it some thought while bending to pick up the next article of clothing and dip it in the water. "Oh, how about 'Jesus Loves Me'? Surely, you all know that one."

"Yeah!" they chimed at once.

"Only let's all sing this time," Benny suggested.

And so they did. When Maggie chanced a look at Luke, she caught him singing along and grinning from ear to ear.

Chapter Seventeen

Around mid afternoon, Charlotte and Stanley relieved Maggie and Luke of their supervisory responsibilities in the laundry room—and none too soon, in Luke's opinion. Why, if he had to listen to one more whining remark from Noah Price about having to do girl's work, or Peter Kramer's sarcastic comments about Julia Zielinski's oversized pantaloons, or Ricky Campbell's complaints about how hard it was to turn the crank on the wringer mangle, he might well have considered borrowing Mr. Bingham's pistol again—just for the scare factor, of course. Yes, Julia Zielinski had a small weight problem; yes, the crank needed a good oil job; and he'd even admit he didn't like the chore of washing clothes any more than the next fellow. But that did not erase the fact they all had to do their parts, and moaning about it didn't get the job done any faster.

He had only to glance at Maggie Rose, Little Miss Optimism herself, who had a knack for turning drudgery to delight, apathy to adventure, gloom to gladness, to boost his spirits. He reminded himself that these children had not been brought up with such responsibilities when they lived on the streets, and he realized, too, that the tasks were foreign to him, as well, having been spoiled by Aunt Frances and a childhood of few duties, if any.

From Maggie's wailing rendition of "Blessed Assurance" to "Jesus Loves Me," and, yes, even to "Johnny, Get Your Gun," after which they'd all wound up laughing, she'd managed to brighten everyone's moods, his included. As a matter of fact, he rather enjoyed watching her in action with the youngsters—he admired the way she related to them.

With chagrin, it even occurred to him he might be admiring her far more than was proper. She was, after all, someone he'd never see again once his time at Sheltering Arms came to a close.

Late that day, and after a game of checkers with little Dag Haskell, Luke retreated to his room to work on his article. He should have finished it by now, he mulled, but instead, he'd written only the first few paragraphs.

> The name Sheltering Arms Refuge is probably foreign to you. I know I had never heard of it—until I was given an assignment I neither wanted nor readily accepted. Eager to appease my employers, however, I found myself at Sheltering Arms, where I walked in the shoes of an orphan. Founded and run by Mr. and Mrs. Henry Bingham, this refuge houses orphans and abandoned children, providing shelter, food, and, perhaps most important, a nurturing environment. As many as twenty-three children stay here until they're able to board a train that will lead them to prospective families and the promise of a fresh start. Sheltering Arms is a haven of hope and security, a sanctuary for the lost, and an escape from a ruthless, often sadistic society.
>
> They look at you with wary eyes, these orphans, these gems of untold worth, hesitant to believe you could be anything but a menacing threat to their

survival. This belief is based not on unfounded paranoia, but on experience, for many of these children have pasts fraught with abuse, neglect, and even forced prostitution. In their minds, adults are the enemy.

He read and reread the words, thinking them a good start, particularly since they rang of such truth. He'd had brothers Ricky and Stuart Campbell front and center on his mind when he'd written them, primarily Ricky, though, the spunkier of the two.

But now, Maxine Ward and Clara Warner joined the ranks of images in his mind, along with baby Christina, Noah and Emily Price, young Rose Marie Kring, the Zielinski sisters, and all the other youngsters he had gotten to know. He determined to write an article that would stir the city into action, whether financial or physical. According to Mr. and Mrs. Bingham, New York had its share of overcrowded orphanages, all of which needed plenty of assistance. Even now, he listened to the noise filtering up through the registers—sounds of crying babes, fussing teens, pattering feet, squealing toddlers, and an unusually sharp reprimand from Mrs. Bingham, followed by the slamming of a door—and it hit him afresh how very much these children needed the guidance of loving parents. He put his pencil to the paper again and scribbled down the words as they came to him.

You see them every day on your way to work—destitute waifs, street Arabs, as they're often called. You pass them as you carry your briefcases and umbrellas during the morning commute, a newspaper tucked under one arm. You might even take a moment to ponder their existence and, while doing so, drop a coin into the tin container they hold at the ready. You may have bought a box of matches from one of the girls or allowed a boy to shine your shoes and thought well of yourself for providing a dime for their efforts. But you failed to look into their eyes, didn't you? For to do that might prompt you into further action. No, your meager coin is enough for now, you say.

You will not read actual names in this essay, for anonymity is imperative to protect the innocent, although most of the residents at Sheltering Arms have experienced enough in their short lifetimes to know the other side of virtue. Sadly, before these little wanderers found a home at Sheltering Arms, they had tainted views of "normal"—which, for most of us, means two loving parents, plenty of food on the table, warm beds, and someone to kiss us good night. To them, "normal" meant scrounging in waste barrels for their next meal, begging on street corners for blankets and clothing, perhaps running from alcoholic parents and the worst kind of physical abuse, and maybe even stealing a loaf of bread and an apple from the local grocer.

Even the babies, the ones left on doorsteps of rescue centers, hospitals, and police stations, already know the darker side of life—that feeling of separation from loved ones—and yet they lack the ability to ascertain the implications of what that will one day mean for them. Their futures could well lie in the hands of people like you and me.

A fracas on the floor below prompted Luke to lay down his pencil. He sucked in a yawn and pulled himself up, stretching taut muscles and raising both arms toward the ceiling. The article had forced him into serious brooding. He wanted to challenge his readers into doing something, but what? How could he expect more from them than he himself was willing to give? True enough, these children needed help, but what could he do besides write this article and paint a picture of cold reality? He had neither the time nor the passion or wherewithal to do much more than that. Forget that Aunt Frances had left him her entire estate, including her cavernous apartment.

He had come to Sheltering Arms Refuge for one reason—to research a subject and report his findings. Beyond that, he did not intend to involve himself in an emotional way.

But was it already too late?

A rumble of excitement sifting through the air and the ongoing scuffle downstairs made him look at the door. But it was the drumbeat of feet parading past his door and the squeals of "Uncle Herbie's here! Uncle Herbie's here!" that prompted him to open his door and hurry down the stairs on the heels of Gilbert Garrison, feeling like a child himself.

𝒦

Herb Wiley, Virginia Bingham's brother, looked exactly as Maggie remembered when he'd visited Third Street Church in Sandy Shores. Tall and lean, with graying hair and a pencil-thin mustache, he greeted each child who came running to him with a gentle pat on the head and an easy smile. He reached both hands in his bulging pockets and brought out treats of peppermint sticks, lollipops, an assortment of rock candy, and wrapped taffy. The children gathered around him like he was Saint Nicholas himself, eyes filled with eagerness and wonder.

"Herb Wiley, I do declare, you always show up just before the supper hour," said Mrs. Bingham, gliding out of the kitchen with a coffee cup in hand. "You'll ruin these children's appetites."

"Aww, Gin, one piece each won't hurt 'em." He stepped forward to plant a kiss on his sister's round cheek. "You youngsters promise to clean your plates tonight?"

"We promise!" they cheered at once, pushing closer to have a look at his offering.

"Just one apiece, for now," he said with a wink, allowing each child to take his pick.

"Did you bring us any toys this time?" asked Millie, the whites of her big brown eyes fairly glowing against her dark skin.

He bent his knees slightly and tapped the tip of her nose. "I most certainly did, but you'll all have to share, you know."

"We will, we promise! What'd you bring us?" several asked at once. Even the bigger children, while hanging back to give the little ones first pick at the candy in Uncle Herbie's big hands, perked up at the mention of new toys.

"Well, let's see here. There's books, puzzles, some train cars for the boys, a couple dolls in there, some jumping ropes and doll blankets...oh, and I think I saw two or three balls— all donations collected during my travels."

"Yow!" they screamed in unison.

"My stars in glory!" Mrs. Bingham laughed, plugging her ears at the din of happy children. "Gilbert, you and Sam are closest to the door. How about going out to Uncle Herbie's rig to bring in those boxes?"

"Yes, ma'am!"

"There's three of 'em!" Herb called after them as everyone clustered around the windows to watch the boys run down the front steps toward the parked rig.

Herb tipped back on his heels and looked at Ginny. "I swear, you get more petite every time I see you, sis."

"What I get is wider, Herb Wiley, so it gives the appearance that I'm shrinking instead."

He arched his gray eyebrows at her. "Sort of like one of them optical illusions?"

"Exactly," she giggled, taking a sip from her coffee cup.

"Stop," Henry said, stepping up to slip an arm around his wife's shoulders. "I like my Ginny just the way she is, and if she's gettin' a little wider in places, well, then, it just gives me more to squeeze."

"Oh, pooh!" Mrs. Bingham swatted at her husband. The other adults present—Charlotte, Stanley, Luke, and Maggie—all looked on with amusement. Maggie wondered if anyone else found the couple's flirtation as endearing as she. Glancing around, she saw Charlotte and Stanley and discovered them standing close, her arm brushing against his side as she twisted back and forth, attempting to coax baby Christina into taking a nap. Luke allowed his own gaze to connect with Maggie's, and the two exchanged a brief smile. As expected, her stomach took its usual tumble before righting itself. Mercy! She must be more careful to check her growing attraction.

Herb's gaze fell on Maggie and Luke. "Meet our latest additions to Sheltering Arms," Mr. Bingham quickly put in. "Maggie Rose Kane, the young woman from Michigan we told you about, and Luke Madison, a reporter for the *World*. He's doing a piece about the children here."

"Really?" Herb lifted Maggie's hand to his mouth and lightly kissed the back of it. Why, she'd never experienced such gallantry, and she didn't quite know how to handle it. In return, she curtsied but then wondered if she'd chosen the correct response. She needn't have worried, though, for the gentleman's attentions immediately shifted to Luke, who stuck out his hand in greeting. As the two shook hands, Herb asked, "You're writing an article, are you? You ask me, a little publicity for Sheltering Arms could be a wonderful thing. This article going to be running anytime soon?"

Luke gave a light chuckle. "If I ever finish it." *Interesting*, Maggie thought. More than once, she'd wanted to ask him about the status of his piece. It seemed he spent most of his time working outside with Stanley and Mr. Bingham, playing games with the boys, and helping run errands. This led her to believe that the writing took place after everyone else retired for the night.

As the two men spoke quietly, the Garrison boys returned with two big boxes, dropped them on the floor with a loud thud, and then ran back out for the third. With wild excitement, the children started squealing and ripping through each crate in search of the perfect find. "Boys and girls, be patient," Mrs. Bingham urged them. "Remember, these items are to be shared." But her quiet order fell on deaf ears as, one by one, each child claimed an article. Little Emily snatched up a hand-sewn doll, Maxine, Clara, and Audrey ran off with a jump rope, Vivian and Jenny Pelton chose a few books, and Billy Harper and Dag Haskell seized the same ball, making a pact to toss it back and forth outside.

Mrs. Bingham shook her head. "Don't go far, younglings. It's almost suppertime." But if anyone heard, they didn't let on. Some still searched busily for just the right plaything, and others had already disappeared with their discoveries.

"Ah, so I'm not too late," Herb said, looking at His sister while rubbing circles into his belly. "For supper, that is."

"Pfff," she snorted. "Like I said, you always plan your visits around mealtime, Herb Wiley."

"Well then, that must mean I'm smarter than I look!" That earned the tall man a good laugh.

In the kitchen, several volunteers busied themselves with supper preparations, one setting the long table, another carving meatloaves and slicing tomatoes, and still another mashing a big kettle of potatoes.

"Take a chair while I get you some coffee," Mrs. Bingham said.

"I'll help," offered Maggie.

"I don't need waiting on," Herb protested.

Thus, everyone meandered to the stove in search of a mug and proceeded to wait his or her turn at pouring the hot brew. Luke fixed himself a cup of tea instead, borrowing water from the steaming kettle at the back of the stove and dropping tea leaves into the stainless steel tea strainer. Maggie could not help but watch the way he moved—he wasn't clumsy, but he didn't seem to have overwhelming confidence in his dexterity, either. She wondered how adept he was in the kitchen. Had his aunt always catered to his needs—or another woman, perhaps? A housemaid? With chagrin, she realized she still had much to learn about this news reporter from the *World*.

"Tell us about your journeys, Herbert," Mr. Bingham said, pulling back a chair for His wife before sitting down himself.

"Oh, my. Where should I begin? Let's see, in the past two months, I've visited churches in Illinois, Indiana, Ohio, and Pennsylvania. How's that for starters?"

"And have you been successful in raising funds for our children?" Mr. Bingham asked.

"That and more," Herb said. "Several expressed interest in setting up donation centers around their cities, places where folks could drop off gently used articles of clothing—coats, shoes, boots, and the like."

"Oh, that would be wonderful!" Mrs. Bingham exclaimed. "The children are in such need."

One by one, the adults situated themselves around the table. Normally, Mrs. Bingham would have been scurrying about the kitchen with the volunteer staff, but one of the ladies insisted she enjoy a visit with her brother, convincing her they had things well under control. Surprisingly, Mrs. Bingham acquiesced and sat down.

Luke sat in the chair next to Maggie, and when he stretched out his lanky legs under the table, his knee brushed her skirt, making her heart throb at a wild pace.

Ridiculous, she told herself. *Utterly so!* Particularly since he appeared completely entrenched in Herb Wiley's words and not affected in the least by their close proximity.

Maggie gave an inner sigh and straightened. One would think she'd landed herself back in grade school the way her heart carried on. And another thing. Luke Madison did not profess to know her Lord in a personal way. She told herself to stop romanticizing about a man who didn't share her faith.

Later, when the kitchen had cleaned, the supper dishes had been washed and put away, and the volunteers had left for the day, the children enjoyed a bit of evening leisure time while the adults gathered in the sitting room off the parlor area for further conversation. Whether by sheer coincidence or by design, Maggie found herself sitting next to Luke on the floor beside a glowing fire. Warm September evenings had given way to a chill that called for a cozy blaze in one of Sheltering Arms' many fireplaces. Charlotte, Stanley, Mr. and Mrs. Bingham, and Herb had situated themselves on the four wingback chairs and settee, so Maggie and Luke lowered themselves to the floor, Maggie tucking her feet under her long, full skirt and Luke stretching out his legs and crossing them at the ankles, his hands sprawled flat on the floor behind him for support.

Conversation topics varied from the rescue of Clara Warner to the weather to the November presidential election to the upcoming opening day of the New York subway system. Every so often, a toddler squealed or whimpered, or a spat over one of the new toys ensued in another room, requiring Mr. Bingham to make temporary departures to settle the matter. Charlotte also walked out of the room more than once to check on the children, finally returning with baby Christina on her hip. Maggie wondered if she would have a difficult time parting with the child when the time came to hand her over to her new parents.

"How are the plans shaping up for the train excursion?" Herb asked.

"Reverend Miles says plans are well underway," Mrs. Bingham responded. "Millie, I'm afraid, is one who will have to stay behind. Poor thing's skin color dictates that."

"That simply isn't fair," Maggie said. "Surely someone would want her."

"Frankly, I'm just as happy to keep her under my care a bit longer. She'll have a hard go of it when she and Audrey part ways. Those two are like two little peas in a pod. Nope, we're not in any hurry for her to go, and if no one steps forward, then she'll stay here indefinitely."

"That's very generous of you," Herb said.

"Pfff, nothing generous about it," Mrs. Bingham said. "We're simply doing what God would have us do. Matter of fact, I don't like to think about any of the youngsters leaving us—the Lord knows I grow so attached—but they must go to make room for another batch. Our ultimate purpose here is to see to everyone's immediate needs, then get them situated in suitable Christian homes with loving parents." She gave her head a slow, regretful shake. "Why must there be so many homeless waifs?"

"These are hard times," Stanley said. He looked wistfully at the sleepy baby in Charlotte's arms, then lifted his gaze to Charlotte. Maggie thought it was a tender exchange. "The city simply can't handle the huge influx of immigrants. Unfortunately, destitution leads to desperation, and, in many cases, parents believe they have no choice but to give up their children."

"It's horrible," Maggie said. "Sometimes I feel helpless."

"But you've been more helpful than you know," said Mr. Bingham. "Your coming here has meant a great deal to all of us, and it's clear the children love you."

"All any of us can do is trust the Lord to meet the needs. He hasn't failed us yet," said Herb. "Everywhere I go, people are eager to do what they can to help."

"It's because you're so convincing," Maggie said. "I wouldn't be here if it hadn't been for your visit to Third Street Church in Sandy Shores last winter."

Herb nodded. "Well, I don't remember what I said exactly, but I thank the Lord it was enough to compel you to come. It must have been hard leaving your family."

Instant tears welled up in her eyes, as did an uncomfortable lump at the back of her throat. All eyes came to rest on her, making her feel especially vulnerable. "I'll admit, I miss my family, but I haven't experienced a moment of regret in coming. Had I ignored God's call, I would have missed out on so many blessings."

"And isn't that the way it is when we fail to obey the Lord's gentle nudging?" Mrs. Bingham said. "Why, there'd be no Sheltering Arms Refuge if Henry and I hadn't listened to the Lord some seventeen years ago when my grandfather willed this house to me. Goodness, what would the two of us have done with this big ol' house? We knew almost immediately we had to fill it with children."

"And where would I have landed without the two of you?" Stanley asked, expression thoughtful.

"Or I?" asked Charlotte, caressing Christina's downy head as she spoke. "Like Maggie, I sensed God's call to this place. It seemed to pull me in like a magnet from the first moment I heard about it."

Others nodded and reflected silently in the seconds that followed.

"Well." Luke, the one who'd contributed the least to the conversation, shifted his position on the hard floor and cleared his throat. "I should probably go work on that article."

He started to rise, but at the same moment, an urgent-sounding knock on the front door got everyone's attention. "Well, who could that be?" Mr. Bingham asked, glancing at his pocket watch, then getting up to answer the door.

In seconds, it became clear to all that something was amiss, especially when they overheard Mr. Bingham say, "Oh, dear. Have you called the police?"

Chapter Eighteen

Everyone, including some inquisitive children, gathered around the rather stout Reverend Miles, anxious to know why their pastor would be making a house call so close to bedtime.

"I'm afraid it was the police who notified me," Reverend Miles said. "They know of my affiliation with Sheltering Arms Refuge."

"What's happened?" Luke asked, his reporter persona immediately falling into place.

The reverend's lightly whiskered face wrinkled in bafflement as his eyes swept over each face in the room. He squinted and chewed his lower lip, nervously wringing his hat with one hand. With the other hand, he scratched the back of his head. "There's been a situation—a mighty serious one."

"What sort of situation, Reverend?" Mr. Bingham asked.

"It's—well, there's a woman at the parsonage. The Mrs. is with her, of course. She's been, um, badly beaten, I'm afraid."

"Oh dear, poor thing. Who is she? Anyone we know?" Mrs. Bingham asked, stepping closer.

"I—well, perhaps the children oughtn't hear."

"Oh, you're right, of course," Mr. Bingham said. "Boys and girls, time to scoot."

"I'll tend to them," Charlotte offered, already corralling the small troop of children. "It's near bedtime, anyway."

"Yeah, come on, boys. Make haste," Stanley said, motioning with his arm.

"Aww, do we hafta?" asked Sam Garrison and Bernard Munson in unison.

Stanley frowned. "Yes, you 'hafta.'" Then, leaning closer to Luke, he muttered, "Fill me in later."

Luke nodded and gave his attention back to the reverend, noting that Maggie did the same, her brow furrowed with concern. No doubt, their minds traveled in the same vein. As the children sauntered off with Stanley and Charlotte, Sam whined, "It was just gettin' to the good part. Are we gonna find out the rest o' the story?"

"I have no idea," Stanley answered. In the adjoining room, the older boys, who'd started a chess tournament earlier, still sat engrossed with their game, evidently uninterested in what the reverend had to say—unless they'd decided to listen with one ear.

"Who is this woman?" Mrs. Bingham asked again.

"She's from some seedy place over on East 74th called Miss Violet's Saloon," Reverend Miles said with a hushed voice. "I believe she said her name is Floretta. Didn't catch the last name, though." Luke's chest heaved as he made eye contact with Maggie. She put a hand to her mouth to squelch any sound.

"Oh, my goodness," said Mrs. Bingham.

"Here's the strange thing," he continued, leaning forward. "The police merely dropped her off at my house, seeming not to want to even question why she'd been beaten. They claim she's mentally unstable—a lady of the night in deep need of spiritual counsel. Of course, I'm certain they're right on both counts. According to one officer, she kept repeating her wish to be taken to the Sheltering Arms Refuge, but they refused, of course, and I'm mighty thankful they did. The last thing you need here is some woman of moral decay stirring up trouble. Besides, you wouldn't want the children seeing her in her current state.

"At any rate, since the police are well aware of my work with the orphanage, they kindly—may I use the word *dumped?*—her on my doorstep. Naturally, I tried to question her while Coreen worked at dressing her numerous wounds, but she simply won't talk to me. She says she only wants to talk to the man 'what came' to the saloon last night. She used those exact words, too. Now, since I'm fairly confident none of the men here would be visiting an establishment like that, I'm more than sure the woman is off her rocker."

Reverend Miles scratched his head again, dipped his chin, and squinted. He turned his gaze on Mr. Bingham. "Am I safe in assuming none of you would've gone to that place?"

Mr. Bingham shifted his weight. "Not exactly, Reverend."

The reverend's brows shot up, one slightly higher than the other. "Want to shed some light on the subject?"

"Perhaps you should come in and have a seat so we can discuss it."

"Yes, and I'll get us something hot to drink," said Mrs. Bingham, bustling off to the kitchen.

"Excuse me, Reverend, but I think I can explain," Luke said.

"And I," said Maggie.

"You?" Reverend Miles turned around on his way to the sitting room, his eyes revealing utter confusion.

"I think I should like to hear this story," said Herb Wiley, the tiniest hint of amusement lining his tone.

They all retreated to the living room and sat down—everyone but Mr. Bingham, that is. He chose to stand next to the fireplace, one hand resting on the mantel. Mrs. Bingham returned with a tray of steaming cups of coffee and proceeded to pass them around as Luke began to speak. He described the rescue of Clara Warner—how the woman named Floretta had offered to help, how Maggie had stowed herself away in the back of the rig and ended up playing a major part in the plan, and how Clara had leaped off the roof to freedom in the very nick of time, with Byron and some other thug chasing after their wagon and yelling obscenities, then threatening to make Floretta pay for participating in the rescue.

At the conclusion of his account, Luke stood up. "If you don't mind, Reverend, I'd like you to take me to your house. I need to talk to Floretta."

"Well, yes, certainly, if you're sure you want to get involved." The man stood up himself, huffing slightly as he hoisted his pants around his paunch. He looked like the type who never turned down a slice of pie while calling on parishioners.

"I'm already involved."

"As am I," Maggie announced, rising to her feet. "So, I'll come, too."

Luke nearly laughed. "I don't think so." He had to admire her for her grit and stubborn will, but he definitely didn't need her tagging along. Hadn't she caused him enough grief already? "You have responsibilities here."

"I'll tend her younger ones," Mrs. Bingham said. "It might be helpful to have a woman along when dealing with this—this—I don't even know what to call her."

"Hussy?" Mr. Bingham put in.

Mrs. Bingham gave a glum nod. "Call her what you will, but she's still a human being in need of a Savior."

"Well, amen to that, of course," the reverend muttered. "In fact, I should have said it myself, but I'm afraid I've let my eyes blind me to the truth. I know God loves the sinner with the utmost compassion, but if you'd seen the way this woman is dressed, rather, *un*dressed…well, you might understand why I nearly forgot to think of her as actually redeemable."

Luke's gut turned over in a sickening way when he recalled how close Floretta had come to opening her robe in front of him.

"I was there last night to help with Clara's escape," Maggie quickly asserted. "Therefore, I hold a certain amount of responsibility for this woman's predicament. I want to see if there's anything I can do to help her. She may just need someone supportive to hold her hand while you talk to her."

"Someone to hol—." Maggie Rose Kane was something else. Now, besides gritty and stubborn, she had a soft heart for prostitutes? Luke didn't quite know what to think of her. He tried to imagine Annalise having this level of compassion. Oh, she'd always been delightfully fun and friendly with all the customers at Engel's Restaurant, but now that he thought about it, he didn't remember what sorts of things made her passionate; what things drove her to put others before herself. She'd been a wonderful woman, yes, and he'd loved her—still did—but for reasons he couldn't explain, her face had been dimming in his memory, and it scared him. He didn't want to forget one single aspect of her person. And blast it if Maggie Rose Kane had anything to do with his fading recollections!

And what of his former obsession and resolve to carry the *General Slocum* investigation to its conclusion? With chagrin, he realized he hadn't even thought about that in the past few days, so wrapped up had he been in Clara Warner's situation. Good grief, something had happened to bring about this change in him. Somewhere along the line, he'd started caring for the orphans at Sheltering Arms. For crying out loud, he even felt a swell of sympathy for Floretta, a loose woman!

"It might not hurt," said Reverend Miles. "I'm sure the Mrs. could use a little help in removing those bloody clothes— well, what remains of them, that is. I'll have to warn you, the lady is not a pretty sight."

Luke's resolve started caving in on him. What they were saying made sense, but it irked him no end to admit it. He didn't want the little miss from Michigan sitting next to him on the rig, no matter how short the span between Sheltering Arms and the church parsonage, and he certainly didn't want to entertain the possibility of her slender shoulder making contact with his arm or those long, blonde locks of hair flying freely in the breeze. At the same time, the notion of looking at a scantily clad Floretta, bleeding from who knows where, and trying to draw information from her didn't bode well, either. Yes, he was a news reporter and accustomed to squeezing details out of folks, but it wasn't every day he interviewed a streetwalker.

"You make a good point," he forced out.

"Of course he does," Maggie said. "Besides, my being there will be a comfort, you'll see."

Maybe to her, he thought.

K

Luke had become more and more adept at driving the rig. He'd even learned to navigate the grooves and potholes made by the hundreds of wagon wheels and horses' hooves traversing the dusty streets. Because of the late hour, traffic was lighter than usual as he followed Reverend Miles to the parsonage, Maggie sitting tall beside him, every so often trapping her flyaway hair with one hand. For some reason, she'd decided against a bonnet, and more than once, those golden tresses slapped him between the eyes. Whereas most women tended to bind their hair up in knots with ample waves, she usually pinned hers back with combs or bound it with a bright ribbon. He tried to remember exactly how Annalise had worn her coal-black hair, frowning when he couldn't form a clear picture in his mind's eye.

"Who do you suppose beat Floretta?" Maggie asked Luke as they made the turn off Dover and onto the worn, two-track driveway leading to the parsonage, the preacher parking his rig close to the well-lit, two-story structure sitting prettily next to the brick church before motioning at Luke to park behind him.

It was the first bit of conversation either had offered on the short drive over. In fact, they might have walked, but the air was downright cool, and since the preacher had driven, Mr. Bingham had suggested Luke do the same.

"I'd guess that big bruiser named Byron did the deed. It might've even been a group effort." Maggie trembled visibly, and for the first time that night, he looked her square in the face. Okay, she had a lovely countenance—delicately carved contours, a full mouth, sparkling blue eyes, and an exquisite little nose. He forced himself to look away.

"She may be a terrible sinner, but she didn't deserve a beating. Nobody does," she whispered.

"I agree." And he did. He draped the reins over the brake handle and stepped down from the rig, turning to assist her. When she put her hand in his, he felt a strange and unexpected jolt—a hot sensation surged through his veins, something he couldn't quite identify and didn't want to try. She jumped down, and for the span of three seconds, they looked into each other's eyes, she straining upward, he tilting his chin downward. The faintest scent of tuberose drifted past, and he couldn't tell if it came from her or from the nearby garden.

"You coming?" the preacher asked.

A jolt of a different kind had him whirling on his heel. "Yes!" he called back, mortified to have been caught staring at this tender shoot of a woman—and by the preacher, of all people.

K

Nothing could have quite prepared Maggie for the sight of Floretta. It took all she had to hold down her supper when she first laid eyes on the pathetic woman, blood trickling from her helplessly crooked nose that looked to be broken, blackened eyes swollen to mere slits, cuts and slashes covering her face, arms, and hands. Her lips puffed out like two pink pillows. She lay on a narrow cot in a small guest room on the parsonage's first floor, covered by a thin sheet, while Mrs. Miles tended her many wounds.

Maggie whispered a prayer for strength and courage as she approached the bed, Luke quietly following. She'd heard his sudden intake of breath at his first glimpse of Floretta, and she knew the sight had shocked him equally. Reverend Miles hovered quietly in the doorway.

At their entry, Coreen Miles looked up and smiled, then crooked her index finger at them in quiet invitation. "Someone's here to see you, Floretta," she said in a hushed voice, lowering her face to the woman's ear before stepping away to give Luke and Maggie some space.

Very slowly, Floretta turned her head. Maggie couldn't help the slight gasp that emerged from her throat, but Luke's gentle touch to the center of her back brought untold comfort. In fact, it settled her nerves almost entirely.

"Floretta, my name is Maggie Rose Kane," she said, laying a gentle hand on the woman's shoulder and praying she'd found a spot that didn't hurt. "I work at Sheltering Arms Refuge." The woman gave a slight nod and tried to open her mouth. "Don't speak just yet. I only want to say I'm very sorry you had to take such a beating. I'm quite sure it came as a result of your helping to rescue Clara Warner. Am I right about that?"

Another slow nod spoke volumes. Maggie and Luke exchanged a hasty look, and he seemed content to let her keep talking. Her eyes returned to the battered woman, and like an arrow shot from heaven, an unfathomable surge of love soared straight from her heart, prompting her to cover Floretta's bruised hand with her own. "You told Reverend Miles you wanted to talk to the man who came to the saloon last night. I hope you don't mind that I came along. I—I wanted to see if I could help. It was a brave thing you did, you know—helping Clara like that. We appreciate it more than you know."

Some kind of light dawned in Floretta's slit of an eye. "Y-you're the one—what got caught in that—t-tussle downstairs." Maggie nodded. "Yo'r the brave one, missy." She spoke slowly and with effort. "Ain't many women who'd come marchin' into Violet's like the way you done. I heard 'bout it from one o' the girls. They said you was this feller's wife."

She felt a blush rush up her cheeks. "No, I'm—well, we had to make up something on the spot." Heat traveled up her neck. Oh, dear. Now the preacher knew her to be a liar. "I didn't exactly march into the saloon, Floretta. It was more like somebody dragged me in."

"Don't matter. You was plucky is what I was told."

Plucky. She'd been called many things, but never plucky. She rather liked the word, now that she thought about it. "Listen, Floretta." She leaned closer, despite the unmistakable stench of blood, and marveled at the newfound compassion pouring forth from her heart. "Are you able to talk to Luke about what happened? We want to help in whatever way we can."

"I—I'm beyond help, I'm afraid, but you—you folks is the innocent ones. I just wanted to warn y', is all."

"Warn us?" Luke sounded mildly alarmed. He squatted down next to Maggie. "From what—or whom?"

Floretta wheezed and swallowed. Maggie worried she needed the kind of care that only a doctor could provide. With a great deal of effort, Floretta opened her mouth. "They—they are plain b-bad, Miss Violet's dogs." This she muttered in nothing more than a whisper, impelling Luke and Maggie to move in closer. "They beat me till they thought I was dead." For a long moment, everything went still.

"Oh, Floretta, you're safe now," Maggie reassured her, patting her bruised hand. She heaved a long, labored breath and tried to open her eyes. Maggie read intense fear behind the swollen lids. "They made me tell them—where you took—Clara."

Luke frowned, then turned to look at Reverend Miles. "Do you have a telephone, Reverend?"

"I certainly do. Shall I call the police?"

Luke nodded and ran a nervous hand through his hair. "They need to make a return visit. And tell them to send an officer to Sheltering Arms."

"Of course," the preacher said, making an about-turn.

"And could you call Dr. Hesselbart, too?" Maggie asked.

"I've done that," he said, pausing. "He's delivering a baby right now, but he promised to make this his next stop."

"I—ain't needin' no doctor. You should oughta jes' let me die."

"Hush," Maggie soothed, patting the woman's arm. "We won't let you die, Floretta. You're safe now."

But in her heart, Maggie couldn't be sure any of them was out of harm's way.

Chapter Nineteen

It was a relief to return to Sheltering Arms and find it safe and quiet, especially when Luke had expected trouble. He had driven the rig faster than he probably should have, Maggie jostling against him as he navigated the bumpy road. There was no telling what those thugs who'd beaten Floretta into the ground were capable of doing next, particularly if Violet paid them for their dirty deeds, as Floretta claimed. But were they actually malicious and degraded enough to march into an orphanage? Oh, he had no doubt they were evil, but a plot like that would take careful planning, not to mention brains—and that's where he figured they fell short. Even the police said they doubted the oafs would have the courage to follow through with their threats. Still, they promised to do daily and nightly patrols at the Refuge, keeping an eye out for anything suspicious. When asked if they planned to arrest the hoodlums who'd beaten Floretta, they said they would if she pressed charges, but, of course, she wouldn't for fear they would come after her.

During the course of the police visit, Luke had asked about the "old bat Violent." Couldn't they shut her down?

One of the officers actually grinned at that and shook his head. "You kiddin'? Her placard says 'Miss Violet's Saloon.' We start shutting down one bar, we gotta shut 'em all down. Talk about an uproar!"

"But she runs a house of prostitution upstairs."

The officer nodded. "I understand what you're saying, but without proof—."

"Proof!" Luke had nearly burst a vein in his neck when he yelled, prompting Maggie to place her hand on his arm and make a shushing sound. He pulled away from her soft touch and gestured with his head at the bedroom where Floretta lay on a narrow cot. "Why don't you ask her?"

"I already did," the older officer said. "I questioned her pretty thorough-like while you were out here. Unfortunately, she told me Miss Violet's Saloon is just that. A saloon. Nothing illegal about that, I'm afraid."

"She's just scared," Luke said, shaking his head. "So, how do you explain there being a young girl upstairs?"

"According to Floretta, those are upstairs apartments, and the girl had no way of taking care of herself. Said something about her roommate leaving her in the dust."

"That was Maxine Ward. She escaped out a window," Maggie put in.

"No one ever filed a report, far as I know," the officer said.

"The girl begged Henry not to," Luke said.

"And this Henry fellow complied with her wishes?"

"To a point," Luke answered. "He reported the incident without revealing the girl's identity. Whether he was right or wrong isn't the issue. The fact is, that place needs a thorough investigation. I can tell you this much—those are not apartments above Violet's place. They're rooms with beds and washstands where prostitutes entertain paying customers."

They ignored that, and the one who'd conducted the supposed interrogation merely sighed. "Look, Floretta says you offered to give the girl a place to stay where she'd be well taken care of, and she merely assisted you in seeing that the girl got put on your rig. Said living above a saloon was no good place for a young girl. 'Course, I agree with her."

"If that were true, and Clara had been free to leave at will, why did she leave with only the clothes on her back?"

Both officers shrugged. With down-turned lip, the younger of the two said, "Maybe that's all she had."

"And why were we chased?" Luke added, refusing to drop the matter.

"Maybe they didn't like the fact you were kidnapping an innocent girl."

"Are you crazy? They were keeping her upstairs—holding her captive."

"Was the door locked from the outside?" the older fellow asked.

"What? No." Unfortunately, they had him there. Clara had clearly been the one who'd locked the door. His shoulders dropped. Maggie was standing so close that he could hear her short, unsteady breaths. He knew it must've taken every bit of effort on her part to let him do the talking.

"Look." The older of the officers lowered his chin and his voice. "You give us some solid proof, and we'll take this a step further. We'll get a warrant and search the place. Without a warrant, though, our hands are tied."

"We might be able to haul those little girls in for questioning," the younger one said.

Luke put his foot down on that one. "Nothing doing. Those girls are leaving on a train in a few days. I do not want them involved in this investigation. They've had enough grief in their twelve or so years."

Both nodded. "You're probably right on that count," the older one said.

Silence engulfed the room, and all that anyone heard for the span of ten seconds was the ticktock, ticktock of the giant grandfather clock in the far corner of the parlor.

"You say you work for the *World?*" the older one asked.

"I do. I'm working on a piece about Sheltering Arms."

"Humph," he said. "You plannin' on mentioning anything about good ol' Violet's place in this here article?" A sinister gleam made his eyes look liquid. "Might work to everyone's favor 'cept Violet's if you was to include something about this little incident—the one in which the victim was too scared to press charges for fear of retaliation. Just a thought, mind you."

Two days later, Luke still mulled over the officer's words. For the moment, his only consolation was that Clara Warner remained safe at Sheltering Arms, and that the thugs had not shown up to reclaim her. It angered him plenty the way the situation had turned out, with nothing resolved and no arrests made. Perhaps his only recourse was to reveal the ugly secret behind Miss Violet's Saloon, although he'd have to figure out a way to do it without disclosing Maxine or Clara's names. Something like that could very well get the attention of a judge.

K

An air of excitement mixed with apprehension whistled through the walls of Sheltering Arms as most of the children prepared for the train trip west. The older ones knew about the big event, and they helped with the final details of packing and making ready, while the younger ones went about their day with hardly a care. Luke wondered how they'd fare once they had been passed into the arms of total strangers. His gut did a flip just thinking about bidding these youngsters good-bye. There was innocent and bright-eyed Rose Marie Kring, and then Audrey Wilson, Julia and Sofia Zielinski, and the Pelton sisters, to name a few of the girls who had become especially dear to him. He realized with chagrin he would miss them all. And of the boys, he'd particularly miss Allen and Peter Kramer, Billy Harper, Samuel Garrison, and Stuart and Ricky Campbell—yes, even Ricky, with all of his impishness.

Luke sat on his bed, pillow propped behind him, legs crossed at the ankles, his notebook in his lap. He was thinking how to proceed when a light rap at his open door made him turn his head. "Hey, come on in," he said to Stanley.

"Didn't mean to disturb you. How's the article coming?" Stanley leaned in the doorway, arms folded.

"This? Oh, slowly, I guess. I probably should have finished it by now, but there are so many dimensions to it that I don't quite know which way to approach it. For instance, how specific do I get? Do I tell any one child's story, or do I keep it general? Should I write about Clara's rescue, and if I do, how do I keep her name out of it? And what about Floretta? She has nothing to do with Sheltering Arms, and yet, she has everything to do with it. I guess my main concern is, will I capture the essence of Sheltering Arms and its mission? Will my meager words make any difference the day *after* the story hits the press?" Luke rolled his pencil between his thumb and fore-finger and pondered his own words while gazing at the wall.

"Wow!" Stanley whistled between his teeth. "I wouldn't want to be in your shoes. I can barely write my own name, let alone an entire newspaper article. I wouldn't sleep for days—make that weeks—if I had to come up with some story for the whole city to read. It would wind up in the funny pages, for sure."

The two exchanged a chuckle. Stanley moved in and sat at the foot of Luke's cot, stretching his legs out before him and studying his feet. "You've changed since you came here, you know that? I don't know exactly what it is, but you're not as, well…angry. If I had my guess, I'd say these children have softened your hard edges." He grinned. "Am I right?"

Luke felt his eyebrows shoot upward. He tilted his face to one side and rubbed his scratchy chin, grinning slightly. "I probably wouldn't argue with that. It's sort of a mystery to me how it's happened, but these youngsters have wheedled their ways into my heart. I never saw it coming."

"Interesting. It happens, you know. You think you won't grow attached, but all of a sudden, it's too late. Happens to me every time we get a new batch of little hooligans. By the way, you going to church tomorrow? It's the last time most of these children will be here before we head out with them on Monday morning."

Until now, Luke had avoided attending Dover Street Chapel with the rest of the household, wary of setting foot inside its doors for fear of what would happen to his emotion-ally barricaded heart. But it somehow seemed necessary to break down and attend, considering it was the children's last full day at the refuge. Besides, he'd made a sort of vow to the Lord to drop some money in the plate for helping get Clara out of Violet's Saloon. It was best not go back on a promise to the Almighty.

"Yeah," he heard himself say. "I plan to go."

Stanley breathed a sigh and pushed himself up. "That's great. The children will like having you there." He started for the door, then turned. "You're doing a good thing by writing that story. I know that whichever way you decide to go with it, it'll be exactly as it should be, especially if you ask the Lord for guidance. Have you done that?"

Now it was Luke's turn to whistle through his teeth. "Uh, I'm sorry to say I really haven't."

Stanley scratched the back of his head. "I bet if you do, it'll flow a lot easier."

"You think?"

He grinned again. "I know."

K

Maggie hurriedly brushed her own hair, sticking two shiny red combs behind each ear, then started in on the lineup of girls wanting their own locks either plaited or pulled back before church. Most of them were more than able to take care of their own needs, but since her arrival at Sheltering Arms, they'd taken to her fussing over them. Even Maxine had plopped herself on Maggie's bed to watch the hair styling, her own hair having been neatly braided for a change. Ever since Clara had come, Maxine's entire persona had changed—she'd gone from cynical and depressed to downright joyful, from apathetic about her appearance to diligent about washing her face daily and wearing clean, pressed dresses. Goodness, she'd even started being nice to everyone, including Vivian Pelton. Would wonders never cease?

"Have a seat, little princess," Maggie said to Rose Marie, holding the chair for her so she could crawl up onto it. The freckle-faced youngster complied, settling into place and turning her back to Maggie, sitting as tall as her tiny frame would allow. Maggie took up the child's long brown hair and began brushing it, noting its silky feel between her fingers. My, but she would miss this little one—and all of her other charges, for that matter. But she didn't want to talk about it lest she prematurely stir up the pain of separation. Already, there were those voicing their fears about leaving, some pleading to stay back. "But you will be so much better off with a real family," Mrs. Bingham had said to more than one in as soothing a voice as she could muster. Maggie could only imagine the unsettling worry building up in some of their little hearts. And then there was Maxine, who took the opposite stance. "It's gonna be like heaven to see the countryside," she'd announced over the evening meal. "I hope somebody wants t' adopt me. Wouldn't it be grand t' be adopted, Clara?"

"I—I guess," Clara said, still cloaking herself in shyness. Maggie would have liked the chance to get to know her better before handing her over to strangers. The Lord knew she'd probably seen more of life in her few years than all of the children put together. What thoughts must be running through her head now that she'd finally found a safe haven at Sheltering Arms, only to be shuffled off to parts unknown? The Binghams had discussed extending her stay with them, giving her a chance to adjust before forcing her on the train, but Luke had put the brakes on that idea, claiming the best and safest thing for both Clara and Maxine was to get them far away from the city and their former existence, not to mention Miss Violet and her thugs. The sooner they both made fresh starts, the better. Maggie had to agree. She could only pray the Lord would shield the girls from further danger.

Vivian Pelton entered the room filled with girls awaiting Maggie's attention. She sported a new plaid jumper that had been donated by the women's guild, and her brown hair was pulled back with a coordinating red ribbon. She looked as pretty as a portrait; it was no wonder Allen Kramer watched her with special care whenever she entered a room. Her sister Jenny followed on her heels, equally attractive, albeit in a different way. Whereas Vivian's beauty was obviously physical, Jenny's came from her spirited, spunky personality. The two seemed always at each other's throats, bickering constantly, but if someone else picked on either of them, the other would defend her sister like a feisty bulldog. In some ways, their silly squabbles reminded Maggie of her relationship with her sisters. Rarely did a day go by in her childhood that Grandmother Kane didn't settle some dispute or another. Some days, Maggie swore she'd sell both Hannah Grace and Abbie Ann at auction, but let anybody speak a negative word about either one of them, and she'd have the unfortunate person's throat.

"Hey, we can help with their hair," Jenny offered.

"That would be wonderful!" Maggie said. "Bring in a couple more chairs."

They did so, and the next thing she knew, there were twelve girls crammed into her tiny room, all putting in their requests for braids, plaits, or other styles.

The sun shone on their backs as the entire brood of them made the four-block walk to church, some carrying little ones in their arms or pushing baby buggies, older children holding the hands of younger ones, and some of the boys galloping ahead independently.

Maggie found herself walking alongside Luke, surprised yet pleased to see he'd decided to attend church. Several feet ahead of them, Charlotte and Stanley walked side by side, Charlotte pushing baby Christina in the buggy and Stanley carrying little Lillian. Charlotte's lighthearted laughter carried through the air, making Maggie wonder what Stanley had said to elicit such a joyous sound.

Although the sun shone brightly overhead, the crisp air reminded Maggie of autumn's impending arrival. Would New York's trees have the same vibrant colors as those of Michigan when the leaves started turning?

Luke interrupted her thoughts. "You ready for the big train ride?" He kicked a stone with the toe of his boot and made it sail across her path.

"I don't quite know what to expect," she answered. She glanced up at him, struck by how dapper he looked in his white dress shirt and tweed trousers, his dark locks falling in their usual fashion across his high forehead, hands tucked deep into his pockets as he strolled. She ordered her heart to stop slamming against her chest.

"You're not alone," he said, issuing a grin that showed his nice teeth. "I know much preparation has gone into it. Ginny says the women's guild has donated new clothes for all the children to wear on the train. I guess it'll be important for them to look their best when they arrive at the various stations. And, I heard that Reverend Miles has arranged for everyone, adults and children alike, to stay in homes along the way. It should be quite an experience for all of us."

"I'm sure you'll be taking plenty of notes for your article."

"That's my plan."

"When do you think you'll be done with it—your article, that is?"

"Trying to get rid of me, are you?"

"What? No." She felt a blush creep above her neck.

A low chuckle coming from his chest prompted her to look at him again. He wore a peevish grin. "You've become my partner in crime, you know. Never can tell when our next opportunity for adventure may come around."

"I think I can wait."

Their arms brushed ever so slightly.

He nodded. "I heard you went to see Floretta yesterday. You shouldn't have gone over there alone."

"I didn't. Stan went with me."

"Stan? Oh. I just assumed…."

"I'd intended to go alone, but Stan would have none of it, and neither would Henry. I guess they were right. Besides, Papa made me promise never to venture out on my own, although I think that's a bit stringent."

"Your father sounds like a smart man. New York City is no place for a beaut—er, young woman like yourself to be out roaming alone."

Hearing his near confession that he found her attractive warmed her to her soul, but it did no good to dwell on it. He had quickly rephrased the sentence, which meant he'd likely misspoken.

"I would gladly have taken you," he said. "I would personally like to ask that woman why she changed her story to the police. She made me look like a fool."

Now, that got her dander up. "You know very well why she did that, Luke. You said so yourself—she's afraid for her life. If it ever got back to Violet that Floretta went to the police, she'd sic her big bulldogs on the poor woman, and this time, those thugs would make sure she never talked again, let alone breathed."

He seemed to think on that. "I hear Dr. Hesselbart said she's lucky to be alive."

"Indeed he did. Floretta suffered several cracked ribs, but aside from that, she had mostly bruises. I hope she never returns to that awful place or that wretched lifestyle."

Luke shrugged and gave a troubled look. "It's all she knows. I heard her say it. Don't know how a person like her can ever change."

He'd opened the door for discussion, so she walked through it. "The Lord can change her heart, Luke. She is just the kind of person He longs after—someone with a bleak outlook who doesn't know where to turn, someone downtrodden and lost." She stole another glance at him, noting the square set to his jaw as he looked straight ahead. "Not only that, but He especially hears the cry of the bitterly brokenhearted."

Luke snorted. "You wouldn't be preaching at me, would you, Miss Kane?"

"Of course not, Mr. Madison."

K

The little church buzzed with *amens* as Reverend Miles delivered his message of hope to the people. Luke had been shocked to see Floretta sitting in the second row with Coreen Miles, looking much more alive than she had looked mere days ago, when he'd wondered if she'd even live. Now, though she still bore the bruises of an awful beating, at least she was upright—and looking mostly attentive to the preacher's words. Luke was confounded to find himself acutely engrossed in the sermon.

"There may be those of us here who do not have a keen understanding of the Father's love—perhaps because your earthly father failed you," Reverend Miles said. "But I have good news, my friends. Your heavenly Father loves you. He is not cruel and vengeful, as some would think, but full of compassion. Most of all, He longs for a relationship with each of us. How is this possible, you ask? It is quite easy.

"The Bible tells us in the third chapter of Romans that all of us have sinned and fallen far short of God's glory, but if we confess our sinful state, we may know His forgiveness through simple faith in His Son, Jesus, who offered up His very life as a sacrifice for our sins.

"Perhaps you have known much disappointment in your lifetime, whether young or old. You may have suffered unfathomable grief and pain, and because of that, you see little hope for tomorrow. It is even possible you blame the Lord for all your misery. Please allow me to reassure you, the Father has little to do with the wrong in your life but everything to do with the right. Think of it! In an instant, you can move from misery to mirth, from gloom to gladness, from bitterness to *betterness!*" The manufactured word created a stir of appreciative *amens*. Luke shifted in his seat, hoping to ward off the growing conviction that he'd been running from this God of love. He'd attended church with Aunt Frances all his life and even called himself a Christian, but now that he pondered his wretched, bitter heart, he wasn't sure he'd ever known this God the Reverend Miles spoke about, at least not in a truly personal sense.

Leaning slightly forward, he glimpsed Maggie Rose with hands folded in her lap, head bowed as if in prayer. When they'd arrived at the church, three little ones had tugged at her to come and sit with them, and she had followed, situating herself in the midst of them all. He'd ended up on the same bench but farther down, sandwiched between Ricky and Sam. Charlotte and Stanley sat in front of him, their shoulders touching, a sleepy child on each of their laps.

While Luke listened, he couldn't quite take his eyes off Maggie. Something told him that besides praying for the children and for Floretta, she'd sent up a prayer to the heavenly Father on his behalf.

And the notion made his heartbeat accelerate.

K

Sandwiched between Mr. and Mrs. Bingham in the fifth row, Maxine and Clara clasped hands, Clara squeezing extra tight when Reverend Miles talked about the difference God could make in a life when a person started trusting Him. Yes, they'd had hard lives up until now, Clara and she—most would call them deplorable—yet, somehow, here they both sat in Dover Street Chapel, getting a second chance. It was a miracle, Maxine decided. She had Mr. Madison and Miss Maggie to thank, of course, but Clara said God had a big hand in it, too. Wiping away a rare tear before anyone could detect it, Maxine let the notion of God's amazing love wash over her.

And in the preacher's closing comments, she did something she'd never done before: she asked Jesus into her heart. It wasn't a big, emotional moment, and she figured she'd have to give it a few days to see if it even stuck. The main thing was, she felt an undeniable sense of relief—and, well, freedom—when she whispered the prayer.

Surely, that had to mean something.

Chapter Twenty

The walk back from church did not end up being nearly as leisurely as the walk to church, for during the course of the morning service, the sun had gone into hiding, giving way to threatening rain clouds. Several steps ahead, Mr. Bingham urged the children to walk at a faster pace. It was a challenge for little Emily Price, who'd finally fought off her nagging cough but had yet to regain all her strength—and her weight. Clara held her hand, trying to pull her along, while Maxine carried two-year-old Cora Van Sanden. Without forethought, Luke moved forward and swept Emily up into his arms. The child awarded him a surprised look but then grinned and clasped her hands about his neck. She couldn't have weighed more than a couple of feathers, and he was glad the Binghams had decided to keep her and her brother at Sheltering Arms a while longer.

"Oh, I'm glad you're carrying her." Maggie and Rose Marie caught up to him, holding hands and swinging them as they walked. "I was just about to do it myself, but you beat me to it. Did you like the sermon?"

No hedging with this woman, he thought. "It was fine." He wouldn't tell her how the reverend's words had put him on edge, forcing him to search his soul. No, he would keep that matter to himself. He would also keep to himself the fact he'd caught himself looking at her almost constantly over Ricky's head.

"He's certainly not afraid to speak the truth. I like that in a preacher, don't you?" The first drops of rain started to fall, and they still had another block and a half to go. Luke quickened his pace, but Maggie kept in step with him, prattling on and paying no mind to the worsening weather. "I mean, some preachers are all about making their congregations feel comfortable just so they'll return every Sabbath. But not Reverend Miles. No, he simply preaches the Word of God, and woe to the people who don't appreciate it. That's something to be admired."

He glanced over at her. Blonde locks, once tucked neatly behind red combs, now fell in disarray around her flushed face as she hurried along, little Rose Marie clinging tightly to her hand. He wondered if she had a clue how lovely she looked with her wide skirt flaring around her ankles and her blue eyes sparkling with passion. He certainly wouldn't tell her, though—and woe to *him* for noticing! He refused to fall for someone he wouldn't even see again once he had returned to his job at the *World*. Besides, his heart still belonged to Annalise Engel, as it always would.

"And did you notice Floretta sitting up front with Mrs. Miles? My, it did my heart good to see her in the service, didn't it yours?" she prattled on. "Afterward, I went and talked to her, and she seemed so much stronger than she was two days ago. After I left her side, I noticed a few other women gathering around to offer kind words. Some would shun a woman like that, but a true Christian is commanded to love even the worst of sinners, just as Christ does. I think it's quite amazing to watch God at work among His people, don't you? Sometimes, just knowing someone cares about you is enough to start a body on the road to healing. I imagine that's how it is with Floretta. I wonder if anyone's ever truly cared about her before."

Luke had opened his mouth at least three times to respond, but she never gave him the chance. He figured it was just as well, since he didn't know what to say, anyway, especially with regard to her comment that kind words could catalyze recovery in a body. He wondered if the same rang true of the heart. She rattled on about how the women of the church had been dropping off hot meals ever since hearing about the new boarder at the parsonage. "Don't you think it's a marvel what these women are doing?" she asked. He glanced down at her. Talk about a marvel. He was looking at one. The woman was a regular ball of vim and vigor.

Drops of rain were pelting their heads and shoulders, so he stepped up the pace. "We're going to get soaked."

"Is that all you can say?" she demanded, having no trouble keeping up with him. Rose Marie trotted along, surprising them both with her stamina.

A small grin formed on his lips. "You don't give me much of a chance, Miss Kane."

"What? You can cut me off at any time."

"Really?" Now he chortled aloud.

"What I mean to say is—."

Now the rain was falling even harder. Horsemen galloped past, and drivers slapped their horses into faster gaits, their wagon wheels throwing mud for several feet in every direction. Squeals of both delight and despair echoed through the air. Emily giggled with glee as she bounced along in Luke's arms. Ahead of them, Charlotte paused to draw a blanket over the baby buggy, then quickly caught up with Stanley.

Just then, a clap of thunder sounded, and a flash of lightning streaked the skies. Screams of surprise rose up. Luke grabbed Maggie by her free hand. "Come on!" he shouted through the noisy torrents of rain. "Run!"

Without ado, they set off through the deluge, rain soaking their clothes, their boots splashing through puddles that soaked them even more. Fortunately, they were bringing up the rear, so Luke had everyone in his sight as they sprinted in the direction of Sheltering Arms, Maggie and Rose Marie managing to step in every puddle along the way, giggling like two silly schoolgirls.

When Sheltering Arms Refuge came into view, Luke vowed it was the prettiest sight in all of New York.

K

Maggie could think of nothing to match the invigorating feeling of running through the rain, especially with Luke Madison pulling her along by his strong grip and Rose Marie hanging on to her other hand for dear life. Of course, it all came to a halt as soon as they got inside. Mrs. Bingham started issuing orders to the children to leave their wet shoes and boots at the door and march upstairs to change into dry clothes before they all caught their deaths. Maggie shook the rain from her cape and hung it on a hook, then slipped out of her leather lace-up shoes with the pointy toes. Out the corner of her eye, she watched Luke assist a couple of youngsters with their boots, secretly hoping he might look her way. She didn't know what she expected. A tender glance? A look that conveyed an ulterior message? Good grief, was she losing her marbles? All he'd done was hold her hand for a thirty-second sprint up the rain-soaked street. Still, as simple gestures went, this one had lingering power.

Later that same day, after helping Mrs. Bingham and Charlotte pack up meals for the train ride—carrot sticks, pickles, jelly sandwiches, beef jerky, apples, grapes, cookies, and fruit juice—Maggie went to her room to write a letter to her family. After composing it, she sat on the edge of her bed to reread what she'd written.

September 15, 1904

Dear Papa, Grandmother, Abbie Ann, Hannah Grace, Jesse, and Gabe,

Life here at Sheltering Arms is never dull. Today, we all got caught in the worst rainstorm ever on our way back from church. It came as a big surprise, especially since our walk to church had been a sunny one. I happened to be walking next to Luke Madison, the newspaper reporter I told you about, when he suddenly grabbed my hand in the midst of the downpour and took off with me and six-year-old Rose Marie. In fact, the whole of Sheltering Arms, including Henry and Ginny, raced up the street. We must have been quite the sight to anyone who happened to be driving by.

The orphanage has been a whirlwind of activity as we've been preparing for our train ride west. We are leaving for the station at seven o'clock in the morning, which will mean getting everybody up and moving by five-thirty, quite a feat for nineteen children and four adults.

We have had many exciting events occur here at Sheltering Arms, but I shall tell you all about them at Christ-

mastime. Is it silly for me to say I am already anxious for the day when I shall see you all again? Christmas does feel like an eternity away when I consider it is not even October yet. I'm sure this nearly two-week train trip will make time appear as if it's flying, though.

It hardly seems possible that the trip is already upon us. On our way to Lincoln, Nebraska, our final destination, we will stop in Columbus, Ohio, and Springfield, Illinois, where we shall see if any of the citizens are of a mind to adopt a child or two. Please pray that all will go smoothly and that no child will feel the pangs of rejection.

Reverend Miles has made all the arrangements. As is usual, Sheltering Arms will have an entire train car reserved for the travelers. It will be situated at the rear of the train, in front of the luggage car, which is a very good thing, indeed. They plan it purposely that way so that few passengers will pass through our car, meaning we will have less exposure to bawdy songs, cursing drunkards, and incessant smokers, not to mention squalling babies— other than our own, that is. I'm sure baby Christina, one-year-old Lillian, and two-year-old Cora will have their moments. Four-year-old Emily, the one I told you had been sick with a bad cough, will remain at Sheltering Arms, as will her brother, Noah. She still needs time to recuperate, although I'm happy to report she is greatly improved, thank the Lord.

I miss you all so much. I will admit I even miss your silly jokes and antics, Abbie Ann!

Hannah, do write and tell me how sales have been at Kane's Whatnot. Speaking of that, how is business at the upstairs library? Has there been any further discussion at the town council meetings about erecting a new building for the library? And have any new books come in for old Mr. Fisher? I'm almost certain he's read every title available, and some more than once. I do so miss volunteering my time at the library, even if it often meant working alone because no one could abide my habitual singing. I've shared my vocal talents here a few times, but I still get the strangest looks—even from the children. Why, last Sunday morning, right in the middle of singing "The Comforter Has Come," a rather bulbous boy standing next to his mother turned around to grant me a beady-eyed glare, as if I'd just committed some heinous crime. Mercy, what has become of parents these days? Don't they teach their children that it's improper to gawk at strangers?

Papa, how is the insurance business doing? Have you sold many new policies? I miss your warm embraces and words of wisdom.

Gabe, I do hope you are keeping the peace as sheriff of Sandy Shores and that you've been able to keep your gun in your holster. I shall never forget all the terrible happenings of last fall when that awful McCurdy gang rode into town. But you were the city's hero, and now, you're my brother-in-law, which is altogether a wonderful blessing.

Jesse, are you and that rascal Billy B Hiles staying out of trouble? I hope you're taking your schoolwork very seriously. You once told me you wanted to be a lawyer someday so that you could make new laws to help orphans. You do know, of course, that this will require a lot *of studying on your part? You are certainly smart enough to handle it, I know. I don't mean to preach, Jesse; I just want to encourage you to stay true to your passions and trust the Lord to give you wisdom every step of the way. You are never too young to ask for His guidance, you know.*

Grandmother, I miss you ever so much. If only I could have just one more of your tender squeezes. Oh, my gracious, I do believe I'm tearing up, so I best conclude before I soak this parchment right through.

I shall be sending you postcards along the way, but I am sad to think I will not be receiving mail from you for the next several days. Please write to me anyway so that I will come back to New York with a mountain of letters awaiting me.

All my love and best wishes to each of you,
Maggie Rose

Chapter Twenty-one

Grand Central Station buzzed with loud voices, hissing engines, squealing whistles, and screaming babies. At the last minute, Mrs. Bingham had decided to hold back Bernard Munson and Benny DeLuca on account of fevers and coughs, and so, in the end, nineteen wide-eyed children, including Clara Warner, stood at the platform awaiting instructions to board the roaring locomotive.

Each child wore a new set of clothes donated by the church guild and carried one tiny suitcase, another guild offering, containing all his or her earthly belongings. To Luke, they presented a somewhat pathetic picture, all lined up like soldiers awaiting orders from their captain before heading off to war. Suddenly, he wanted to reassure them of their bright futures, but he knew he had no business making empty promises.

Maggie stood surrounded on all sides by little girls, some clinging to her arms and others to her skirts. She reached out her hands to smooth down one girl's flyaway hair, pat another's rosy cheek, or bend at the waist to whisper something. They watched her closely, as if she were their lifeline. Not for the first time, Luke stood at a distance to admire the courage she emanated but then shook off the notion that she had started growing on him.

A train whistle echoed through the station, forcing up a cloud of smoke and steam from the engine. Its suddenness gave even Luke a jolt, so it was no wonder that little Cora Van Sanden started to scream, prompting Christina and Lillian to follow suit. In their usual motherly fashion, Maxine and Vivian stepped forward, Maxine taking Lillian from Charlotte so that she could tend to Cora, and Vivian cradling baby Christina in her arms. Stanley had enough to worry about keeping Billy Harper, Dag Haskell, and Sam Garrison corralled, while Luke saw to it that the bigger boys—Gilbert Garrison, Peter and Allen Kramer, and the Campbell boys— stuck close by. In her normal fashion, Clara followed behind Maxine, ever her faithful shadow.

Standing slightly back, Mr. Bingham, Reverend Miles, and Herbert Wiley were engaged in conversation with the train conductor, no doubt making final arrangements for boarding the orphans and their four adult escorts. Stanley held a brief- case given to him by Reverend Miles. It contained important instructions with regard to the children and their trip—the station platforms where they were to wait for their connections, the churches in Columbus, Springfield, and Lincoln where they could expect a hot meal and a night's accommodations, and application forms for prospective parents to complete.

"When do we get on this big ol' engine?" Ricky asked, hands shoved in his pockets, face contorted in its typical gri- mace. By now, Luke had learned the boy's tough façade was a way to conceal his insecurities.

"Whenever they give the word, buddy. If you look down the line, you'll see none of the other passengers have boarded, either."

"How many hours we gotta stay on this thing?"

"More than you or I want to think about right now."

"What time's your watch say?" Not ten feet away from them, there was a large clock protruding from the wall with a face on both sides so that people coming and going could view the time. Next to that, a large blackboard listed the trains by number and departure time, and people dressed in suits and rags alike came up to check the train schedule. To synchronize his timepiece to the one on the wall, as well as to appease Ricky, Luke withdrew his pocket watch.

"It's 7:26."

"What time's ar' train leave?"

Luke breathed a sigh for patience. "I told you—7:45. We should be able to board anytime now, I would think."

Luke glanced around at Mr. Bingham and, in that moment, saw a figure slip behind a large cement beam—someone waiting to board, no doubt. He didn't give the matter much thought, too preoccupied keeping watch on his boys. But when the figure reemerged, hat pulled low, face darkened by its rim, something like a heavy stone plummeted to the pit of Luke's gut. It wasn't Byron, but the man could have been his double. Looking like a bar bouncer with his broad-set shoulders, the fellow perused the overcrowded station, where hundreds of folks were milling about, awaiting their connections.

Cora's cries had died down, but Lillian's still continued at maximum pitch. Maxine and Charlotte exchanged bundles. When Luke glanced over, he noted Maggie still offering words of comfort to her young charges, her arms wrapped around a frightened Rose Marie Kring and an awestruck Audrey Wilson. He told himself he watched Maggie too much, and yet one could never be too careful. She had assisted in helping to rescue Clara Warner, which made her as vulnerable to retaliation as Floretta and he.

Another whistle sounded, and the conductor gave the word that boarding could begin. "All aboooard!" he boomed in his well-trained voice. A flurry of excitement rippled through the crowd as folks pushed forward to reach the train cars—all but the residents of Sheltering Arms Refuge, that is. Mr. Bingham, Reverend Miles, and Uncle Herbie gathered the children together in a circle.

"Come closer, please," he said. Everyone did as told, and the next thing Luke knew, he was rubbing shoulders with Maggie in the tight circle.

The reverend made a careful study of each solemn, youthful face. "You are about to embark on a great adventure, my dear, young friends," he told the orphans. "May the Lord go with each of you as you depart for places unknown. Let's join hands with the people next to us and thus unite our circle as I speak a prayer on your behalf."

Luke hadn't counted on this, but lest he sound like one of the whining boys who had to hold the hand of a girl, he quickly took Maggie's hand. She gazed up at him and smiled, making his heart knock crazily against the wall of his chest. His other hand remained free, so he reached out and snatched Peter Kramer's, amused by the boy's mortified expression.

Not until now had he ever hoped that a prayer would drag on forever. Whether the sound of the preacher's words, monotonous yet sincere, or the very solemnity of the moment was responsible, he couldn't be sure. He just knew that he wanted to hold Maggie Rose Kane's hand as long as he could.

Of course, at the final "Amen!" Peter Kramer wrangled out of his grasp; quite naturally, he dropped Maggie's hand, as well. But rather than reveal his disappointment, he looked in the other direction. And that's when he saw him—the lurking man, the one resembling Byron—leaning against the big cement post not seventy-five feet away, wide-brimmed hat still riding low on his face to hide his searching eyes.

"Stay here," he whispered.

"Where're you going?" Maggie asked, surprise in her tone. "We have to board the train!"

With eyes focused straight ahead, he advanced. "I'll be right there. Get on."

"But…." Maggie watched as he broke away from the circle. He headed for where the man was standing, wanting a closer look, but a woman crossed his path, maneuvering a baby buggy with one hand and hauling a toddler along with the other. To avoid colliding with her, he paused to let her pass, and when he looked up again, the man had vanished. He blinked and shook his head. Surely, he hadn't imagined it, and yet….

He stopped in his tracks to scrutinize the bustling station and its sea of people of every color, size, shape, and age, each carrying a piece of luggage, a newspaper, a handbag, a trunk, or even a child. He rubbed the back of his neck then, turned back to the train, worry nagging at his mind.

"Luke," said Mr. Bingham, approaching from the side. "You take good notes now, you hear? We'll expect to see that article when you return." The stout man gave him a playful pat.

"I'll work on it, that's for sure," he said, somewhat distractedly. "Tell Ginny I'll be missing her pies."

"I'll do that."

Luke looked again in the direction where he'd seen the shifty man, but he'd definitely vanished.

"You okay? You're looking a bit pale."

"No, I'm—it's just—I thought I saw someone familiar."

"Where?"

"There." He pointed. Feeling foolish for his undue fretting, he shrugged. "But I guess it was just my imagination."

"Guess so." Mr. Bingham patted Luke's shoulder and shook his hand. Reverend Miles and Uncle Herbie concluded their final instructions for Stanley before ushering him to the train steps, then turned to Luke to bid him farewell.

The last of the group from Sheltering Arms to board the train, Luke turned around once more as he climbed the steps and made a final scan of the station, then nodded at the three men. With a whooshing noise, the big door closed behind him. He moved down the narrow aisle, discovered an empty seat next to Maggie, and nearly sat in it—until Julia Zielinski scooted into it ahead of him. *It's just as well*, he thought to himself.

"Luke, come sit back here!" called Sam. Luke stole a glance at Maggie, but she was already engaged in conversation with a few children, arms wrapped around their shoulders to draw them close, no doubt trying to ease their worries. He moved down the aisle, seating himself next to Sam and plopping his briefcase into his lap. It wouldn't hurt to do some work on his article once the train got underway. Sam jumped up from his seat and tried to open the window, as he saw other children were doing. It seemed they wanted to hang their heads outside and wave a final good-bye to the men standing on the platform. He reached up to lend the boy a hand and, in so doing, looked down to see—who else?—the "lurker." The creep had sidled up to the train and was looking up at his window. In that moment, Luke recognized him as Byron's companion, the other man who'd chased after his rig on the night they'd kidnapped Clara from the saloon.

"Have a nice trip," the thug mouthed, his narrow expression wickedly probing.

With a less than cordial shove at poor Sam, Luke whipped the window up and pushed his head out the opening. "What do you want?" he growled.

"Me? Nothin'." The man's big shoulders heaved up and down. "Just keepin' an eye on things is all—and seein' a friend off. You keep your eyes open, you might even get a glimpse of 'im on the train. Matter of fact, I'd watch my back, if I was you." To this, he flashed Luke an evil grin, revealing one blackened tooth, and started to cackle.

Luke's brow furrowed as several thoughts turned over in his head. "Just what friend did you happen to see off today?"

He lifted one brow. "Oh, why don't you think on it? I wouldn't want to spoil your little guessing game."

The louse! Luke pushed past Sam and moved into the aisle, making a dash for the door.

"Sorry, fellow, but this train is leaving," said one of the officials, stepping in front of him to block his exit.

It took every bit of self-control not to shove the little man on his fanny. He practiced steady breathing. "I have to get off."

"You'll have to take a seat."

"There's a man—I need to speak with someone out there."

The conductor's expression went rock hard as he puffed out his chest, his buttons nearly popping with self-importance. He had to look up quite a distance to meet Luke's eyes. "I told you to take a seat, sir."

The train lurched forward, its engine hissing and popping. Several of the children gasped in surprise. Luke grabbed hold of a bar to maintain his stance.

"Luke, what's going on?" Maggie asked from behind him.

He turned to look at her, seeing deep worry in her eyes. Through the window beside her, he spotted Mr. Bingham and the other two men waving at the children. With no time to explain himself, he leaped in front of her, sprawling across her lap, and yanked open the window. Maggie gave an audible gasp. "Henry! Henry!" he yelled.

The stout fellow started walking alongside the train, brows quirked in question. "What is it?"

"I need you to call the police!" he hissed, trying to keep his voice down yet still be heard. "Tell them to meet me in Columbus."

"Wh—what on earth for?"

"There's a man here—at the station. He's been watching us the whole time."

"Where?" Mr. Bingham made a hurried perusal but, seeing nothing noteworthy, looked back at Luke, all the while quickening his pace to keep up with the train's chugging.

Desperate to explain himself, Luke yelled, careful to enunciate as clearly as possible. "Listen to me! I have a hunch there may be some trouble ahead!"

"A hunch?" Mr. Bingham yelled back. "What sort of trouble are we talking?"

"Don't ask. Just—just call the—you know." He couldn't repeat the word for fear the children would hear.

Mr. Bingham gave a fast nod. "Yes." Coming to the end of the platform, He screeched to a halt. "Be safe!" he called after the train, hands pressed together as if for prayer.

Caught up in the excitement of a speeding locomotive, the children were oblivious to Luke's final conversation with Mr.

Bingham. They chattered a mile a minute, some still hanging their heads out the windows and squealing with enthusiasm until Stanley put a stop to it.

Thankfully, Julia Zielinski had already vacated the space beside Maggie. Luke collapsed into the seat and stared up at the ceiling, gulping large breaths of air and then releasing them slowly in measured sighs. He didn't have to look at Maggie to know she had a number of questions on the tip of her tongue. In fact, a peripheral glance confirmed it: her arms were folded, her blue eyes full of inquiry, eyebrows raised above them. He had to respect her for giving him a moment to collect his thoughts.

He closed his eyes against the sudden pangs of a headache.

"All right, what's going on?" Maggie finally whispered, settling back against the seat, her shoulder rubbing against his arm.

He might have known the silence between them wouldn't stretch on forever. He opened his eyes and turned his head, shocked to discover her face mere inches from his. There went that mysterious thudding against his chest again.

He sniffed. "It could be nothing. Or—it could be something," he whispered.

She arched her right eyebrow, her shapely lips pursed in annoyance. "That tells me a great deal. What was all that hurried talk with Henry? I couldn't hear for all the noise and commotion going on about me."

He sighed. "That's just as well."

She cleared her throat, arms still tightly folded. "Oh, no, you don't. If the children are in danger, I deserve to know about it—and so do Charlotte and Stanley."

He tugged at his earlobe and winced. Unfortunately, what she said made sense.

𝒦

A tight knot rolled over in Maggie's chest as Luke told her about the man at the station. "And you're sure he is the same man you saw the night we rescued Clara?"

Luke nodded slowly, then braced his head against the seat. She turned her body to face him, then realized that they were mere inches apart. She told herself it was necessary so that they could speak without the children overhearing, but that didn't erase the fact that their close proximity flustered her. Why, at this range, she could observe all of his facial features, like his clean shaven jaw line and square chin, dark, appealing eyes hooded by long, curved eyelashes, firm mouth, and classic nose. She even discovered a tiny scar just under his left temple and longed to ask him how he'd acquired it. As the train chugged along, the sunlight illuminated his handsome face, which was shadowed periodically by trees or buildings they passed by. There was no doubt about it—she enjoyed looking at him. But it ended there. It had to. For all she knew, he was still faithful to his deceased fiancée. And then, there was the matter of his faith—or, rather, his lack thereof.

"What do you think is going to happen? I mean, what did that fellow intend when he said you should watch your back?"

"I'm not sure, but it can't be good, whatever it is. I'm going to make a thorough search of this train, starting with the front car and making my way to the back. I intend to look every single passenger in the eye."

"That doesn't sound like a good idea, Luke. What if you come face-to-face with Byron?"

"That's exactly what I'm hoping will happen."

"And what do you plan to say to him? You haven't had as much as a minute to devise a strategy, and already, you want to go looking for him? This could be dangerous. That Byron is a big monster with no scruples."

He turned his head, and their eyes met, his gleaming with slight amusement.

"Do I detect a lack of confidence in my abilities?"

"Well, no—not exactly. But—what if he wants to fight you?"

His mouth quirked at the corners. "Then he would probably win. There could be a lot of blood."

"This is no laughing matter, Luke Madison."

"Who's laughing?"

"You look ready to."

His slight smile dissipated. "Has anyone ever told you that you have lovely blue eyes?"

"What? Well, um, I suppose my papa told me once—when I was a little girl, but—oh! We are not discussing my eyes, for goodness' sake!"

"We're not?"

She could not believe he'd just paid her a compliment in the midst of a tumultuous situation. "This is a matter for the train authorities, Luke. I think you should go straight to the engine room and speak with the engineer or conductor or whoever is in charge."

"Is that what you think?" He turned to face her and reached up to take a few strands of her hair between his thumb and forefingers. "You make a very convincing argument, Maggie Rose Kane."

Chill prickled up her spine and raced back down again. *Dear Father in heaven, I believe I'm turning to mush. For goodness' sake, what should I do? I feel a growing attraction to Luke, but he doesn't know You as Savior and Lord, so therefore, I can't allow myself to care for him.*

Her misgivings were offset by a response she seemed to sense in her heart: *My child, judge not, lest you be judged. Allow Me to work in the situation, and entrust your heart to My care.*

It seemed like a good idea, even a scriptural one, so she swallowed down a hard lump and practiced quiet, slow breathing. *I'm trying, Lord. Help me to trust You.*

Luke continued studying her face with a look of admiration, and Maggie felt herself blushing under such scrutiny. Suddenly solemn-faced, he turned and faced the front of the train, as if annoyed by something.

He's a hard man to read, Lord, Maggie continued her prayer.

I see into the soul, My child. You must step back and allow Me to deal with him.

"I need more evidence before I talk to the conductor," Luke said with a pensive frown, resuming the topic at hand.

Maggie cleared her throat. "And just how will you go about doing that?"

"I told you—I'll need to search the train. If he's onboard, I'll confront him—ask him what his business is and where he's headed. If it looks like he wants to create a fuss, I'll go straight to the conductor."

"But what if he won't talk to you? What if he jumps up and punches you right there on the spot? I think you should speak to the conductor beforehand, bring him with you on this—this search."

"You are full of ideas, Maggie Kane." He grinned an impish sort of grin. "Have you seen the conductor? He's an odd little fellow."

"Oh."

Out the corner of her eye, Maggie caught sight of Stanley coming up the aisle.

"Hey, you two, is this a private discussion?" he teased. "Did I see you saying something to Henry back there, Luke? Anything wrong?"

Luke looked up. "You would have to ask that."

The train switched tracks, throwing Stanley into a teetering stance. He grabbed hold of a pole to stay upright.

Maggie took that as a cue that Stanley needed to sit down. "Here, Stan, take my seat. I believe Luke has some things he needs to talk about with you."

Rising, she quickly slipped past Luke without another word and made her way to the back of the car. Seeing an empty spot next to Charlotte, probably Stanley's, she decided to sit down and fill her in on the latest developments concerning that big brute, Byron, and his good-for-nothing accomplice.

Chapter Twenty-two

I f "Big Bad Byron" was anywhere on this train, then Luke would eat his boot! He'd started at the first car and eyeballed every passenger, finding no one who as much as resembled the beastly Byron. He'd even loitered whenever he'd encountered a vacant seat, waiting for the absent person to return.

It was a painstaking process, and it didn't end with just one pass through the train. Every time they stopped at a station, Luke started the search all over again, surveying the new passengers. It got so folks started recognizing him and either saying there was nobody new in the car or pointing out the latest passenger. Luckily, no one seemed interested enough to ask why he kept returning; they just gave him cursory nods and went back to reading, tending to noisy children, conversing, smoking their smelly cigars and pipes, or sleeping.

After returning from his fourth pass through the train, Luke dropped into a seat next to Ricky and sighed, confident he could now relax.

"Why you keep walking through this train, anyways?"

He settled his head against the seat and closed his eyes. "I need my exercise."

"Can I go with you next time?"

"Nope."

"Why not?"

"Because I said so."

Ricky heaved a loud breath. "Adults always say that. 'Because I said so,'" he mimicked in a singsong tone. "I need my exercise too, y' know. Bein' trapped on this ol' tank ain't my idea of fun."

"We've been on it for only three hours. You'll have the chance to stretch your legs when we get to Columbus. We're spending the night there."

"Is that where folks is gonna look us over t' see if they wanna take us home?"

Luke's heart did an uncomfortable flip. It could not be easy for these children, wondering where they'd wind up. He hated thinking of leaving any of them with complete strangers, but it appeared to be the way the system worked. "That's one stop, yes," he answered. "Tomorrow, they'll take us on to Springfield, Illinois, and, after that, Lincoln, Nebraska."

"That's where I wanna live. Lincoln."

"Oh, yeah? Why Lincoln?"

"It reminds me of my favorite president. Abe, that is. He started the Civil War and stopped slavery."

Keeping his eyes shut to the hubbub around him, Luke gave a slow grin. "I wouldn't say he actually started the war. No president would want that legacy resting on his shoulders. Speaking of old Abe, he had a love of book learning. Are you anxious to start back to school again?" Schools had resumed in New York a week ago, but Mrs. Bingham had not sent the orphans, thinking it best they start attending after they had gotten settled with their new families. She'd start

Millie Sargent, Noah Price, Bernard Munson, and Benny DeLuca next week.

"I don't mind. Long as I get me a good teacher."

Truth be told, Ricky Campbell had grown on him, albeit by mere particles. Luke folded his arms across his chest and allowed his mind to drift. Shoot, if Ricky quit talking, he might even take a three-minute nap. Three seats back, Maggie started leading the children in a lively rendition of "The Farmer in the Dell." He groaned to himself. The woman couldn't carry a tune in a bucket, and someone really ought to tell her. Not that he minded it all that much. If anything, it added to her childlike charm. Childlike, yet thoroughly woman. He didn't know what he'd been thinking earlier when he'd snagged a lock of her hair. Something in her sea-blue eyes had simply compelled him to do it. Thinking back, he realized it'd been plain foolish. Not for the first time, he told himself that once he returned to his life at the *World*, she and everyone else at Sheltering Arms would dissolve into the furthest recesses of his memory.

"…someone'll want Stu an' me?"

Coming back to the present, Luke opened one eye to peer at Ricky. "What's that?"

"I said, do you think there's anybody in Lincoln who'd want Stu an' me? We ain't got much t' offer, and I guess I can be pretty ornery."

He chuckled, even though Ricky's question demanded respect for its legitimacy. "Things might work in your favor if you would practice getting rid of some of that orneriness."

Ricky actually smiled, revealing his big, budding front teeth. "I don't know as it'd come natural for me. A person like me's got t' work at bein' nice."

At this, Luke gave a hearty laugh.

K

When noontime rolled around, the children had grown weary of traveling songs and were complaining about empty stomachs, so Maggie decided to go to the baggage car, where they'd stored their supplies—blankets and pillows, meals of non-perishable foods, books, games, toys, soap and towels, and a number of other miscellaneous items Mrs. Bingham had determined they would need for their journey. Looking behind her, she spotted Charlotte feeding Christina her bottle and Stanley slowly rocking a cranky Cora back and forth on his lap. Luke, situated three rows ahead of her next to Ricky, appeared to be resting. Beside her, Jenny Pelton sat staring out the window, mesmerized by the passing scenery.

"I'll be back shortly," she told her. "I'm going to go get our lunches."

"You want me to help?" Jenny asked.

"Oh, would you? I imagine the boxes will be somewhat heavy, but between us, we should be able to manage."

Boxes, trunks, crates, and large pieces of luggage belonging to the passengers lined all four walls of the baggage car, leaving only an aisle in the middle by which to navigate and blocking a great deal of light coming through the windows. Maggie knew right where Stanley and Luke had stacked their cartons, so she and Jenny made their ways back, every so often grabbing hold of one of the stationary poles to maintain their balance when the train lurched. A shuffling noise at the rear of the car caught their attention.

"I heard something. This place is dark, not to mention spooky," Jenny said.

"It's just a bunch of goods, honey. I imagine something shifted in its box, that's all. Nothing to worry about." It was best to remain calm, Maggie decided, even though she had the same sense of creepiness skipping across her nerves. "Let's see here." She bent to read the words on the cartons, squinting as she sought to identify the one saying "Sheltering Arms Meals." "Ah, there it is!" she announced, discouraged to find it wedged beneath two other crates. "Why wouldn't they put the food crate on top?" she wondered aloud with slight irritation, knowing that she and Jenny would have to lift the other two boxes down in order to reach the one they wanted. "Here, you take this side, and I'll take the other," she instructed Jenny. Together, they moved the top crate—not an easy feat, considering its heavy wooden frame.

"What is in this thing?" Jenny asked after they had lowered it to the floor.

The lettering indicated some manufacturing company. "It's not even our box," Maggie said, puzzled by that. "I thought the men said they stacked all our things together."

Next, they went for the other crate, this one lighter, and last, the carton of their meals.

The train took a wide curve in the tracks, also passing over an uneven section, which sent both of them into sprawling positions. Jenny plopped on top of a passenger's big trunk, and Maggie grabbed ahold of the big manufacturing carton to keep her footing. They looked at each other and let go a spurt of nervous giggles. "Are you okay?" Maggie asked. The young girl nodded. At the back of the car, a loud thud caused their heads to turn.

"What was that?" Jenny's eyes grew round as apples.

Maggie shrugged, hiding her wariness. "I haven't a clue. Probably something not stacked quite securely enough." She glanced toward the back. "Should I go check?"

Jenny's eyes remained wide. "Are you fooling? I want to go back to our car, and the sooner the better." The girl looked panicked.

"Okay, then, let's hurry up with this box." They bent to retrieve it, both taking an end and lifting.

"Need help?" came a masculine voice.

Without taking a second to assess from whence the voice came or to whom it belonged, both girls let out a breathy gasp and dropped the box, just missing their toes, then sighed with relief at Luke's shadowy figure in the aisle. He wore a puckish grin. "Did I give you ladies a fright?"

"A fright? More like you sent my heart into spasms!" Jenny exclaimed, clutching her chest. "It's spooky enough back here without you sneaking up on us like that. This place is full of bizarre noises."

"I wasn't sneaking, and what do you mean by bizarre noises? What sort are we talking?" Luke advanced down the aisle.

"Something fell back there," the girl said, pointing. "And it gave me the creeps. In fact, now that you're here, I'm going back. Is that okay, Maggie?"

"Sure, it's fine, honey." *Except for the fact that it will leave me alone with Luke.* Her heart thrummed an uneven rhythm, more from excitement than from fright. "I'll return in a minute. Tell the others to prepare for lunch. If they all behave themselves, there'll be cookies for dessert."

Jenny gave a nod and hurried off, pushing open the big door and stepping through it, then closing it behind her.

Maggie gazed at the door. "She's a bit overdramatic, I'm afraid. Yes, there was a noise back there, but I'm sure it was merely a box that shifted and fell. Hopefully, nothing valuable broke, or the owners will be quite dismayed. This train is not what you'd term a smooth ride."

"It's always bumpier at the back of the train."

"Oh, I didn't know."

"I'll see if I can figure out what fell."

"Yes, that would be good."

To give him space to navigate past her, Maggie pressed back against the stacked boxes, but the narrow aisle made it difficult for the two of them not to touch in the process. He paused and looked down, and their gazes held briefly, his breath grazing her cheek. Suddenly, the rocking, swerving car seemed filled with tremulous feelings—the sort that precede a first kiss. Could it be that he contemplated such a thing? In an instant, her heart leaped to her throat, and she brought her hand up to clutch the place where it pulsed nearly out of control.

And that's when it happened—the car went as black as a burnt skillet.

"Oh, my!" Sheer instinct prompted her to reach into the dark, and when she did, Luke's hand caught hold of hers and squeezed gently, drawing it to his solid chest. "It's just a tunnel. Pennsylvania has a number of them. We should come through it in a few seconds. Just hold steady."

When she might have wriggled free of him, she instead relished the warmth of his long-fingered hand over hers, coarse and calloused from working outside with Mr. Bingham and Stanley. It didn't feel like the hand of a newspaper reporter. She swallowed a lump of anticipation and prayed silently, *Lord, give me strength.*

With a tentative glance upward, she noted the faintest flickering rays of light dancing over his profile. The end of the tunnel couldn't be far off now. She counted her breaths, one every two seconds, and told herself to settle down, lest she faint dead away.

"Your hair smells sweet," he said in a low, smooth voice, his face dipping dangerously close.

Tiny shreds of resolve melted like ice on a spring day. She could hardly believe the teaspoon of lemon juice she'd used that morning while lathering her locks still left its scent. And to think she'd almost decided not to bother. The chug-a-chug of train on track overpowered her thudding heartbeat, and tiny traces of light bounced off the boxes and crates. Would this tunnel never end?

He lifted his free hand to stroke the hair from her temple, and she quivered with expectation. In the slowest of motions, he bent and kissed the underside of her jaw, her cheek, her earlobe, her eyelids. Then, like that pause between lightning and thunder, he hesitated before tilting his head and kissing her on the mouth. His hands slipped behind her, making faint movements that sent the fabric of her dress whispering across her skin.

At first, she stood straight and unyielding, frozen as a stick in the snow, but when his hands spread wide on her back to draw her closer yet, and he continued pressing his lips to hers, she conceded, falling into him like a powerful wave breaking on the shore, throwing her hands around his neck.

In her wildest imaginings, she had not anticipated the colliding force to her body brought about by a first kiss, had not fancied it wreaking such havoc on her balance or her ability to think straight. Why, every morsel of common sense she could muster dictated she should pull away. *He does not serve the Lord with total abandonment. I must…stop….*

But then, larger amounts of foolhardiness crept in to cloud her thinking. *This feels so right. I'm falling in love.*

Common sense said, *I cannot love a man who doesn't share my values and passions.*

Foolhardiness said, *I never knew a kiss could be like this, or that one man's arms could feel so warm and shielding.* Another minute, and she would be proclaiming her undying love for him, no matter the abruptness of it all.

The kiss ended when light burst upon them and the train's whistle echoed from afar. Luke suddenly dropped his hands to his sides and stepped back, snapping to attention much like a soldier might do for a superior officer. A look of disgust and disappointment washed over his expression and, after that, clear regret.

"I'm—s-sorry about that. I don't know what possessed me. I think I forgot for a moment where I was, and—well, I wasn't thinking straight, that's all."

Maggie couldn't explain why her thudding heart came nearly to a standstill as she set about collecting her bearings. He'd forgotten where he was? Did that also mean he'd had someone else in mind when he was kissing her? His precious Annalise, perhaps? *Lord, how could I be so naïve as to picture myself with Luke Madison? Forgive me for jumping so far ahead of You.*

She lifted her chin, pulled back her shoulders, and dared to look him full in the face. "Well, if it's any consolation, my clouded head was equally to blame. Rest assured, it won't happen again."

At this, he lifted one dark brow a notch, opened his mouth, then promptly snapped it shut again. After three seconds, he said, "I guess I'll check on that sound you heard back there."

Despite her trembling nerves, she did not waver in her gaze. "Yes, why don't you?"

He gave her another long look before swiveling on his heel and heading down the long, narrow aisle. She watched with dulled emotions as he inspected the trunks and cartons on either side of him. At the end of the car, he disappeared behind the last row of cargo. She experienced a few moments of anxiety when he didn't return, but then he finally emerged, at which she released a long-held breath.

"I found a big wooden crate lying on its side. Don't know if it shifted and that's what you heard, but at any rate, I shoved it back in place. Label said 'Carson Freight.'"

"So, you saw nothing suspicious?"

He shrugged, avoiding her eyes, obviously still regretting that shared moment of intimacy. "Not particularly."

She sniffed, determined not to reveal the hurt lying just beneath her skin's surface. "Well, that's good, then, isn't it? Shall I help you carry the crate of lunches into our car?"

"I think I can manage it alone. How did you and Jenny lift it off that stack, anyway? It had to be awkward."

"It was on the bottom," she said. "The hard part was getting to it."

"Actually, when we loaded everything, I set it on top of the two other boxes," he corrected her.

"Actually, you put it under them," she argued, her dander rising of its own accord.

He looked directly at her, eyes narrowed in contest. "I put it here." He rested his hand on top of a box marked "Sherwood Manufacturing," then hastened a quick glance at it—and then at another. Wrinkles spread across his forehead as he bent down to read the words. "I thought I put it here, anyway. Where're the Sheltering Arms boxes?"

She pointed at the boxes on the other side of the aisle.

His frown grew. "That's not where we put them. I distinctly remember Stan and Henry placing this wooden crate on the bottom right here. The reverend hefted this one up, and I put the food crate here. Somebody obviously came in afterward and readjusted things."

"Who would do that?"

He lifted his shoulder in a perplexed shrug. "No idea."

"It's strange."

"Not really. Somebody just did a little rearranging, that's all. Maybe the conductor didn't like the way something was stacked, and so he made a few adjustments."

"Are you going to ask him?"

"No point to it. It's probably nothing of great concern."

The train lurched again, causing them both to teeter. He reached out a hand to steady her, but she quickly pulled away, recalling what had happened the last time she had accepted his assistance. She wasn't about to fall into that trap again.

Once steady on her feet, she quickly turned on her heel and headed up the aisle toward the passenger car. He gave an audible sigh when he bent to lift the food crate.

Chapter Twenty-three

At exactly four o'clock that afternoon, they passed through a little town outside of Columbus, Ohio. *It can't be long now,* Luke thought, glancing out the window at several rows of houses and a couple of small businesses peppering the landscape. The train's whistle sounded, alerting folks of its approach. Baby Christina squawked, something she'd been doing on a steady basis for the past two hours. Luke's head ached with tension. Ever since lunch, the children had squirmed and fussed, the older ones included, asking how much longer, whining from fatigue, and wrestling in the aisles. More times than he could count, he and Stanley had refereed one spat or another.

Maggie had not granted him so much as a single look since their kiss in the baggage car. Of course, his bigger fumble came about with his pathetic attempt at an apology. What woman wants to hear a manufactured excuse after such an amazing kiss? True, it shouldn't have happened, for it complicated matters in unimaginable ways, but he at least could have found something better to say than, "I forgot where I was." What bothered him most was the hurt he'd seen in her face, followed by the stubborn façade she'd immediately erected.

He tried analyzing the kiss, rationalizing its occurrence, but he came up short of ideas, other than the fact that she'd been downright tempting—and vulnerable. Admittedly, he'd taken advantage of the situation, and now, he would pay for it by suffering her deliberate silence. This was an uncomfortable state of affairs, considering the cramped conditions that would characterize their next several days. Perhaps he could manage a way to justify his actions to her, but that would be tough, especially since he didn't quite understand them himself. *I do not have feelings for Maggie Rose Kane*, he told himself. As a matter of fact, he'd been thinking about Annalise when he kissed her—hadn't he? Sure, there weren't many women lovelier than Maggie, but that didn't mean she attracted him in a romantic sense. *Did it?* Besides, he didn't come close to deserving a beautiful woman like Maggie, someone compassionate, dedicated, fervent, and, yes, even strong. Shoot, he'd need to get his life turned in the right direction—facing God—before she'd ever think about him seriously. *Not that I want her to think about me seriously*, he said to himself. He tried putting Annalise's china-doll face in his head, but the image kept fading in and out.

Lord, I am a pathetic case. I don't know what You want from me or how to discover it, he prayed silently.

I want your heart—all of it. It's no more complicated than that. The two-sentence response to his musings hit him dead-on, awaking in him an unspecified need. What had made him think it? *Who* had made him think it?

He gave his head a swift shake, frowned, and watched a row of two-story houses with neat little fenced-in yards go by in mesmerizing succession. The cops would be waiting for him at the train station, and he had nothing to report—another cause for his tension headache. Had he completely missed the mark concerning Byron? And if he had, then what had the lurker meant when he told him to watch his back?

Then, there was the matter of the rearranged crates in the baggage car. He'd sloughed it off in Maggie's presence, but it did continue to nag at him. Luke had told Stanley about it, but he'd merely shrugged and repeated what he'd told Maggie: the conductor or another passenger had probably moved things around to make room for additional cargo.

He decided to go give the baggage car one more search before the day's journey ended. Rising, he passed Allen Kramer and Vivian Pelton, their heads together in quiet conversation. He knew they had serious feelings for each other and wondered how they would handle parting once they received their home assignments. Advancing up the aisle, he passed Maxine and Clara, each holding a little one on her lap. Maggie sat three rows behind them, squeezed in between Audrey Wilson and Rose Marie Kring, her arms around their narrow shoulders as she whispered words of comfort. She didn't favor him with the slightest glimpse, despite the fact she had to have seen him coming. He shook off the memory of their kiss.

Stanley stood at the back next to the train washroom and bounced Christina in his arms, giving a weary-looking Charlotte a reprieve. He certainly had a way with little ones. Heck, he had a way with Charlotte, as far as Luke could tell. He couldn't understand why the two of them didn't just admit it—they had eyes for each other. As he drew near, Stanley arched an eyebrow. "Everything all right?"

"I'm going to check that baggage car once more."

"Should I come with you?"

"No need. I don't foresee any problems. Just want to give it one more look-see before I talk to the police in Columbus."

"Ah, yes, the police. If Henry followed through, as I'm sure he must've, then they'll be waiting at the station. Did you give the conductor or engineer some forewarning?"

"I mentioned it to the conductor after he asked me why I kept walking through the cars looking at all the passengers. He said he'd alert the engineer, but whether he actually followed through remains to be seen. He never made his way back here to let me know. Truth is, I don't think they care much. They've probably dealt with so many tussles on these trains that my conjecture is minor. I have no proof, and so far, nothing's happened to change that."

"Well, let's hope it stays that way," Charlotte put in. "It'd be much better if that fellow's intention back in New York was just to cause you alarm. After all, you did kidnap Clara, meaning you outsmarted them, and they can't be too happy about it. My opinion is, they want you to know they're plenty mad, but that's where it ends. It's not like you broke any law in taking her, so they can't report you to the authorities. Moreover, what good would it do them to chase all over the country after her and Maxine when they know very well you'd bring their actions to the attention of the authorities? They'd have to be fools to do that. No, I have to believe they will let the whole matter drop."

"You make some very strong points. I hope you're right." Luke turned to Stanley. "She's a smart woman. You ought to grab her up."

Luke glanced down at the pleasant-looking woman, noting the way she tipped her face up to meet Stanley's eyes. In that moment, Luke swore he saw love pass between them.

"I've been thinking the same thing, actually," he said with a sly grin. Charlotte blushed and looked down at her folded hands.

Well, now, isn't that something? Luke thought.

Baby Christina snuggled into Stanley's shoulder and closed her eyes. Luke reached up and rubbed a knuckle over her soft cheek. "Looks like Christina's finally conceding her need of a nap."

"It's about time," Stanley said, resting his chin on her downy head. "This trip has been hard on her—and on Charlotte."

"Well, you've been a great help to her—Charlotte, that is. No doubt you'll both hate giving this one up."

Charlotte raised her head again and nodded, her silence speaking volumes.

Luke smiled. "Well, I best get back to that baggage car for one more look." The train's whistle sounded. "I think we're coming into Columbus."

Stanley moved aside, allowing him to pass. Luke pulled open the door, shut it behind him, and stepped across the short platform between the two cars, reaching the baggage car door in two steps. It took a bit of muscle to open these doors, but he did it with little effort. His eyes had to do some adjusting to the darker car, but once they did, he received the shock of his life.

"Hey!" he yelled across the car. "What do you think you're doing?"

There was great commotion when they reached Columbus and Luke hauled a bedraggled-looking stowaway off the train by the scruff of his neck and passed him to the police. According to Luke, he'd been helping himself to the food supply for Sheltering Arms and rifling through all the baggage, looking for money and anything else of value. Evidently, the police recognized him, because one of the officers called him by name. Maggie overheard the officer telling Luke and Stanley that it wasn't the first time they'd caught the sponger riding the trains. He often emptied the largest container in the baggage car and made it into his bed, but this would be the last time, for they were hauling him off to the county jail. Of course, that explained the strange noises Maggie and Jenny had heard earlier; it also accounted for the fact that they'd been short a few lunches today. The sponger had been hiding out back there the entire time! Even now, while riding aboard one of three horse-drawn coaches escorting the children and adults to the First Methodist Church of Columbus, she shivered to think about it.

"Well, at least that leg of the trip is over, and we arrived unscathed despite that—that leech stowed away in the car behind us," Charlotte said, as if reading Maggie's very thoughts.

Maggie smiled and nodded as they bounced along, a babbling Lillian Reese in her lap. Snuggled in on either side of her were Rose Marie and Audrey. Charlotte was perched in the seat facing her, Christina asleep in her arms. Julia and Sofia Zielinski shared her seat, Sofia leaning over her sister to gawk and point out the window every so often, bantering back and forth with nervous excitement.

"Luke certainly has shown himself the hero on more than one occasion," Charlotte commented. "First, in his rescue of Clara, and now, with his discovery of that stowaway. Sheltering Arms owes him a great deal."

"Yes, he's quite the dandy, isn't he?"

Charlotte raised one sculpted brow. "You're not impressed, I take it."

"What? Well, I wouldn't say that. It's wonderful what he's done."

"But…?" she pressed.

How could Maggie begin to explain herself? That dratted kiss had turned her mind to pure mush. Why ever had he done it, and worse, why had she allowed it, even relished it? Mercy, only a promiscuous hussy would have fallen so willingly into his arms. She couldn't even count how many times she'd prayed for forgiveness, as much as she knew that one time sufficed in God's eyes.

She wanted to confess how very proud Luke made her, risking his life as he had to save Clara Warner—never mind that she'd played a minor role—and then wrestling down a thieving stowaway to bring him to justice. But she dared not confess such a thing, lest Charlotte see through her, perhaps even identify the love for Luke Madison that she hid in her heart.

Charlotte leaned in closer to whisper, "You were saying?"

"I—just meant to say that Luke is a—a definite asset to Sheltering Arms." She swallowed and added, "A *dandy* one."

"Ah, so that's what you meant to say, is it?" Charlotte narrowed her blue eyes and quirked her eyebrows, tilting her head inquisitively. She stared at Maggie for a few seconds. "Maggie Rose Kane, I do believe you've fallen for the newspaper man."

"What?" she said in a shrill whisper. She threw a hasty glance at the older girls, relieved to find them still engaged in excited chatter. "That's utterly—."

"Ridiculous?"

"Yes."

Charlotte nodded, a mischievous smile turning up the corners of her rosy mouth. She leaned back in her seat and tipped her chin the other direction, as if weighing in all the evidence. "You don't lie very well, Maggie."

Maggie heaved a sigh of resignation. "I know. I've always been bad at it."

Charlotte moistened her lips while adjusting her sleeping bundle, eyes trained on Maggie. "Well, now, what do you plan to do about this crush you have?"

Maggie opened her mouth. "I…." She clamped it shut, then opened it again to finish her thought. "Nothing. Absolutely nothing. There's nothing I can do."

How had it come to this? One second, she'd had her secret love locked up, safe and tight; the next, it was exposed like a front-page headline in the *World*. Dash and drat! That was the trouble with women. They could always read one another's hearts. If the Zielinski sisters had overheard, though, they didn't let on. Maggie suspected their minds weighed heavy of their own thoughts, and rightly so.

"I suppose you're right," Charlotte murmured over Christina's head. "After all, he's just here to do research. I expect he'll be going back to his beloved newspaper and his own apartment in a few weeks."

"Exactly." It peeved her that his absence at Sheltering Arms would create a void in her heart.

"And besides, you'll want to marry a man who shares your zeal for children, not to mention your devotion to the Lord."

She could only nod, for those were her thoughts exactly— not that she'd entertained any serious notions of marriage. "Yes, someone like Stanley, I suppose. Wouldn't you think? Of course, he appears to be taken." *Two can play this little game*, she reasoned. Charlotte glanced hurriedly out the window, trying to hide her smile but failing. Maggie leaned forward, coming as close to Charlotte's ear as possible without allowing the squirmy Lillian to slip off her lap.

"Wasn't it mere weeks ago you visited your beau in Boston?"

"If you'll recall, I told the girls that he isn't my beau—at least, not anymore. We've come to an understanding, Clyde and I. Our two families tried for years to bring us together, but it's clear we prefer to remain just friends. As a matter of fact, he confessed to me last month that he'd fallen in love with a young woman he met at the university. I'm thrilled for him."

Maggie sat back in her seat. "You're not hurt by the news?"

"More like relieved, actually. It made things much easier to confess I'd done the same—fallen in love with another, that is."

Maggie gasped. "Oh, Charlotte, I knew it. I just knew it! You and Stanley are meant to be together. You'll be married soon, then?"

Inside the coach, things grew still as several pairs of female eyes came to rest on Charlotte's blushing face. Maggie wanted to retract her words, but how could one call back a waterfall?

Finally, eleven-year-old Julia shrugged. "It's no big secret, Miss Charlotte. All us have known for months."

"You have?"

"Sure," Sofia said. "We all saw the writin' on the wall."

At that, the women burst out laughing. Apparently, this was not the day for withholding secrets.

"Look!" Julia put her forehead to the window and pointed. "There's a whole slew of folks standin' outside that church we're pullin' into. What you s'pect they're doing?"

Charlotte dipped her head to see out the window, and Maggie did the same. True enough, people were standing in large clusters, eyes wide with enthusiasm to welcome the three coaches packed with newcomers.

"I suspect they're here to see you," said Charlotte.

K

On the lawn behind the Methodist church, several tables were spread with the picnic dinner a group of women had prepared—vegetable soup, thick-sliced bread, apple wedges, and a variety of pies. The orphans ate as if this was the first meal they'd had in weeks. Actually, Luke did the same, for he had skipped lunch altogether so that there would be enough food for the children, even though some had been stolen by that sponger. Now, his stomach satisfied, he sat in the shade of a drooping, ageless oak and worked on his article while Maggie, Charlotte, and Stanley helped the youngsters prepare for their moment in the spotlight, the "distribution"—that time when they would each parade up to the church platform before countless spectators in hopes of finding a family. Not all of them looked enthusiastic about the prospect, but if they hoped to go home with new parents, they had no choice. The whole process put Luke in mind of an auction. Who would take the prize for best appearance? Who would find suitable homes tonight, and who would board the train for Springfield in the morning?

I will call her Catherine. She is roughly 12 or 13; I can't tell you her exact age, for she does not know it herself. Catherine has no family, having been deserted and then shoved from one person to another until the day she found herself begging at the front door of disaster. She thought he meant to help her, this man who offered her food and shelter, but instead, he meant to profit from her poverty—by selling her to a house of prostitution in the Upper East Side, an establishment called Miss Violet's Saloon, owned and operated by Miss Violet Harding....

"What you writin'?"

Luke glanced up from his pad of paper and set his pencil down. Looking about as tidy as any gangly teen could look with her hair pulled back in two tight braids and her new plaid jumper fairly hanging on her gaunt frame, Maxine awarded him a curious stare.

"Why don't you come and see for yourself?" He patted the grassy area next to him. She advanced in slow motion. "You look nice, by the way."

The tiniest glint flickered in her blue-green eyes. Someday, she would be a beautiful woman. She sat down with a *plop* and gathered her skirts about her. *But first, she'll galumph through this graceless phase,* Luke thought, smiling to himself.

"That your article?" she asked when he put the notebook under her nose.

"It is—what I have of it so far, anyway. Remember I told you I'd discuss it with you before handing it off to my editor?"

She sniffed and took the notebook in hand. "That'll be hard to do if I get adopted."

"Well, you're right about that. Somehow, I thought I would've finished it by now, but it feels like there's still more to see and learn. Sorry about that. We can discuss what I've written so far, if you'd like."

She nodded and set to reading. His heart thudded against his chest as if she were the critic he most had to please—and, perhaps, she was. Within minutes, she laid the notebook down, allowing him to breathe with relief.

"So, you're goin' to talk about Miss Violet's place?" she asked in a hushed voice.

"That all right with you? As you can see, I've changed Clara's name."

"Yeah, I saw that." She looked overhead where a cluster of birds sat perched on a branch. Forehead scrunched, she kept her eyes trained on them. "What name you gonna give me?"

"What's that?"

"Ain't you goin' to talk about me when you tell the story? I'm the one who tol' you 'bout Clara in the first place."

"I thought you didn't want me to mention you."

"Well, as long as you can do it without lettin' on who I am, then I s'pose it's okay."

"Really? It'd make the story more interesting, and I'd be careful not to reveal your identity. I'm thinking if I do it right, this article could make quite an impact on folks. Might spur them into donating to Sheltering Arms, or perhaps to another agency around New York. The city needs to know about the problem of homeless children, not to mention the cost involved in providing for them."

She seemed to ponder his words. "I've always liked the name Susan."

"Susan?"

"Yeah, for my fake name."

"I can do that."

They sat in a warm blanket of silence, the afternoon sun shining its rays through the branches while the birds chirped.

Smells of vegetable soup still wafted through the air as the volunteers went about cleaning up the remains of the picnic supper and dressed-up children walked solemn-faced around the churchyard, careful not to soil their new clothes.

"Do you pray?" Maxine asked, breaking into his thoughts with a question that seemed out of the blue.

"Wh—do I…? Yeah, sometimes. Do you?"

"I do now, 'cause I asked Jesus into my heart."

"You did? Recently?" He didn't know why the news made him want to fidget.

"How did that come about?"

"I listened close to the sermon for a change and realized I was a sinner. I did it all on my own, too—asked Him into my heart, that is. You're the first person I told."

"I am? Well, what do you know? I'm honored." He smiled admiringly at her. Then, he pulled a long blade of grass from the ground and studied its perfection, knowing in his heart that Someone had created it. Trouble was, that same Someone allowed tragedies of the worst magnitude, and that's where the problem lay. Like a flash, the ugly memory of the June 15 boat disaster anchored itself in his mind. Would he never come to grips with it? Never reach a point of letting go long enough to receive the lesson God had for him, if indeed there was a lesson to be learned?

Annalise, I miss you, he mused.

"Yeah, so I'm starting to feel some better about my life and stuff."

A misting in his eyes had him briefly turning his face the other way. "That's great," he managed, amazed by the depth of his emotion wrought by her confession. The young lady had made some serious changes just since the rescue of Clara Warner.

In the distance, a train whistled. Luke glanced across the churchyard and spotted Maggie conversing with one of the volunteers, one hand making animated gestures as she talked, the other wrapped securely around the front of Rose Marie, holding her close. A thrill of remembrance rushed through him—the feel of his lips pressed against hers, his arms encircling her feminine frame, her mesmerizing citrus scent wafting over him—and it gave him pause. How did it happen that in one second, his beloved Annalise could fill his thoughts, but in the next, Maggie Rose was all he could see, touch, and smell?

"You think that ol' Byron's still goin' t' come lookin' for Clara and me?"

The blunt question landed Luke squarely back in the present. He gave his head a quick shake. "Nah. It'd be downright stupid of Byron to come after you at this point." He did not intend to tell her how he'd suspected Byron to be on the train. "I mean, he'd have nothing to gain from it, except maybe a salvage of pride. But then, I'd have the law all over him. So, no, you needn't worry." In fact, he'd stopped worrying about Byron himself, for the most part, especially since he hadn't a single piece of evidence to prove he'd jumped aboard the train. He thought about the stowaway he'd wrestled with on the baggage car and dragged off the train by his ear. Once that fiasco was over, he'd actually relaxed.

"That's what I thought." She looked at her hands, clasped in her lap, and twisted her face into a frown. Overhead, the birds silenced themselves, as if to eavesdrop.

He dipped his face to see into her eyes. "Unless you knew something he didn't want you to know. That would be the only reason I could think of that he'd come looking for you."

There followed a long, intense silence. Maxine kneaded her hands in a fretful manner, and Luke suddenly tamped down his own brand of worry. Finally, she looked up. "Well, then, there is one little thing."

Chapter Twenty-four

W hat one little thing might that be?"

Maxine winced, as if it pained her to go on. "There's this guy who comes in the saloon a lot. He's part owner or something. Byron was arguing with Violet one day, sayin' something about that feller shouldn't ought t' come around so much. Said he's diggin' his own grave— whatever that means—and he ought t' be more discreet 'fore he gets 'em all in trouble."

"I thought Violet was the sole owner."

"Naw. That fellow and Violet are partners. I think Byron would like a piece of the pie, but he probably ain't rich enough, or he doesn't got the smarts for it. Anyways, he got mad when he saw me standin' at the counter—said I was listenin' in, and it weren't my business. I told him I wasn't listenin', and even if I was, it was boring stuff. Truth is, I saw that fellow and Violet pass a lot of money between 'em."

"What's his name?"

She shrugged and started to stand. "I can't remember. 'Sides, it probably don't matter."

"Wait a minute, young lady." He snagged her by the arm and pulled her back down beside him. Apprehension and surprise pooled in her shiny, silverish eyes as she looked at his hand still wrapped around her skinny forearm. He quickly released his hold. "Sorry. You know I wouldn't hurt you."

She gave a nod and exhaled slowly. "I know."

"So, this man. You sure you don't remember his name?"

She gnawed on her lower lip and shook her head, crumpling her eyes into slits. "It's—something like Horace Blackstone—or Blakely." She scratched her temple. "Or maybe it's Bramley or Brawley. Horace Brawley. I tol' you, I can't remember. I think he's somebody important, though."

"What makes you say that?"

"'Cause some other guys in black suits always come in with him, sort of like his watchdogs."

"You mean bodyguards."

"Yeah. One of 'em looks sort of like Byron. Big and ugly, that is."

Luke pondered her words, his mind racing with possibilities. "This guy you think is part owner—what does he look like?"

"I don't know. Why do you want to know?"

"Because now you've raised my curiosity, Miss Ward. I'm a newspaper reporter, remember?" He tried making light of the situation by nudging her gently with his elbow. "Humor me, okay?"

A few seconds passed while she thought on it. "Well, he's older 'n you, I s'pose, sort of tall, has dark brown hair and a skinny moustache that curls up at the ends, and a little beard, a goat-something."

"Goatee?"

"Yeah, that's it. That's about all I can think of, 'cept that he sits at the gamblin' table a lot. And he likes the women. He usually gots a different one 'bout every night."

He pictured him now—the familiar-looking man he'd seen that night when he'd rescued Clara. He summoned up the memory of him stopping on the stairs to gaze down at him, almost as if he, too, had a sense of knowing Luke but couldn't recall just how. Unfortunately, Luke still couldn't place him, and until now, he had forgotten all about him. Who was he, and what significance, if any, did he play? Moreover, why did he travel with bodyguards?

"Children, gather round. I need to talk to all of you." Stanley gained everyone's attention, including that of Luke and Maxine, with his deep, clear voice. "I want to give you all a few more words of instruction before the town meeting takes place and then say a prayer for you."

K

Maggie's heart pounded with anxiety as all the pews in the little Methodist church started filling. She looked at the gold watch her father had given her for her eighteenth birthday. The seven o'clock meeting would start in less than fifteen minutes, and anyone else who entered would have to stand at the back. From her seat in the third row, she had a good view of the children on the stage. Rose Marie sat in a chair too high for her, legs swinging back and forth and squirming, making Maggie wonder if she should have taken her out to the necessary one last time. The child peered over the crowd of people, and Maggie caught her eye, giving her as reassuring a smile as possible. She was thankful when Maxine, seated next to Rose Marie, reached down to give her hand a squeeze. Clara, wide-eyed and pale, if not a tad faint, looked ready to bolt, and she may have, had it not been for Maxine's whispered words, whatever they were.

Lord Jesus, Your will be done tonight. Please calm these children's nerves and shepherd the right people to each of them, matching them with the best possible homes and families.

No sooner had she uttered the prayer than a female voice behind her said, "My, look at them all sitting on the stage in a neat little row, feet crossed, hands folded in their laps so nicely. Aren't they sweet?"

"Doubt they're quite as sweet as they look," another retorted in a loud whisper just as baby Christina cut loose a hair-raising scream from Charlotte's lap. Poor Charlotte had her hands full trying to quiet the baby at the front of the church. She didn't look the least bit ruffled, though, Maggie thought, not like she would be if *she* was the one sitting in that row of chairs, a hundred pairs of eyes gawking at her. "Wouldn't you think that girl would leave the stage?"

Maggie turned slightly to catch a peripheral view of the women seated behind her, noting they all wore flowery hats and were dressed to the nines, as if the occasion called for it. As Uncle Herbie had promised, folks would come out in droves just to watch the proceedings, more curious about the New York orphans than they were eager to adopt them.

"I wish I could take one home with me, but Harold would have my hide," the first one said, giggling. "That brood of ours practically eats us poor as paupers. Last thing he said to me when I walked out the door was, 'Esther, don't you even go getting any notions 'bout bringing home another mouth to feed.'" The other ladies laughed.

"He's smart," one of them said. "We're livin' in hard times. Don't imagine it'd be cheap or easy to take in some stranger's child, especially one all grown up."

"Those big ones could help on the farm," the one called Esther said in a reasoning tone. "And the bigger girls could cook and do house chores, not to mention tend to the babies."

Maggie wanted to turn completely around and give them all a giant piece of her mind. Didn't they know these children needed love first and foremost? That the assignments of chores would come later, once the newcomers eased into their family settings?

"Well, I'm plumb too old for takin' on another youngun," another one of the women chimed in. "I done raised my litter. Orville would have a conniption."

Maggie was about to give the women a stern look when Luke entered her pew. He squeezed past three people she didn't know and sat down beside her, his shoulder brushing hers as he settled back against the pew, arms folded across his chest, lanky legs spread, as if his sitting there was the most natural thing in the world. She certainly hadn't expected this, but much as she hated to admit it, it did feel rather nice, his musky scent making her somewhat dizzy.

"Well, now, I can't even see," the woman directly behind Luke grumbled.

If he had overheard—and only a deaf man wouldn't have—he ignored the remark. "You okay?" he whispered in Maggie's ear, so close that his breath effected a chill that ran up her spine.

"I'm fine, thank you." She trained her eyes on the fidgeting children, trying not to let on that his closeness rattled her. On either side of them and behind, the conversations continued.

"Really? I notice you've been casting me the same kind of looks you might give a bad rash. Wouldn't have anything to do with that kiss we shared, would it?"

"Shh. This is neither the time nor place for discussing—that—that—."

"Kiss. You can't even say the word."

"Stop it."

"You're still thinking about it, then."

"I most certainly am not. We both know it was a mistake, and for your information, I have not wasted one second of my time dwelling on it." *But I have wasted several hours,* she amended in her head. "Now, would you kindly drop the matter—and move over, while you're at it?"

He'd been leaning against her side. "Sorry, not possible. These are cramped quarters."

She glanced around him and said in a hissing tone, "Then you shouldn't have crowded in here."

He did nothing about adjusting his position but merely gazed forward. "How many do you think will go home with new families tonight?"

His question drained her of her indignation and actually made her go limp to remember her anxiety. She raised her shoulders and then let them slump. "I have no idea." In the front row, a young couple happily held Cora Van Sanden and Lillian Reese in their laps. "It looks like at least two of the babies will go home with that couple by the name of Ferguson. They sent in their application two months ago and traveled a hundred miles to get here. I don't know about the rest of the children, though, do you? Seems to me, most folks are just here to see a show, the way they're all laughing and conversing."

He looked around. "It does appear they're here out of curiosity more than anything else."

Just then, Stanley walked to the podium. As if on cue, Christina hushed, almost like she sensed something important in the works. One by one, folks ceased their chatter and faced forward.

"Good evening, folks. The people of Sheltering Arms Refuge want to thank you for coming out tonight."

⌒*K*⌒

Stanley gave a five-minute history of Sheltering Arms Refuge, then introduced the children, telling something special about each one and taking care not to go into detail about their sordid backgrounds. The girls stood and curtsied in the manner in which Charlotte and Maggie had taught them; the boys bowed at the waist. Their fine comportment evoked several "oohs" and "ahs" from the audience, who applauded lightly after each introduction. Even Ricky complied with the rules they'd established beforehand, as much as he didn't want anyone from Columbus adopting Stuart and him. No, he'd set his heart on Lincoln, Nebraska.

Stanley explained that the children would go home with their prospective families for a trial period. If, during that time, a child or a family felt the match unsuccessful, and if no amount of counseling could rectify it, the child would either return to Sheltering Arms or take another placement. In the beginning, Sheltering Arms required biweekly letters of correspondence to ensure healthy adjustments and scheduled two home visits in the first year, tapering off in subsequent years if all went well.

After Stanley's talk, those folks interested in fostering or adopting children were invited to come forward and pose questions to individual children. Those who had come merely to watch the proceedings were asked kindly to stay put or to be excused. Luke heard Maggie's sharp intake of air as a few folks stood up and walked forward. Instinctively, he put a steadying arm around her shoulder, more to soothe his own apprehension than anything. To his surprise, she did not pull back but rather leaned into him, if only a fraction. They seemed to draw on each other for support. He'd underestimated the poignancy and suspense of watching potential parents select a child. At what point had these children come to mean so much to him?

"Oh, dear Father, please have Your way in these agonizing decisions. May each one be made with heartfelt prayers for guidance from You," Maggie whispered.

"Yes, amen," Luke agreed, his chest pounding through his shirt, his face close to Maggie's as he said it. "Make it so, Lord." He couldn't believe how easily the prayer slipped past his lips or how genuine it felt to utter it. Maggie lifted her face to him, her eyes shimmering with tears.

"It'll be all right," he assured her, pulling her closer to him. "Keep up those prayers." She nodded and quickly focused her attention back to the children.

It was fascinating to observe how a couple seemed drawn to a particular child, and the child to the couple. For instance, Audrey Wilson, expression initially wary and guarded, eyed an approaching couple in their mid- to late thirties. When the woman bent close to whisper something in Audrey's ear and then gently touched her shiny braid, it didn't take long for a shy smile to emerge on Audrey's face. And just like that, all three of them were laughing as though they'd all landed on an amusing topic when, really, they were just testing the waters of a new beginning.

A lump the size of a peach pit lodged in Luke's throat at the realization they'd be saying good-bye to Audrey. And then there were Julia and Sofia Zielinski, both sitting pretty as could be, when a husband and wife and a little girl about six years of age stepped forward to introduce themselves. Julia did most of the talking while Sofia listened, eyes moving from the man to the woman and then to their daughter, who was hiding behind her mother's skirts. What was going on in the sisters' minds? Were they thinking of what might have been, had their own family not fallen apart? Were they asking how they'd ever come to be put in this awkward position of counting on strangers to care for them?

Allen Kramer and Vivian Pelton looked detached from the whole event, sitting at the end of the line, huddling close and whispering. This had to be difficult for them, Luke mused, given that their childish hearts belonged to each other. Unfortunately, they were too young to have things their way. In time, they would probably forget their bond. He wished Stanley would tell them to sit up and pay attention. He didn't want them missing out on the chance for a placement.

At evening's close, it looked like Audrey Wilson, the Zielinski girls, babies Cora and Lillian, and seven-year-old Billy Harper would have new homes. With the help of the Methodist minister, who was responsible for advertising the train's stopover in Columbus, Stanley reviewed legal documents and numerous details with the adoptive parents and families. Meanwhile, everyone else gathered around the children who had been placed to bid them farewell. Maggie quickly left Luke's side, mentioning something about taking Rose Marie to the outhouse before she had an accident. He nodded, noting how the poor little thing had jumped from her chair and set to doing a little "dance" that could mean only one thing.

And that's when he noticed the man standing in the shadows by the front side exit, face mostly hidden by his low-set, wide-brimmed business hat. Luke spotted something oddly familiar about his stance—the way he posed as if for a camera, shoulders drawn back in a professional air, arms slack at his sides.

Blast! He should have known better than to blink, for that was all it took for the mystery man to disappear.

Chapter Twenty-five

"All aboooard!" the conductor bellowed at seven-thirty the next morning, rain pelting the overhang under which everyone was huddled for protection. Jagged fingers of lightning flashed across the sky, followed by deep, guttural claps of thunder, making the electric light bulbs inside the station flicker off and on.

How strange to be boarding the train with six fewer orphans—strange, but good, Maggie told herself. To her great relief, Audrey, Julia, Sofia, and Billy had left with waves and smiles. No tears had been shed, and for that, she was thankful. Even the babies had only cooed and giggled. All that remained was to trust the Lord that the children had been handed off to the best families possible.

From the look of the overcrowded station, it appeared the entire city of Columbus intended to ride the passenger train heading for Springfield, but in actuality, many were just bidding loved ones good-bye. At the conductor's call, the travelers made a dash for the train, covering their heads with everything from umbrellas to newspapers to scarves and hats. As she and Luke, Charlotte, and Stanley herded the orphans toward their car at the rear, Maggie wondered if Luke planned to check the baggage car for stowaways. He certainly had his eye out for something the way he'd been gazing off ever since arriving at the station that morning, scrutinizing everyone who passed and failing to engage in conversation, even when Stanley or one of the children addressed him. She couldn't help but wonder what busy thoughts filled his mind.

"How long's our train ride today?" Maxine asked in an unusually cheerful voice.

"Almost as long as yesterday's, I think," Stanley said. "You're sounding very chipper this morning."

Maxine made it to the door first, with Clara on her heels. "Why wouldn't I be?" she chimed. "Just because it's raining ain't no call for being grumpy."

"My!" Charlotte said, stepping up behind Clara with Christina in her arms, the baby's head covered by a downy blanket. Stanley followed her, trailed by Maggie, and Luke brought up the end of the line. "It's so nice to hear you talk that way."

"Me and Clara decided to be on ar' best behavior," Maxine supplied while choosing a seat in the middle of the car. She plopped down next to the window, and Clara fell in beside her. "'Course, Clara don't have to work at it like I do. She's jus' naturally nice."

"I think you're plenty nice," Clara said in her usual soft manner. "It's just that you got that inborn impulse to disagree with folks."

Stanley laughed out loud. "What will you two do without each other? Seems to me Clara brings out the best in you, Maxine."

"We plan to pass letters back and forth," Clara said. "If God answers ar' prayers, we might even end up in the same town, so's we can visit each other sometimes."

"Now, wouldn't that be ideal?" Charlotte exclaimed, settling into a seat a few rows ahead of the girls. Stanley sat down next to her. By now, it seemed understood that they would share a seat.

Christina wriggled and fussed in Charlotte's lap, so she handed her to Stanley and pulled a bottle of milk from her satchel. With the baby's first suckle, she quieted and relaxed against Stanley's chest. He grinned. "I have the touch. Babies just naturally love me."

"Oh, please," Charlotte giggled. "Any baby would love you if you stuck a bottle in her mouth."

Maggie smiled at their banter and took the seat directly behind Maxine and Clara, inviting Rose Marie to sit with her. Ever since rising that morning, the little girl had been especially clingy and quiet. She'd slept poorly in the big feather bed they had shared at the parsonage, waking up every hour and needing attention. *Poor dear*, Maggie thought. What must be going on in her young mind? "Will somebody pick me at the next place?" she'd asked Maggie at 3:30 that morning.

"I don't know, darling," she'd answered, gathering the girl's tiny body in her arms and drawing the blankets up around her chin, wanting to encourage without giving false hope. "We will have to wait and see."

"What if somebody I don't like chooses me?"

"Well, now, you won't know you don't like them right off. You'll have to think positive thoughts. Don't worry, honey. I've been praying that God will place all of you with exactly the right parents. All we can do is trust Him in these matters."

That seemed to satisfy her for the time being—that is, until she awoke an hour later to ask the same questions all over again.

Maggie placed her satchel on the floor and situated herself in her seat. Rose Marie gave a little shiver, lay her head in Maggie's lap, and closed her eyes. It was certainly no surprise that the little girl was tired. Maggie wove her fingers through her damp tresses and sighed. Vivian and Allen raced past, calling dibs on the last seat, no doubt anxious to spend as much time together as possible in these final hours. Maggie couldn't help but wonder how they would handle their parting.

Luke was last to board the car, and not a second too soon, either, for just as he landed in the seat directly across the aisle from Maggie—his face altogether too grim, even considering the sunless skies—the train's whistle sounded, and the lengthy stretch of iron and steel started rumbling down the tracks.

An hour into the ride, Maggie started thinking Rose Marie's forehead felt warm to the touch. Moreover, every time the train took a curve or hit a snag in the tracks, she moaned and clutched her belly. Wanting to express her concern to Charlotte, but not wishing to disturb Rose Marie, she remained seated and whispered a prayer that whatever ailment had befallen the poor child, it would quickly run its course.

As if sensing something was amiss, Luke raised his eyebrows at her. "Everything all right?" It was the first time he'd acknowledged her since boarding the train, so intent had he been on writing in his notebook. She'd have liked to be a little bird looking over his shoulder.

She gestured at Rose Marie and mouthed, "She feels hot."

He quickly laid down his notebook and pencil and moved across the aisle, placing a hand on Rose Marie's forehead.

His face crinkled with concern. "You're not kidding," he murmured.

"What can we do for her?"

"I'll go back and get some water," he said. "A cool cloth would probably feel good to her."

"Yes, a cool cloth. That would be a comfort. Shall we tell Stan and Charlotte?"

"Not yet. No point in causing a stir."

Maggie nodded. "You're right. It's probably just a little tummy ache. I'm sure she'll be feeling fine when we arrive in Springfield."

Luke studied the girl for a few seconds, his forehead still crumpled with concern. "I hope you're right."

But she wasn't. By the time they arrived in Springfield, poor Rose Marie had emptied her stomach three times, the first being the worst in that most of her breakfast landed in Maggie's lap. Luke made fast work of cleaning up, running to the baggage car to rinse out a rag in a bucket, then rushing back to the passenger car to wipe the mess from her skirts. With no time for feeling self-conscious, she did as he instructed, stayed put to care for Rose Marie, while he tended to her needs in a completely selfless, efficient manner. In the meantime, children groaned at the dreadful odor, and Dag Haskell, having a weak stomach, heaved his breakfast, as well. "Everyone move as far away as possible," Luke said in an authoritative voice. "And if the smell bothers you, cover your noses. We'll have this taken care of in no time."

But "no time" still amounted to fifteen minutes. Charlotte handed Christina to Maxine so she could help Luke, and Stanley saw to Dag, who started recovering immediately once Clara began fanning his face with a newspaper. Unfortunately, the air never completely cleared, and Maggie suspected the floor would need a good scrubbing, not to mention her long flowing skirts. She could hardly wait to retrieve her change of clothes from her satchel.

"I don't feel so good," Rose Marie whimpered weakly when the train rolled into Springfield, its high-pitched whistle signaling their arrival, the locomotive's wheels screeching to a stop. Outside, the rain sliced against the windowpanes, ruthless and unrelenting.

Maggie put her arm around the ailing child and drew her close, sympathy running deep. "I know, sweetheart, but you'll soon be good as new, you'll see."

"When?" She hiccupped and brushed a hand over her forehead. Her blue eyes seemed almost too large for her pale, oval face that angled up at Maggie.

Maggie dropped her chin to the child's downy head and made eye contact with Luke. "Soon," she whispered.

He smiled and mouthed, "You okay?"

She nodded and mouthed back, "Fine, thank you."

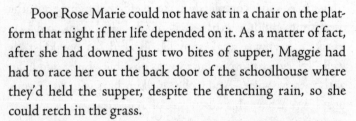

Poor Rose Marie could not have sat in a chair on the platform that night if her life depended on it. As a matter of fact, after she had downed just two bites of supper, Maggie had had to race her out the back door of the schoolhouse where they'd held the supper, despite the drenching rain, so she could retch in the grass.

Twice as many people filled the Springfield City Hall that night as had shown up at the Columbus Methodist Church, which meant double the noise and excitement and double the dankness of the crowded room. Luke kept an eye out from the back of the room for the elusive stranger who'd poked his head in the door of the Methodist church last night, but he never spotted him, making him think that he'd overreacted yet again. He needed to get a grip on himself before he went completely crazy. He was beginning to think he had as vivid an imagination as a mystery novelist.

Stanley delivered much the same speech as he had the night before, but with six fewer orphans to introduce, his presentation ended much earlier. When he issued an invitation for folks to step forward for a look at the available orphans, only ten or so couples moved out of their places. Maggie tried to remain calm, especially for the sake of Rose Marie, who was curled up like a kitten in her lap. Luke noticed the concern on her face, momentarily regretting his decision not to sit with her. But then, he pulled his brow into a rigid frown, realizing that somewhere along the line, he'd assumed the responsibility of easing her cares—and he didn't like it. He didn't see himself in any kind of position to look after her, not with his heart still so raw over his loss of Annalise and Aunt Frances. Besides, wouldn't she consider him a poor risk in light of his pathetic lack of spiritual wisdom and maturity, not to mention his lack of commitment? He shook his head for even pondering the question, leaned against the wall, and turned his attention to the front of the room, where folks had struck up conversations with various children.

One couple approached Dag but quickly walked on when he announced in a shrill voice that he'd thrown up that day. The Pelton sisters drew some attention, but Vivian put on her most aloof face—until another couple initiated a conversation with the Kramers. Luke imagined the teenagers' elation if they were to wind up in the same town. But soon, those couples moved down the line to speak to the rest of the children. It appeared they wanted to weigh their options. Again, the concept of an auction came to mind, and Luke had the strongest urge to shout from the podium that every one of these children deserved more than a cursory glance. When a rather corpulent woman demanded Stuart Campbell open his mouth so she could determine the condition of his teeth, Luke really had to exercise self-control. Suddenly, he found himself saying a prayer much like the one he'd heard Maggie whisper the night before. "Lord, please direct the right people to the children best suited for their homes and families. If they are not in this room, then may we all board the train together in the morning."

And that is exactly what they did—with the exception of Dag Haskell, that is, who wound up going home with a Baptist family, and the Garrison boys, who went home with a friendly middle-aged couple who owned a large dairy farm five miles out of town.

And when they boarded the train bound for Lincoln bright and early the next morning, there were still ten orphans in need of homes.

Early morning light bathed the sleepy train occupants in a reddish glow, but its brightness did not produce the warmth of a midsummer day. No, today's sunlight felt more like the true beginnings of autumn, crisp and chilled, yesterday's rain having ushered in a wave of cool, brisk air.

Maggie covered Rose Marie's thin shoulders with a blanket, drawing her close. At least the child's temperature felt normal, and her breakfast of lightly buttered bread had stayed down thus far. She'd even slept the full night through, which was more than Maggie could say for herself; the lumpy mattress they'd occupied in a kind parishioner's extra bedroom gave her a chronic backache. Then, too, there was the worry over all the children who still needed homes, even though she knew in her heart that God had a perfect plan for each of them and that worrying wouldn't accomplish a single thing.

She brushed her fingers through Rose Marie's hair and thought about how much she'd come to love her—and all the children, for that matter. But she especially loved Rose Marie. Part of her secretly wanted to bring the little girl back to Sheltering Arms, where she could keep a protective eye on her until the next train set out in the spring. But then, she told herself how much better a permanent residence would be for Rose Marie, and the sooner, the better.

A solemn air filled the car. Gone was the unmatched enthusiasm of Monday morning, when they'd first set off from New York, and Maggie suspected that the lack came from fatigue, as well as apprehension and insecurity. While none of the children had said as much, she had to believe they were asking themselves why no one had picked them back in Columbus or Springfield. Luke must have had the same sense, for from three seats back, she heard him comment that Lincoln, Nebraska, was a big city. "I bet folks will come out in droves tonight."

"Sure, a ton will come to gawk at us," Jenny said. "They just want to see what orphans look like—see if we have crossed eyes or an extra arm."

"Jenny Pelton, don't be crude," her sister scolded.

"Well, it's true! Why else would they fill up the city halls and churches if they didn't intend to take one of us home? They just plain want to gawk, that's all. I, for one, feel stupid sitting up on that platform like some kind of doll on a shelf while customers try to choose which one of us has the prettiest face."

"That's not what they're doing, sweetie," Maggie said, turning around. "It's true, folks are curious, but not in a bad way."

Luke nodded. "Remember, too, that six of you are siblings, and Sheltering Arms holds strictly to the policy that brothers and sisters are to be kept together. A lot of families just aren't in a position to take more than one child."

"Don't matter to me if they keep us together," Peter said. "Ol' Allen's probably goin' to up and marry Vivian one day soon, anyways. I heard 'em say that no matter who winds up takin' us all in, soon as Viv gets of age, they're goin' to elope."

"Which won't be for at least another year and a half, silly," Allen said.

Maggie caught Luke's eye, and they shared a brief, tentative smile. "In the meantime, you and I stick together, little brother, just like Viv and Jenny are going to do."

Allen's words came as a relief to Maggie. She'd been worried the young couple might do something rash, like run off together. It pleased her to see that Allen was thinking sensibly.

"Hot diggity, then!" Peter exclaimed.

Allen laughed. "I guess you want me around more than you care to admit, huh, little brother?"

"Long as you don't boss me from mornin' till night."

"Well, now, don't go expecting the impossible."

As the banter continued, the children's spirits seemed to lift. By noontime, even Rose Marie had started acting like her old self again, and the lunch the ladies' guild had packed for them went straight down her gullet and stayed there.

Lincoln's train station came into view at a quarter to five. It seemed a mob of folks had turned out for the train's arrival—men and women, boys and girls, most of them wearing expectant faces. Maggie peered through the smudged glass, not wishing to awaken Rose Marie from her all-too-brief nap until the last possible minute.

"How're you holding up? You tired?"

Maggie turned at the sound of Luke's voice. "I'm fine, thank you."

He chuckled. "Do you know you almost always say you're fine?"

"I do? Well, the alternative would be to sulk, I suppose, and what would that accomplish? I much prefer to keep a positive outlook."

"Even when the situation doesn't call for it—like yesterday, for instance, when that little one tossed her cookies all over your skirt?" He gestured at the child in her lap.

She smothered a moment of laughter with the palm of her hand. "Oh, my. That was a disaster. You were very kind to come to my rescue as you did. It couldn't have been pleasant for you. And, now that I think on it, I don't think I've adequately thanked you."

His eyes gleamed with mischief as he turned toward her and leaned across the aisle, speaking in a low, dusky voice. "Did you have something in mind—for thanking me more thoroughly, that is?"

"What? Well, I...."

"Perhaps another meeting in the baggage car?"

She raised her chin and put on her best glare. "I think not."

"You can't tell me you haven't thought about that kiss."

"Would you kindly stop bringing that up?"

"Why? Because it bothers you that you can't stop thinking about it?"

She opened and closed her mouth, unsure of how to take him or even what to say. Oh, how it perturbed her when he said things purposely to ruffle her.

His chuckle evolved into a gale of laughter. Failing to see the humor in the moment, she ignored him and reached for her cape, which was draped over the seat in front of her, and looked out the smeared window to see where folks were milling about, awaiting the train's complete stop.

"Don't worry, Miss Kane. I understand entirely that you are far superior to me on a spiritual scale. Kissing me again would go against your principles."

She jerked her head around to look at him, but he'd already risen from his seat and moved into the aisle.

Oh, Lord, that man is such a bafflement to me. I hate that I love him.

Chapter Twenty-six

L uke berated himself for his loutish behavior. How could he be so callous and downright rude to such a lovely person, taking such pleasure in watching her blush and squirm? Talking with her—just looking at her, in fact—forced him to look within, and he didn't like what he saw. Since the *General Slocum* disaster, he'd turned hard about matters of the heart.

Lord, if I am ever going to heal from the inside out, I need to learn to trust You and submit to Your divine will for my life— whatever it is and wherever it takes me.

The sudden, silent assertion slammed against him like a sledgehammer, and, for a moment, he felt numb. Where had it come from, this newfound revelation? It occurred to him then that God was knocking at his heart's door, but something kept him from opening it fully. Was it fear, or just plain stubbornness?

As soon as the children and adults had gathered on the train platform, a number of folks approached them. Leading the pack was a middle-aged fellow in a dark, wrinkled suit, his belt buckle coming just below his portly belly, a smile stretching from one sagging jowl to the other. Next to him was a woman of similar age, but she was more smartly dressed. "Is this the group from the Sheltering Arms Refuge?" the man asked in a gravelly voice.

"Yes, sir, it is," Luke answered, since the fellow had directed the question at him.

The man removed his bowler hat. "Well, fine to see you. I'm Reverend Joseph Ardmore of the Park Street Presbyterian Church, and this is my wife, Helen." He extended a hand. "Might you be Stanley Barrett?"

"No, sir," Luke said, shaking his hand anyway, then smiling and nodding at the man's wife. "I'm Luke Madison, a newspaper reporter for the *New York World.* I'm just along for the ride, helping where I can. Stan is—well, he's the one handing the baby to that woman over there."

Spying the two men talking, Stanley quickly wove his way through the cluster of children and adults to get to the preacher. "I'm Stanley Barrett." He stuck out his hand. "Reverend Miles tells me you two are old friends."

"Ah, yes, yes—I went to college and seminary with that old whippersnapper." He shook Stanley's hand like it was a stubborn pump handle. "'Course, we had to part ways once I went Presbyterian and he took the Methodist route." He said this with a poker face but in seconds gave way to a burst of laughter. "I'm just joshing you, son. Herb and I have stayed fast friends for years. Matter of fact, I've been in contact with him for the past several weeks concerning this train of orphans. Folks are excited to meet them. And here's the proof." He made a sweeping gesture with his arm toward the cluster of people surrounding the children, all smiling and nodding. "Brought along our church consistory and several other members to help welcome you to our fine city."

While the group waited for the train personnel to empty out the baggage car so that Luke and Stanley could claim their boxes, several people stepped up to initiate conversations with the orphans. It pleased Luke to see a man strike up a chat with Stuart and Ricky, and the pastor's wife seemed especially interested in engaging Maxine and Clara. As usual, little Rose Marie clung like a magnet to Maggie's side, big round eyes surveying everyone present, perchance envisioning how it would be to go home with them. As if sensing her fear, Maggie bent down to pick her up. Rose Marie wrapped her legs around Maggie's waist and rested her head on her shoulder. Luke suspected the girl still carried a trace of yesterday's illness.

"Well, perhaps we should mosey toward our carriages," the reverend announced once the conversations had died down and they'd claimed their belongings. Volunteers kindly offered to carry the crates so that Luke and Stanley could tend the children. "They're parked on the other side of the street, so we'll walk through the underground tunnel to get there. Best all stick close together, though, as this is a mighty busy place. It wouldn't be wise if we lost someone."

"We're goin' through a tunnel?" Stuart asked. "Hot diggity!"

The preacher grinned. "That we are, and then on to the parish hall for a nice supper before our seven o'clock meeting. You do like chicken and mashed potatoes, I hope? The ladies of the congregation have been working hard all day to prepare a meal."

"You bet we do!" Stuart answered on everyone's behalf.

"As long as you got gravy to go with the taters," Peter tacked on.

"Oh, my, yes," the preacher said, glancing back to give the boys a wink. "Come to think of it, I believe the ladies doubled the recipe just in case a couple of famished lads showed up."

They started moving through the crowded station, and Luke stepped up beside Maggie. "I'll carry her," he said, opening his arms to take Rose Marie. Happily, she went into them, encircling his neck with her arms.

"Oh, thank you," Maggie said. "She might be a little thing, but she still gets heavy."

After that, they walked in silence, listening to the chatter going on around them.

There were more than enough carriages and volunteer drivers, so Luke, Maggie, and Rose Marie were the only passengers in one of them. Luke placed the girl on the seat facing them, and she immediately rose up on her knees to peer outside.

Just as he reached across Maggie's lap to close the door, the preacher poked his hand inside the cab. Out of breath, he spoke with a sheepish tone. "This telegram came to the parsonage earlier today. I'm sorry I forgot to give it to you immediately after we met. Plain slipped my mind."

Luke took the envelope with mild curiosity. Who would be sending him a telegram? "No problem," he assured him. At that, the preacher nodded and closed the cab door.

Luke didn't open the telegram that instant; rather, he fingered it for the first few minutes of the ride as he answered Rose Marie's endless questions. "What's that building?" "Who lives there?" "What does that say?" "How come that lady's carryin' a umbrella when it ain't rainin'?" "What's those people sellin'?"

After her questions finally tapered off and the child simply took to gawking at all the sights, he broke the envelope seal and unfolded the thin piece of paper within. Although Maggie didn't inquire, he knew her curiosity burned like fire just to know the telegram's contents. He squinted and scanned the words.

> Threat could be real. Floretta made several confessions. Some NY congressman is investing in houses of prostitution. Floretta has not named names. He may be watching you. Call police if situation warrants. Praying for you all. Henry

He folded the paper, digested its contents in his head, then unfolded and reread it.

"Is everything all right?" Maggie asked over his shoulder.

Luke scratched his head and gazed out the window, as if to find answers there, then exhaled deeply and angled her a glance. "I'm trying to make some sense of this telegram."

"What do you mean? Who sent it?"

"Henry. Here, you can read it."

He handed it over. She read it quickly, scowling in confusion. "I don't understand. What does he mean about the congressman and then Floretta making confessions?"

Slowly but surely, his stomach turned in an unsettling way as a realization set in. The man he'd spotted at Miss Violet's Saloon was the very man he'd seen standing in the doorway of the Columbus Methodist Church. No wonder he looked familiar. And his name wasn't Horace Bramley, as Maxine had guessed, but Lewis Blackwell, the congressman up for reelection, despite controversial allegations that he might be involved in tax evasion and fraud. And now, he was investing money in prostitution rings across New York City? Incredible! What other wrongful acts did this shyster engage in, this congressman who represented his fair state in the country's capital? Owen Perry had assigned him to investigate the allegations some months ago, but he'd been too engrossed in the *General Slocum* case to give it his full attention, so his friend, Nathan Emory, had promised to look into it. Oh, he wished the telephone service stretched from New York to Nebraska instead of stopping in Chicago. He might get some decent answers if he could just talk to Nathan or Owen.

In the minutes that followed, Luke told Maggie all that he knew about the matter, including what Maxine had revealed the day before. From what Maxine had said, and now with what he gathered from the telegram, who else but Lewis Blackwell could be the "mystery man" of whom he was now certain he'd caught a glimpse or two during their journey?

"What possible reason could he have for being on the train?" Maggie asked.

"I'd like to know the same thing. Wouldn't you think with an election coming up, he'd want to stick close to home and spend as much time as possible gathering votes?"

"It does seem odd—provided it's truly Lewis Blackwell you've spotted."

"Oh, it is. I've seen old newspaper clippings with his photo attached. It may have taken me a while to place him, but having seen him in the saloon that night, I'm convinced I've also seen him on this trip. He's always lurking, as if he has some sort of plan up his sleeve and can't wait to see it play out."

"What do you think it is, this plan? And why would Henry start out the telegram with the words 'threat could be real'? What does he mean by that?"

"Believe me, I'd like to know. All I can say is, I've seen an evil look in Blackwell's eyes, and it's clear he's up to no good.

Maybe he thinks I'm out to destroy him, although until now, I had no reason to suspect him of anything because I failed to recognize him."

"He doesn't know that."

"True." He thought for a moment. "Might be he's just so mad about my kidnapping Clara that he means to make me pay."

"You think Miss Violet's involved?"

"Without a doubt. Wouldn't surprise me if she's wrapped the congressman around her finger, much in the way she has Byron."

They both ruminated that thought, taking a moment to gaze out the window. Pedestrians waited on the curb to cross the road, some with packages in hand, others with newspapers or briefcases. Women held tightly to their children's hands as they navigated the busy sidewalks. Two dogs wolfed down a few scraps of meat a butcher had tossed on the sidewalk.

"I'd like to know what confessions Floretta made—and to whom," Luke said, thinking aloud.

"Maybe she finally talked to the police, told them that Violet's Saloon is more than just a saloon."

"More likely, she just talked to Reverend Miles and Henry. Since she still won't reveal the congressman's name, it's obvious she's running scared—too scared to talk to the cops."

"Then she's to be commended for talking to anybody. I'm glad Henry thought to send you the telegram. You do plan to call the police, right?"

"I already cried wolf once by having Henry notify them to meet me in Columbus. I don't think I'll make that mistake twice."

"But that time, you were looking for Byron, not some New York congressman. This could be big news, Luke, if not dangerous information—too dangerous to keep to yourself."

"Or it could backfire. Cops don't cotton to false alarms."

The carriage jostled over potholes and crevices, making Maggie and Luke bump against each other. Luke mulled over their words, glad he'd had someone with whom to discuss his thoughts. Although he still had questions, their exchange helped give some clarity to the situation.

He took a deep breath and tried not to worry. "Well, anyway, thanks."

"For what?"

He touched the tip of her straight little nose. "For being so helpful and perceptive." Throwing caution to the wind, he added, "And might I say, downright pleasing to the eye? Makes talking to you a satisfying experience, if I may say so." Her expression froze, as if he'd just said the sun and moon were one and the same. He chuckled. "What? You're not used to flattery?"

"Certainly not from you."

He brushed a finger across her cheek. "Well, then, I've been remiss." No doubt about it, he had her stumped. Blast if he wasn't stumped himself, but that didn't stop him from continuing. "You have a lovely sprinkling of freckles, too."

"They come from my Grandmother Kane." The way she swallowed—as if a rock had just gone down her throat—told him he'd unnerved her. She quickly glanced out the window. What was with him? Hadn't he just berated himself back at the station for taking pleasure in watching her squirm?

"Maybe I'll meet her someday."

She jerked her head back in surprise, her blue eyes analyzing his casual remark. "My grandmother? I don't see how that would be possible."

He shrugged. "Never can tell when I might jump a train to Michigan. From what you've told me about your family, I think I'd like to meet them." She looked as shocked as he felt. *Go easy, Madison.*

He pivoted his body to face her directly. "It still amazes me that a young woman like you would trade in her comfortable life in Sandy Shores to work with orphans in New York City."

She cocked her blonde head to one side and frowned. "First of all, twenty is not so young. Goodness, Hannah Grace married at twenty-one, and she didn't seem the least bit young, in my opinion. Of course, marriage is the furthest thing from *my* mind."

"Of course." He tried not to look at her full lips.

"And, second, as I've said before, I would not have missed God's calling for the world. It's an adventurous thing to serve the Lord, Luke. One never knows where it might lead."

Adventurous? How intriguing. His admiration for her jumped several notches.

With the jostling back and forth of the cab, their noses came dangerously close to touching. His throat nearly dried up with thirst. "I know I'm not what I should be in terms of spiritual maturity, but I'm beginning to see I need to set my goals higher, work toward being a better Christian."

Her expression turned reflective, and there he went again, looking at her lips. "Then the first thing you have to learn is that no amount of work is going to accomplish that goal. Salvation is not something you work toward; it's a gift.

Simply receiving it with a repentant heart will draw you closer to your objective, Luke. And once you surrender everything, including your bitterness over losing Annalise, you'll find yourself on an altogether different spiritual plain."

He blew out a big dose of air and pulled back from her. They weren't the words he'd expected to hear. In fact, he should have been angry with her for mentioning his loss. What did she know about it anyway? Strangely, though, the remark didn't anger him. Rather, it seemed to captivate him. With his head propped against the wall of the carriage, he gave her a hard look. "See what I mean about your perceptive mind? You nailed me."

Her smile sagged a bit as she raised one blond eyebrow. "Luke, it doesn't require a genius mind to recognize you came to Sheltering Arms with a giant chip on your shoulder. And, might I add, you've shown that chip mostly to me?"

"I've done that, have I?"

Rose Marie had dropped back down to her seat and was pressing her head against the window, looking groggy enough to drift into another nap, judging by the way her eyelids drooped. Sunlight cast its silvery glow across her angelic face, and Luke realized that he didn't have a disparaging bone in his body toward Rose Marie or toward any of the other children. Even Ricky's somewhat crass behavior had ceased to bother him. Moreover, Henry, Ginny, Stan, and Charlotte had begun to feel almost like family. Yes, why indeed did Maggie Rose Kane bring out his irritability?

As if a two-ton boulder had rolled down a cliff and barreled into him, the answer plowed into his head. He had feelings for this woman—powerful ones—and he didn't deem himself equipped to deal with them. To ward them off, he often put up strong defenses to protect his heart.

"From the first day we met, it seemed you had a bone to pick with me." She pulled at an invisible thread in her skirt, then smoothed down the material. "You disliked me right off."

"Huh?" In a nervous gesture, he scratched the back of his neck. Who was squirming now? That she was under the impression he disliked her nearly knocked him off his seat.

"I did not dislike you, Maggie Rose, and I don't now. I think you're—very special. Shoot, I kissed you, didn't I?"

"I can't believe you said that!" With certainty, he knew he'd chosen the wrong words. Again.

The affront she felt made her frown deeply. "People who merely like each other, which is how I view us—merely friends, that is—have no business kissing! And that is exactly why it will never happen again."

"I'm sorry you took what I said in a negative way. I didn't mean it to come out like that. The kiss meant something to me. It was nice, don't you think so?"

Her chin jutted forward. "It doesn't matter what I thought of it. It's behind us."

"So, you did like it."

She leaned forward in her seat. "Oh, look, we're coming up to the parish hall—and the church is right next door," she blurted out.

He gave a bored glance out the window, then turned his eyes back to her flushed face. "Maggie, I want you to know—you're important to me." There! He'd admitted it.

She stretched forward to touch Rose Marie's arm. "Wake up, sweetie. We're here." From up top, the driver called out a command to his horse, and the carriage slowed to a stop.

"Did you hear what I said, Maggie?" He'd just laid himself out on the table like a sacrificial lamb, and she ignored him.

She left the seat to sit with Rose Marie and nudge her awake, sweeping a palm across her forehead. "At least she doesn't have that fever anymore. That's a relief." Clearly, she meant to dismiss him.

"Maggie…."

She peered at him over Rose Marie's head, and the look she leveled him was very firm. "We should probably get something straight, Luke. I think you're a nice person, but in all fairness, we are merely friends."

Merely friends. She had certainly made a point of emphasizing those final words.

"I came to New York with incredibly clear direction from the Lord, and I am quite passionate about carrying out my mission. I cannot allow a simple kiss to divert my attentions, and I'll thank you to remember that."

Simple kiss? Had she really said that? If memory served him right, there had been nothing simple about it.

"You're right," he said, not meaning it. He fully intended to kiss her again. Some very strong sense told him God had ordained it to happen, and the fact he'd come to that conclusion threw him for another giant spin.

She opened the door of her own accord and jumped down, taking Rose Marie with her. On a whim, she turned, looking ready to get in one last word. But the excited yelps of youngsters disembarking their carriages after having been trapped all day on a train distracted her, swallowing up whatever she had planned to say.

Taking Rose Marie by the hand, she swiveled on her heel and walked away.

"Thanks again for talking over that telegram with me," Luke called after her.

She looked back briefly. "You're entirely welcome. I'd take care, if I were you."

Maxine and Clara ran up to her and Rose Marie, and the four walked hand in hand to the front door of the parish hall, from where the aroma of roasted chicken wafted out and reached even Luke's nose.

Watching her walk away, long skirts billowing and golden hair flying, he wondered what bothered him most—the notion that Lewis Blackwell might intend to harm him, or the idea that Maggie Kane considered him nothing more than a mere friend.

Chapter Twenty-seven

P ark Street Presbyterian Church buzzed with excitement as folks filled the pews just minutes before the start of the evening's proceedings. On stage were Maxine and Clara, the Pelton sisters, Stuart and Ricky Campbell, and the Kramer boys. They were bookended by Rose Marie, looking frightened as a kitten in a bear cage, her feet swinging back and forth while she sucked her index finger like it was a lollipop, and Charlotte, holding a squirming, screeching baby Christina. As a matter of fact, her wails had caused a stir of amusement in the audience.

"How are you feeling now?" Luke whispered in Maggie's ear, his warm breath tickling her cheek. Even after her rather emphatic declaration that their kiss had been a mistake, he'd still plunked himself right next to her at the supper table, and here he was again, beside her in the pew at the back of the church. She'd been forced to choose a seat near the door because, sad to say, her stomach had started doing strange things ever since supper—gurgling, burning, and turning over—and she worried that she might have to make a run for the necessary behind the church at any moment. It would appear her worst fear had come true; she'd caught Rose's

Marie's dread illness. To make matters worse, her aching body felt hot and out of sorts, and all she wanted to do was find a cot on which to lie. To be sure, Luke's strong shoulder looked tempting enough to lean against, but, of course, she would resist.

"The same as I did when you asked five minutes ago."

"Oh. I'm sorry."

"Don't be. There's no help for it. By tomorrow, I should be good as new. I just wish I could sit closer to the front. I'm worried about Rose Marie. Look at her—she's wearing the most forlorn face, the little darling."

"She'll be fine, you'll see."

She gazed up at him. His square-set face hadn't seen a razor since early that morning, and a dusting of whiskers gave him a rugged allure. To her great despair, she longed to run a finger along his jaw to test its roughness. "I've been praying that just the right couple would come along to claim her."

"And if they don't?"

"Then I will happily put her back on the train. God has a plan for each of these precious children, and I don't presume to know it. In some cases, His plan might very well mean bringing them back to New York with us."

He considered her words. "I believe you're right. Still, I have a good feeling about tonight."

"You do?" She managed a weak smile. "You've seen no sign of the congressman, I take it?"

"No, he's not here. Believe me, I've been on the lookout for anything suspicious."

He looked like he was about to say more, but the clock chimed seven, cutting off his words. It was time for the meeting to begin. Stanley stepped forward and gave his well-practiced speech, enrapturing everyone present, so that when the time came to invite folks forward, the couples who left their seats outnumbered the available children. Unfortunately, that was about the time Maggie's roiling stomach prompted her to run out of the church.

Outside, a cool blast of evening air brought an instant measure of relief. She was thankful Luke hadn't followed her out. She needed to find a place to plant herself—an inconspicuous spot, like a nice patch of grass under a tree, where she could moan about her miserable circumstances without calling attention to herself. Oh, she hated that she couldn't stay in the church to keep an eye on Rose Marie. What if everyone descending upon her caused undue stress? Perhaps she wouldn't know what to say, so she'd remain silent. If only Maggie could be with her to help her through the process. "Please, Lord, give Rose Marie a sense of calm and confidence, as young and helpless as she is. May she somehow know You won't let any harm come to her."

Following a path to the privy, she noticed a copse of trees about ten yards beyond that. *Perfect*, she told herself, willing her stomach to stop pitching and swirling.

Dusk had moved in, and the setting sun created long, dark shadows on everything that obscured it. A flock of birds that had perched on the church roof chose that moment to take flight for places unknown, the presumed leader squawking instructions. While it'd been a touch windy earlier, now the air lay still and heavy, allowing sounds to carry. Across an open cornfield behind the church, a dog barked, and from the opposite direction, a door slammed shut. As Maggie picked her way down the narrow trail, something else caught her attention—the sound of low voices in the distance exchanging words. She slowed her step, thinking the voices might be coming from behind the privy.

"If we're gonna do away with 'im, it's gotta be tonight, boss. You said you wanted to get the deed done whilst he's furthest from home, and this is as far as that train's goin'. No one'll suspect a thing if we make it look like a' accident. You can't have him goin' back to New York and writin' that article 'bout you. You'll lose your standin' in congress, for sure, not to mention the money you been usin' to fund your—um—side ventures."

Maggie stopped dead, her heart thumping so hard it nearly broke free of her chest. She clamped a hand over her mouth and fought down a chill, barely able to breathe. Bile, strong and bitter, collected in her throat. What to do? If she proceeded to the cluster of tall trees, they would spot her. If she went into the outbuilding, they would hear the door open and close. And if she turned and ran, why, they would certainly chase her down. On the other hand, if she remained, still as a statue, they would continue strategizing, and she would be apprised of their scheme.

"It's certain he's figured out by now who I am. We made clear eye contact the other night at Violet's place, and I'll not forget that look he gave me of utter disbelief. If there've been any rumors flying around about me, he'll surely validate them the minute he gets back to New York. By now, I'm convinced that little minx Maxine has filled him in on every last detail about my business dealings with Violet Harding. Nosy little thing always did have a big mouth. Why, I can almost see the headline now: 'New York Congressman Found Guilty of Fraudulent Use of Government Funds'!"

"Good thing Byron and his boys shut Floretta up." He gave a devilish chuckle.

"Yeah, well, they better've shut her up for good. That woman could do me some serious damage."

"They claim they left her for dead. I ain't heard nothin' to believe otherwise."

"Good. Now all I have to concern myself with is getting that reporter out of the way. I'm not worried about Maxine or Clara. Who'd believe them over a United States congressman?"

"Exactly. But they might believe a reporter. That's why we best settle this matter once an' for all."

"You're right." A short pause followed. "So, what sort of *accident* did you have in mind?"

"Me? I thought *you'd* have a plan in place."

"I expected *you* to do the planning. Why do you think I hired you?" His stern, authoritative voice carried over the still air. Maggie slowly turned to see if anyone else may have heard, but all she saw were a couple of uninterested dogs sniffing around the churchyard. Out of sight, in front of the church, one of the horses that was hitched to a wagon neighed and snorted.

"So I could carry out a job you'd have outlined ahead of time," the hired thug hissed back.

Maggie heard the congressman clear his throat and spit. With all her might, she held in the need to hurl, keeping her hand firmly clasped across her mouth.

"I don't know the first thing about killing someone, you idiot. That's your department. I thought we got that settled when I passed you that bag of cash back in New York."

"Well, I been waitin' for you to tell me how you want it done. Thought you said you wanted it to look like a' accident."

"I do, you simpleton. But I thought you'd have a method up your sleeve." He cursed. "If I'd have known you were going to have a leak in your head, I would have hired somebody else."

"Well, there ain't that many methods for faking a' accident."

She pictured the congressman taking a couple of hard swallows to tamp down his anger. "Do you have a gun?" he asked in a monotone voice.

"'Course I do. I always carry one."

"Then use it, smarty."

"But I thought you said you—?"

"Never mind what I said, just get the job done, you hear me?"

If ever the time had come to vanish from the premises, it was now. She had to get to Luke—and fast. Trouble was, when she turned, she stepped on a twig, snapping it in two. And to top matters off, what little she'd had for supper that night chose that moment to spill out on the grass at her feet.

"What in the—?" the thug spat out.

In terror, she lifted her skirts and set out running; unfortunately, though, she wasn't fast enough to escape the thug. Before the word *scream* even registered in her head, one of his hands snagged the back of her dress and yanked her backward while the other reached out to snatch a fistful of her hair and jerk her around, clamping a firm, smelly palm across her mouth. Frantic, she kicked and flailed, managing at one point to move her face in such a way as to let go the shortest scream in all of history.

"Shut up, you little—."

"Kill her," the congressman said. "Now."

"What? You can't be serious," his hired man said. "You don't just kill a woman in cold blood and not expect to hang for it."

"She knows too much."

"How do you know she wasn't just walkin' out to the johnny? Didn't you just hear her throw up?"

Maggie fought for air, a dizzying sensation clogging her head and messing with her ability to keep her thoughts straight. *Lord Jesus, help me*, she prayed silently.

"She's with those orphans, fool. Don't think Madison didn't tell her all about me."

In her wooziness, she managed to give her head a fast shake. "Uhh," she moaned.

"Give me the gun," the congressman ordered.

"What? You're crazier than I thought."

"Give it to me."

"You've lost your ever-lovin' mind."

There was a scuffle of sorts, and then the sound of gunfire—a loud, thunderous, ear-splitting crack that made everything and everyone fall silent. For a split second, Maggie feared she'd been shot, what with the way her ears buzzed and her head swam. Was she just too numb to feel the blood oozing from her hot, aching body? She felt her body sag weakly against the hired killer.

"Drop that gun, Blackwell, you good-for-nothing chiseler. And you—let go of her—now!" came a familiar voice. Sweetly familiar. *Luke. Oh, dear Father, I will never have the chance to tell him I love him. Would You tell him for me?* "So help me, I swear I will kill you both," he was saying, his voice increasingly distant, almost like an echo. Still, it had a velvet ring to it, like the sweetest song she'd ever heard.

"I am a United States congressman."

"You are a United States disgrace, that's what you are. Now, put your hands above your heads, both of you, and step away from her. Slowly." He kept his gun aimed at them.

"Maggie, are you all right?" As fine as his voice sounded to her ears, she did not have it in her to respond. She was dying, and the blessed thing about it was, she didn't have an ounce of pain from the mortal wound.

As she slowly slid to the ground, the sounds of pounding feet and loud voices echoed through the air. "What's going on?" "Call the police!" "Is there a doctor anywhere?" "I'm a doctor. Step aside." And finally, "Sweetheart, hang on," spoken by Luke, her darling Luke. But what was she thinking? He wasn't hers to love, not as long as he didn't trust Christ as Savior.

Besides, she reminded herself, *I'm not long for this earth.*

⌒K⌒

"Will she be all right?" An angel with a voice much like Rose Marie's hovered mere inches from Maggie's face, her cool breath brushing her cheeks like silk. If this was heaven, the Lord had sent her straight to bed upon first entering the pearly gates. A layer of confusion covered her already clouded thoughts.

"She needs some space, honey. Here, come sit on my lap." Even in her foggy state, she recognized Luke's voice, comforting and kinder sounding than she'd ever thought possible.

Lord, what is happening to me? Am I somewhere between earth and paradise? But if that's the case, why is my body burning up and my stomach feeling the awful need to retch?

Someone laid a cool, damp cloth on her forehead. "Doc Haverstock says we need to get this fever down. Soon as that happens, she'll start coming around. She's in a delirious state right now, mumbling about the pearly gates one minute and spiders the next." This came from a woman whose voice she didn't recognize. "The aspirin should soon work its magic— that is, if she'll keep it down long enough."

"Thank you, Mrs. Ardmore. You've been a great help."

"Oh, goodness, Mr. Madison, it's my pleasure taking care of her. And with darling Clara and Maxine to assist through the night, why, we'll have her better in no time."

"It's all my fault," Rose Marie whimpered, her voice sounding distant.

"No, it's not, sweetheart," said Luke. "She merely caught your illness."

If only Maggie had the strength and wherewithal to put a word in edgewise. But she felt herself drifting back into a dark cave.

A cave where spiders and wiggly things dangled in her face.

They did not board the train the next morning. Instead, Luke and Stanley rode into the city with Reverend Ardmore, first to give further statements at the police station, then to send a wire to Mr. Bingham from the telegraph office.

Luke dictated the telegram: "We are safe. Stop. Congressman Blackwell and hired killer behind bars awaiting trial. Stop. Most children adopted out except for Campbell boys and Rose Marie. Stop. Maggie ill with fever. Stop. Start back when she recovers. Stop. Will inform you of future developments. Stop. Luke. End."

"You do know that telegram will drive Ginny to utter distraction," Stanley said later on their drive back to the parsonage. "She won't rest until she's heard every last detail. She'll wonder why the congressman's in jail, what transpired between the two of you, what's wrong with Maggie, how the Campbell boys and Rose Marie are doing...."

"Well, I sent a wire to Owen Perry, a more extensive one, so they'll be reading an article in tomorrow's *World*. 'Course, there's still a lot we don't know, especially with regard to Blackwell's shady business ventures. But it will all come out in time, now that the cops have started an investigation. Hopefully, to the great disadvantage of Violet Harding."

"Indeed," Stanley said. "That woman deserves to go behind bars herself."

"I can't agree more." An overcast sky threatened additional rain as the threesome rode past businesses and industries, dodging traffic and pedestrians. "How is Charlotte, by the way? I saw her crying when she handed Christina over to that young couple last night," Luke said.

"We both shed a few tears, as a matter of fact. But the truth is, that couple's been praying for a baby for seven years. Christina could not have fallen into more loving or grateful arms. There are mixed feelings all around—never fails when we take these train trips. You tell yourself not to grow too attached, but next thing you know, you've gone and done it. In the end, Christina will be much better off. It's always our intent to provide temporary homes, not permanent ones. Someday, Charlotte and I hope to...."

Luke angled his head at Stanley when he stopped in the middle of his sentence.

"Have your own brood?" he coached.

Stanley's mouth curved into a sheepish grin. "You might say so, although I shouldn't be talking about it in her absence. Nothing's official, mind you. There's a lot to talk over with Ginny and Henry—like where we would live, for starters. If we were to marry, would there even be a place for us as a married couple in that house, and what would our roles be? Henry would have to hire someone else to take over the boys' floor. It gets complicated when you start analyzing the details. Char and I are passionate about working with homeless children, but whether the Lord wants us to remain at Sheltering Arms or start our own institution is the question. We're waiting on His divine guidance."

"I can't imagine that Henry and Ginny wouldn't want you staying on. I'm sure there's a place for both of you, but I do admire your seeking God's direction. Exactly how will you know when He's made it clear to you? I mean, obviously, He doesn't speak in an audible voice anymore."

Stanley gave a lighthearted chuckle and looked at the preacher stationed between them on the seat, his large-set arms handling the reins with practiced finesse, bouncing up and down with their rutted ride. "Reverend Ardmore could answer that better than I could, but for me, it's an underlying sense that I'm moving closer to the Lord rather than further away when I desire His will. If you truly aspire to know it, He reveals it in different ways—in His Word, while you're in prayer, or through the wise counsel of other believers. What do you think, Reverend Ardmore?"

The reverend kept his eyes on the road, a grin poking out from under his mustache. "I think you'd make a mighty fine preacher, that's what I think."

They all laughed now, relieving some of the tension brought on by the morning's affairs. After all, it wasn't every day Luke filed a report at the police station regarding threats made to his life. Even now, he couldn't quite get the order of last night's events out of his head—how he'd sat at the back of the church awaiting Maggie's return, then worried she might not come back, might need his assistance, then ironically rubbed the handle of Henry's gun, which he'd tucked deep in his pocket. Yes, Henry had insisted he take the pistol on the train. "Never know when there might be a scuffle," Henry had said. "I'd rather you handle it than Stan." Of course, he'd kept it locked up tight in his luggage the entire time—until last night, when something—or *Someone*—had told him to remove it. No doubt about it, that nudge had come from God. Maggie might very well have been shot otherwise. There was no telling what that maniac, Blackwell, was capable of doing.

"You're right, of course. Discerning God's will for your life is a process that requires complete surrender," the reverend was saying. Luke refocused on his words. "I've always been of a mind that if I have a surrendered heart toward God and long to know His will for my life, then I'm living it—His will, that is. He knows our desires, and as long as we go about living with hearts to serve and please Him in the best way we can, which includes discerning His will in every situation; then, all that's required is merely to trust Him to close and open doors as needed."

"You make it sound so simple," Luke said. A drop of rain landed on his forehead, prompting him to scan the darkening sky.

"Well, I wouldn't say that. God never promised His ways would be easy. Matthew 7:14 in the Bible says, '*Strait is the gate, and narrow is the way, which leadeth unto life, and few there be that find it.'* That says to me that a lot of folks find it much easier to take the sinful path than the righteous one. Living a Christian life calls for sacrifice."

"Sacrifice?"

"Well, maybe not in the literal sense," the pastor said, "but in the human sense. We are called to lay down our lives for our brothers and sisters—that is, be willing to give our all for the sole purpose of spreading the gospel message, exuding Jesus, if you will. Sheltering Arms Refuge is a perfect example of that. Look how much the Binghams have given up by turning their home into a refuge for lost children."

"They wouldn't think of it as sacrifice at all," Stanley said.

"Probably not," Reverend Ardmore agreed, giving a tug on the reins to direct the pair of horses down a pebbled street. Luke remembered the street from their ride into town. They couldn't be more than a mile from the church and parsonage now. "When one is passionate in his work, it can feel quite effortless. There is true joy in serving God with your passions."

Luke thought that over. He liked his job at the *World*, but would he call it passion that compelled him—or a simple need to stay busy? Yes, reporting on the daily news excited him; it even offered a certain sense of gratification when he was assigned a good story. But did it fill him with contentment and purpose? Would he be fulfilled living out the remainder of his days researching and writing news stories? A gentle tug at the heart told him there had to be something more out there.

And something else told him Maggie Rose Kane played into the picture.

Chapter Twenty-eight

I will call her Catherine. She is roughly 12 or 13; I can't tell you her exact age, for she does not know it herself. Catherine has no family, having been deserted and then shoved from one person to another until the day she found herself begging at the front door of disaster. She thought he meant to help her, this man who offered her food and shelter, but instead, he meant to profit from her poverty—by selling her to a house of prostitution in the Upper East Side, an establishment called Miss Violet's Saloon, owned and operated by Miss Violet Harding and Mr. Lewis Blackwell.

Luke reread the last portion of his article, tapping his pencil on his notebook as he pondered how to continue. He was seated at a little table in the parsonage parlor, and though he was trying to concentrate, the closed door to the bedroom where Maggie was sleeping kept him from doing so. It didn't help that and Clara and Maxine were jumping rope in the front yard and squealing with glee, their sheer happiness at being invited to live together with the Ardmores lending to their overabundance of energy and excitement.

"They're quite something, aren't they?" Mrs. Ardmore said, fluttering into the room, feather duster in hand. She headed straight to the little table to dust circles around Luke's stacks of papers, then bent over to clean the shelf by his feet. She stopped to look out the front window and watch the girls at play. "I knew from the minute Joseph told me their story that we just had to open our home to them."

Luke watched the girls, surprised by Clara's agility with the rope. So far, he'd observed her to be only quiet, wary, and distrustful. Now, however, she fairly bubbled with life. "They are certainly beside themselves with joy. Don't be afraid to put them to work, though. They're used to chores—well, at least Maxine is. Clara arrived only a few days before we swept her away on that train."

"Yes, I heard about your brave rescue. Thank you for risking your life like you did."

It was odd how, at the time, he hadn't considered the risks all that serious. He knew only that he had to get Clara out of that rotten saloon. Maybe that's what Reverend Ardmore had meant when he'd said that passion makes a job seem effortless. He continued tapping his pencil in thought.

"I'll give them a few days to adjust to their new environment and just be, well, little girls," Mrs. Ardmore said. "From what I hear, they lost a good chunk of their childhood, poor things. Well, Joseph and I have raised a brood, so we know a thing or two about it. We'll treat them with kid gloves for a while, at least till we've gained some measure of trust, and then we'll start assigning them a few chores."

"You'll get along fine," Luke said. "Maxine can be a little belligerent at times, but Clara's on the shy side."

She chuckled. "Joseph will take care of that." She moved on to dust the chair arms of the wingback chairs on either side of the fireplace, followed by the mantel. "I wish we could have taken sweet little Rose Marie, as well, but Joseph and I both thought two girls were enough for a start."

"Rose Marie will be fine. She'll be boarding the train back to New York, as will the Campbell boys."

"What will become of them?"

"They'll stay on at Sheltering Arms until someone offers them a home or they're old enough to go out on their own."

"Oh, my. They're just young fellows, those boys, aren't they?"

A knot caught in Luke's chest. He'd seen the look of dis-appointment in Ricky's eyes when no one had selected his brother and him, but the truth was that there just weren't enough folks equipped to handle siblings. The older Kramer boys had gone to a farm where, undoubtedly, they'd be put to work, and the Pelton girls had gone home with a couple who already had baby twin girls. Luke guessed that the mother needed help with them. But Stuart and Ricky were only ten and twelve, and while Ricky had some brawn on him, he also carried a large chip on his shoulder, which started showing when it became apparent no one was planning to take him and Stuart home. There was one elderly woman who'd said she wouldn't mind taking just Stuart, but Stanley had denied her request, insisting the siblings stay together. She'd pursed her lips in a straight line, taken a gander at Ricky, who by now was folding his arms in defiance, and given her head a quick shake. At that point, Ricky had bolted from his chair and thumped out the back door, yelling, "This whole thing is stupid!"

Unfortunately, Luke had not had the wherewithal to deal with his fit, still too preoccupied by the night's events, not to mention worried over Maggie's faint due to her high fever. All told, the scuffle outside the church had delayed the placing out proceedings by a good hour or more, putting nerves on edge and sending several folks home prematurely—folks who might well have taken a child or two with them, had they not been frightened off by the churchyard fracas. He figured Ricky needed to cool off on his own, which he did. Ten minutes later, he returned and plopped himself down on a back pew, chin jutting out, forehead creased with a frown, hands tucked deep in his side pockets. By then, several folks who'd lagged behind engaged Luke in conversation, wanting to know everything the police had said to him before hauling off the congressman and his hired man in their wagon.

"How old are those boys?" Mrs. Ardmore asked from the next room, having completed her dusting in the parlor.

"What? Oh, Stu and Ricky? They're ten and twelve," he answered, dragging himself back to the present.

Just then, Reverend Ardmore exited his office, Bible under his arm. "I'm going to make a house call on old Burton Franks, Helen. I'll be back in an hour." To Luke, he said, "Say, you wouldn't want to use my office while I'm gone, would you, young man? Looks like you're trying to write that article."

"I would be much obliged, sir, if it's no trouble."

He flashed him a look of merriment and whispered, "That wife of mine can talk an ear off an elephant. You best get yourself some privacy."

"What are you saying, Joseph?" Mrs. Ardmore called from the other room.

"Nothing, dear. Where is everyone, by the way?"

Helen poked her head around the corner. "Those Campbell boys have been holed up in the attic sorting through some of your old war scrapbooks and who knows what else all afternoon, and little Rose Marie is curled up in bed sleeping with Maggie. Little thing refuses to leave her side."

It was almost too good to be true, Maxine thought, Clara and her having been chosen to live in the same house—and with the reverend and his wife, no less! They would have been happy to pass letters back and forth, but now they would be talking at the breakfast, lunch, and dinner table, not to mention walking to school together beginning next Monday. No doubt about it, God had answered their prayers! To make matters even better—well, perfect, actually—that dumb congressman was in jail, so she and Clara were forever safe!

Oh, she knew there would be less-than-perfect days—days when she wouldn't want to obey all the rules or finish her chores or do her schoolwork. There even might be times when she and Clara would get on each other's last nerve. And, most likely, old memories would crop up now and then to turn her into a regular grouch. But with God's help, she planned to make the best of things, thank Him daily, and do her best to be a good, likeable, obliging girl.

Maxine watched Clara handle the jump rope, getting the knack of twirling it over her head and skipping over it. For never having jumped rope before, the girl was picking it up quickly.

Just then, the front door opened, and Reverend Ardmore stepped outside, granting both girls a wide smile.

"Hello, Reverend Ardmore," the girls said in unison, Clara coming to a breathless standstill. Men still made her nervous, and it always took Maxine a while to trust anybody new.

Hitched at a post in the driveway, the reverend's horse neighed and pawed impatiently at the earth. The reverend stopped in front of the girls and surveyed their faces for a moment, his kind eyes crinkling at the corners. "You may feel free to call the Mrs. and me Helen and Joseph, if you like—or Mother and Father—whichever makes you comfortable. We just want you to know that you can depend on us."

They nodded and watched him mount his horse. His smile still in place, he turned the creature around, waved, then headed up the street, the *clip-clop* of hooves making a pleasant sound on the brick street.

Clara finally released her breath. "Maxine," she whispered, "I do believe you and I have crossed heaven's threshold."

K

Lewis Blackwell is the New York congressman up for reelection this November. He has been indicted on charges of tax evasion and various other illegal entanglements, and now, he is suspected of engaging in the exploitation of girls and women for profit. He and a hired man followed a train of orphans from Sheltering Arms Refuge west with the intent to silence this truth-telling reporter for good. His scheme was foiled, however, and Mr. Blackwell is now in the custody of police, awaiting trial. I protect the innocent, but the guilty I fully expose.

Luke considered the wisdom of that last statement until he thought about everything that scoundrel Blackwell stood for, how he'd duped the citizens of New York—not to mention the United States. No, the fool deserved not one ounce of sympathy for his frankness. It was his responsibility to expose the truth.

He studied the tip of his pencil, as if therein lay all the ideas for the remainder of his article. Outside, squeals of delight coming from Maxine and Clara made him smile in spite of himself. Next door, he knew Maggie must surely be trying to rest, but something told him their peals of laughter provided music to her ears. He longed to peek in on her, but propriety kept a tight rein on his desires. All of a sudden, he put pencil to paper and let the words begin to flow.

I first learned about Catherine from another young lady named Susan (not her real name), who escaped from the sordid upstairs quarters at Miss Violet's Saloon, where she and Catherine were held and required to entertain male guests. She'd begged Catherine to come with her, but the girl had refused, held back by a sober estimation of the grave repercussions, should they be discovered.

Susan found her way to Sheltering Arms Refuge, still raw, hurting, and bearing unfathomably deep emotional wounds. I learned of her friend, Catherine, and her plight. Immediately, I felt compelled to act. Whereas I had been unable to save the loved ones I lost on the General Slocum when it burned in June, I realized I could rescue one innocent girl from a house of horrors. And rescue her I did, with the indispensable assistance of two brave women: one, an employee of Sheltering Arms, and the other, an employee at Miss Violet's Saloon.

I will not go into the details of our rescue for fear of jeopardizing future seizures from similar establishments. There will surely be more, for I have had only a taste of what it is to free an innocent victim from the clutches of evil, and now that I've sampled its sweetness, I cannot put it out of my mind.

How is it feasible that a city of millions has let a problem of this magnitude go unchecked? Homeless children wander the streets by the hundreds, perhaps thousands. Where is the outcry for justice? We prosecute those who do us harm, like murderers, thieves, and marauders, but close our eyes to these innocent children against whom more grievous injustices are done every day. Where is our compassion for these precious lost and forgotten emeralds with hidden talents and untold potential?

Luke laid down his pencil, the tip having gone dull with use. *A dull pencil is a useless tool. How much more useless for the kingdom of God is an unrepentant heart?*

What? Like a streak of lightning breaking through a gloomy sky, the words flashed across Luke's brain, etching themselves into the darkest regions of his soul. What in the world? More like, what in heaven? Where had such words even come from?

In an earnest search for meaning, he lifted his face and prayed silently, *Lord, what is my purpose on this earth? Do You want me to help homeless children? Do You want me to keep reporting the news? Do You have a plan for me, Lord?*

Foolishly, he waited for some sense that God had heard, some sort of sign. "Are You trying to tell me something, God?" These words he hissed aloud. "Or is my heart too dull and lifeless to hear Your voice?"

Pieces of that final conversation he'd had with Nathan Emory the day Owen had kicked him out of the office replayed in his head. What was it? *"I'm hoping that, someday, you'll see that in the middle of your pain, there is a balm to be found. You'll find it the day you start trusting Christ."*

For reasons he could not explain, a tear rolled down his cheek, followed by another—and another. Visions of the *General Slocum* and its passengers—Annalise, Aunt Frances, and Zelda Engel included—danced across his mind, their faces jubilant at first, but quickly changing to fright as flames of death engulfed the paddleboat. Why did he have to think these dreaded thoughts now? Why, when he'd just begun to lay them all down? Just when he'd turned a corner on his grief? He had even started entertaining the notion of falling in love again.

Why, Lord? Why?

As if to accentuate his sudden change in mood, a rumble of thunder rolled in the distance, and the rain that had been only a threat earlier started coming down in sheets. He heard the front door open and slam as two overexcited girls stomped their feet on the rug by the door, still erupting in giggles. Mrs. Ardmore quickly shushed them and took them to the kitchen to help her bake a batch of cookies.

He spotted a tattered Bible on the preacher's desk. One part of him felt like covering it with another book so he wouldn't have to look at it. Another part prompted him to open it to the place the reverend had bookmarked.

He yanked up the book and opened it to the passage the pastor had underlined, Proverbs 3:5–6: *"Trust in the* Lord *with all thine heart; and lean not unto thine own understanding. In all thy ways acknowledge him, and he shall direct thy paths."* *Hmm,* he thought. *That's well and good.* But then, his eyes moved on to the following verse: *"Be not wise in thine own eyes: fear the* Lord*, and depart from evil."*

He clamped the book shut, folded his hands, and blinked back more tears. Then, he prayed the only words that came to mind. "Lord, if You are there, please help me find my way back to You."

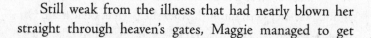

Still weak from the illness that had nearly blown her straight through heaven's gates, Maggie managed to get herself dressed and make a bit of sense of her tangled mass of hair. *My, but she looks like a ferret in a fry pan*, she mused, leaning into the mirror. She turned at the sound of a gentle rapping on her door, but the sudden movement made her dizzy, prompting her to plop into the nearest chair.

"Oh, my goodness, child, you're still unwell." Mrs. Ardmore rushed to her side, touched cool fingers to her brow, and exclaimed, "You shouldn't be traveling today."

Maggie smiled shakily. She liked the woman and appreciated all her efforts to nurse her back to health. But she could not continue to burden her, and, the truth was, she longed for home—Sheltering Arms Refuge, that is. It shocked her to realize how much she longed for it, even though she also craved Grandmother Kane's comforting touch.

"I'll be okay, really. You've already done so much for me, and all of us, for that matter. Thank you so much."

"Oh, pooh," the woman said with a flick of her wrist. "Having all of you here, crowded as it is, has been pure delight for the reverend and me. I'm just sorry it couldn't have been more pleasurable for you." Taking Maggie by the arm, Mrs. Ardmore helped her to her feet, but all her fussing produced quite an audience: Charlotte and Stan, Maxine and Clara, the ever present Rose Marie, Reverend Ardmore, Ricky, Stuart, and her precious Luke, of whom she'd seen little in the past few days. Even now, he stood at the back of the group, as if wary of catching her dread illness. She dared not let her eyes dwell too long on him.

"We'll take very good care of her, Mrs. Ardmore," Stanley said, stepping forward to take Maggie's other arm.

"Yeah, we'll see she gets back to Shelterin' Arms safe an' sound," Stuart said, sounding like the perfect little man. Oh, how it pained Maggie that no one had offered to take Ricky and him. Even now, she detected regret in Ricky's eyes, even though he stood at the doorway in front of Luke looking brave and unaffected.

"And I will personally see that she drinks plenty of water," Charlotte added, facing Maggie with a sympathetic smile. "I just read an article in the *Ladies' Home Journal*, of all places, that water is one of nature's finest healing agents. Who would have thought?"

"Well, I don't doubt it. After all, she's lost plenty of it over these last few days," Reverend Ardmore said. "Stands to reason her dehydrated body would need some replenishing."

"I hope I don't catch that pitiful ailment," Maxine said. "Your stomach must be sore as a boiled toad after all that—."

"Shh, Maxine!" Charlotte shushed, laying a hand on Maxine's arm.

"Well, I mean—I felt bad for her, an' all," she revised.

"Of course you did, dear," Mrs. Ardmore said. "We all did."

Oh, my stars and planets! Had the entire household heard her awful retching in the middle of the night? If she could have melted into the braided rug beneath her shoes, she would have done so that instant.

"I holded her head, 'cause that's what she did for me when I throwed up," Rose Marie said in her tiny voice.

Maggie touched the darling girl's cheek.

"Oh, sweetheart, you are such a gem for doing that," Charlotte said. "I'd have done the same, but I thought Mrs. Ardmore was tending to her."

"She was—she did," Maggie hastened. "Oh, you all have been wonderful. And, now, could we please quit talking about me?"

A tiny glance up at Luke revealed a hint of humor in his eyes. Goodness gracious!

The ride east had a certain solemnity to it. Whereas they'd used the car closest to the baggage compartment on the way out, they now took seats in a car closer to the front of the train, everyone seeming wrapped up in his or her private thoughts. Even those riders she didn't know from Adam kept their faces hidden in books and newspapers or closed their eyes to the passing scenery. Luke and Ricky sat three seats ahead of Maggie and Rose Marie, Charlotte and Stanley were two seats back on the other side of the aisle, and young Stuart perched directly in front of her and next to an elderly man who smoked a cigar, even in his sleep. The odor drifted through the air and turned Maggie's already ailing stomach, making her think of the craggy-faced man she'd met on the train to New York back in August—Mort Dempsey. She remembered how quickly her heart had turned from fuss and fury over his smoking to near tenderness once she had heard his story. A hasty glance around the car made her ponder the vast number of stories behind all the faces. *Lord, give me a heart of passion for people, that I may love them with the kind of love You so graciously show me on a daily basis,* she prayed silently.

She closed her eyes and drifted off to sleep, Rose Marie snuggled close against her side.

She had no idea how long she slept, but she came awake when Luke set Rose Marie on his lap and settled down next to her. She must have started, for he immediately touched her arm. "Sorry to disturb you. I just got up to walk around a bit and thought I'd check on you. You all right? And don't dare answer with, 'I'm fine.'" He grinned and leaned closer.

Lord, guard my heart. "But I *am* fine; weak as a two-legged stool, mind you, but fine." He frowned. "All right, then—*almost* fine," she corrected herself.

He chuckled, and my, it fairly pealed like the finest bell. She'd missed him! *May as well admit it*, she thought.

"I'm sorry you got so sick," Luke said, holding Rose Marie as she quietly played with a cloth doll Mrs. Ardmore had given her before they'd set out. "You got bit pretty badly by that nasty bug. I sat with you that first night, but you didn't know it."

"What?" Maggie jerked forward. "You did not."

"I did. Of course, so did Mrs. Ardmore, Charlotte, Maxine, and Clara. Pretty much everyone took a turn putting a cold cloth to your forehead."

She tried to recall that evening, but about the only thing that came to mind was the mass of spiders she'd distinctly seen dangling in front of her face. Spiders with big, black, bulging eyes. Oh, and there was that moment when she'd walked through the pearly gates—or, at least, had thought she'd gotten a glimpse of them. She shook her head in dismay.

"Well, thank you very much."

He briefly touched a knuckle to her cheek, sending chill bumps down her neck. "You are very welcome," he whispered.

"And since we're on the subject, might I thank you for saving my life when that awful fellow had me in his clutches? Once again, I found you to be quite handy with a gun."

"And, once again, I must admit to no particular skill on my part. Must be that folks just find the sound of the gun and the sight of its barrel poking down their noses somewhat intimidating."

"You do have a way of putting on the sternest face when you set your mind to it."

"Is that so?" His chuckle intensified as he lowered his hand to finger Rose Marie's long braid in a tender fashion. Maggie found it strange how his gentle handling of the girl created the deepest sort of longing in her heart for him. If she wasn't careful, Luke Madison would be her complete undoing. She must make every attempt to steer clear of him in the days to come.

Pressing ahead, she said, "Truth be told, my memory's foggy, but I do know I overheard that awful Mr. Blackwell threatening to do you in. It was my intention to give you fair warning, and I would have, too, if that evil hired man of his hadn't caught hold of me by the hair and tried to strangle the breath out of me. I think it was my sprint through the churchyard that caused my faint."

"You had a raging fever and didn't even know it," Luke said. "The doctor said it reached a height he hadn't seen in some time in adults. Everyone prayed you through it."

"You included?" she asked.

He paused, and she held her breath. Finally, he gave a slow nod. "Me included."

Chapter Twenty-nine

No one appeared happier than Virginia Bingham when the hired coach rolled in to the circular drive of Sheltering Arms Refuge late one afternoon. In a flash, the front door flew open and out she came, carrying a bundle wrapped in a blanket. Mr. Bingham and several other children of different sizes, shapes, and ages followed behind. Maggie's spirit soared at her first glimpse of Millie Sargent, Bernard Munson, Benny DeLuca, and Emily and Noah Price when they jumped off the front step and came barreling down the walk to meet them. They were a welcome sight, making her realize afresh that the terms *Sheltering Arms* and *home* had somehow become nearly synonymous. It wasn't that she didn't look forward with eagerness to the day she would return to Sandy Shores for a family visit, but, for now, God had granted her such peace about living in this big house with people who needed her. She took a deep breath and tasted the joy of her passion.

Charlotte jumped out before the carriage had come to a complete stop, and Maggie surmised it was due to the precious bundle Mrs. Bingham was cradling. If anyone had the inborn gift of nurturing, it was Charlotte Decker. She'd been unusually quiet on the trip from Lincoln to New York, no doubt missing baby Christina more than words could express, but here she was again, preparing to make herself vulnerable to another needy infant. She hurried toward the house with Stanley at her back. Ricky and Stuart jumped down next, then Luke. He turned to help Rose Marie, but she leaped to the ground unassisted.

"Well, okay then," Luke said, laughing quietly when the girl set off. Then, he turned to Maggie and reached up a hand, which she gladly took, her wobbly legs demanding assistance. He bent his arm at the elbow, and she tucked her hand into the curve of it.

"I didn't get took by any family!" Rose Marie blurted out as she marched up the path to the front door, her cloth doll dangling at her side.

Mrs. Bingham placed the infant in Charlotte's eager embrace and opened her arms wide to the dejected child, meeting her halfway. "Well, glory be for that!" she exclaimed, pulling her close. "I got to thinking that life here at Sheltering Arms would be rather dull without you! I know Millie and Emily are happy to see you." A solemn-faced Ricky walked past Mrs. Bingham to peruse the new wide-eyed residents, putting on his best scowl.

Mr. Bingham patted him on the shoulder. "Welcome home, Ricky," he said.

Mrs. Bingham released Rose Marie and focused her attentions on Maggie. "My dear girl, you look as frail as a one-winged dove. Whatever did you catch?"

Maggie laughed in spite of herself, going willingly into Mrs. Bingham's arms and savoring the warmth of them against the cooling, late September air. "The doctor tells me influenza."

"Well, you're home now, and the first thing I intend to do is feed you some chicken soup. Then, we'll make some introductions, and after that, it's off to bed with you."

"What?" Maggie pulled back from her. "I just got here, and you're already sending me to bed?"

"Well, if it suits you, you may recline on the sofa, but I can tell from the look of you that you haven't had a decent night's sleep for some time."

She must have looked worse than the mirror had indicated the previous morning. She supposed that's what happened when one spent several nights curled up on a train seat. For that matter, none of the other riders looked that rested, either. "That would suit me well," she said. "But, please, don't treat me like an invalid. Goodness, you'll have me so spoiled I won't want to lift a finger."

"Oh, pooh, everyone needs a little spoiling now and then."

At that, Mrs. Bingham turned Maggie's body toward the house, and together, everyone filed inside.

K

Dear Papa and Grandmother,

I trust you received my postcards from Ohio, Illinois, and Nebraska. I certainly received your much-welcomed letters upon my return to New York. What a wonderful treat! Our trip west was mostly successful in that we left with nineteen orphans and returned with only three; successful in that we found so many wonderful homes for most of the children, but somewhat sad for those we did not. If I had it within my means, I would adopt them all.

Do you think I'm foolish for saying that? I especially love little Rose Marie Kring. Perhaps someday you'll meet her.

Oh, how I miss you all. Do you know I am already marking the days off until I come home for Christmas?

I must tell you that while in Lincoln, I contracted the most dreadful case of a fever and chills, accompanied by an awful stomach ailment. I acquired it from Rose Marie, who recovered within twenty-four hours. Sadly, I cannot say the same for myself. In fact, my illness caused a delay in our return, prompting the whole lot of us to stay a few extra days. Thankfully, the Presbyterian parsonage is a rambling old house, and, while it was crowded, Mrs. Ardmore insisted every one of us stay holed up with the reverend and her. (So that you do not worry, I am much improved since our return to Sheltering Arms two days ago.)

There are several new residents at the refuge, and I am still learning all their names and personalities. This is an ever-changing environment. It is beyond heartbreaking to see so many orphans and half-orphans needing our services, but I am so proud and pleased to be able to offer what little I can to make their lives a trifle easier. (Thank you for giving me your blessing, Papa. There is no doubt the Lord intends to teach me much as I fulfill my duties here.)

Those children who are old enough, a dozen or more, attend school daily, thereby freeing the workers to assemble meals, keep up with laundry, sweep floors, change bedding, and so on. It is different now that the school year is upon us. In the summer months, the children did more chores, but now, their primary duties are making their beds in the morning, tidying up their spaces, and keeping up with their schoolwork. Some of them are so distracted by their new environments it is difficult for them to concentrate.

I have a strong suspicion that Luke Madison, the reporter for the World, *will not be staying on much longer. Lately, he has seemed more distant and aloof. I think perhaps he feels his time here is quickly drawing to a close. By now, I'm certain he must surely have completed the research for his article. (I'm afraid I shall miss him when he leaves.)*

Oh, there is so much more I could tell you, but most of it will wait until I see you in December. Never fear, though, I shall keep you abreast of all the most important information.

I love you both. Please send my love to Abbie Ann, Hannah Grace, Gabe, and my precious nephew, Jesse.

Fondly,
Maggie Rose

By design, she did not mention Congressman Blackwell and her near-death encounter with him and his accomplice, ruling it best to keep some matters to herself. Now, all she had to hope was that the news of Mr. Blackwell's misconduct would not reach Sandy Shores, Michigan.

K

"How's school going for you, Ricky?" It was an afternoon in mid October, and Luke and Ricky were tossing a baseball back and forth in the backyard. In the corral by the barn, the cows were mooing, and the refuge's stray pooch, Charlie, lay curled under the shade of an ancient oak, while a few chickens picked at the ground in search of a seed or two. Cool breezes dislodged the gold and orange leaves collecting on the branches and sent them floating to the earth, creating a crunchy blanket.

The boy shrugged. Lately, he'd been despondent, and Luke could guess why. His friends, Peter Kramer and Gilbert Garrison, were gone, and a whole new batch of orphans and half-orphans had taken up residence at Sheltering Arms. Oh, Bernard Munson, Benny DeLuca, Noah Price, and, of course, Stuart were still here, but all of them had more affable personalities than Ricky, and they had been quick to make new friends. Ricky, on the other hand, had developed a side to him that Luke hadn't seen before. Whereas he'd once been downright ornery and irritable, he now wore a long face denoting a deep depression, never reserving so much as a hint of a smile for anyone and retreating as much as possible. In fact, it had taken some serious effort on Luke's part to convince the boy to come outside with him.

It'd been almost a week since their return, and Luke worried what would happen to the boy after he left. Stan could spread himself only so thin, what with new boys arriving almost daily. The last he heard, the numbers had climbed to eleven girls under Maggie's care, thirteen boys under Stan's, and five in the nursery with Charlotte. It appeared that additional staff would soon be necessary; either that, or another facility in which to house some of the children.

"It's okay."

"You need any help on your homework tonight?"

"Nope."

"Are you learning lots of new things every day?"

Ricky never caught the ball, no matter how direct Luke's aim; therefore, most of their conversing took place while Ricky chased after the ball. Luke managed to catch most of Ricky's pitches, despite having to dive for the ball in several instances.

"Naw. It's boring."

About all he'd gotten from the boy these days were three- and four-word replies.

"Who's your teacher?"

"Don't remember his name."

Luke found that hard to believe. More likely, he just didn't want to discuss it. This time, when he caught the ball, he let it fall to the ground. "You want to go rub down the horses?"

"I already did that when I got home from school."

"Oh."

Without so much as a farewell, Ricky tucked his ball glove under his arm and headed for the house.

Luke caught up to him. "Hey, let's sit on the steps and talk a minute."

"About what?"

"I don't know. Just stuff, I guess. Whatever you choose."

Ricky shrugged again, then sat down by the back door. These days, the doors remained closed to the outside elements. Clearly, fall had arrived in its colorful uniform, bringing with it plenty of chilly air. Luke pulled his coat collar up around his throat and plunked down next to Ricky, long legs extended, but not before glancing through the window for a glimpse of Maggie. She was standing at the stove stirring a kettle, her blonde hair falling about her shoulders, her blue skirt cinched at her small waist with a white apron. He couldn't help but let his gaze linger on her for a few seconds.

Since the arrival of the new residents, she'd jumped head-long into assisting Mrs. Bingham and the volunteers with the added responsibilities, not to mention chipping in when needed with Charlotte and her wee charges. In the evening hours, she helped with homework and read to the smaller children before heading upstairs shortly thereafter to get them all tucked into bed at a decent hour. Luke rarely saw her again after this, figuring she used that time to write letters to her family and rest in the privacy of her room. After her bout with influenza, Dr. Hesselbart ordered rest and more rest to prevent a serious relapse. Mrs. Bingham had agreed, of course, but Maggie was nothing if she wasn't stubborn. Daily, he watched her with new wonder and respect, while he tried to figure out how in the world he could ever win over someone as pure and wonderful as she, someone so committed to meeting the needs of others. What made him think she'd even have a minute to spare for him if he did want to court her? Although, when he looked at Stan and Charlotte, he observed them having plenty of time for each other in the evenings. He scoffed at his ridiculous musings. For all he knew, Maggie had not the slightest desire to encourage his advances. After all, she had an important mission to fulfill at Sheltering Arms. Where would he get the notion he might begin to complement her passions? No, that would have to come straight from God.

"You leavin' Shelterin' Arms pretty soon? I mean, you got that newspaper article all wrote up?" Ricky initiated. If there was one thing the orphans at Sheltering Arms lacked, it was proper grammar. Luke offered a weak smile. "I'd say it's pretty much wrapped up, yes." He rubbed his hands together to warm them up.

"So, they got that congressman guy?"

"There'll be a trial, of course." The news had hit the papers, including the *Times*, but the *New York World* owed Luke for having run the piece ahead of everyone else. Owen Perry had called it great journalism, and he couldn't stop singing Luke's praises for the well-dictated wire he'd sent through Western Union in Lincoln. Luke could barely remember sending it for all the stress he'd been under. "A first-rate reporter lays aside his worries and fears and reports the news, young man," Owen had said on the telephone just yesterday. "I'm thinking you might be ready to come back to the office a little sooner than I originally projected. You're sounding a lot stronger. You want to come in and talk about it?"

Owen's affirmation should have filled him with anticipation, but instead, it had put him in a kind of quandary, one he couldn't quite set to words, at least not on the phone.

"Yes, sure, I'd like to come in and talk about it, Owen. Thanks for that."

Ricky scraped his shoes in the dirt, digging a hole with the toe of his boot. The movement brought Luke back to the present. "Is that ol' lady goin' to jail?"

"What's that?" Luke asked, crossing his ankles and shoving his hands into his pockets.

"That lady I heard you guys talkin' about, the one who owns that tavern. Is she goin' to jail?"

"Oh, her. Well, they'll run an investigation of her business dealings, find out how much she and the congressman were in cahoots, yes. But it could be some time before we discover if they plan to prosecute her."

"Well, I say they ought to throw her in the poorhouse," Ricky said matter-of-factly.

"You do, huh?" Luke had no idea how much Ricky knew about Maxine and Clara's involvement at Miss Violet's Saloon, or if he'd just surmised a story on the basis of his limited knowledge. He decided not to enlighten him. As for Floretta, she'd been staying on with Reverend and Mrs. Miles, and the last he'd heard, she'd been cleaning the church as a means of paying back the warmhearted folks for their show of unconditional benevolence. According to the reverend, it would be a while before she gained enough confidence to strike out on her own, though. "What she needs is purpose," he'd told Luke just that Sunday. "Something to prove her value in God's eyes. Right now, she doesn't see it, and no amount of my wife or me telling her she is capable of leading a good life is going to make her turn the corner. It's something she must do on her own—with the Lord's guidance and direction, mind you."

"Well, she certainly did a good thing in talking to you about that crooked congressman, Blackwell. That ought to make her feel good about herself."

The reverend gave a slow nod. "You'd think. But when folks have repeatedly been made to believe they have no value, it takes a great deal more than someone telling them they did a good job. They literally need to catch themselves in the act of providing compassion and goodwill to another human being."

Even now, Luke pondered the reverend's words, wondering about their full meaning.

"So, that means you're leavin' for good?" Ricky asked.

The very question set his mind to spinning—and mostly around thoughts of Maggie.

"Well, I—I don't know as I'd say 'for good.' Those words sound so final."

He'd taken to reading his Bible on a nightly basis, but every day, he thought about how far he had to go to measure up to Maggie Rose Kane's standards. To be sure, Annalise had held to her Christian faith, but seldom had they discussed their personal beliefs, and they never would have thought to pray together. Here at Sheltering Arms, a prayer was said before every meal, before bedtime, and in between, if the occasion arose. It gave him pause to think how willing Annalise had been to marry him, despite his lack of spiritual maturity. Had she planned to work on reforming him after their wedding, or had she merely considered it an unimportant factor?

Somehow, he needed to figure out a way to get Maggie Rose alone to discuss his feelings—if he could even find a way to understand them fully himself—before he left Sheltering Arms, whether for good or not. Besides, he just had to get in another good kiss, didn't he? How else did one ever learn if the grief over a lost loved one had lessened?

"Well, it figures," Ricky mumbled. "Everybody leaves around here."

Sudden pity for the boy welled up from his innermost parts. "Not everybody. You have Mr. and Mrs. Bingham, don't forget, and then there's Stan."

"They don't want me stayin' here."

"What in the world makes you say that?"

"They keep puttin' me on the train, don't they?"

"Well, it's true they'd like you to find a permanent home, but Henry and Ginny would never force you to leave."

He lifted his shoulders and dropped them with a sigh, his frown firmly in place. "Next time, I swear, I ain't comin' back. Me an' Stu'll set off on ar' own."

"Don't even think such a thing, Ricky. Stu is too young for setting out, no matter how capable you may think you are of taking care of him. Harm could come to you. Besides, you need to stay in school."

Luke recalled the brief story Stan had told him a while back about Stuart and Ricky's mother dying in Central Park, and how the police had found the boys sprawled across her body. From there, they'd landed in Sheltering Arms and had been here ever since, having taken exactly three train rides east since in hopes of finding a home. His heart pinched with regret for all they'd been through. He'd at least had Aunt Frances and Mrs. Jennings to dote on him. Even if "dote" wasn't the proper word, he had never wanted for anything— except maybe the closeness and warmth of family.

The unvarnished fact was that he had more money than most of the supporters of Sheltering Arms Refuge put together, and yet it sat in a bank, untouched and gathering more interest than dust on a deserted windowsill. No one, not Owen Perry, not Nathan Emory, not Stan, not even Henry or Ginny could imagine the vast wealth left to him by Aunt Frances. Shucks, did he even know the grand total of all his assets? He didn't *need* to work at the *World*. Realistically speaking, he could live the remainder of his days as a hermit and never lack food or shelter. His deceased uncle had left Aunt Fran a veritable fortune, but since her death, he hadn't wanted to think about it, much less do anything with it.

Not until now, that is. He could be putting it to good use.

Chapter Thirty

The second Saturday in October shone clear and sparkling as a crystal goblet. The cool breezes of the past several days had chosen to let up, distinguishing this as one of the warmest, most brilliant Indian summer days Maggie could recall. More than once that morning, while sweeping leaves from the front step, dusting windowsills, or straightening library shelves, she had caught herself in a joyous refrain, caring not whose ears it fell upon. In the backyard, the merry squeals of children at play filled the air.

"Is that a song you're singin', or what?" asked Lyle Forkner as he sauntered through the room on his way to the library. A boy of about fourteen, he'd arrived at Sheltering Arms with his two younger sisters while Maggie and the others had been on the train. Like all the others, they had a sad story, but Maggie had asked Mr. Bingham to spare her the details, and so he had. Destitute and sadly neglected—that was all she needed to know.

"Is that a song, did you say? You don't recognize it?" came a velvet-lined voice from behind.

She whirled, dust cloth in hand. Luke approached with some sort of basket under his arm, Mrs. Bingham trailing with a coy smile.

"No," Lyle said, stopping midway to the library. "Should I?"

Mrs. Bingham walked up behind Maggie and untied her apron strings. "Wh—?

"My dear boy, that was 'Ida, My Sweet Apple Cider,' right, Maggie?" Luke asked, chortling in that sly way of his.

"I—yes, it was."

Luke dipped his chin and looked Maggie head-on, a boyish smile turning his mouth up at the corners. "And didn't I hear you singing 'In the Good Ol' Summertime' just before that?" Before giving her a chance to reply, he straightened and pulled her arm through his while shifting the mystery basket to the other.

"Wh—? Um…." Maggie swallowed down a lump of embarrassment, if not plain confusion, then quickly arched her eyebrows at Lyle. He shrugged as if to say, "Don't ask me what's going on."

"Here, you'll need this," Mrs. Bingham said, stepping forward to hand her a wrap. "It may get chilly later."

"What? Chilly? What are we doing?" But even as she asked the question, Luke whisked her toward the door.

At the entryway, she turned in time to see a smiling Stan, Charlotte, and Mr. Bingham peek their heads around the corner. "Have fun," they called, waving wildly.

The last thing she noted before Luke closed the front door behind them was Lyle's perplexed facial expression.

Most surprising was the beautiful red brougham carriage waiting in the circle drive. She slowed her pace, staring in astonishment, then halted altogether. "Luke Madison, whatever you have in mind, I'm not dressed for it. Look at me." She glanced down at her plain, gauzy-sleeved housedress with the low, rounded neckline, a blue cotton getup she'd donned to do her chores. It wasn't her worst dress, but it was far from elegant. Why, she hadn't even done up her hair in a fashion suitable for riding on a rig with leather seats and shiny paint. What in the world?

He paused and gave her a sweeping glance. "You look beautiful from top to bottom, madam. And if you're worried that I plan to take you anywhere formal, you can relax. That's not my style. Besides, what do you think I have in this basket?"

He held it up.

"I haven't the foggiest idea."

"A picnic, my dear."

"A pic—." Her throat caught. No one, certainly not a man, had ever taken her alone on a picnic. The very notion set her heart to fluttering. "But, I don't—I have children to tend to—there are tasks…."

Luke laughed. "Just get up there, Miss Kane. It's time you had a day off from work."

"A day off? But—."

"You're full of protests today, aren't you? How about you sit back, take in the scenery, and enjoy a little leisure? Ginny and Charlotte have everything under control."

"They do?" She let him ease her closer to the fully enclosed carriage. Its driver was perched high atop a box seat, wearing a dark suit and tall hat, and the black satin horse hitched to the front was pawing at the ready on the pebble drive. Why, she'd never ridden in this sort of carriage before. She would even venture to say that no one in all of Sandy Shores, not even the famous doctor, Ralston Van Huff, had ever even seen such a fancy contraption.

With tentative steps, she inched forward, allowing Luke to help her up. Her utter joy and exhilaration were almost more than she could tamp down.

Merciful heavens! I've entered a fairy tale.

"Where to, Mr. Madison?"

"Central Park, Elger. We'll start at the zoo."

"Yes, sir." Elger snapped the horse into a comfortable gait. *Central Park? The zoo?* Ever since arriving in New York, she'd wanted to visit the zoo, but she'd always thought they'd take the children. She hadn't imagined an actual picnic date with Luke Madison. Her pulse took a foolish leap.

Lord, again, I ask that You would guard my heart. Not for an instant do I wish to run ahead of You, came her silent prayer.

My dear girl, He seemed to say in return, *entrust your life into My very capable hands. I will lead you in the path you should go. Is not My Word hidden in your heart, that you may know My wonderful plans, plans to prosper you and not to harm you? Trust Me, My child.*

Yes, Father.

K

As they traveled west on 65th Street, Maggie trained her eyes on the sights along the way, and Luke realized he didn't know much about courting. What he'd had with Annalise had fallen into place like magic, dating one day and discussing marriage the next. Looking back, he remembered little about worrying over saying just the right thing or acting a certain way with her. One day, he'd walked through the doors of Engel's Restaurant, spotted a beautiful woman, and felt an instant connection with her. She'd waited on his table, lingered to visit, and laughed at his jokes. In time, they'd discovered they had a lot in common, so he kept returning. From then on, the bond between them had strengthened, growing into love. He'd had no angst or worries about trying to impress her. In fact, he'd always believed he held the cards in the relationship—not because he wanted to be in control, but because she relinquished it. He always knew where he stood with her, and vice versa.

Maggie Rose, on the other hand, stumped him; she had his stomach tied up tighter than a towel in the wringer mangle. Oh, he'd given the impression of being calm and collected by asking his aunt's old carriage driver, Elger Braun, to dust off the brougham and drive it over to Sheltering Arms. He'd even shown his cleverness in bringing Charlotte and Ginny into his scheme, Ginny going so far as to pack them a lunch of turkey sandwiches, canned fruit, cookies, and a jar of orange punch. Why, he'd even made sure to include a tablecloth and eating utensils!

But his sense of ease and refinement stopped there. Inside, he was nervous as could be. First, he truly didn't know his own intentions; he couldn't even get his heart untangled enough to recognize what it was feeling. Why, just four months ago, he'd been engaged to another woman! Second, he had no notion of what she thought of him. He'd kissed her, yes, and she'd definitely responded, but a few weeks had passed since then, and for all he knew, she'd let the incident fade from her memory.

He sent up a silent prayer of his own. *Lord, it's been a slow journey finding my way back to You, but I believe I'm getting there. Give me keen ears to hear Your voice and learn Your plans*

and purposes—and to know whether those plans include Maggie
Rose Kane. Most of all, Lord, help me not to waver from the path
You've carved out for me.

The apparent response was instantaneous. *My son, trust*
Me with your whole heart, He seemed to say. *Remember the*
promises you have gleaned from My Word in these past days, how
I long to bring hope and healing to your broken spirit. Blessed is
the man who trusts in Me alone.

Yes, Lord.

Elger navigated the carriage into Central Park's entrance
at 5th Avenue and 65th Street, then gave a clarion "Whoa!"

"Are we here?" Maggie asked, her childlike voice nearly
stealing Luke's breath away. It had been a long time since he'd
looked at New York City through eyes of awe. What he could
learn from Maggie Rose through simple observation!

"We are, indeed." He gathered her wrap, secured the
handle of the picnic basket, and reached for the door, but
Elger beat him to it.

"Allow me, miss," he said, extending his gloved hand to
Maggie. For the briefest instant, his mind burned with a
memory—Aunt Frances slapping his hand as a young boy for
reaching for the door ahead of Elger. "Why do you think we
pay him to taxi us around, Luke? You must learn to sit like a
gentleman and await his services." Aunt Frances had always
been strict about following proper protocol, but she'd had a
generous spirit, so he couldn't fault her entirely. As a matter
of fact, the nostalgic recollection put a dull ache of longing in
his heart to see her again. She may not have been an overly
demonstrative person when it came to showing affection, but
he'd never doubted her love for him.

Maggie giggled with excitement, which generated a
glint of warmth in Elger's eyes as he helped her down. Luke

grinned and stepped down behind her, and Elger tipped his hat at Luke. "I'll wait right here for your return, sir. No need to hurry."

"If you'd rather come back in a couple of hours that'd be fine, Elger. Why not go have a cup of coffee and a good chat with some of your cronies?"

He nodded. "I'll do that, sir. Thank you, sir."

Luke sighed as the man returned to his box seat. Some habits never died. To Elger Braun, Luke would always be his superior, no matter that the man had to be pushing seventy, albeit a spry seventy. He smiled down at Maggie and looped his arm. "Which do you want to see first, the monkeys or the bears?"

"Oh, the monkeys, of course!" she said without the briefest pause. "Their silly antics put me in mind of Abbie Ann."

He lifted one brow. "Your sister?" She gave three fast nods. He laughed. "I think you should tell me about her on the way to the monkey house. In fact, I want to hear about your entire family."

"You do?" She smiled with apparent delight.

They set off walking, her arm through his, and he started to relax.

K

Maggie could not have imagined a more perfect day if she'd orchestrated its every second herself. From the monkey house to the bear caves to the bird sanctuary, and even in the reptile quarters, they hadn't once stopped talking. Luke would ask her a question, and she'd answer, then shoot one right back at him. He even confessed to having cracked open his

Bible more often, as of late. Her heart sang, but she carefully kept her excitement to herself.

"What prompted that?" she asked, feigning nonchalance.

"I had a sort of experience, I guess you'd call it, in the reverend's office back in Lincoln. I was working on my newspaper article, and the words were flowing nicely, when, suddenly, my pencil went dull; absolutely quit producing graphite."

He ended his thought there and turned his attention to some kind of African bird species. Surely, he meant to tell her more. "Your pencil went dull?"

He laughed. "It's kind of a long story, but I think there was a lesson in there for me. I'm still trying to figure it out, actually, but it had something to do with a life lacking passion and purpose being about as useful to God as that dull, pointless pencil was to me." He stopped and gave her a sheepish look, sinking his hands deeper into his pockets. "I can tell by your face that what I just said made no sense whatsoever to you."

She stared at him while a dozen exotic birds flitted about their heads in the bird sanctuary. "What? Are you joking? It made all the sense in the world. In fact, it was profound."

They kept up a lively interchange for the next hour or more, every so often finding something new to discuss at length or to laugh about.

"Shall we sit?" Luke asked later when they came to a vacant bench beside a quiet stream, having viewed most of the animals in their habitats. At the water's edge, a couple of swans preened their feathers.

"That would be nice." Overhead, birds and squirrels kept up a constant chatter while, across a field, enthusiastic children set off on a run, their parents trying to keep up. Crisp leaves of many colors lay in their path, crumbling beneath their tread. A boy threw a ball a distance, and a big brown dog bounded after it.

They sat down on the wooden bench, their sides fitting snugly against each other, and Luke placed the picnic basket on the ground at their feet. His thigh brushed against Maggie's skirt, making her insides tingle with excitement. "You couldn't have picked a better day for this outing."

"Are you happy you gave in?" he asked.

"Extremely. Have you ever known it to be so warm in October? If I close my eyes I can almost imagine it being July."

"It's a gift, all right, but I would have stolen you away for the day, regardless of the weather."

"You've had this planned for a while, then?"

"Oh, a few days. Of course, when Ginny got wind of it, she had to drag Charlotte into the plan, and the next thing I know, the whole lot of them have jumped onboard. The picnic lunch was Ginny's idea, but I called Elger of my own accord." He seemed proud of that fact.

"Elger. You've known him a long time?"

"He was my aunt's driver for many years, as long as I can remember. He took her everywhere. That woman wouldn't walk a block to the food market if her cupboards were empty, which is an oxymoron in itself, considering she had shoppers to keep her pantry stocked and cooks to prepare our meals."

"And do you still have someone seeing to your needs— when you're home, that is?" In all their discussions today, he hadn't mentioned his past. All she had to go on was the story he'd told her several weeks ago about the *General Slocum* disaster and the losses he'd suffered. She longed to know more about it, including whatever he wanted to tell her about his beloved Annalise.

"Naw. I make do on my own."

"You cook?"

He grinned and picked a yellow leaf off his sleeve. "I didn't say I cook; I said I make do."

"So, you subsist on bread and butter, in other words."

He tossed his head back and let out a hearty chuckle. "I'm very good with a bread knife."

"'*Man shall not live by bread alone*,'" she quoted in jest.

He laughed again. "You sure know how to whip out the Scripture." An awkward pause ensued. "I also take my meals out a lot. Annalise's family owns a restaurant, so I go there— or used to."

He had provided the opening, so she walked through it. "It must be hard for you to go there now. I don't know if I could do it."

He nodded, bent over to uproot a long blade of grass, and looked out over the park, elbows propped on his knees. "It's different, that's for sure, but I mainly go to check on Heinz, Annalise's father. I haven't been down there since coming to Sheltering Arms, though. I should get back there."

"I'm sure he appreciates your visits."

"They're good for both of us."

It felt like stepping on hot coals to keep the conversation moving, but she had to ask. "Do you miss her terribly? Annalise, I mean?"

He shot her a pointed look, and for a moment, she thought he might tell her to mind her own business. She waited for the harsh response. "She was a beautiful woman," he said instead, his eyes trailing after the same boy and his dog that had been playing for several minutes.

For the next few minutes, he talked about Annalise—her flowing, ebony hair and charcoal eyes, her sparkling persona, and the way she loved people. Maggie made a self-conscious sweep of her platinum hair, tucking several loose strands behind her ears and thinking about the dreadful contrast she must make to his lovely Annalise. "When customers walked through Engel's door, they came to see her," he said with a proud smile. "The food's great, mind you, but Annalise and Zelda, her mother, were the true drawing cards. The restaurant's nothing special—sort of run-down, actually—but it's got charm, just like the neighborhood. Don't know if the neighborhood will survive, though."

He went on to talk about the German community that made up the Lower East Side, how many men had up and left after the tragedy, some even committing suicide for lack of hope. Tears welled up in Maggie's eyes for all the pain and suffering so many had endured, but mostly for Luke's. She dabbed at her wet cheeks, wishing for the handkerchief that was tucked in her apron pocket back at Sheltering Arms.

As if suddenly coming out of a dream, Luke snapped to attention and looked at her. "Gosh, what's wrong with me? I'm sorry for going on like that."

"No, no, it's good. You needed to get it out, and I—well, I've wondered. Thank you for trusting me enough to share about your past."

He shifted in the bench to face her better, then took her face in his hands, rubbing her tear-streaked cheeks with the pads of his thumbs. "I seem to have a knack for making you cry."

She shook her head gently and bit down on her lip. "I wish I had a tougher façade."

"What?" He lowered his head to look into her eyes, hands still cupping her face, thumbs now stroking her jaw line. "You have a tender core like no one I've ever known, and it's a trait to cherish."

She gazed through bleary eyes at his features and thought she saw a smile playing around his mouth, until something in his expression intensified, and he moved in closer. What to do with her wildly thumping heart was the question. Surely, he could hear it! She put a hand to her pounding chest, as if that would slow its violent pulsations. In a quivering second, his lips met hers, soft and supple and terribly warm. His chest pressed gently against her hand, and his arms encircled her, pulling her close. For the life of her, she couldn't breathe. In many ways, the kiss matched the one they'd shared on the train, but in a million other ways, it didn't. This one implored her to look deeper, to sing louder, to reach higher, to cling tighter, and to fall further.

Had she reached the point of no return with this man, then? The point at which she could no longer rein in her heart?

One kiss turned into kisses, and she cared not who passed by, what they might think, or what remarks they would make. A dog barked, a horse neighed, and a baby squealed, but all of it was lost to her as she took a perilous leap into the unknown.

All that was left to do was pray the Lord would cushion her fall.

K

She was everything he needed and more. Soft, passionate, beautiful, sweet, and precious. Despite the total impropriety of kissing her in broad daylight, and in a public place, no less, he couldn't help himself. He loved the delicate feel of her, the way she fit against him like a lost and found puzzle piece. She slipped her arms around his neck, and, despite the burning heat of the day, a shiver scurried up his spine. He couldn't think straight; he could barely even breathe. He whispered against her lips, telling her she meant everything to him. The kiss intensified. She whimpered something in return. He muttered back, "Annalise."

Suddenly, as if recovering from a cruel blow, she pushed hard, putting space between them, her blue eyes showing the tortured dullness of disbelief. She stared for several seconds, unblinking, breaths coming out in awkward spurts.

"What?" she asked. Luke's heart thudded loudly in his ears. He had to think what he'd said; had to get his bearings. He wiped a hand across his sweaty brow and stared back, terrified that what he'd thought in his head might have come out of his mouth. Had it? Had he actually whispered "Annalise" when he'd clearly meant to say "Maggie"? His mind fairly whirled in unspeakable confusion. He had been thinking only of Maggie when he'd kissed her so completely, hadn't he? His throat clogged with tumultuous tension.

"I think we should go, don't you?" She sniffed and stood up.

"Maggie, I think I can explain. Let's get out the picnic lunch Ginny packed and talk about—."

She put up her hand to stop him. "There's absolutely nothing to explain, Luke. In fact, I wouldn't want you trying. Really, I'd just like to leave."

He jumped to his feet. "No, I—I want to tell you what I think happened. I was actually thinking—."

She laid her hand on his arm and applied pressure. "It's all right. The plain truth of the matter is that you still love her, Luke. You love her. She is still the first face you see when you wake up in the morning."

"No."

"Yes. And I wouldn't expect it to be any other way." She swallowed hard, and the tears in her eyes were inconsolable. "But here's the thing. You cannot hang on to both of us at the same time. I am not Annalise, nor do I wish to walk in her shadow."

"I know that. I don't—."

She squeezed down harder, almost to the point of making him wince. "So, I think that what needs to happen is for you to go."

"Go."

She took a long, labored breath and nodded. "When we get back to Sheltering Arms, I want you to pack your bags and say good-bye." His heart cinched. "Please," she tacked on.

He stared down at her for ten seconds, blinking back his own bitter tears. Finally, he nodded. Because he knew she was right.

He wasn't over Annalise Engel.

Chapter Thirty-one

The days grew shorter and colder as October turned to November. Life at Sheltering Arms Refuge took on a heartening sameness that Maggie clung to for strength and assurance. No one could term it "monotonous," though, for, truly, no two days were alike. But the ironically predictable variety made living at Sheltering Arms a rewarding experience. It had its challenges, yet she daily thanked the Lord for opening the doors of opportunity for her to pour her heart and soul into her work. While she missed Maxine, Clara, Audrey, and the Zielinski and Pelton sisters, she quickly discovered she had little time for dwelling on their absence and hardly a chance to feel lonely. The new girls required her utmost attention and affection as they learned to adjust to their new surroundings. And then, of course, there was Rose Marie, who had to be taught in small increments that, while she remained dearest to Maggie's heart, there were others who needed her attention, as well. She seemed to grasp that—as well as any six-year-old mind could.

There were tears, displays of anger, and disputes to settle between the girls, but there were also many moments of laughter and fun, and all of it combined brought the truest sense of satisfaction to her frayed and tattered heart.

Yes, her heart had frayed—more like shredded—since Luke's departure from Sheltering Arms. Saddest was his lack of communication, not only with her, but also with the rest of the staff. Mrs. Bingham fretted and stewed over his abrupt exit, saying she wished she could have given him a proper farewell, and wasn't it strange the way he up and vanished like nobody's business? "I asked him to go, Ginny," Maggie had divulged at the kitchen table on his second day of absence. She'd followed up with a detailed account of their kisses on the train and in the park. The children were in school, and the little ones were taking their naps, when Charlotte had walked in midway through the confession. Maggie had invited her to sit and listen, and by the end of the tale, all three women had been a blubbering mess.

"It will all work out as God intends," Mrs. Bingham had assured her, using the corner of her apron to dab at her eyes. "I'm sure the Lord will use this time to speak to his heart."

"He needs more time to mend," Charlotte had inserted. "He's suffered a great loss."

"I knew just from the way he talked about Annalise at Central Park that he still loves and misses her so much. I am no match for his beautiful fiancée."

"Don't sell yourself short, young lady," Charlotte had said. "You are prettier than anyone I know."

"Oh, goodness, I'm as ordinary as they come."

"Well, if you're ordinary then I'm Mrs. Fanny Face," Mrs. Bingham had put in, causing a sudden spurt of laughter to erupt among them.

When their giggles had died down, Maggie had sighed loudly and tapped her fingers on the rim of her empty teacup. "Well, all I know is, I can't live in another woman's shadow."

"Ha! None of us would want that," Charlotte had said before swallowing her last sip of tea. "I'm actually thankful Stanley never had a proper sweetheart. I am his first and last love, and, really, he's the only man I've ever loved in the true sense. What I had before was nothing but a silly crush."

Maggie had never even had a crush, unless she counted Walden Greenbrook from fourth grade.

And so it went, the three of them voicing their opinions and thoughts yet solving nothing.

On Thanksgiving Day, hordes of volunteer cooks and servers from Dover Street Chapel banded together to prepare the annual feast at Sheltering Arms Refuge, declaring it a day off for all staff. Mrs. Bingham hardly knew how to act when Mrs. Miles shoved her out of her own kitchen, directing her to go and find a place to relax. Never had Maggie seen so much food or heard such commotion as the women basted turkeys, peeled potatoes and yams, baked breads and muffins, and whipped up a smorgasbord of tasty treats. While several worked in the kitchen, others set up tables, using the library and parlor for extra seating, and many of the older children chipped in, eager to help get the meal underway.

To Maggie's great delight, Floretta also came, but rather than work in the kitchen, she mostly rocked babies and played games on the floor with the young ones. Maggie watched, fascinated by how well she related to the children, and how they seemed equally drawn to her.

"She missed out on child rearing," Mrs. Bingham whispered from behind her. Floretta had taken to reading a picture book to a group of children on the braid rug in front of the fireplace. "It's a shame, too, because she's a natural with them."

"She's making up for lost time," Maggie said.

A reporter from the *World* by the name of Nathan Emory showed up at 1 p.m. to take some pictures of the children and interview Mr. and Mrs. Bingham about the annual Thanksgiving festivities. Feeling certain she'd heard Luke mention his friend Nathan in passing, Maggie wanted to ask him about Luke—how he was doing, whether he'd returned to his job, how he looked, and when he planned to release his article to the public. But then, she worried he'd recount her interrogation to Luke, which meant he might relate how she had come across as sorely distressed and downhearted. She decided to retreat to her room during the interview.

All in all, the day had been a great success, mainly because it raised the children's spirits, made them feel special, and reminded them there were people who loved them and cared about their futures.

For Maggie, however, it was a day of reflection and utter loneliness. Oh, no one would have suspected it for a minute, her slump in mood, for she hid it well, making sure to laugh at all the right junctures, join in lively conversation at the dinner table, enter into a game of charades in the parlor, and challenge some children and adults in a carom tournament, in which she came up far short. No, she made sure to hide the fact she missed her traditional Sandy Shores Thanksgiving, where she would have partaken of Grandmother Kane's best recipes and enjoyed friendly banter with her darling sisters and precious Papa. It would have been her first Thanksgiving spent with Gabriel and Jesse, too, and the notion that the lot of them were having a grand time in her absence pained her to her toes.

And then, there was the matter of Luke. Where had he spent the day? With Annalise's family, perhaps—or, worse, alone? Her chest fairly burned with the memory of their kisses. Daily, she prayed for a way to stop thinking about him.

After tucking the girls into their beds, reserving Rose Marie for last so she could give her an extra long snuggle, she tiptoed down the hall to her own room. Mrs. Bingham reached the top of the stairs as Maggie opened her door.

"I've been thinking," she said.

"About what?" Maggie whispered, motioning her to come inside.

Mrs. Bingham stepped through the door and closed it behind her, leaning her plump body against the frame. She bit her lower lip.

"What is it? What's wrong?" Maggie asked, thinking by the look on Mrs. Bingham's face that surely she'd done something terrible.

"Nothing's wrong, dear." She swallowed. "Other than it's time you went home to your family."

"What?" she nearly shrieked. "Why? What have I done?"

"Oh, heavens to Betsy! There is no one more dedicated or zealous than you. We love you, darling, but both Henry and I think it's time you went home—just for a short while, mind you."

"I do—plan to go home—just before Christmas."

"I know, I know, but we think you should go home sooner. It would do your heart good."

Shocked, Maggie opened her mouth to protest, but nothing came out.

For the next few minutes, Mrs. Bingham talked, listing all the reasons why Maggie needed to spend some time with her family. Luke Madison was the primary basis for this belief, but she pitched out several more: Maggie was fatigued, still recovering from her bout with influenza, facing emotional upheaval over her brush with death, and still learning the ropes of a sometimes thankless job. While she talked, a river of tears flowed like rain, tears Maggie hadn't known existed.

"Watching Floretta with the children today cemented my idea. She will take over for you in your absence."

"But...."

"She'll be fine. Mrs. Miles thinks it's exactly what Floretta needs, and I tend to agree. Who knows? Perhaps we'll find a permanent spot for her here at Sheltering Arms."

"You mean to replace me?"

Mrs. Bingham gave her head several fast shakes then chortled. "What? You, my precious girl, are irreplaceable."

Relieved, Maggie wiped her eyes and tried to adjust to the idea of returning to her family and Sandy Shores. "I'm going home? I'm really going home?"

Mrs. Bingham smiled and nodded. "Not forever," she added, waving her index finger under Maggie's nose.

"But...oh." Her heart suddenly plummeted.

"What is it?"

"I—I can't leave Rose Marie. May I take her with me? She won't know what to do without me."

"She has her school lessons."

"I'll see that she stays caught up in all her subjects. She's a smart little girl."

Mrs. Bingham looked thoughtful, but only for a span of three seconds. "Somehow, Henry and I already knew you'd want to take her," she said with a glint in her eyes.

Oh, my! Home. How good it sounded. She gave Mrs. Bingham a hard, fast squeeze, and just like that, her spirits soared.

Luke Madison could just pine after his Annalise for as long as he wanted. As for her, she was getting on with her life. With the Lord's help, of course.

K

With briefcase strapped over his shoulder, Luke strode up the busy sidewalk, weaving in and out to avoid running into pedestrians who appeared not to be watching where they went, men's noses buried in newspapers even as they walked, women looking down at their children, dragging them along by the hand.

He could be taking the city's new underground transit system back to his apartment, as he had done a couple of times, but the walk to and from the New York World Building did his heart good; it gave him plenty of time to process his day and to plan for the next.

Cold, blustery air burned his face as he mapped his course up the street. He might have bought a horse and reached his destination faster, but a horse required food and care, a stall, and plenty of room to roam, as he'd discovered at Sheltering Arms. His two-story brownstone apartment, sprawling and well equipped as it was, did not provide for horses, and, if all went as planned, this commute between his home and work would soon meet its end, anyway. Of course, Owen Perry didn't know that, nor did his good friend, Nathan Emory. In fact, only recently had even he started picturing the whole scenario, aided by God's keen direction, brought about by his heartfelt prayers and many dedicated hours of delving into his Bible. At long last, he'd reached a point of total surrender to the Lord and, in the process, discovered a fiery, continually growing passion for Him.

Ever since his return to work as usual at the *World*, Owen had been after him to hand in his article, which he'd finally titled "Forgotten Emeralds: The City's Lost Treasure." "It's not done yet," Luke kept saying.

"How is that possible? You've been working on the darn thing since August."

"I know, but—I feel like the end hasn't been written yet," Luke said.

"Well, that's obvious," mumbled Owen, showing his prickish side. "Get to writing it, why don't you?" Luke couldn't blame the guy for his impatience. After all, he'd been more than generous by allowing him a leave of absence to straighten out his tattered life. Anyone else might have gotten the boot.

"It's almost there," Luke said. "I can feel it."

And he could. In fact, he could almost taste it.

As had become his habit, Luke scanned the streets for treasure—stray children, in other words—asking God to lead him in his search. Whenever he spotted them, he stopped to talk, ask them about their stories, and inquire as to whether they had a family, a place to call home. Most of them were working for their parents, begging for coins, selling wares, shining shoes at their makeshift stands, or playing small instruments in hopes of earning a penny for their talents. Occasionally, he'd run across a homeless urchin and direct him to the nearest shelter, Sisters of Mercy, sometimes even taking him by the hand and walking with him up the wide expanse of stairs to knock on the big front door. That was until last week, that is, when Sister Mary Constance had taken him aside, quietly explaining that their quarters had filled and asking if he might consider taking the next orphans he found to another shelter.

"And where might that be, Sister?" he'd asked.

She'd shrugged and bit down on her plump lower lip. "I'm afraid the city needs more shelters, Mr. Madison."

Yes, more shelters. But first, *awareness*. His article could provide that. As he walked up the street, bumping shoulders with humanity, he cemented the final words of his commentary in his head so that the instant he walked through the doors of his apartment, he could pull out his notebook and set to finishing the dratted thing, once and for all.

And after that? Well, tomorrow, he planned to take a taxi over to Sheltering Arms to visit Maggie Rose Kane and declare his love to her, that's what. In the past six weeks, he hadn't stopped thinking about her. Why, if he were to put a single drop of water in a cup for every second he thought of her, he'd have run out of cups long ago, not to mention water. The truth of the matter was, he'd lost his heart to her forever, and the time had passed for proving it. But would she accept his confession as truth? Would she even agree to see him?

The Thanksgiving Day interview at Sheltering Arms had been Nathan Emory's idea, and Owen had jumped on it, thinking it would make a relevant connection with Luke's article. In fact, Nathan had invited Luke to come along, but he had declined, thinking his sudden appearance could cause a stir. After all, he'd left abruptly all those weeks ago, taking only a few minutes to say good-bye to everyone and offering what hardly qualified as a satisfactory explanation. He wondered how Maggie had handled things the next day and prayed his exit hadn't caused her undue stress. He also worried about Ricky, hoping to right things with the boy just as soon as he had reconciled with Maggie. *First things first*, he kept telling himself.

Thanksgiving Day had started quietly, but late in the afternoon, he'd rung up Heinz Engel, not surprised when he'd answered the restaurant phone. "Come over, come over," Heinz had said. "Everyone is gone. I'm just cleaning up." And so he'd put on his coat, hailed a cab, and made a run to Engel's, even though the CLOSED placard hung in the window. Heinz had waved him in, and for the first time, the jangle of the bell above the door didn't prompt him to look for Annalise. Rather, he'd thought how grand it would be to bring Maggie Rose to meet Heinz sometime. As a true test, while sipping on a Coca Cola and downing a salami sandwich, Heinz's specialty, he'd told him he'd fallen in love. Heinz didn't so much as flinch; he just smiled while puffing long drags from his pipe and said, "Well, now, this is good news, no?"

"It is to me, Heinz, but I wasn't sure—how you'd take it."

Heinz flapped his wrist. "You must bring her to me, this woman."

"What? Really?" Luke tossed back his head in disbelief. "I wouldn't want to—what about Stefan and Erich?"

"Pfff. They can think what they want. This is your life, and you deserve every happiness. This woman—she is Christian, no?"

Luke closed his eyes and breathed deep. "She is the epitome of one. I've found my way back to the Lord, Heinz, and while she isn't the *reason* I came back to Him, she played a very large part in my rediscovery—more like discovery—of God's love."

Heinz sighed. "Now I know I must meet her."

"Will you still be here, Heinz?" He held his breath while Heinz took his sweet time answering.

"I will be here until the Lord says otherwise, Luke."

"Good. That's good. And your sons?"

He took several more drags of his pipe, then grinned over its stem. "They will do what they will do."

It had been the blessing Luke needed. In many ways, it felt as if he'd closed the book on one chapter of life and opened it to a new one. Now, if only he could get Maggie Rose on his page.

"Lord, please, I have so much I need to tell her, plans I want to share with her. Your plans, Lord. *Our* plans."

He had his notepad in hand and a freshly sharpened pencil at the ready almost before he got through the door. Once done with his rough draft, he would drag out his trusty Number 5 Underwood and type it off. Finally, Owen Perry would have his article.

The jury was out on whether he would approve of the final few paragraphs, though.

K

Maggie heard sounds coming from the Kane kitchen and awoke before opening her eyes. Instinctively, she reached for Rose Marie, but she found the space beside her empty.

"She's downstairs having a heyday with Grandmother."

Her eyes shot open, especially with the rocking motion of the mattress when Abbie Ann's body dropped across it. "Are you ever going to wake up, sleepyhead?" her sister asked, reclining and laying her head on Maggie's stomach. "It's late, you know."

"What time is it?" Maggie asked, yawning. She began combing her fingers through Abbie's thick, inky black hair, reveling in the feel of it. My, but she'd missed her baby sister.

"Nine."

"Nine o'clock? I've slept till nine o'clock in the morning?"

"No, nine at night, silly. Of course, it's morning. Grandmother said you needed your sleep. You've been through the wringer. I heard about that awful gangster fellow attacking you in the churchyard—Papa told me you relayed the story to him last night in the library. And then, to think you got that terrible case of influenza! Grandmother says those germs can hang on in the body for some time. You're worn to a frazzle, sister dear. I'm glad those Bingham folks sent you home. It'll do your soul a world of good to be able to relax and do nothing but concentrate on regaining your strength."

"I think I regained it last night. Goodness, I don't remember the last time I slept till nine o'clock. Why aren't you at the Whatnot, by the way?"

"Hannah Grace is working today, and Jesse's helping her. He's become quite the little businessman behind the cash register."

"He's not in school today?"

"He had the day off. Some sort of teachers' meeting all day."

"Oh, I'm sure that tickled him. I'll walk Rose Marie over there today. She and Jesse will get along grandly, I can tell."

"He'll show her the ropes. Of course, Dusty is there. He's become the Whatnot mascot, always lying on the rug by the door and raising his head just long enough to greet folks before drifting back to dreamland. Silly mutt."

Maggie giggled just picturing it. A year ago, Papa wouldn't have allowed a dog in the store. Strange how Jesse Gant Devlin's arrival on the scene had changed so many things in the Kane household. The dog also freely roamed Grandmother's domain whenever Jesse brought him over, another miracle in itself.

"Say, I meant to ask you how Micah and Katrina Sterling are doing these days. She must be due to have that baby most anytime, right?"

"She isn't due for another month, actually, but I think she'll deliver sooner. She's not been feeling at all well. Pains in her side and back and general fatigue."

"I'm sure that's to be expected in the final stages, wouldn't you think?"

"The doctor says not. Truth is, he can't figure why she's having pains. They ought to get an opinion of someone other than Huffy, don't you think?"

Huffy, as Abbie referred to him, was really Dr. Ralston Van Huff. He had been Hannah Grace's beau until Gabriel Devlin came riding into town almost a year and a half ago. Abbie had never approved of him, and, as it turned out, her instincts had been right. Of the three sisters, Abbie outperformed them in wit and winsomeness, but now that Maggie thought about it, she probably took the prize for female intuition, as well.

She considered Abbie's words. "It might not hurt for her to see another doctor, if for no other reason than to learn that all is well."

"I've said the same, but she insists she doesn't feel like traveling a distance."

"What does Micah say?"

"He's fine with whatever she thinks is best. Frankly, I wish he'd be more forceful, and I told him so. I don't think he likes me very much. I'm always butting in."

Maggie smiled, tipping her chin downward. "Katrina may be your best friend, my darling sister, but she is Micah's wife, and you absolutely cannot interfere with that."

"I know." Abbie cleared the worry from her throat. "Have you heard? We've been invited over to Ambrose and Norma Barton's house for supper tomorrow night."

"But it's not even Christmas yet. We usually go there for caroling and her famous Christmas cherry punch and cookies."

"I think your coming home earlier than planned called for an occasion. Mrs. Barton wants us all there by six o'clock, Gabe, Hannah, and Jesse included."

"Oh, that sounds lovely. I can't wait."

They lay there for scant moments, and for a second, Maggie wondered if her sister hadn't fallen asleep, using her body as a pillow. She would have liked to reposition herself, but she couldn't bear to move, so pleasant was the experience of being close to her sister—just like old times. Oh, how she'd missed home. At the same time, she missed Sheltering Arms. In her mind's eye, she pictured Mrs. Bingham scurrying about the kitchen, Henry and Stan doing chores in the barn, the babies crawling around at Charlotte's feet, and Floretta chipping in, still getting acclimated to her new surroundings.

Then, of course, her thoughts never strayed far from Luke. Oh, what a scoundrel he was for stealing her heart, never mind that she'd given it freely.

"So, tell me about this Luke Madison character."

Character, indeed. Goodness, had she been thinking aloud?

Before she knew it, she had spilled the entire contents of her heart to Abbie, starting with the first time she'd laid eyes on him right up until that last kiss, which had prompted him to whisper the name of Annalise.

"That must have hurt, him calling you by his fiancée's name, but I'm sure it was a mistake. He's probably pining over you this very moment."

"Ha! He's had six weeks to pine, then."

"And heal. That sort of sorrow takes time to recover from, Maggie Rose."

"You sound like Charlotte and Ginny."

"Okay, now you have to tell me about them—oh, and Stanley and Henry, too. And then you must elaborate about Sheltering Arms. I've read your letters, mind you, but there's nothing like hearing it straight from the horse's mouth."

"Excuse me? Do you dare call me a horse?" Maggie picked up a pillow and thumped Abbie on the head. One never did that sort of thing to Abbie, though, without expecting retaliation.

"More like a nag!" Abbie gibed, sitting up and grabbing another pillow with which to lambaste Maggie.

And so it went, this jousting match with pillows, until Grandmother entered the room, hands on her hips, lips pursed in pretend admonition. Rose Marie's feet stood planted on the floor, her eyes round with shock, probably because she'd never seen this frivolous side of Maggie.

"Come here, little one," Maggie said, curling her index finger at Rose Marie. "Let's you and I gang up on Abbie Ann."

Rose Marie gave an impish grin, and in a split second, she sprang onto the bed. The three of them set to tickling one another and squealing like little banshees.

Out the corner of her eye, Maggie spotted Grandmother Kane shaking her head and chuckling quietly before turning on her heel and leaving the room.

K

Owen Perry stood behind his desk and greedily plucked the article from Luke's hands, putting Luke in mind of a dog snagging a ham bone off a dinner table. Luke took a step back and plopped into the one and only chair facing Owen's cluttered desk, steepling his hands under his chin and watching his boss's expression.

"This is good," Owen muttered, eyes eating up the page. Then, "Oh yes, I like this," then nodding. "Mm-hmm, this should give folks something to chew on." He read on, every so often throwing out a comment, turning pages as fast as his eyes scanned them. On the last page, though, Luke noted a distinct change in his facial expression as the fellow slowly lowered himself into his chair. "It's a fine piece, excellent journalism. It will definitely gain public attention. But—I don't understand. Is this—are you—?"

Luke nodded and pulled a folded piece of paper from his briefcase. "I'm afraid this is my letter of resignation, Owen. Nothing personal, mind you. Just something I have to do."

Owen unfolded the letter and read it, gazing intently at each word. Finally, he stood up again and extended his arm across the desk to shake hands with Luke. "I hold myself responsible for this, you know."

"How's that?"

"If I hadn't sent you off to that blasted orphanage…." He said the words in jest, smiling under the surface. "You're a fine journalist, Luke. Talented. You sure you're making the right decision here?"

"I'll be in direct disobedience to the Lord if I don't do it." He wasn't sure how much of that Owen understood, but it helped to get it off his chest.

"The article will appear in one of next week's issues, can't say which day. I do know this, though. It's front-page material." He still had Luke's hand in a firm grip. When their eyes met, Owen's had a glossy sheen to them.

That afternoon, Luke packed up the few personal belongings that remained in his desk, visited with friends and acquaintances in a few other departments, answered questions of his colleagues, and then allowed Nathan to help him carry a couple of large boxes out to his waiting taxi at the end of the day.

"Don't be a stranger, Luke," Nathan said, shoving the box in the wagon's back compartment. Luke did the same with his crate. They faced each other and shook hands, then simultaneously went for a hug instead.

"I never stopped praying for you the whole time you were at Sheltering Arms."

"Then I have you to blame," Luke teased him. "Seriously, though, I appreciate the prayers. I needed to work through a lot of things."

"The *General Slocum* case is getting a thorough investigation."

"So I've read," Luke said.

"Shouldn't be long before they get the trial underway. I hear they're working on the jury selection."

"Should be quite a process," Luke said, nodding. It wasn't that he didn't still read every article he got his hands on that dealt with the case, but his obsession no longer ate a hole through his heart. Nor did it consume his every waking moment. No, he had the present to think about now—and the future, whatever it involved.

He just couldn't help but pray it involved Maggie Rose Kane.

Chapter Thirty-two

W hat do you mean, she's not here? Is she out running errands?"

"No, she's gone," Mrs. Bingham said. "Come in out of the cold before you freeze us all out, would you?" She snagged him by the coat sleeve and pulled him inside, the brisk wind catching hold of the door and slamming it shut.

"Gone?"

"Luke!" Stanley hurried into the room, nearly knocking him over with his strong, lengthy handshake, quickly followed by a strong slap on the shoulder. "'Bout time you came back. What took you so long?"

"Is that Luke I hear?" Mr. Bingham emerged from the kitchen, coffee mug in hand. "Well, glory to heaven!"

Floretta peeked her head around the corner. "Hello, Mr. Madison."

"Floretta! What—?" Floretta had a sleeping baby in her arms. A complex web of confusion clouded his thoughts.

Charlotte whipped around the corner next, a toddler in tow. "Well, lookie here," she said, all smiles and good cheer. "Everyone's in school today—everyone but Ricky, that is.

Poor thing's up in his room with the sniffles. You ought to go peek in on him."

"I will," Luke said. "But, first, where is she? Where's Maggie?"

"Why, in Michigan."

His heart sank clear to his toes. He could hardly believe it. He might have guessed it when he first met her. On first glance, he'd seen her as delicate and naïve, and he had pegged her for not lasting the month—the week, even. But soon, he'd seen her strength of purpose and hardy spunk; he'd recognized the zeal with which she loved and served the children, the boundless energy and excitement she applied to every task. And just like that, she'd picked up and gone back to Michigan? His head stirred with a thousand questions.

"She went home?"

"Hey, when is that human interest story going to appear in the *World*?" Stanley asked, oblivious to Luke's question. "I've been checking the paper every night since you left."

"Yes, did you finish it?" Mr. Bingham asked.

"Why?" he asked.

"Just curious."

"No, why did she go back to Michigan?" He tried to keep his impatience from leaking out. "Is she coming back to Sheltering Arms?"

"Well, of course," said Charlotte.

"She'll be back," Stanley affirmed.

"Henry and I just thought it would be good for her to spend some time with her family," Mrs. Bingham answered. At these consistent responses, Luke whistled a sigh of relief.

"Luke?" All heads turned to see Ricky standing in the kitchen doorway, a glass of water in his hand, hair hopelessly disheveled.

"Hey, buddy!" Luke stepped through the tight circle to approach the lad, turning around at the door. "I'll be back down in a bit to tell you what's been happening in my life, but first, I've got to catch up with this young man."

"Ain't nothin' much to tell," Ricky said with a shrug. Luke winked at his audience, then put a hand on the boy's shoulder and followed him up the stairs.

In his room, Ricky tossed himself on his rumpled lower bunk and motioned at Luke to take a seat. Luke lowered himself to a straight-back wooden chair and gave the room a quick scan, noting three other beds all neatly made. "I guess you've got some new roommates, huh?"

"A couple. Rex sleeps on that upper bed"—he pointed across the room—"and some feller by the name of Howard on the lower. Stu sleeps above me."

Luke nodded, clasped his hands, and propped his elbows on his spread knees. "You getting along okay—aside from that cold you've got there?"

Ricky shrugged and forced a cough. "It seems kind of weird with you gone. I was just gettin' used to you."

Luke grinned. "Likewise. Hey, I wanted to tell you I'm sorry about all that. I left in somewhat of a hurry, but, well, I've been thinking a lot about you and Stu."

"Yeah?" The boy wore a doubtful expression.

"In fact, I'd like to propose something to you—just to see what you think about the idea."

This got Ricky's attention. He turned on his side and propped his head up on his pillow. "I'm listenin'."

K

A whistle sounded, alerting Sandy Shores' citizens of the train's arrival. Luke scanned the assembly of folks on the platform, many preparing to board and others eager to greet incoming passengers. He gathered up his belongings—a suitcase, a dark wool overcoat, a black scarf, a pair of leather gloves, and a day-old newspaper. The woman he'd been seated beside was taking the train further south, to Benton Harbor. She smiled up at him. "You take care now, young man, and I hope things work out for you with the young lady. I can tell you this much just from chatting with you: she would be a fool to say no."

A low chuckle came up from his throat. He couldn't believe he'd divulged so much to a perfect stranger, but his rattled nerves had set his mouth in motion. Fortunately, chances were slim that their paths would cross again. "Well, I thank you for your vote of confidence, ma'am. About all I can say is, it's in God's hands."

She nodded, putting him in mind of Mrs. Bingham with her round face and jovial spirit. "No better place for it." He scooted past her. "Oh, and may the Lord bless your new endeavor, as well."

He waved and disembarked the train. The platform bustled with conversing people, everyone seeming to know each other. *Truly the benefit—or the bane—of small town life,* he thought, smiling to himself. So, this was Maggie's stomping ground. He took a moment to inhale the fresh, clean air. Somehow, he could see himself coming here, year after year with her, growing accustomed to the relaxed atmosphere, the slower pace, the beautiful channel leading out to Lake Michigan, the miles of open sky.

Fresh snowflakes drifted down in a lazy fashion, not sticking to the earth but threatening to if the temperature dropped any further. He set down his suitcase, wrapped his scarf around his neck, and slipped into his coat, hurriedly buttoning it to his throat to block the biting breezes coming off the water. Sticking his hands into his fur-lined gloves, he did a quick survey of his surroundings. Seeing a hotel across the street called Sherman House, he picked up his suitcase, dropped the newspaper into the nearest waste receptacle, and headed over. Just as soon as he had freshened up, he'd inquire as to the location of Kane and Perkins Insurance Office, Maggie's father's place of business.

First on his agenda was to have a man-to-man talk with the father of the woman he hoped to marry.

∽K∽

Maggie dabbed at her moist eyes with the linen handkerchief her father had retrieved from his desk drawer. She might have known telling her father about Luke Madison would trigger another flood of tears. Goodness, when would she ever learn to start carrying her own hanky for such occasions? Jacob Kane dragged a chair closer to the one Maggie had plunked herself into and took her hand in both of his.

"Darling Maggie Rose, you are so much like your mother, do you know that?"

She sniffed, then blew her nose loudly into the fresh linen cloth. "I am? But you've never told me that. How am I like her?"

He sat back and closed his eyes for a few seconds, face tilted upward, as if reviewing all of his memories. Slowly, his gaze came to rest on her face. "Besides her loveliness, you inherited her passionate spirit, her earnest faith in humanity, her undying resolve and strength of character, and her tender, affectionate heart. It is no wonder that when you fall in love with a man, you do it with all your being. That is the way you carry out every aspect of your life, my dear—with your whole self. Unfortunately, that kind of devotedness sometimes leads to a sorrowful heart because you run into someone who doesn't love you with the same vehemence."

"Oh, Papa." She fell into his arms and let another batch of tears fall and soak into the shoulder of his scratchy wool jacket. "I love him so, but I see what you mean," she cried. "I gave my heart away too readily. He'll never recover from his grief, and now…"—she sobbed the harder—"neither will I."

"There, now." He patted her cheek with his smooth palm, rocking her in a gentle manner. "I didn't mean to imply he doesn't love you, Maggie. I've never met this man, so I can't presume to know these things. One thing I do know, though." He pulled away slightly and looked into her eyes. She gave another hard sniff. "He's suffered a hard blow, and you cannot expect him simply to erase the memory of it. Perhaps that is why he's stayed away for these many weeks. He must learn how to allow a piece of his late fiancée to remain in his heart while loving you at the same time." She frowned as she absorbed his words.

"I'm not saying he should allow her memory to cloud what he feels for you, but you mustn't try to stifle it, either. That would only build resentment between you." He pursed his lips in thought and tipped his face at an angle. "After your mother's passing, I wouldn't have minded remarrying, but I simply never found another woman to love. But on the chance I had, how would it have been if my second wife had never allowed me to mention Hattie? Can you imagine how strangling that would have been for me?"

She gave a slow nod as his words sank in. She went back into the warmth of his arms, gaining strength from his support.

"If you seek the Lord's guidance wholeheartedly, and if Mr. Madison does the same, then you shall find your way back to each other. But it must be in accordance with God's will and His perfect timing. Do you trust Him, dear daughter?"

She gave her eyes one last sweep with the handkerchief, then angled her face upward and nodded. "Yes, Papa, I do. With all my heart."

He kissed her forehead. "Good. Now then, you best get back over to the Whatnot, pick up that sweet little charge of yours, and go meet Jesse at the schoolyard as you promised." Jacob checked his pocket watch. "School lets out in less than half an hour."

"Yes, Papa."

"And don't forget we're to go to the Bartons' for dinner tonight."

"I know, Papa."

He grinned and pulled at his beard. "You might want to fix that puffy face of yours, or you'll be having to repeat your entire story to Hannah Grace, and poor Jesse will be stranded for hours."

"Silly Papa! Did you think I wouldn't have already told my sisters and Grandmother about my sorry state?"

He looked slightly abashed. "Why am I always the last to know these things?"

Chapter Thirty-three

L uke did not dawdle on his way to Jacob Kane's insurance office. He quickly learned that one never dawdled in Michigan during the wintertime, not with the way the wind nipped mercilessly at the nose and ears. He had never been much for hats, but he could have used one today.

He hastily read the signs on storefronts and businesses, anxious to reach the second block, Jellema Newsstand, Moretti's Candy Company, Hansen's Shoe Repair, DeBoer's Hardware, and, up ahead and across the street, Kane's Whatnot. He stopped and gawked, his firmly planted feet seeming stuck to the wood planks of the boardwalk. *Kane's Whatnot.* His heart throbbed as he resumed his step. Kane and Perkins would be just past the intersection and across from the Whatnot. Now, wouldn't that be something if he ran smack dab into Maggie Rose in the middle of Water Street?

A bell above the door jangled to alert a middle-aged secretary of his arrival. She glanced up, laid aside the fountain pen with which she'd been writing, and folded her hands. "May I help you, sir?" Beside her was a mountain of paperwork, no doubt insurance forms of every kind.

"I'm here to see Jacob Kane, ma'am—if he's in, that is."

"You don't have an appointment, then?"

"No, ma'am. Do I need one? I mean, I'll be happy to come back later, if he's busy."

"Oh, no. I think—let me see." She quickly pulled out a large, spiral notebook, opened it to a particular page, and ran her index finger down a chart column. "He seems to be available. I thought I saw him walk out a while ago, but now that I think on it, I believe he just walked his daughter as far as the door. Mercy, when I get my head buried in a project, I seem to be blinded to all else." She looked up and granted him a toothy grin. "Do you ever get like that?"

"Yes indeed." He shifted his weight, his pulse quickened by the mention of Jacob's daughter. Had it been Maggie Rose?

She pushed back from her desk, the chair legs protesting against the marred oak flooring. "Let me just see if he's free to see you." She took three full steps before turning abruptly, her long skirt flaring at her heels. "Well, gracious me, where is my brain today? Who shall I say is calling?"

"Luke Madison, ma'am. He probably doesn't know who I am. Would you just tell him I'm a friend of...."

"Mr. Madison?" A booming voice carried from the hallway, followed by the sound of hurried steps. An instant later, a man of medium height and build, with graying hair and a beard and neat-as-a-pin mustache to match, emerged in the portal, silver eyes wide and disbelieving. "Well, as I live and breathe!"

"Sir?"

"Come, come," he gestured with his head, grinning beneath his mustache. "I have some probing questions for you."

To say the fellow's reception surprised him would be an understatement. Luke was baffled and befuddled. Did Maggie's father have him confused with someone else? He shot the secretary a glance, but all she did was issue a smiling nod and waddle back to her desk.

K

Maggie readied herself and Rose Marie for their evening at Ambrose and Norma Barton's place. My, it would be good to see Mr. and Mrs. Barton again. Through the years, they had been the kindest of neighbors, always taking special interest in Jacob's daughters, inviting them over to play games or listen to the phonograph. When they were younger, Mrs. Barton would often summon the girls to help her bake a cake or decorate cookies. Of course, they never turned down such an opportunity, as it always meant licking spoons and bowls afterward. Perhaps because they had no children of their own, the Bartons had latched onto the Kane girls right from the start. And Grandmother never minded, for whenever someone took the three lively girls off her hands, it afforded her a break.

"You look mighty pretty," said Rose Marie, gaping at Maggie through the mirror from her place on the vanity bench while Maggie did up her hair in fresh French braids. It had been good to shuffle through her closet to find a gown, and she had finally chosen one of shimmery blue satin with long, puffy sleeves and a high lace collar. She had so many fine dresses to choose from and so few opportunities to wear them, especially now. Why, to wear something fancy at Sheltering Arms would be most silly, particularly because she usually wound up with several soiled marks on her clothes by day's end. Not that she missed any of her lovely gowns. No, God had filled her with such passion for working with the city's underprivileged waifs that she'd learned months ago to put more frivolous desires far behind her. That didn't, however, obliterate the joy of dressing up on occasion for the sheer sake of showing her femininity.

"And you look mighty pretty, too, my sweet girl. But you shall look even prettier once I finish these braids and we get you into that lovely new dress we picked up for you at the Whatnot."

"I never had a new dress before."

Maggie plaited the second braid to the tip, finishing it off with a silver barrette. "Well, now you do, and I shall see to it that you get a few more. How would that be?" She bent to kiss Rose Marie's perfect forehead.

"Can we always live together?" Rose Marie asked, eyes as round as moons staring back at Maggie.

Maggie's heart dipped and turned, for she'd been thinking about this very idea. More than anything in the world, she wished to adopt Rose Marie Kring. She went down on her knees and faced the child, taking her hand. "We need to find you a permanent home, darling girl. Right now, my home is at Sheltering Arms, so I can't promise you you'll always live with me. But I can promise you this: you will always have a home right here"—she placed a hand across her chest—"in my heart."

The Edison phonograph played a lovely orchestral tune as the Kanes and Devlins filed into the Bartons' parlor, Ambrose and Norma scurrying to hang everyone's winter wrap or cloak on a wooden hanger in the small room off the parlor. Snow had started to collect on the ground, and so they all stomped their feet on the braid rug before moving further into the house.

"For mercy's sake, don't worry about a little snow," Norma said, ever the gracious hostess. She turned to Maggie first and swept her into a tight hug. Then, stepping back, she gave her a full perusal. "My, you are even prettier now than when you left in August. What a lovely blue gown you're wearing! Matches your eyes to a tee." Next, she looked at little Rose Marie. "And who might this child be, all dressed in raspberry red? A fairy princess?" She bent at the waist to tweak Rose Marie's petite nose. The girl smiled but looked to Maggie to make the introductions.

"This is Rose Marie, one of my dearest little friends. She rode back with me from New York. We intend to show her a real Michigan Christmas."

Not wanting to be excluded, Jesse crowded in close to Maggie. She wrapped her arm around his shoulder. "Oh, and Jesse, of course, my other dear young friend."

They sat down to a dinner of tender beef roast, mashed potatoes and gravy, boiled vegetables, cranberry salad, and an assortment of breads. Conversation ran the gamut from the recent presidential election, which Theodore Roosevelt had won by a landslide, to life at Sheltering Arms, to this year's football team at the University of Michigan. Once the topic switched to sports, the women went off on their own, discussing current trends in clothing, swapping favorite recipes, and talking about the latest books they'd read. Norma stepped out momentarily and returned with a white porcelain coffeepot to refill the china teacups. Once an avid reader, Maggie could claim only to having recently completed reading the New Testament and a variety of children's books. Her work at the refuge certainly affected her life on many levels. Goodness, she hadn't the time for even thinking about sitting next to a cozy fire to read a book for the sheer enjoyment of it.

Despite their lively discussions, Maggie could not help but notice how distracted her father seemed; perhaps jumpy better described his mood, particularly when the grandfather clock struck eight o'clock.

At the final chime, Jacob looked directly at Maggie. "Sweetheart, I was just telling Ambrose here about a book I've been reading on the life of Theodore Roosevelt. It's sitting on the dining room table. I wonder if you might run home and get it for me."

It seemed a strange request, but she was glad to comply. "Um…yes, of course." She laid her napkin beside her dessert plate and prepared to excuse herself.

"I can get it!" Abbie Ann offered, pushing back her chair and jumping up.

"No!" Jacob nearly roared. The room quieted, and Abbie slowly sat back down. Her father cleared his throat. "What I mean to say is, well, Maggie is—closest to the door."

Maggie nodded, not quite understanding his logic but not questioning it, either. "I'll be right back, then. It's on the table, you say?"

He relaxed. "Yes."

"Can me and Rose Marie go with her?" Jesse asked, getting ready to bolt from the table. The children had sat so patiently while the adults talked nonstop on issues they knew nothing about. Surely, they would both benefit from getting out of the house.

"Sure," Maggie said, while Jacob's simultaneous reply was, "No!"

Again, the room went stock-still as several pairs of eyes came to rest on Jacob. No doubt about it, he had something up his sleeve. *He probably wanted to plan some sort of event in honor of my homecoming,* Maggie surmised, *and getting me out of the house is the only way to discuss it with the whole family. Oh, what a sweet Papa! And silly for thinking he could pull the wool over my eyes that easily. Doesn't he know I see right through him?*

"I shall return as quick as a wink, then." Norma rose. "Don't bother, Mrs. Barton. I can fish my own coat from the wardrobe."

Outside, the snow had started to accumulate. She pulled her fur collar up tight around her neck and pointed her face downward to avoid the worst of the wind, cutting across the two yards and making fresh footprints. The Kanes' porch light glimmered its welcome, and the snow-covered arborvitae cast a long shadow on the lawn. As she drew nearer to the house, a movement caught her eye—there was something, or *someone*, huddled on the top step. Her heart nearly slammed through her chest as she pivoted to make a beeline back to the Bartons', a flashback of the awful man who'd snagged her in Lincoln adding urgency to her flight.

"Maggie, stop. It's me, Luke! Maggie!"

What? Stopping abruptly, she turned, squinting in the dark to make out the approaching figure. Her throat closed up tighter than a drum as she tried to force air through it, her tongue frozen to the roof of her mouth. Was she dreaming? She heard nothing but the crunch of snow beneath his feet and the trees rustling in the wind. In the distance, an owl gave a haunting hoot.

"It's me," he repeated in a hoarse whisper, coming into clear view now.

She inclined her head and tried to wade through her fuzzy thoughts, not believing what her eyes said were true. "Luke?"

He reached out a gloved hand to her, but she refused to take it, still not grasping that he stood mere inches away.

"Could we go inside? Please?"

He looked wonderful, even in the shadows, with snow collecting on his head of thick, cocoa-colored hair. It looked to have been recently cut, but it wasn't so short that it didn't still fall in wisps across his forehead. His smart-looking overcoat and wool scarf enhanced his dapper appearance. "What—are—you—doing here?" she asked in spurts.

He smiled in the dimness. "Well, for starters, I brought you a draft of my article. I thought I'd have you read it before it hits the newsstands."

She reveled in the sound of his voice, its smooth, deep, gentle tone caressing her senses. She could have stood in the frozen air for hours and been warmed by its rich timbre. "You came all the way from New York to show me your article? Now?"

He nodded. "Well, I know the hour is a little late, but... well, I didn't want to interrupt your plans entirely. I knew you'd already arranged to have dinner at the neighbors' house. Anyway, do you think we could go inside where it's light—and warm?"

"I—I'm supposed to take something back to my...." She crooked her thumb at the Bartons' place and stared at him, still dazed. "Wait a minute. How did you—?"

He chuckled and tugged gently on her sleeve. "I'll explain once we get inside. And for what it's worth, you don't have to take any book about Theodore Roosevelt back to your father."

She stopped short. "What? He's in cahoots with you?"

He laughed again and pulled her toward the house.

K

He helped her out of her coat, breathing in her flowery scent and thinking he'd never seen a lovelier creation than this woman standing before him. She was wearing some kind of shimmery blue getup with ballooning sleeves and silver buttons up the bodice, finishing at the neck, and her golden locks cascaded down her back in soft waves, held back at the temples with blue beaded combs. She had barely breathed more than a few words to him, and he feared she might even be angry for the interruption. After all, he hadn't spoken to her in weeks, and suddenly, he showed up on her doorstep on a blustery December night. What must she be thinking? Feeling out of his element, he lifted a silent prayer for courage.

Once he deposited their coats on the walnut coat tree, they stood staring at each other, he looking deep into her marine blue eyes, she seeming to search his for some kind of explanation. He longed to enfold her in his arms, kiss her hair, touch her cheek. Instead, he rubbed his hands together, suddenly tense and timid.

"Okay, I confess. My reason for coming is twofold—well, maybe threefold. First, I want to show you my article. I've sent a copy to Maxine for her approval." He produced a folded set of papers from his hip pocket, worn and frayed around the edges by now, and handed them to her—all but the final page, that is. This, he'd reserved to read aloud to her. She chewed her lower lip, gave him a tentative look, paused, and then walked to a velveteen settee in the living room and slowly lowered herself. He followed along but chose to sit in a nearby chair.

His heart thumped erratically while she read with intentness, making his mind fly in a million directions. What was she thinking as she read? Was his presence a distraction? Should he give her privacy? Was she happy to see him or still too shocked to process his presence? Would he be able to convince her of his undying love? Moreover, would she say yes to his "big question"?

Unlike Owen, who had inserted remarks while reading through the exposé, Maggie read in silence. She remained expressionless, save for licking her plumpish lips and nodding ever so slightly from time to time. In fact, the only sounds he detected were his own breathing, the ticktock of the grandfather clock in another room, and the shifting, whistling winds whipping around the corners of the house.

After what seemed like an hour, Maggie lowered the papers to her lap and looked at him, tears pooling in her eyes. "It's very good," she whispered. "Is it true, this part you wrote here, when you say, '...for I have had only a taste of what it is to free an innocent victim from the clutches of evil, and now that I've sampled its sweetness, I cannot put it out of my mind'?"

He nodded and unfolded the sheet he held in his hand. "And there's more. May I read the rest of it to you?"

She wiped her eyes and sniffed. "Please do." This is what he loved about her; besides having a zealous heart, she exuded tenderness and compassion.

He cleared his throat, slid forward in his chair, his elbows propped on his knees, and proceeded to read.

> Once you've lived among orphans and seen life
> from their point of view; once you've played their
> games, eaten their food, cried their tears, traveled

on a train with them in search of families; you cannot remain the same. No longer can you walk the streets of New York City and remain oblivious to the plight of the homeless children around you. I know, because this happened to me. Every day, I find myself on a mission of sorts: I look for wide-eyed wanderers with dirt-specked noses and smudged cheeks, dressed in filthy garments, and sporting shoes with their toes poking out of the ends (if they even have shoes, that is). When I find them, I approach them and try to initiate conversation. If they don't trust me, I walk away, knowing I will return the next day, and the next, and the next, until I've finally earned their trust and can take them by the hand and lead them to a safe place.

At this point, Luke uttered another silent prayer, swallowed hard, and glanced up at Maggie. Finding her attentive, he continued.

After many years of writing for the *World*, I am leaving journalism behind to embark on a different career path: providing a temporary home for homeless children, much like Sheltering Arms Refuge. It shall be the Frances Connors Children's Relief Center, in honor of my late aunt, whose generous bequest to me makes this plan possible.

It is odd but not uncommon for tragic circumstances to give rise to a new beginning. After losing my aunt, my fiancée, and her mother in the *General Slocum* disaster this past June, I thought my life was lost, as well. But God had other ideas, taking my useless, broken, and tattered soul and mending it for use in His kingdom. As Romans 8:28 wisely says, *"We know that all things work together for good to them that love God, to those who are the called according to his purpose."*

I shall forever recall the *General Slocum* tragedy with regret and sadness. But I shall also think of it as the catalyst that caused me to redirect my focus, taking it off my bottomless pain and putting it where it could do some actual good.

Perhaps you suffer from some unfathomable sorrow. Why not consider channeling the energy demanded by self-absorption and self-pity and involve yourself in a course of action that will make a positive impact on others? Ask yourself what you can do to help our forgotten emeralds, the city's lost treasure.

You can make a difference in a child's life today. An account has been established at the New York State Bank and Trust Company to support the orphans of this city. Should you find it in your heart to donate to this account, you may be assured your contributions will serve the children of Sheltering Arms Refuge and a number of other children's relief agencies around the city.

Chapter Thirty-four

Maggie's whimpers gave way to sobs. Luke tossed the article aside and fairly leaped from his chair to the settee, pulling her into his arms and whispering soft assurances in her ear. "Maggie, sweet, darling Maggie, I've gone and done it again; I've made you cry. Why am I so good at that?"

She might have laughed at the desperate tone of his voice, and she did, in fact, expel a pathetic chuckle. Again, she had nothing to wipe her eyes on but the edge of her sleeve. Luke scrambled to search his pockets but came up empty-handed. "Here." He offered up his own sleeve.

This spurred giggles between her sobs. "Oh, Luke, I can—hardly believe it. Y-you're actually quitting your job at the *World*? But, are you s-sure that's what you really want to do? I thought you enjoyed reporting the news."

"I'd rather read it any day than report it," he confessed. "I'll admit, news fascinates me, but it's not my passion. I came to Sheltering Arms and saw folks with true zeal, and it made me long for a purpose of my own.

"I've been reading my Bible, praying daily, and seeking God's guidance. Yes, I finally reached a point of surrender,

Maggie, and not because I knew it would please you or Ginny or Henry—or anyone else, really. I did it because my life was empty, lacking direction.

"I still remember. It was the first day of November, and I dragged myself out of bed, determined to go to a little city church around the corner from my apartment. Somehow, I had to figure out my life; decide how to make it less painful. You see, I'd been living in a hole of self-pity for some time, and I needed to claw my way out to survive. My losing Annalise and Aunt Fran was just the tip of the iceberg.

"From the moment my parents died and my aunt took over, I felt cheated, resentful, like I didn't rate very high on God's love scale."

"Oh, Luke, I didn't know you felt like that." Maggie swallowed a painful lump in her throat.

"Aunt Fran was a good person, don't get me wrong, but she wasn't my mother, and even at the tender age of six, I could tell she wasn't too keen on the idea of raising me into adulthood. It molded me into the person I am today, skeptical and cautious.

"Well, on my way to church that morning, I spotted a little boy, probably not much older than six or seven. He was kicking stones to pass the time. I walked up to him and asked him where his parents were. He shrugged and said his father hadn't been home in days. As for his mother, he claimed he didn't have one. He looked scared as a rabbit in a snake hole.

"It was the strangest thing, Maggie," he said, frowning down at his shoes, then directing his gaze back at her. "When I looked in that little boy's eyes, I saw me.

"As long as I live, I'll never forget that feeling of his fingers wrapping around mine when I reached out to him. I took him to the Sisters of Mercy, and last I heard, his father hadn't returned. He either deserted or got caught up in some illegal scam or another. We may never know. But this I do know—God put that child in my path that morning so I could get him to a safe place.

"Anyway, that was my turning point. I knew I had to make my life count for something, and what better way than to give children a little ray of hope?"

Now they both had tears streaming down their faces. Maggie stood up, dashed to the buffet, and drew out a couple of linen napkins from the bottom drawer, handing one to Luke. They sat there blowing their noses like a couple of ninnies.

Luke cleared his throat, but when he spoke, his words still came off sounding choked and raw. "I slipped into the service late that morning, just as the pastor was delivering his closing remarks about forgiveness and letting go of the vile, loathsome thoughts we fallen humans tend to cherish. Everything flashed before me in that moment—my own orphan state and the anger I carried because of it, my recent losses and the added resentment they brought, my failure to surrender to God—to just say, 'I trust You, Lord. Whatever that means, wherever it takes me, whatever it brings my way, I trust You.' That was my pivotal moment, Maggie, just giving it up and admitting my need for a Savior."

She sniffed. "Oh, Luke, what a beautiful thing. I—I hardly know what to say. I mean, it's so amazing the way the Lord has worked in your life."

There followed a pause while he took a long breath. She closed her eyes against another torrent of tears. Suddenly, he reached for her hand and held it in his lap, linking his fingers with hers. "Since then, I've been seeking more specific directions as to how I might get this children's home under-way. There's still some legal rigmarole to wade through in terms of transforming my apartment into a refuge facility, and I know I'll have to make a few structural changes to some of the upstairs rooms." He took another breather and swept his gaze over her face. "And then, there's the matter of finding someone to help me manage it."

Her breath caught in her throat. "Oh."

He leaned back, sizing her up with a somewhat impish glint in his eye. "You wouldn't have any idea whom I might ask, would you?"

Did he mean to insinuate…? Her heart thrummed. "I would have to give that some thought. Perhaps you might run a newspaper ad?"

"Humph." He looked thoughtful. "It would have to be someone with a bit of experience. And passion. That's a must for the job."

"It would be foolish to hire someone lacking enthusiasm," Maggie conceded. "And then, of course, whoever you hire must have a deep love for children and a heart for sharing Christ's love."

He leaned forward to tease her earlobe with his thumb and forefinger. "I wasn't thinking of *hiring*, necessarily," he whispered.

She feigned surprise. "You expect someone to work for no salary?"

He kissed her temple. "Oh, make no mistake. The pay will be outstanding." His lips trailed tiny kisses down her cheek and across her jaw line. She shivered, enthralled by their gentle sparring. "In fact, it just occurred to me you might like the job."

"Me?"

Suddenly, he rose to his feet and grasped her hands, drawing her up with him. He leaned to kiss her fully, then wrapped his arms around her to pull her close, the pleasant sensation fairly exploding through her veins. As always, when he kissed her, her mind started scurrying in countless directions. What to do? How to act? Where to put her hands? How to breathe, for goodness' sake?

"Yes, you," he muttered against her lips. "In case you haven't figured it out yet, I love you, Maggie Rose Kane—you and only you."

She leaned her head back and looked at him, eyes brimming with tears of joy. She loved him equally, of course, but before she could say the words, she had to make one thing clear. "I don't want you to forget her, Luke."

He tilted his face. "Maggie…."

"I mean it. Annalise was a very real part of you."

He kissed her forehead with utmost tenderness. "Would you be my wife?"

"It was wrong of me to expect—what?"

He held her at arm's length. "Would you be my wife?" he repeated, taking careful time with each word.

"Oh, Luke, I—but—are you ready? I mean, it's been only…."

He clutched her arms and looked her square on, giving into a sigh. "All right, yes. Annalise will always live in one tiny corner of my mind. But she is a memory, sweetheart—not a living, breathing entity. I love you, Maggie Rose, and that is the plain truth. Now, would you kindly tell me you love me back?"

She paused to study the inherent strength in his face, the dark, compelling eyes that drew her in, the swath of hair that refused to stay in place. She reached up and raked her fingers through his hair, finding it silky. "I love you back," she whispered.

"Really?" He looked surprised at not having to prompt her further.

She nodded. "More than life."

Their lips met, long and thoroughly this time, and they separated only for brief periods of time so they could each catch a breath of air. Every kiss grew in intensity, the knee-weakening, heart-stopping, nerve-shattering kinds that left two people feeling wilted and spent.

In one moment of reprieve, Maggie pulled back, breathless. "Oh, my goodness! You'll have to seek Papa's permission—for my hand, that is."

"Silly girl." He kissed the tip of her nose. "What do you think I did this afternoon? As a matter of fact, you and I missed seeing each other in his office by about fifteen minutes. Your father and I had a nice, long chat. I'd say he approves."

In preparation for another kiss, he took her face in his hands and brought it slowly toward his own, but just before their lips touched, she put a hand to his chest and pushed back gently. "Rose Marie," she muttered.

"Yes?" he asked, mouth parted.

"I must bring her with us."

"Fine."

"Fine? Just like that? You don't mind?"

He shook his head. "What would you think of inviting Ricky and Stu, as well?"

"I think we should!"

"Phew, that's good, because I already talked to Ricky, and, well, he's ready to move in tomorrow. The boy needs a second chance, and I think we can give it to him."

She stood on tiptoe and kissed his solid chin. "You are a fine man, Luke Madison, and it would be my honor to be your wife."

He dropped his hands to the small of her back and gathered her into his tender embrace, nuzzling her neck and sighing. "It will just be the five of us—until we get settled."

"*Just* the five of us?" She started to giggle.

He tossed his head back and chortled. "And then, I suspect it will be six." He planted a kiss on her right cheek. "And then seven," he added, kissing her left one.

"And maybe eight, depending on whom the Lord sends our way," she inserted.

He pulled back and gave her a flirtatious glance, eyebrows arched. "And nine, when you count the baby. For there will be a little Madison mixed into the bunch—and maybe more than one."

Unspeakable joy bubbled over as Maggie turned her chin upward for more melting kisses. When God had called her to Sheltering Arms Refuge, He'd had a twofold plan in mind.

My, what an all-knowing, all-forgiving, all-sufficient, divinely clever God.

Reverend Cooper, the pastor of the Third Street Church of Sandy Shores, married Luke and Maggie Rose on the hottest June day on record. Despite the heat, folks filled up every available pew, the women armed with fans that never stopped moving, giving the appearance of a whole swarm of butterflies.

At the front of the church, an electric fan served to keep the bride and groom as comfortable as possible, but by the look of the sweat trickling down the groom's face, it didn't appear to be working. The beautiful bride, adorned in a classic gown with a low, scalloped neckline, a gathered waistline, and a chapel-length train decorated with embroidery, beaded appliqués, and intricate pearls, appeared not the least bit ruffled by the heat. If anything, her radiant appearance made a body forget about the soaring temperatures. From every corner of the church, folks had "oohed" and "ahhed" at the sight of her when she came floating down the center aisle on Jacob Kane's arm, the flower girl and ring bearer, Rose Marie and Jesse, having arrived ahead of them to join a very pregnant Hannah Grace, Abbie Ann, Gabe, and Nathan Emory at the front of the church. Of course, the groom, standing center stage, beamed in awe and wonder at his beautiful bride.

Grandmother Kane fairly glowed with pride from her seat in the second row; behind her, bearing proud smiles of their own, were Henry and Ginny Bingham. Stanley and Charlotte had been married in April and were now living on the main floor across from the nursery at Sheltering Arms. They had stayed behind to hold down the fort, along with a young fellow they'd hired to live on the third floor. Helping them were a host of volunteers, as well as Floretta, the other new full-time employee at Sheltering Arms.

It had been a long time coming, this day of matrimony, for when two hearts love with utter totality, the waiting can be tedious. But waited they had, and had stayed plenty busy in the interim, Luke overseeing the renovation of the apartment to make it ready for orphaned residents, Maggie making wedding plans. She had traveled back to Michigan twice during the six-month period to appease Grandmother

Kane, who had claimed a bride needed to be present in the planning. Still, she had worked at Sheltering Arms until one week before the wedding.

Luke had kept a curious eye on the *General Slocum* case, though not an obsessive one, for he'd learned that time truly does a masterful job of healing. When the one-year anniversary of the tragedy came around, he mourned, yes, but not just for what he'd had to endure, but for what the city as a whole had suffered. The investigation continued, and no one could predict when it might conclude, but Luke had learned to surrender the situation to God.

Luke's news piece, while not winning national awards for excellence in journalism, did earn local acclaim. As a result, several charitable societies and church groups organized events to raise funds for the fast-growing account at the New York State Bank and Trust Company, which had been established for the sole purpose of benefiting homeless children. The attention given to the problem of dispossessed children stirred many a heart into action, which had been Luke's aim when he'd submitted the article to Owen Perry. That, and seeing Congressman Lewis Blackwell and saloon proprietress Violet Harding brought to justice. And he had! Less than a month ago, the fellow had been sentenced to a minimum of fifteen years in prison. For her part, Violet, while not forced to serve jail time, was ordered by the courts to pay fees and penalties in excess of $30,000. Naturally, every customer walked out on her, and the last Luke had heard, her business bore a CLOSED sign. Someone had come along to ransack the place, knocking out every window and door in the process.

The ceremony was blessedly brief, but the kiss was not. Upon the pastor's final words of pronouncement, Luke cradled his wife's face in both his hands, gave a lazy smile, and slowly, methodically, and reverently brought his lips to meet hers. It seemed the onlookers forgot to breathe as the whole place went momentarily silent. Outside, even the birds that'd been keeping up a constant chatter through the open windows hushed their songs.

From five rows back, the Bartons sat shoulder to shoulder. "Oh, my body and soul!" Norma hissed in Ambrose's ear when Luke came up for air at last and turned his blushing bride to face her audience. "Have you ever seen anything like it?" She pressed a hand to her thumping heart.

Ambrose grinned and slid an arm around his wife, drawing her closer to his side. "Not since the last Kane wedding. I wonder when Jacob will be giving Abbie Ann's hand in marriage?"

Tilting her gaze at Ambrose, she gave her head a decisive shake. "Oh, well, that will be a long time in coming. Abbie's an independent little critter. It will take a special man to capture that one's heart."

He gave a thoughtful nod. "You're probably right."

As the bride and groom passed by during the recessional, their faces glowed with jubilant hope.

Outside, the birds resumed their summer song.

About the Author

Born and raised in west Michigan, Sharlene MacLaren attended Spring Arbor University. Upon graduating with an education degree, she traveled internationally for a year with a small singing ensemble, then came home and married one of her childhood friends. Together they raised two lovely daughters. Now happily retired after teaching elementary school for thirty-one years, "Shar" enjoys reading, writing, singing in the church choir and worship teams, traveling, and spending time with her husband, children, and precious grandchildren.

A Christian for over forty years and a lover of the English language, Shar has always enjoyed dabbling in writing—poetry, fiction, various essays, and freelance work for periodicals and newspapers. She remembers well the short stories she wrote in high school and watched circulate from girl to girl during government and civics classes. "Psst," someone would whisper from two rows over, always when the teacher's back was to the class, "pass me the next page."

Shar is an occasional speaker for her local MOPS (Mothers of Preschoolers) organization; is involved in KIDS' HOPE USA, a mentoring program for at-risk children;

counsels young women in the Apples of Gold Program; and is active in two weekly Bible studies. She and her husband, Cecil, live in Spring Lake, Michigan, with their lovable collie, Dakota, and Mocha, their lazy fat cat.

The acclaimed *Through Every Storm* was Shar's first novel to be published by Whitaker House, and in 2007, the American Christian Fiction Writers (ACFW) named it a finalist for Book of the Year. The beloved Little Hickman Creek series consisted of *Loving Liza Jane*; *Sarah, My Beloved*; and *Courting Emma*. Faith, Hope, and Love, the Inspirational Outreach Chapter of Romance Writers of America, announced *Sarah, My Beloved* as a finalist in its 2008 Inspirational Reader's Choice Contest in the category of long historical fiction. Along with *Hannah Grace* and *Maggie Rose*, *Abbie Ann* will complete Shar's latest trilogy, The Daughters of Jacob Kane.

To find out more about Shar and her writing and inspiration, you can e-mail her at smac@chartermi.net or visit her Web site at www.sharlenemaclaren.com.

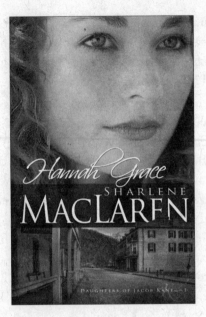

Hannah Grace
Book One in The Daughters of Jacob Kane Series
Sharlene MacLaren

Hannah Grace, the eldest of Jacob Kane's three daughters, is feisty and strong-willed, yet practical. She has her life planned out in an orderly, meaningful way—or so she thinks. When Gabriel Devlin comes to town as the new sheriff, the two strike up a volatile relationship that turns toward romance, thanks to a shy orphan boy and a little divine intervention.

ISBN: 978-1-60374-074-6 ♦ Trade ♦ 432 pages

WHITAKER
HOUSE

Long Journey Home
Sharlene MacLaren

Single mother Callie May is still nursing emotional scars from an abusive marriage when a handsome but brooding stranger moves into the apartment across the hall. In spite of his attractiveness, pastor Dan Mattson has problems of his own—he abandoned his flock and turned his back on God following the deaths of his wife and baby daughter. When Callie's ex-husband shows up to wreak even more havoc in her life, Dan comes to her defense—and faces his own demons in the process. Will Dan and Callie allow God to change their hearts and mend their hurts so they can take another chance on love?

ISBN: 978-1-60374-056-2 • Trade • 400 pages

WHITAKER
HOUSE

Coming in Spring 2010: Book Three in
The Daughters of Jacob Kane Series!

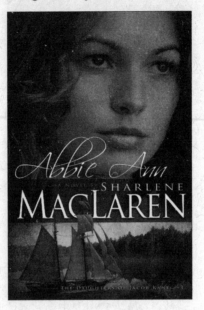

Abbie Ann
Sharlene MacLaren

Abbie Ann Kane, the youngest of Jacob Kane's three daughters, is a busy woman. Between running the Whatnot, the family's general store, being active in the Women's Christian Temperance Union, and assisting the elderly citizens of Sandy Shores, Michigan, she has little time for frivolous matters—even matters of the heart. When the recently divorced Noah Carson comes to town, son Toby in tow, to pursue the shipbuilding business, Abbie Ann tries to keep her distance—especially when his flagrant ex-wife shows up. But God has other plans in mind....

ISBN: 978-1-60374-076-0 ◆ Trade ◆ 400 pages

WHITAKER
HOUSE